# Highway to Hell

MAGGIE QUINN: GIRL VS. EVIL

# Highway to Hell

*a novel by*

## Rosemary Clement-Moore

DELACORTE PRESS

Published by Delacorte Press
an imprint of Random House Children's Books
a division of Random House, Inc.
New York

Visit us on the Web! www.randomhouse.com/teens

Educators and librarians, for a variety of teaching tools, visit us at
www.randomhouse.com/teachers

*Library of Congress Cataloging-in-Publication Data*
Clement-Moore, Rosemary.
Highway to hell / Rosemary Clement-Moore. — 1st ed.
p.   cm.—(Maggie Quinn : girl vs. evil)
Summary: On their way to spend spring break on a Texas beach, college freshmen Maggie
Quinn and D&D Lisa are stranded in a town where some believe a chupacabra is killing
animals, and as the girls investigate they get help from diverse and unexpected sources.
ISBN 978-0-385-73463-9 (hc : alk. paper)—ISBN 978-0-385-90462-9 (glb : alk. paper)
[1. Chupacabras—Fiction.  2. Monsters—Fiction.  3. Psychic ability—Fiction.
4. Witchcraft—Fiction.  5. Demonology—Fiction.  6. Journalism—Fiction.  7. Texas—
Fiction.  8. Mystery and detective stories.  9. Horror stories.]  I. Title.
PZ7.C59117Hig 2009
[Fic]—dc22        2008005304

The text of this book is set in 12.5-point Filosofia Regular.

Book design by Angela Carlino

Printed in the United States of America

10  9  8  7  6  5  4  3  2  1

First Edition

To Ann Boelhouwer, my Oma, the inspiration, in her own practical way, for the awesome grandmothers who appear in my stories.

# 1

Some people think that Texas has only one season, that it's summer all year long. In fact, the Lone Star State does have four seasons: Hot, Humid, Horrible, and Hellacious. But when I decided to road-trip with D&D Lisa to South Padre Island, I didn't think that last one would be so literal.

I shouldn't have been surprised. I'm Maggie Quinn: Psychic Girl Detective. Lisa is an amateur sorcerer. We aren't exactly normal college freshmen. Yet there we were, doing the normal college thing, setting off on a Rite of Passage: Spring Break at the Beach.

An odd choice, since I hate any water deeper than a

bathtub, I already have a boyfriend, and if you couldn't tell from her nickname, D&D Lisa isn't the beer and boobfest type. Neither am I. But we'd wanted to take a road trip, and the destination had started as a joke. Then I pitched an article to the editor of the Bedivere University newspaper—who seemed amused by the whole World's Least Likely Spring Breakers angle—and to my surprise, Lisa went along with it.

In the end, our reasons don't matter, except to explain how we came to be cruising down State Highway 77 in the smallest hour of the morning, even though we knew—better than most—what kinds of things go bump in the night.

I flexed my hands on the Jeep's steering wheel and sank lower into the seat. It was a long drive, which hadn't seemed so daunting until I realized how much of it was through landscape so desolately featureless, it made me think Dante must have visited here before he wrote *The Inferno*.

"If I owned Hell and Texas, I'd rent out Texas and live in Hell."

Lisa paused in fiddling with the radio. "What's that about?"

I shrugged. "Something I read once. Like . . . Did you know Velasquez County has more cows than people in it?"

There was just enough light from the dashboard to see her roll her eyes. "Remind me to never go up against you on *Jeopardy!*"

Under a nearly full moon, the coastal plain was as flat as a silver-gray sea, cut by a black ribbon of highway and a smaller thread of railroad tracks running alongside. Now and then we'd reach a crossroads, where there might be a grain silo, a water tower, or a tiny fruit stand, deserted for the night and only adding to the barren atmosphere.

It seemed like there should be more traffic—other spring breakers, semis on their NAFTA routes, minivans loaded up like the Griswolds' station wagon in *Vacation*—but since we'd passed Corpus Christi, the signs of civilization had dwindled to zero. We'd passed the last minimart an hour ago, and with nothing on the horizon but more road—and eventually Mexico—I was beginning to regret the twelve ounces of Coke I'd downed to keep alert in the unrelieved boredom.

"You didn't have to come with me," I pointed out.

Lisa had given up on the radio and plugged my iPod into the adaptor. "Is it so weird to want to do something normal?"

I glanced at her silhouette, arching my brows wryly. "For you? Yes."

"I'm taking a break from my sorcerous studies. It will be just like the old days, except that instead of sitting around in the caf mocking the jock-headed and lame, we'll be sitting on the sand mocking the drunk, sunburnt, and slutty." She bent her long, denim-clad leg to an impossible angle and propped her foot on the dash. "Besides, I'm ahead on all my coursework, so what else am I going to do? Sit around and play World of Warcraft all week?"

Our friendship had endured four years of high school, freshman semesters spent at colleges half a country apart—not to mention the forces of darkness. In the past year, one of us had summoned a demon, one of us had vanquished it, and our friendship had nearly fallen apart. Then we'd had to team up to defeat a sorority who had the devil on speed dial. Lisa had saved my life, which went a long way toward reestablishing trust between us.

That's a grossly abbreviated summary of events, of course. The important thing is, Lisa isn't a bad person, though she sometimes thinks she is. Really she's just . . . complicated. Which I guess you would have to be to summon a demon, even sort of unintentionally, in the first place.

So I could see her wanting a break from that for a week. As for myself, a feature article for Bedivere U's *Daily Report* was just an excuse. My real reason was tiny, pink, colicky, and possessed of a wail like an air-defense siren.

I'd been an only child for eighteen years, and while I didn't mind sharing the bright center of my parents' universe, I'd been completely unprepared for the disruption that my infant sister brought to the house. Lately I spent long hours away on campus, or at my boyfriend's apartment. But with school out for the week, and Justin going out of town, too, I was at loose ends. I would have jumped at a chance for a trip to the moon.

Lisa clicked through my playlists, looking dissatisfied with the selection. "You're going to have fun this week, right?"

I glanced at her doubtfully. "Surrounded by the drunk and disorderly? We are going to study the natives, not to become them."

"Which does not preclude having a good time. You're not going to be all goody-two-shoes?"

"What does that mean?" Since I had already taken the unprecedented step of lying to my parents about our departure time in order to avoid the "Two girls driving alone at night" speech, I really didn't appreciate being called a killjoy.

"Don't get pissy. I just don't want you to mope around because Sir Galahad isn't there."

"Sir Galahad" is my boyfriend, Justin. He and Lisa had

started off on a bad foot, though they've since reached a kind of détente. Lisa, in her D&D terminology, says that Justin is a Lawful Good Paladin. She doesn't always mean it as a compliment, but it's absolutely true, so it's hard to take offense.

"Just because I have a boyfriend doesn't mean I *require* a guy to be happy. And if I ever do, just shoot me." Needling me was Lisa's way of breaking up the monotony of the drive, but that didn't stop me from getting defensive. "Besides, it's good to have some time apart."

"You're sure?" She prodded me like a bug under a microscope. "It doesn't irk you he's spending the week with this buddy of his?"

The only thing more provoking than Lisa in a good mood was Lisa in the throes of boredom. "Why should it *irk* me?"

"It's your first school break as a couple." She was fishing, and I was determined not to take that bait.

"Henry's been his best friend since forever. They're going to hang out and do guy stuff. It's not any different than you and I going off to do girl stuff." I shot her a look. "Not that I can remember why that seemed like a good idea."

"Because we're best friends." Lisa unplugged my iPod and replaced it with hers. The screen cast her face in a cool glow, at odds with her devilish smile. "And when I take over the world, I'll appoint you to a place of distinction in my Council of Evil."

"Can't wait."

The music had started low—a distinctive, almost tribal, drumbeat. Bending her other leg to join the first, Lisa tapped her bare toes on the dash and drummed on her knees along with the Rolling Stones.

"You have got to be kidding me," I said.

Lisa just grinned and sang along with Mick. " 'Please allow me to introduce myself, I'm a man of wealth and taste . . .' "

"Sympathy for the Devil." I slanted her a look of disbelief. "You have a sick sense of humor."

All I got was a wider grin and more lyrics. " 'Pleased to meet you. Hope you guess my name.' "

"That might have been funny before you took up sorcery as a hobby."

"One little demon summoning," she said, as the chorus began, "and you never let me forget it."

If she was going to Hell, I guess I was, too, because the outrageous irony dragged a laugh out of me. She bobbed her head, tapping the beat on her knees. This was why we were still friends, as much as because of the saving each other's lives and teaming up against Evil stuff.

Abruptly, Lisa dropped her feet to the floorboard. "Brake lights."

I peered into the darkness beyond the Jeep's headlights. "I don't see anything." Only road and more road.

Drumbeats nearly drowned out our voices. "There! Dead ahead."

I glimpsed twin red beacons in the silver-gray darkness. But in the instant it took for me to shift my foot to the brake, the lights disappeared.

"Where'd they go?"

"There!" Lisa pointed into the field. How had that car moved so fast? The gleam of red seemed to be moving off-road, across scrub and between the shadows of scraggly mesquite.

"How . . . ?"

"Maggie! Look out!" I slammed my foot on the brake. Lisa braced herself with a hand on the dash and another on the roll bar. I could see it now—something huge lay across both lanes, too close to swerve around. The Jeep hit the yielding bulk of the thing; a lower-profile car would have smashed into it. But the off-road tires of the Wrangler went up and over, tilting precariously to one side. The whole vehicle shuddered as something scraped the undercarriage to the tune of tearing metal.

We hit the ground on the other side. There was a sharp crack, and my teeth rattled as we spun out, tires squealing like a tortured soul. The flat gray Purgatory of South Texas whirled past the windshield as I released the brake and turned the wheel into the spin, my right arm burning in sharp protest. Careening onto the shoulder, we came to a stop facing back the way we'd come.

The headlights illuminated the great misshapen carcass of a horned animal, dead in the middle of the highway. In the anticlimactic quiet, the Rolling Stones played on.

"Pleased to meet you. Hope you guess my name."

# 2

Lisa's hand shook as she clicked off the iPod.

"What the hell is that?"

"Cow, I think." Though my first guess from the size of it would have been buffalo. But then, all I knew about cattle came from the movies.

No question the cow was dead. Its big head was twisted almost all the way around and one horn looked half torn off, possibly from meeting the undercarriage of the Jeep. The asphalt was darkly wet.

"Did *we* kill it?" I asked in a guilty whisper.

"I don't think so." Lisa sounded dazed. "Did you hurt your arm?"

Until she said it, I didn't realize I was cradling my right arm against my chest, holding it protectively with my left. "I had to turn the steering wheel pretty hard."

The sharp aching pull was dulling quickly. I wiggled my fingers, the flare of the injured nerves racing up and knotting in my chest. The puffy red scar that ran nearly from my elbow to my wrist was a souvenir from last December. Eventually the scar would fade, but my hand would always be weak, and always protest when I asked too much of it.

I took a deep breath and let it out, letting some of the pain go with it. "Are you okay?"

"Yeah. No harm done."

Right on cue, the Jeep gave a sputter, then died.

"Okay." My voice sounded high and tight in the silence of the desert. "Let's not panic."

"We're not going to panic." Lisa stated it as fact. "We're going to get out of the car and check the damage."

Another deep breath. "Yes, Obi-Wan Kenobi."

She was right. No point in freaking out until I knew the extent of the damage. Grabbing the flashlight that I kept between my seat and the center console, I opened the door.

Beside the Jeep, the ground fell away steeply from the shoulder of the highway, and I had to slide down until the prickly grass scratched at my ankles, and the toes of my flip-flops sank into the sandy soil. I could smell gasoline, carried on the warm air. That couldn't be good.

Lisa joined me as I crouched to shine the light under the Jeep. "See anything?"

"Yeah." A direly mangled hunk of metal hung from the undercarriage, dripping some liquid steadily onto the earth. "But don't ask me what it is, other than bad."

Something stung my leg. I slapped at it, and found a mosquito the size of a quarter squished on my palm.

"Let's get out of the grass," Lisa said, and I didn't argue. We retreated to the road, where the wetness on the pavement gleamed iridescent in the spill of the headlights. Over the metallic tang of blood, the petroleum stink was thick.

"It—the cow, I mean—must have torn the gas tank." I contemplated the carcass, the broken ridge of its spine and the scars on its red-brown hide. "Do you think that other car hit the cow first? Maybe it went off the road." Shielding my eyes from the Jeep's beam, I scanned the dark landscape, but saw no taillights, or any other sign that we weren't the only people in the entire world.

In the near distance, a coyote yipped, and another answered. Lisa gathered her hair into a ponytail and lifted it off her neck. "Some psychic you are, not to see this coming."

I glared at her and slapped another mosquito. "That might be funny if we weren't stranded at the corner of No and Where." That wasn't the way my mojo worked. "Why don't you just whip out your cauldron and conjure us a new gas tank?"

"Don't be silly. I don't take my cauldron with me on vacation." She reached into the pocket of her jeans. "Fortunately, I have my magic cell phone."

I headed for the tailgate. "And I have an emergency kit in the back of the Jeep."

She raised a sardonic brow as I passed. "And you say you can't see the future."

My gift was not foresight; it was overpacking. I believed in being equipped for as many scenarios as possible. Nancy

Drew never got caught without her flashlight and magnifying glass, and neither would I, if I could help it.

I also had flares, a first-aid kit, reflective triangle thingies, a whistle, one of those thermal blankets that looks like something from *Star Trek,* and enough bottled water that, added to the copious amount of snacks we'd brought, made it unlikely that Lisa and I would have to resort to eating each other before someone found us.

The Jeep lurched and I jumped back, my heart thudding against my ribs. But it was just Lisa, climbing onto the front bumper and holding her cell phone skyward.

"What the hell, Lisa? Are you summoning the mother ship?"

"Looking for a signal."

My peripatetic heart plummeted, all the way to my gut. "You're kidding me."

"About being stuck in Nowhere, Texas? *Not* a laughing matter."

Scrambling to grab my own mobile from the dashboard, I stared at it in disbelief. Not even zero bars. Just a "no signal" message across the screen.

The isolation was complete. I stood in the middle of the highway, the island of light cast by the headlamps the only outpost of reality. What if, like some episode of *The Twilight Zone,* the world had ended, only Lisa and I didn't know it?

"We should turn off the headlights," Lisa said calmly, "and save the battery."

That's what we did. What we always did, really: put off blind panic with sensible action. Well, action, anyway.

I turned off the lights and put on the hazard blinkers. In

the intermittent red glow, my eyes adjusted to the moonlight, which made it seem less like a wall of dark separated us from the rest of the world. Lisa assembled the reflective triangles into pyramids and put them around the Jeep. I grabbed the flares and the flashlight, and steeled myself to approach the cow.

My flip-flops stuck to the asphalt; with each step, the rubber soles released with a sucking pop. The smell of blood grew worse as I neared the carcass, and the Maglite wavered. I swallowed, hard. It was going to be a long time before I could even think about eating a hamburger.

Sensible action, Maggie. Barfing is not sensible.

The cow lay on its side, head twisted unnaturally toward the sky, glassy eyes reflecting the stars. Lips pulled back from flat, herbivore teeth, and a thick tongue hung out. Blood pooled from the neck, which gaped open, muscle and glistening sinew exposed in the beam of my flashlight. I thought at first that the laceration was from the Jeep's impact, but the edges of the cow's hide didn't look torn from a shearing force. The flesh had been . . . incised.

The word popped into my head with a clarity that wasn't random. Incisor. Tooth. Fang. I stretched out a curious finger and touched the blood, thick and clotted on the ground.

*Hot, crimson spray on white, sharp teeth. The sensation of it flooded my mouth, coated my tongue with salt and copper.*

I reeled back, met pavement, and kept going, crab-walking away as fast as I could. I'd dropped the flashlight, and couldn't see anything but red-tinged blackness. My lungs gasped for air, yet nothing came in but the stench. I was drowning in it.

"Maggie! Snap out of it."

Light hammered my eyes. I flung up a hand to shield them from the flashlight beam that Lisa pointed at my face. Her gaze went to my upraised hand, and I looked at my palm, coated with blood, sticky and cold.

"There was so much of it." My voice sounded distant and strange.

"Well, duh, Mags. What did you expect?"

Not sympathy, obviously. My brain slogged toward a retort, but my stomach had already reached a state of full-scale revolt. I stumbled to the dry grass beside the road for a humiliating digestive retrospective.

By the time I was done swearing I'd never eat Twizzlers again, Lisa had gone to the Jeep and returned with Handi Wipes from the glove box. She offered one silently, and I cleaned my face and hands.

"Thanks."

"Don't mention it," she said dryly, and handed me the last of my Coke. I uncapped the bottle and washed the acrid taste from my mouth with a little high-fructose nirvana. Thank God for artificial flavoring.

I'm not much of a badass demon slayer. Superheroes always have a cool origin story, but not me. I'm not on a quest for vengeance or atonement. I'm not the Chosen One. I'm just a girl who can see things that most people can't.

That's what clairvoyance is. My Gran calls it "the Sight," but it's more than that. All my life I've had freakily accurate hunches, great intuition, even though I haven't always listened to it. Then last year, I started to sense things. It began with dreams of something stalking my classmates, and then I was *seeing* the thing in real life.

After that, I paid attention to my intuition, and worked on focusing on those feelings. But last fall, my weirdness got a major boost when I met the sorority from Hell. I started getting flashes when I touched things. Not just vision, but sound and smell and taste. Emotion, too. You know how you can tell your parents stopped arguing right before you came into the room? Like that, times a thousand.

I thought it might go away after Lisa, Justin, and I dealt with that particular baddie. But the sensory flashes seemed to be a permanent development. Mostly I pick up little things—moods, recent events—and usually it isn't intrusive. I can tell when the barista who hands me my coffee has had a fight with her boyfriend. I know who's calling me without looking at the caller ID. But this was the first time since December that something had, literally, knocked me on my butt.

So, needless to say, I was almost more shaken up than I was grossed out.

Lisa started back toward the Jeep. I fell in alongside, keeping a careful distance from the carcass. "I'm an idiot. I know."

She stopped, facing me with her hands on her hips. "You knew it didn't die peacefully. What did you think would happen when you touched it?"

I shot her a cranky glare and sank into the passenger seat. "Tell me again why we're friends?"

"Who else is going to tell you, 'Don't poke the dead cow, Maggie, because you might get a vision of its horrible and violent death'?"

A shiver ran through me, like my body was trying to shake off the image. "It was awful. So many teeth."

She paused, maybe picking up on my disquiet but not ready to ask. "Probably a coyote."

That was how we were going to play it. Lisa rejected my unspoken suggestion that this was something . . . other than normal. I let it go, for now. Middle of the night, middle of nowhere—we had plenty to worry about without my adding the eerie to the mix.

"Probably so," I said, and tried to sound convinced.

Lisa picked up the flashlight she'd set aside. "I'd better go put up the flares. Stay here and don't touch anything else."

"Yes, ma'am." I saluted her Roman-centurion style and she went back to business. I sat in the dark, slapping mosquitoes and jumping at the unfamiliar noises of the wilderness.

My arm ached, and I rubbed the knotted muscles along the ridge of the scar. I used to think of myself as two people. Logical Maggie: honors student, journalism club, yearbook photographer. Nothing weird there, except maybe my obsession with science fiction movies. Freaky Maggie had stayed nicely compartmentalized until I'd needed her.

But try finding out that the natural world, all that stuff you learn in physical science, is only part of the picture. There's this whole other stratum of *super*natural reality, with its own rules, that the rest of the world has no clue about.

If my experiences last fall had done anything permanent to me—other than the damage to my right arm—it was that I'd been forced to integrate the parts of my self. Freaky had to work with Logic, or I was going to wind up dead. Worse, people I loved would be hurt. You can't come back from that.

15

Which meant that I could pretend for a little while that I believed that we were only dealing with coyotes, but I couldn't entirely let it go.

∗   ∗   ∗

"Car!"

I jolted out of a not-quite-doze, glimpsing Lisa's back as she swung out of the Jeep. It took me longer to untangle my brain and my legs. By the time I joined her on the road, she was waving the flashlight in the direction of an oncoming vehicle.

"What are we going to do if it's an axe murderer?"

Lisa kept her gaze on the rapidly approaching headlights. "You can always go up and touch him and see what you See."

I eyed her profile. "Do we not have enough on our plate without a side of sarcasm?"

The grille of a large pickup stopped in front of the bovine roadblock, motor churning down to a throaty idle. The door opened, and boots hit the asphalt with a crunch.

It was hard to make out details of the guy, backlit by the truck's headlights. Mostly just a silhouette, tall and whipcord lean. Low at his waist was the gleam of one of those plate-sized silver belt buckles. He set his fists on his hips and whistled.

"Daaaaaang." One syllable, stretched long. "This is some mess. You girls all right?"

Lisa glanced a question at me, and I shrugged. I wasn't sensing a threat, but I wasn't ready to commit myself.

"Ladies?" Cowboy Joe repeated, sounding more concerned. "You okay?"

"We're fine," I said, appointing myself spokesperson. "But our Jeep isn't going anywhere."

"Dead as this heifer, huh?" He circled the carcass with a don't-you-worry-little-lady amble. I saw Lisa's left eyebrow climb, and knew she was thinking something sarcastic, so I jumped in before she could speak it aloud.

"I think the gas tank was sort of . . . gored." I swatted a mosquito that hadn't heard from his friends that I'd already been bled dry.

"What happened?" he asked, heading toward the Jeep.

"The cow was lying in the road like that. We went over the top of it."

"You're lucky you didn't roll over." He crouched to look underneath the car, which gave us an excellent view of the back of his jeans as he bent over. I caught Lisa checking him out, her other eyebrow shooting up to join the first. Not so sarcastic now.

Since I have a boyfriend, my interest in his Wranglers was purely aesthetic. I swear.

He stood and dusted off his hands. As he turned, I got my first look at his face. Tanned skin over sculpted cheekbones, deep-set dark eyes, tidily cropped black hair. He wasn't obviously Hispanic or Native American, but he was definitely the thoroughbred product of a nice mix of bloodlines.

"I can't tell much in the dark, but it's a pretty sure bet . . ."

He hesitated and Lisa finished for him. "That we're screwed?"

"Something like that."

This was not news, but it was hard to hear. I felt light-years away from home. If I'd had even half a bar of signal on my phone, I would have called my mom. But she would just tell me not to be ridiculous. Sensible action, Maggie.

"How close is the nearest town?" At least some part of my brain was functioning.

"Well, Dulcina is not too much farther." He pronounced it with the accent on the second syllable. Dul-SEE-na.

I imagined "not too much farther" could be anything up to fifty miles. "Is there a garage that can send a tow truck?"

Thumbs hooked in his belt, Cowboy Joe considered the question. "There's a garage of sorts. Buck usually takes care of tractors, flat tires, that sort of thing. It's a start."

"We couldn't get a cell phone signal." I pulled my phone from my pocket to check again.

"All kinds of dead spots along this highway." He glanced at his watch. "You don't want to call now anyway. Wake Buck up and he'll charge you an arm and a leg."

"So what *do* we want to do?" Lisa asked, arms folded, hip cocked to the side. "Besides get out of this dead spot in the road."

The guy snuck an up-and-down look at her, which she neither missed nor appreciated. The corners of her mouth tucked in displeasure, but I thought it served her right. Not to mention, I should hold up so well to scrutiny. Lisa was tall and slim, and with her long chestnut hair pulled back, you could see her pretty face and unusual gray eyes.

I'm not saying I'm a dog. I'm short, and with my pointed chin and turned-up nose, I suppose pixie comparisons are inevitable. I get called cute a lot, which isn't a bad thing to be. I prefer to think of my beauty as idiosyncratic, like my personality.

Our knight in shining denim answered Lisa's question

without acknowledging her sarcasm. "Why don't I take you to Dulcina. You can get a room for what's left of the night. Your Jeep is already off on the shoulder. We'll call the state troopers and report the accident, and you can get Buck out here first thing in the morning."

This was an extremely sensible plan, except for the get-into-a-car-with-a-perfect-stranger part. But fortunately I was equipped to deal with that.

"Thanks." I wiped my fingers on my shorts to make sure there wasn't any more cow blood on them. "I'm Maggie, by the way."

"I'm Zeke." He stepped forward and grasped my offered hand without hesitation.

Zeke was the smell of hay and the sweat of hard work, the silky coat of a dog with one brown eye and one blue, the tang of beer with lime, and spicy enchiladas every Sunday with his grandmother.

"Thanks for the ride," I said, unable to stop a smile.

"No problem." He glanced at Lisa expectantly. She stopped goggling at me long enough to supply her name, too. "Nice to meet you both. Why don't you get whatever you need out of your car, lock it up, and I'll see what I can do about this."

Our eyes followed his gesture to the bovine remains. "What are you going to do?" asked Lisa. "It's too late for anything but a barbecue."

He didn't quite laugh. "I can't leave her in the middle of the road for the next car to run into. You two were lucky you weren't killed."

Lisa responded on a droll note. "Yeah. We live a charmed life." She grabbed my good arm and tugged me toward the Jeep. "Come on, Mags."

"Stop pulling," I hissed, letting the diesel engine of Zeke's truck cover our voices.

"What is wrong with you?" Lisa's voice was a harsh whisper. "Did you learn *nothing* from the cow?"

"But you said—"

"I was joking!"

I shrugged. "I figured if anything happened, you could turn him into a frog."

"Very funny."

Maybe not. But I didn't get to yank her chain very often. By the time I'd taken Zeke's hand, I'd felt pretty certain he wasn't a threat. Opening myself up to the psychic slideshow had been confirmation.

It's not the same thing as reading minds. The hyper-intuition isn't an exact science, and neither is the touchy-vision thing. It's really more like a compass heading than a road map. But I'm pretty good at getting a read on someone's nature—what my best friend, in her D&D Lisa days, would call alignment: good, neutral, or evil.

Unlike role-playing characters, most human beings are a mix of all these things—weighted, maybe, to one side or the other. I couldn't tell if Zeke was the kind of guy to cheat on his girlfriend, but I *could* see he wasn't the type to chop us into bits and feed us to his dog. So the situation wasn't as dire as it could be.

A horrible scraping noise and the throaty roar of a diesel engine made me turn, as Zeke used the pickup to drag Old Bessie off the road and onto the shoulder, leaving a gory smear across the asphalt.

Not that dire for us, anyway.

# 3

The blaring of my cell jolted me out of a deep sleep. Fumbling for the phone on the nightstand, I flipped it open without checking the caller ID. "Hey, Justin."

"You were supposed to text me when you got in." The thin mobile connection didn't do justice to his voice, which was normally a warm and congenial baritone. It was neither of those things at the moment.

"What?" My brain felt thick and gummy inside, which meant I'd been dreaming, even if I couldn't remember it yet. Slowly, the unfamiliar room, sandpaper sheets, and stale motel air worked their way through the fog.

"When you got to South Padre." At my befuddled silence Justin continued impatiently. "You were expecting to get there in time for breakfast? And you were going to let me know that your insane drive-all-night plan had not, against all probability, resulted in disaster?"

Memory sharpened to a painful point between my eyes. The road, the cow, the wreck. My vision of flashing teeth, and the sharp-sweet tang of blood, thick in the air. The dream that had only confused me more.

I sat up, head pounding. "What time is it?"

"Eight-thirty. You sound awful."

"Headache."

"Where are you now?"

I glanced around the motel room. Sunlight edged the drapes—a brown, orange, and gold floral hideousness that matched the bedspreads—and when I finally managed to focus on the second of the double beds, I found it empty. The bathroom door stood open. No sign of Lisa but her rumpled covers and open suitcase.

"A town called Dulcina."

"Where is that?"

"The edge of the world, I think." I rubbed my forehead with my left hand, trying to massage out the ache. "You have to promise not to say 'I told you so.' "

A pause, so prolonged that I thought the call might have dropped. Finally he spoke, worry and displeasure vibrating through the network. "Just tell me what happened."

I told the abbreviated version: deserted highway, dead cow, wrecked Jeep, handsome stranger, cranky night manager at the Artesian Manor. Of course, I may have left out the word *handsome,* along with the details of the gore-o-vision.

He didn't say anything about our getting in a stranger's car, blah blah blah serial killer, but cut to the important question. "So did you get a vibe on anything . . . weird?"

Squeezing the bridge of my nose, I willed my thoughts into line. "Zeke—the rancher that rescued us—said a couple of coyotes could bring down a calf."

"But a full-grown cow?"

I sighed, knowing I was at the end of my self-deception. "I don't know."

"Did you dream last night?" I'm the psychic one, but Justin has got decent intuition himself. We're a good team, because he's also as intellectual as Lisa, but not nearly as clinical.

"Yeah. The details are still vague." I sat up, swung my legs over the edge of the bed. No wonder I itched; my legs were polka-dotted with mosquito bites. "Maybe I'll remember more after I shower."

Justin made a grumbling sound. "Are you sure you're not hiding something from me?"

"What could I be hiding? I don't know anything." My reply was snappish, but psychic hangovers coupled with physical misery tend to make me a little cranky. "Sorry. You know how this works. I don't get all the answers. Just more questions."

Justin's sigh was deep, and not with contentment. "So, what are you going to do?"

"Get the Jeep towed back here, I guess. Call the insurance people. Figure out what to tell my parents."

"I suggest the truth."

"Yeah. That'll be fun." I changed the subject. "First I have to go find Lisa."

"Okay. Henry and I will be knocking around the campus, so I may not have my phone on. Just text me or leave a voice mail. I'll check messages."

"I'll keep you posted." I knew I should let him go, but I felt the distance between us keenly, and wanted to hold on a moment longer. "So, how is the monastery?"

"Seminary. Henry's only a pre-theology student."

"I was joking." It depressed me that he didn't realize that, but then, phone connections don't transmit smart-aleck very well.

"Oh." He laughed, more at himself than at my questionable wit. "We went to an all-boys boarding school. This isn't that different, except that the conversation in the dorm isn't all about sports and girls. Not as much, anyway."

Justin's parents were doctors who had died overseas while working for a Catholic relief organization. The only other family he ever talked about—besides his best friend, Henry—was the bishop who became his guardian. Justin didn't discuss the details, but apparently it wasn't as Oliver Twist as it sounded. His parents had a good insurance policy, and the boarding school had given him a scholarship so he could save the money for college. But even so, losing your parents would suck.

"Henry was glad to see you?"

"Yeah." There was a funny note to his laugh, sort of nostalgic, sort of not. "Seminary hasn't changed him as much as I thought it would."

"That's good, right?"

"It is to me. Not sure how the Church will feel about it."

"He sounds like an interesting guy."

I said it offhand, without meaning anything by it. He answered the same way. "You'll meet him eventually."

"Great." And then there wasn't anything else to say. My stomach was rumbling, but I waited in awkward silence, because I didn't know how to end the call. I'd never said the *L* word to Justin, not even casually. But the accident and the miles between us somehow made "See ya! Bye!" a little too cavalier. And "Care about ya! Bye!" was just ridiculous.

"Maggie?" Justin's voice dropped to the warm rumble I knew well. "I'm really glad you weren't hurt."

I smiled and sat on the edge of the bed. My headache almost disappeared. Because his mouth might be saying, "I'm glad you're all right," but everything else was saying those three little words.

"Yeah," I answered. "Me too."

✳  ✳  ✳

The wallpaper on my phone was of Justin, sitting on his sofa with a book in his lap, wearing worn jeans and a faded T-shirt. Normal college-guy uniform. His brown hair was short over his ears, his face clean-cut, but he had a crooked, roguish smile that took him from boy-next-door to boy-next-door-who-you-want-to-watch-mowing-the-yard-without-his-shirt-on-every-Saturday.

Snapping the cell closed, I tossed it on the pillow. I needed coffee before my thoughts got really sappy.

Hot water would help me think through my dream. Not to mention get rid of any lingering cow cooties. Only exhaustion had kept me from taking a shower when we'd checked in.

Scratching absently at a mosquito bite, I looked for a note

from Lisa, found none, and decided that she couldn't have traveled far without a car. Maybe she'd gone to find some breakfast. My stomach growled again at the thought.

I grabbed my toiletry bag and some clean underwear out of my suitcase and headed for the bathroom, only to recoil when I saw my reflection in the vanity mirror. My hair stood up like a tornado had hit it, the dark brown against my pale skin making me look even more washed out than normal. Bloodshot eyes only enhanced my undead chic. Nice.

The bathroom was more humid than old pipes and the Gulf Coast humidity could account for; Lisa must have showered before she disappeared. A pleasant citrus scent hung in the air; my head cleared a little more, and the weight of the almost sleepless night began to fall from my shoulders.

A brown plastic bottle sat on the edge of the tub, like a cough syrup bottle with no label. I unscrewed the lid and smelled lemon and ginger and early spring mornings after a good night's rest.

Lisa was studying international finance at school, but if world domination didn't work out for her, she could make a fortune bottling that stuff for Bath & Body Works. No aromatherapy had ever worked quite like that.

Strange, the things that tempt you. A little magic to make the morning easier. I put the bottle aside and grabbed my own body wash. Maybe I was being a hypocrite. Lisa's arcane studies had saved my life, but sorcery had also put some of my favorite people in the hospital. So yeah, I was unreasonably squirrelly about it. Besides, I had enough freakish trouble without picking up more voluntarily.

As I'd predicted to Justin, the details of my dream

solidified as I worked up a lather of shampoo. I still didn't know what it meant, but at least I had a linear story to tell.

I had dreamed I was at a crossroads, standing under a sky of silver velvet, stars competing against the full moon. In all directions was the mesquite savanna of South Texas; a moist and salty wind rustled the dry grass and leaves like music.

A flash of red grabbed my attention; taillights retreated down the one-lane farm road that crossed the highway. I'd followed them in an effortless run—definite proof that I was dreaming—until the gravel road ran out and I found myself in a field, with a barbed wire fence blocking my way.

It extended in both directions, as far as I could see. The bright metal wire glowed with captured starlight, concentrating it to points at the twisted, sharpened barbs. I reached cautiously toward one of those shining spikes, and felt a tingle as though I'd put my hand near an electrical field. The damaged nerves of my arm began to sting in warning, and I prudently pulled my hand back.

The dream settled one matter. Whatever had killed the cow by the road, this fence was . . . *something*. The barrier didn't have to be literal. It could be a figurative construct. The question was, what did it keep in? Or, for that matter, out?

✳   ✳   ✳

Lisa still wasn't back when I got out of the shower, so I pulled on a pair of jeans and a green Bedivere U T-shirt, slipped on my flip-flops, and went to find some breakfast.

Dulcina wasn't a big town, and from the second-floor landing of the Artesian Manor, I could see most of it. Heck, I could probably see all the way to the Gulf of Mexico if I had a pair of binoculars. The land was that flat. I made for the stairs as I pocketed the key—an honest-to-God metal key with a large plastic tag hanging from it, my room number in big, come-break-into-me digits.

Digit, I should say. There were eight rooms in the Artesian Manor. And from the looks of things, that was seven more than required.

It was an old building, even older than the interior décor indicated. Vaguely Spanish Revival, I guess, with dingy whitewashed walls. Four doors upstairs, four doors down, all facing a parking lot and a fenced-in, empty pool. A cracked concrete path led to the back door of the restaurant/bar that also served as the day office for the motel. This triumph of multitasking was called the Duck Inn, and I hadn't asked if they did room service.

A cowbell above the door clanged as I went in. The morning wasn't hot yet, but the air-conditioner hummed, ready for combat, as sunlight struggled through the tinted windows. It smelled of last night's beer and the last decade's tobacco. The wood floor was scarred and sticky. Booths lined the paneled walls, which were hung with more hunting prints and a few stuffed fowl that justified the pun of a name, but didn't really excuse it.

A Bud Light sign above the bar was dark, and a black-haired woman, whose apron covered a wealth of terrain, was drying glass mugs behind the counter.

My greeting was tentative—it was my first time ordering breakfast in a bar. "Could I get a cup of coffee and . . ." A bagel was probably out of the question. "And some toast?"

The woman thunked a mug on the bar and tucked the

towel into her apron. "You think this is some big-city Star-bucks?"

"No, ma'am," I said, because she reminded me of a scary biology teacher I had in high school, who, it was rumored, would dissect troublesome students like frogs, then feed them to her pet iguana.

"You drive all night, wreck your car, then think you can get through the morning on a little coffee and a piece of bread?"

"Yes, ma'am . . . I mean, no . . . um . . ." I didn't know whether I was more flustered by the lecture or her detailed knowledge of my situation. "I'll have, um—"

"Get the *taquito*." I turned at the sound of Lisa's voice. She peered around the high back of one of the booths and ad-dressed the lady behind the bar. *"Por favor, déle un taquito como que usted me dio."*

The woman's smile made her look much less like a scary biology teacher. *"¿Le gusta a usted?"*

*"Fue muy bueno. Gracias, Teresa."*

*"De nada."* The woman—Teresa, I guessed—turned back to me, smile fading. "I'll bring it to you."

"Thank you," I said. Then added, *"Gracias,"* which aside from *¿Dónde está el baño?* was the extent of my Spanish.

I was a little surprised to see Zeke sitting across from Lisa. He was dressed in jeans and a red T-shirt. Still no cow-boy hat, but in the daylight I could see that it would be a shame to hide his thick, inky hair.

"Hey." I slid into the booth next to Lisa and directed a question to Zeke. "You have nothing better to do on a Saturday?"

"New faces," he said, taking a sip of coffee. "Get tired of looking at the same ones all the time."

"Thanks a lot, Mr. Zeke," Teresa called from behind the bar.

Dull red embarrassment spread over his cheekbones. Lisa pounced right away, like a cat with a new toy. "*Mister* Zeke? Are you lord of the manor or something?"

"No." He leaned back in the booth, maybe guessing—correctly—that the less he squeaked, the less Lisa would bat at him. "My uncle is Mr. Velasquez. I'm Mr. Zeke. It's just a matter of clarity."

"Right," she said. "So what is Zeke short for? Ezekiel?"

He gave in to a sheepish smile. "You should meet my uncle Gabe and cousin Mike."

Lisa laughed in genuine amusement. "Gabriel, Michael . . ."

"Miguel, actually," he corrected.

"Was your dad Rafe?"

"He got off easy with Isaiah. We're just prophets, not angels."

"Were your parents in some kind of cult?"

"Only if you count the Catholic Church."

The unholy laughter in Lisa's gray eyes warned me her reply would be a doozy, but I spotted Teresa on her way over and kicked my friend under the table. She pressed her lips shut as Teresa set down a mug of coffee and a plate. On it was a foil-wrapped cylinder as big around as a Coke can and twice as long.

"Oh, a breakfast burrito," I said, as delighted as I was hungry.

"*Ay chihuahua.*" Teresa flung her gaze skyward. I'd never actually heard anyone say that before.

The *taquito*—which was delicious, stuffed with scrambled eggs, cheese, and sautéed potatoes—claimed my ravenous attention, and Zeke—holder of the latest gossip—had captured Teresa's.

"Do you know whose cow it was on the road?" She lifted the glass coffeepot in a tacit question.

Zeke pushed his empty mug toward her. "Hanging J brand."

"That's too bad." She made a *tsk* sound with her tongue as she poured. "Jorge can't really afford to lose another one."

"He'll lose the calf, too, unless one of the other cows will let it have a teat."

I stopped eating long enough to pour cream in my coffee. "Do you lose a lot of cattle this way?"

Teresa raised her brows. "Hit by cars?"

My eyes went to Zeke. "Killed by coyotes."

She looked at him, too, and he answered with his gaze fixed on his coffee mug. "Looks like she was chased out onto the road. A coyote"—he said it with only two syllables, *ki-yote*—"was my best guess."

Teresa narrowed her eyes. "I've heard of them taking down a calf before, but not a full-grown cow."

There was something argumentative in that, and in Zeke's reply. "Maybe a pack of them ganged up."

"Oh, come on, Zeke." She parked the coffeepot on the table, hard enough to rattle the glass. "You've been riding the herds since you could sit on a horse. Have you ever seen a coyote chase an adult cow away from the group, let alone take it down?"

"If it was sick, or weak for some reason . . ."

She gave a *pffft* of irritated impatience. "There's been a lot of weak cattle around, then, is all I can say."

"Well," said Zeke. "We *are* in the middle of a drought. And even coyotes get desperate."

"Other things might get desperate, too." Her reply was cryptic and significant, as if this was a continuation of a previous discussion.

He set down his mug with a thump that put a period on the conversation. "Teresa, I'm trying to do something about the problem, and your superstitious gossip isn't helping."

Teresa drew herself up to her full height, color blooming in her cheeks. "*Perdóname,* Señor Velasquez. I forgot my place."

Zeke relented immediately, but she had gone, sailing off on her offended dignity. He watched her go, his mouth hardening into a slash of irritation.

"So," I said, the word loud in the awkward lull. The caffeine had kicked in and my brain caught up with the conversation. "Your name is Velasquez like . . . Velasquez *County*?"

"Yeah." He didn't look happy about it at that moment.

The exchange had been interesting, but raised more questions than it answered. "What does she mean, other things get desperate?"

"The ranchers, probably." Zeke finished his coffee in what must have been a scalding gulp. "Could be an insurance scheme."

While I didn't believe this for a second, it distracted me with an awful new thought. "I'm not going to get sued for hitting someone's cow, am I?"

"No. It's the rancher's, or the landowner's, responsibility to make sure the fences are secure. Which is why I'm going out with you and Buck to get your car. I want to see what that fence looks like."

"Don't look so grim," I said. "I'm not going to sue *you*."

He gave me a rueful smile, but I was glad to see some of his humor returning. "Don't speak too soon. You haven't gotten the news on your Jeep yet."

# 4

It didn't seem possible that the highway scenery could be even more boring in the daylight.

I rode in the cab of Buck's tow truck; the mechanic was a nice guy with a slow drawl and no hurry to get anything done. He liked playing tour guide, though, and answered my questions about the landscape.

"Gulf's about ten miles that way," said Buck, pointing to the east side of the highway, which was a little greener than the west. "Stays a little wetter. There's some bird-watching out by the water, and a restaurant about twenty miles up the coast. Some mighty good shrimp there."

There wasn't room for all of us in the tow truck, so Lisa and Zeke were driving ahead in his pickup. Interesting how chummy they'd gotten. Back in her goth days, D&D Lisa wouldn't have sat on the same side of the cafeteria as Zeke the rancher.

"So, Buck. How well do you know Zeke Velasquez?"

"Young Zeke?" He shrugged. "He's a good kid. Got some highfalutin ideas about a few things. Wants to put big ol' windmills all along the water, generate electricity or some such business."

"You mean a wind farm?"

"Yeah. Got the other counties in a pelter. Say the bird-watchers won't come down if there's big airplane propellers interfering with migration."

"Would it? Interfere, I mean?"

Buck shook his head. "Had a bunch of college types down here to check it out. Zeke wouldn't do anything to hurt an animal. He loves 'em. Just got a puppy from him."

I tried to picture the laid-back mechanic with a yapping little dog. "A puppy?"

"Yeah. My granddaughter needed a new one after her last one got killed."

"I'm so sorry." We hadn't had a dog since I was little. Mom had been thinking of getting another one, but then she got pregnant, so I have a little sister now instead. Not exactly the same thing.

"Yep. Coyotes got him. Weren't pretty." He nodded ahead, to the southbound side of the highway. "That your car, little missy?"

I was glad for the distraction from that mental image. The

Jeep, with its safari-brown paint, could have been nicely camouflaged in the desert. Especially since it was missing its black canvas top.

"Where is the top?" Twisting in the seat, I craned to peer across Buck, in case I had simply not noticed the roof of the Wrangler.

"Must have got stolen" was Buck's sanguine answer. "Hope you didn't have anything valuable in there."

"Just that whopping big *part of my car.*"

The carcass of the cow was gone, too, but there were a lot of gooey stains on the road, smeared by countless tires. Zeke put on his turn signal as he approached the median cross-over, then U-turned onto the southbound lanes and pulled onto the shoulder, leaving room for Buck to back the tow truck up to the Jeep. I noticed that, despite my dream, there was no second road crossing the highway there.

Watching for cars, I opened the door and slid out, taking my camera bag with me. There was a lot more traffic on the road this morning. A semi roared by, followed by two cars full of spring breakers.

"Do you mind if I take a few pictures before you load it up?" I asked Buck.

"Suit yourself."

While he went to work, getting out chains and whatever else he needed, I took shots of the Jeep from all angles. The insurance people had been helpful on the phone, but I wanted to make sure I documented everything.

"Where's the cow?" Lisa stood by the pickup, frowning at the dark, icky spot on the highway and the empty grass of the median.

"I called the cow's owner last night and he came to get it." Zeke slipped a pair of funky-looking pliers into his pocket and pulled on a thick pair of gloves. Hauling a partial spool of barbed wire from the back of the truck, he gave Lisa a teasing glance. "You said it yourself. Too late for anything but a barbecue."

She snapped her gaze toward him. "You're not serious."

"Don't you know where your hamburger comes from?"

"Not from roadkill. I hope."

He smiled, but lost his teasing edge. "Don't judge people for salvaging what they can. Jorge's family counts on those cattle for their living. This drought has hit everyone hard."

Buck hailed me from halfway underneath the Jeep, bringing me back to my own problems. "You tore this thing up pretty good, little lady. You're going to need a new gas tank, maybe a new exhaust system. Think you might have cracked a CV joint to boot."

"Do you think you can fix it?" I watched him emerge and dust off his grimy jeans. "Is it totaled?"

"Totaled? Nah." He lifted a sweat-stained cap and smoothed his thinning brown hair. "They haven't changed these old Jeeps much since I learned on 'em in the service. Gotta get the parts down here, though. That'll take a few days."

"A few days? Can't they overnight them?"

"Sure. Overnight to Corpus, then another day down here. That's the quickest we get things, missy. And tomorrow's Sunday besides."

"Okay," I said, trying to sound like I dealt with this kind of thing all the time. I'd gotten the Jeep—not new, but reliable—when I'd gotten my license, and I'd never had so much as a fender bender.

"I'll load 'er up and get back to the shop. I'll know more when I get it up on the lift." I must have failed in my attempt to look calm, because he put a hand on my shoulder. "It'll be okay, little missy. We'll get you set to rights."

"Thank you, Mr. Buck." And I meant it, despite the "little missy" part.

I waited for another Padre-bound car—the rear-window graffiti was a giveaway—to pass, then stepped out into the lane to take a picture of the blood on the road, and the skid marks of the Jeep.

In the daylight, I could see the trail the cow had left as it blundered through the fence and onto the highway. I wondered, briefly, if the tears on its skin could have been from the barbed wire, then discarded the idea. Instinct said no, and so did logic. The gouges had been too deep.

Zeke was stringing new wire with professional efficiency. Lisa stood on the dirt shoulder, staring at the ground with an intensely thoughtful expression.

I started toward her, and she said without looking up, "Watch your step. I think these are animal tracks."

Treading carefully where the dry grass was undisturbed, I joined her. There was definitely some kind of imprint in the dirt, dramatically different from the cow's hoofs. "Does that look like a coyote to you?" she asked.

"How should I know?" I said.

"You were the Girl Scout."

"I was a *Brownie.* In the first grade. We were too busy making macaroni art to do much wild animal tracking."

"Too bad. It might have thinned the weak from the herd."

"I wish I could tell when you're joking." Crouching, I framed the footprint in the camera's lens and zoomed close. Maybe I was no Eagle Scout, but I could tell it hadn't been made by a canine type paw. The impression was sort of thin, with long toes and claws. It looked kind of reptilian, like the footprints in *Jurassic Park*.

"Do you have a quarter?" I asked.

"Planning to make a phone call?"

"No. I want to put it in the picture for a measure of scale."

Lisa dug into the pocket of her jeans. "You watch too much *CSI*."

"I got that from a Jeffery Deaver novel, actually."

"Nerd." She placed the coin near the mini dinosaur track, which really wasn't that mini, except when compared with a T. rex.

I took several pictures, then lowered the camera. "Gila monster?" suggested Lisa.

"Iguana, maybe." Except the print was the same size as my own foot. A five-foot-two iguana, then.

"Touch it," she said. "Maybe you'll See something."

"Geez, Lisa. Are you *ever* going to let me live that down?"

"I'm serious." She crouched, facing me with the track between us. "Maybe you'll See what kind of animal made it."

She was serious, all right. Her gray eyes were alight with studied curiosity. The kind of curiosity that made Ben Franklin tie a key to a kite string. Now I knew how the kite felt.

"You do remember there was barfing involved the last time I touched something icky?"

"How do you even know this footprint is connected with Bessie's untimely end?" Lisa's voice was reason itself. So much so that it made me seem unreasonable for being such a wuss.

"I've never even tried a footprint before, only objects that have a long association with someone."

"There are a lot of sympathetic magic spells associated with footprints. They're very symbolic."

"Nice for them."

"Come on. Aren't you even curious?"

Of course I was. And of course she knew it.

The tow truck started up with a bang. I jumped and Lisa did, too. She fell on her butt, her foot shooting out and obliterating the track. The chugging of the tow truck's winch, the creak of winding chain as it hoisted the Jeep, covered her curse and my laughter.

"What are you girls doing?" Zeke had to yell over the noise of the truck.

Lisa shot me a look I couldn't interpret, so I ignored her. "We found a weird-looking track. Doesn't look like a coyote."

He left the fence and came over to peer at the ground. "I don't see anything."

I thumbed back through the pictures, and held the camera out to him. Shading it with his gloved hand, he squinted at the view screen. "It's hard to tell from this. Could be anything."

"It looked kind of like a lizard, but it was too big."

He handed the camera back to me, his expression friendly but a little too careful. "Are you sure it wasn't a bird? It could have been a hawk, or a vulture looking for leftovers."

On that lovely mental image, I let the matter drop, and Zeke went back to work on the fence. Lisa watched him go, then turned to me, her voice covered by the engine of the tow truck.

"What are you thinking, Mags?"

I turned off the camera and looped the strap around my neck. "I don't know. I have a weird feeling about this."

She gazed at me, her face inscrutable. "You mean, weirder than us getting stranded by two tons of hamburger in the first place?"

"Yeah."

"Come on, Mags." She made a gesture that encompassed the track and the gory spot on the road. "Some animal killed that cow. If not a coyote, then something else. This might be ranch land, but it's still wilderness. Just look around us."

The highway had plenty of traffic, and there were clusters of houses dotted about, set far back from the road. But there was a lot of open ground, too, where anything could live.

The winch on the truck had stopped, and Buck was securing the Jeep in place. I lowered my voice so he and Zeke wouldn't hear. "I had a dream last night. I'm not sure how the cow ties in, but there is *something* going on."

She pursed her lips. "You mean . . . magic?"

"Maybe."

The crunch of Buck's boots on the dry grass stopped me from saying anything else. "You girls want to ride back with me, or stick around with Mr. Zeke?"

"We'll stay, I guess. Unless you need me to sign anything?"

"Nah." He rearranged the toothpick in his mouth. "I figure you're not going anywhere."

He certainly had that right.

# 5

"Hey, Mom."

"Hey, Magpie!" Mom's voice was cheerful. I could hear Brigid wailing in the background. Astronauts in orbit could probably hear her, too. "How is South Padre? Did you get a room with a view of the beach?"

I took in the scenic view from the balcony of the Artesian Manor—the highway, the Duck Inn, the town square, with its dilapidated gazebo, and the water tower looming over all of it. "Not exactly."

"Oh. That's too bad." I could tell she'd gone to pick Brigid up; the baby's cries were even louder, and Mom's voice came in spurts, like she was bouncing her while she talked. "I love the beach. It was such a shame that you never did. After that one trip, we never tried to go again."

I hate deep water. My folks found this out the hard way after they'd shelled out for a Florida vacation when I was six and someone had had to stay onshore with me at all times.

"Well, it's not going to be a problem here."

"Too much other fun stuff to do, I'll bet."

I could see Buck's garage, where the Jeep was up on the rack like a surgery patient. "Here's the thing, Mom. I don't want you to panic. Everyone is okay."

Brigid started crying louder, as if I needed a barometer of Mom's escalating tension. "Magdalena Lorraine Quinn. What's going on?"

I winced at the full-name whammy. "There was a cow in the road. I tried to avoid it, but there was a lot of damage to the Jeep."

She took several deep breaths, audible despite the crying baby. "But you and Lisa are okay?"

"Not a scratch."

"Where are you?"

"A little town called Dulcina. Not much more than a water tower and a motel. There's a mechanic here who can fix the Jeep. I've already called the car insurance people, and the owner of the pasture—the one the cow escaped from—is going to pay the deductible."

I said this all as quickly as I could, trying to show her that I was responsible, that I'd thought of everything. As I talked, Brigid's cries tapered off, and I figured I'd been moderately successful.

"You have someplace to stay?" Mom asked. "Someplace that I don't have to worry about you?"

"Yeah." I rattled off the address and phone number, in case she needed to get in touch and my cell wasn't working. The two-story motel was the high point in town, and reception had been decent here so far, but spotty out on the road. "We're the only guests, so they'll know who we are."

"Artesian Manor. How fancy."

"Oh, Mom. You would have to see it to believe it."

"Well . . ." She floundered for a moment, as if finding her bearings. "I feel like I should be more upset, but it sounds as if you've already got things under control."

Her subtext was strangely poignant. "Why do you say that like it's a bad thing?"

"I don't know." I could hear a sad smile in her voice. "Because you didn't need your dad or me to fix this."

Guilt closed my throat. I had carefully avoided telling her that the accident had happened in the middle of the night, which would mean confessing my initial lie. "Say that again when the car insurance rates go up."

"You can't help hitting a cow." She sighed. "So, what are you going to do in that tiny town?"

"I might try and take some pictures, poke around." I didn't mention anything about investigating weird footprints. "Since I can't write about South Padre, maybe I can get a regional or historical article on this place."

"Or you could have the Jeep towed to the nearest city. At least you'd have things to do there."

On Monday, the garages in Kingsville or Corpus Christi would be open. For that matter, we could continue down to

Brownsville and still get to Padre Island. I hadn't seriously considered the option to decamp, though, for practical reasons. "The insurance won't pay for a tow that far."

"Well, I will, sweetie. This is your first college spring break, and you should enjoy it."

Mom's deep denial regarding the weirdness that happens around me forces her to cling to the idea that I should have normal coming-of-age experiences, like parties and dates and things. This completely overlooks the fact that I never did have parties and dates and things, even before I encountered the forces of darkness.

Her next words proved I had accurately followed her train of thought. "I suppose I'm relieved it was just an accident, and not anything *weird* this time." A pause, while the baby made a gurgling sound. "It *is* just an accident, right?"

"What else would it be?"

She took the evasive question as rhetorical. "Your dad just came in. Do you want to tell him yourself?"

"Uh, no." I wouldn't be able to keep Dad completely in the dark about my suspicions that there was something going on here. It isn't that my dad is any smarter than my mom—they're both sharp—but Mom is more determined to think the world is a reasonable place.

"Then just keep us posted. And you and Lisa be careful."

"We will. Love you, Mom."

"You too, Magpie."

✻    ✻    ✻

Lisa came back from the Stop & Shop with Zeke, her arms loaded with plastic bags. He'd lent us an ice chest so that we could keep sustenance—mainly Diet Coke—in the room, and

**45**

now he carried, with impressively little effort, a ten-pound bag of ice, which he dumped into the Igloo.

"How did the scavenging go?" I asked, looking up from the book I was reading. It was one of several scattered around me on the bed, along with my laptop.

"We won't starve." Lisa pulled a box of Pop-Tarts and a bag of Tostitos out of the sack. "I see your reconnoiter was equally productive."

"I went to the library before they closed for the day." I neatened the books into a stack. "The librarian already knew our story, and took pity on me."

Zeke looked askance at the laptop. "You brought your computer on vacation?"

I raised a quizzical brow. "Doesn't everybody?"

Lisa was loading cans of soda into the cooler, and handed one to Zeke and one to me. "I don't think they're as addicted to their electronics down here, Mags."

"We have high-tech stuff." Zeke popped the tab on his Coke. "Mostly on hunting equipment. Buck has a GPS on his four-wheeler, Gus has an electronic fish finder."

"How about wireless Internet?" I asked. Needless to say, the Artesian Manor wasn't set up with broadband networking. "Any hot spots in town?"

"No. The library has a connection, but they don't open again until Tuesday. You can come into the ranch office on Monday and use our network."

Forty-eight hours without the Internet. I felt a little queasy. "If I'm not dead from withdrawal by then, I'll take you up on that."

He glanced at his watch. "I'd take you now, but I've got to

get back out to the Big House. My grandmother expects everyone there for Saturday dinner."

"And everyone obeys the summons?" My gran only wishes she had that kind of matriarchal power. It's hard just getting my dad's brother into town for Christmas.

"Yeah. Even my uncle comes down from Houston. His presence is required until after lunch on Sunday."

"From Houston?" Lisa asked. "That's got to be six hours away."

"He's got a private plane. There's an airstrip out by the house." At our stares, he added defensively, "What? We need it for the helicopter, too."

I blinked. "I guess it only *feels* like we've gone back in time."

"Well, since Abuelita doesn't leave the property, the world has to come to her." He went to the door, pausing to toss out a casual invitation. "Why don't y'all come out to the ranch on Monday, keep from going stir-crazy."

"Great," said Lisa, my ex-goth, neo-alchemist friend. At least she sounded droll about it. "It'll be loads of fun."

With a grin, Zeke let himself out. I stared at Lisa. "What kind of pod person are you? D&D Lisa . . . on a ranch?"

"What?" Falling onto the bed, she dropped her arm over her face. "Do you really want to test how long until I go all Jack Nicholson in *The Shining*?"

"Did you get a chance to ask him what Teresa thinks killed the cow if it wasn't a coyote?"

"It didn't come up in the conversation."

I flung a pillow at her, but it bounced off her shoulder and flopped limply to the floor. "What's the matter with you? Don't you want to find out what's going on?"

She threw her own pillow at me, with much better aim. "What do you suggest? 'By the way, my friend the psychic girl detective thinks you have a supernatural mystery on your ranch.' You can't just drop that bomb on someone right after you meet them."

"You might also throw in what a complete *witch* you can be." I stacked the library books—*The Wild Horse Desert: South Texas History* on top of *Handbook of North American Desert Fauna*—with more force than necessary. "I really don't understand why you're being such a skeptic. You were there. You saw those taillights disappear into thin air. And what happened when I touched the cow blood. Come on, Lisa."

Sitting up, she swung her legs off the bed and leaned toward me. Hands braced on her knees, she asked pointedly, "So what, exactly, do you think it is?"

I had no answer, so I redirected the conversation, pointing to the desert fauna handbook. "I couldn't find any track that looked like the one by the road."

She shook her head in faux sympathy. "Deductive reasoning is so inefficient."

I sighed. "Too bad there's isn't a *Field Guide to Supernatural Creatures.*"

"Now, that would be a really useful book." She fell back onto her mattress and covered her face with a pillow. "I'm going to take a nap. Wake me up when it's time for dinner."

That put a cap on the discussion. Lisa's skepticism was both irritating and surprising. I supposed it went along with what she'd said in the car, about wanting a week of being normal. And she hadn't said she didn't believe me that there was something weird here, just that there wasn't really a way to bring up the weirdness to Zeke, who seemed to be firmly—maybe even stubbornly—rooted in normalcy.

It didn't help that I didn't have any specific suspicions. All I could do was figure out what we *weren't* dealing with. And as Lisa had pointed out, deductive reasoning was definitely the long way around to a point.

# 6

The Duck Inn looked different after dark. It was crowded, for one thing. On the jukebox, a gravel-voiced man twanged about lovin' and leavin'. Patrons lined the bar and occupied the tables, and neon beer signs made auras of color in the haze of cigarette smoke.

The song ended as Lisa and I came in, right on cue. We stood in silence broken only by the click of the pool balls and the scrape of a fork on a plate. All that was missing was the sound of crickets and a spotlight on our entrance.

The stasis didn't last long. The next song started and the pool game resumed. People went back to eating and chatting over their beer. Lisa and I exchanged glances, then wove through the crowd. It was a bustling night at the only watering hole in town.

Teresa, once again behind the bar, pushed a couple of grease-stained menus at us. "What'll you have, girls?"

The menu was short, and geared toward the carnivore. "I'll have the chicken." I wasn't going anywhere near the beef.

Lisa perused the list a little longer. "Do you have anything without meat in it?"

Teresa gave her a scary biology teacher look. "You want just some vegetables? They don't have any meat in them."

"You don't cook them with bacon?" I'd been in South Texas long enough to get a feel for the cuisine.

"Well, yeah. But just for flavor."

"So bacon is just a condiment?" I asked.

She leveled a scalpel-like stare at me, and I meekly thanked her for taking our order and retreated. All the booths were full, which left us no place but a table in the middle of the room.

Lisa settled into the chair across from me. "And you say *I'm* antagonistic?"

"I'm a slave to my wit." I tried not to stare at the people trying to pretend they weren't staring at us. "Do you think everyone in town is here?"

"Where else are they going to go on a Saturday night?"

Most of the crowd blended together, with a work-hardened, sun-browned uniformity that blurred the lines of ethnicity. I recognized a group of older men, retirement age, who'd been at the same table that morning, drinking coffee. One of them nodded at me, raising his mug in greeting. I gave a little smile in return, encouraged by the friendly gesture.

At the bar, Teresa seemed to be in conference with two men. One was a lanky guy in a cowboy hat, who gestured lazily with a bottle of Budweiser as he talked. The other guy had his back to us, but I could tell he was younger because his shirt was untucked. It seemed to be a generational thing.

I didn't have to guess the subject of their discussion, because all three of them kept darting glances toward our table.

Leaning sideways, I whispered to Lisa out of the side of my mouth. "Keep an eye on the door in case we have to make a run for it."

She sipped her iced tea, looking almost relaxed. "Does it *feel* like we'll have to make a run for it?"

I realized that my deflector shields were at maximum—that was how I visualized my mental defenses. When I pictured them powering down a bit, I realized that, for all the attention we were getting, none of it was threatening. In fact, not all the buzz in the room was centered on us.

The scrape of a chair drew my attention back to the immediate, normal five-senses situation. The younger man from the bar stood by our table, a friendly expression on his tanned face.

"Evening, ladies. How is Dulcina treating you?"

Lisa raised a brow. "Better than the highway did."

The guy chuckled. "So I heard. Word gets around." If my smoke-bleary eyes didn't deceive me, he was kind of cute. Not young-Lou-Diamond-Phillips gorgeous like Zeke, but sort of guy-next-door good-looking. Behind him, I could see

Teresa and Budweiser Man watching avidly, like his bizarro-world wingmen. "Can I buy you a beer and make amends for your lousy introduction to Velasquez County?"

While I debated a few things—our underageness, his obvious but as-yet-unknown ulterior motive—Lisa just said, "Sure."

I shot her an incredulous look as Young Guy went back to the bar. "What?" she said. "He obviously wants to ask us something, so we may as well grease the wheels. Or else eat dinner while being stared at like tropical fish in a pediatric waiting room."

This was so sensible, I couldn't even come up with a wisecrack. It explained why there were no IDs or questions involved in the handover of beer. Junior was obviously the designated representative of the Duck Inn–quisition.

He returned with three bottles under his arm and a plate of food in each hand. "Here you go, ladies."

The food was either really good or I was really hungry. Maybe a mix of both. As we dug in, the guy spun one of the chairs around and straddled it in the same motion. "I'm Dave, by the way."

"Maggie," I said between bites. "This is Lisa."

"Hey! Like Bart Simpson's sisters."

Lisa rolled her eyes so hard, her whole head turned with the gesture. "Wow. We've never heard that before."

Dave missed her irony, intent on his mission. "Been hearing a lot of rumors about your accident," he said.

Here we go. I could sense people shifting in their seats to better catch our reply. Behind the counter, Teresa stood with her arms akimbo, alert for holes in our story. Budweiser Man had swiveled his stool so he could lean his elbow on the bar, the heel of his cowboy boot hooked on one rung.

"So, how'd you manage that?" asked Bud Man from his perch. He had a serious case of hat head, the kind that only comes from wearing a hat while you sweat. Indicating one of the Old Guys at the coffee drinkers' table, he continued. "Carl over there hit a cow with his truck, and it smashed the whole front end. Nowhere to take it but the junkyard."

Carl nodded, and said something unintelligible into his coffee mug.

I glanced at Lisa, and she yielded the floor to me with a gesture. What a pal. "Maybe because the cow was already, um, dead. We just . . ." I pantomimed the Jeep sailing over the carcass like a water-skier on a ramp.

Dave leaned in, elbows on the table. "Could you tell what killed it?"

"Does it matter?" asked Lisa, her brows arched.

Bud Man took a swig of his beer. "Here's our pickle. Zeke Velasquez says it's got to be a coyote, maybe a pack of 'em. Teresa swears it's gotta be something else, but she wasn't there. You actually saw it—the cow, I mean—so we want to hear what you say."

Behind him, Teresa folded her arms under her ample bosom, her expression daring me to side with Mr. Zeke.

"What else could it be?" I tried to keep the question ingenuous. Here was my chance to find out what these folks thought attacked the cow.

"Maybe you saw something in the fields," said Dave, watching my face avidly. "Maybe some eyes looking at you?"

"Eyes?" I didn't remember seeing any, but the idea

struck a bad chord of memory. Glancing at Lisa, I saw that her face was carefully impassive. No one was bothering to grill *her*. "What do you mean?" I asked. "Like, reflecting the light?"

"Maybe," said Dave. I could tell he was trying to elicit a specific answer with his mysterious—and annoying—ambivalence.

"Like for instance," said Bud Man, in a refreshingly normal tone, "coyote eyes are yellow when they reflect the light. Nothing hinky there."

Dave twisted around to glare at him. "Don't lead the witness. I'm trying to let her come up with her own description."

The cowboy at the bar laughed into his beer bottle. "This isn't *Law and Order,* David. You ease up on those poor girls."

It was too dark to be sure, but I thought Dave's ears reddened. When he turned back to Lisa and me, he looked sheepish. "Sorry about that. Anything you remember about last night would be helpful."

"Helpful in what?" I glanced at the bar full of attentive listeners. There was something about their grimly expectant faces, something about the argument between Teresa and Zeke that morning, as if it was an ongoing conversation. I couldn't remember anyone mentioning any dead cows besides the one on the road, but intuition didn't have far to leap. "This isn't the first animal that's died?"

The beat of silence confirmed my guess, and somehow made the situation more solemn.

Bud Man spoke first. "We're in a drought. You're going to lose animals when it gets this dry. Goats. Chickens. Calves usually go first."

"Drought didn't kill my best herding dog," said Carl from the Old Guys' table. "Or Teresa's goats."

Teresa unfolded her arms slowly, with a sense of drama. "All with their throats ripped out."

I swallowed the memory of the blood, the phantom taste of it too recent. "So, what *do* you think it is?"

"*El chupacabra.*"

She whispered the name, whether for effect or in fear. The half-voiced word breathed across the bar to my waiting ear, lifting the hair on the back of my neck.

"El *what*?" asked Lisa, her tone breaking the spell.

Bud Man groaned, a not-this-again sound of annoyance. "Teresa, you're crazy. It's not the chupacabra. That's a load of horse shit."

She reached across the bar and grabbed his bottle. "You don't have to drink in my bar if you think I'm crazy."

He grabbed it back, sloshing beer on the counter. "Yes, I do. It's the only place in a hundred miles."

"Dave believes me," Teresa muttered. "He saw what happened to my goats."

"What is *el chupacabra*?" I asked. The word tickled a memory in my mental file cabinet of useless information.

"It means 'the goat sucker,' " said Dave. "It kills livestock, drinks their blood."

"And you think this goat sucker killed the cow and left it on the road?" I tested the weirdometer in my head, the way you nudge a tooth with your tongue to test if it's loose. No bells went off, but it was hard to think seriously about something with such a ridiculous name.

Especially when Lisa asked, "Wouldn't that make it a cow sucker, then?"

Teresa scowled at her levity. "*El chupacabra* kills whatever it can get," she explained. "With the drought, cows are weak, easier to catch."

The memory clicked. "Hang on. I remember this from an article on the Internet."

"Oh, well then, it must be true." Lisa's tone was drolly dismissive.

I ignored her. "It's like an urban legend. But in the story, someone found a dead animal they couldn't identify."

"You have got to be kidding me." Lisa pushed back her plate and put her elbows on the table. "This is a real animal?"

"Yes," said Teresa and Dave.

"No," said Bud Man at the same time.

"It *is*," Teresa insisted.

My gaze traveled across the three of them, over to the Old Guys' table, then to the audience in the booths. "So, what is this chupacabra thing supposed to look like?"

I'd asked the magic question. Everyone answered at once.

"It's a huge dog-shaped—"

"Lizard . . . like a lizard . . ."

"With spines down its back."

"It can hop like a kangaroo . . ."

"Fly like a bat . . ."

"Stop!" Teresa held up her hands. The voices subsided; their queen had called them to order. "*El chupacabra* is too smart to be seen. It comes out of the darkness to drain the blood of its prey, then disappears. No one sees anything, just a glimpse of glowing red eyes."

The bar had been warm a moment ago, but as she talked, embroidering the words with melodrama, my skin seemed to cool, and I shivered in the air-conditioning.

"Glowing red eyes like . . . taillights?"

Dave leaned in eagerly. "Did you see something like that?"

"We were on the highway," Lisa snapped, too brusquely even for her. "Taillights are a given."

Teresa held my eyes, encouraged by something in my expression. "It gives a hideous scream that makes you nauseated to even hear it. A few people, a very few, have been near enough to smell its horrible stench, like burning sulfur."

My pulse tripped over itself, an instinctive panic of memory. I glanced at Lisa, but her face was stubbornly blank.

"So what about it, city girls?" asked Bud Man, the easy laugh in his voice diffusing the spell of Teresa's words. "Did you smell fire and brimstone?"

"No," I said honestly. I'd smelled nothing but blood and gasoline. The demon in high school had smelled like sulfur and a lot of other gross things. But it had also been intangible, unable to touch things directly. At least it had at first. The problem with learning that there are things in the universe that break what you thought were the rules of reality is that there are all new rules to learn, and no textbook to study.

Dave was asking me another question. "Had the blood been sucked out of it? The cow, I mean."

My stomach turned in memory. "Definitely not. It was all over the ground."

Teresa was undeterred. "Maybe the car came before the creature could drink."

Bud Man rolled his eyes. "And maybe it's not *el chupacabra*. Give it up, Miss T. You owe me a case of beer."

She pursed her lips and swept the empty out of his hand with a broad gesture. "No way. She didn't say it was, but she didn't say it wasn't."

As if that was some kind of signal, people turned back to their private conversations. If folks were still talking about us, the accident, or the goat sucker, they did it among themselves. Music blared out of the jukebox speakers, and I realized it must have been playing all along, only I hadn't noticed.

Dave crossed his arms on the back of the chair he straddled. "So, how long are y'all going to be in town?"

Lisa stared at him coldly. "You can't tell us about a monster, then hit on us. Are you that desperate for fresh meat around here?"

He grinned, unrepentant. "The dating pool *is* awful shallow."

"Still not making any points, cowboy."

I wasn't really listening. I needed to think, and I had to do it away from all these people. Turning to Lisa, I lied abruptly, "We told Justin we'd call at nine o'clock."

We weren't best friends for no reason. She dropped her napkin on the table and didn't miss a beat. "Gotta go, Dave. It's been real."

He rose to his feet in time to pull out her chair. "I'll walk you to your room. Wouldn't want Ol' Chupy to grab you on the way."

Dave was harmless. I picked that up even without touching him. He was a nice, eager guy with a big mouth, and he was totally in the way when I needed to talk to Lisa ASAP.

A man at the Old Guys' table—the one really not old

enough to hang out with them, the same one who had saluted me when the evening first started—spoke up, his voice casual but somehow authoritative. "Don't try so hard, Dave. Nothing will get them between the Duck and their room."

Dave looked unabashed, but he also seemed to back off from us without really moving. "Just trying to be a gentleman, Hector."

The older guy, Hector, had a long face that I couldn't see clearly in the smoke-filled room. He met my gaze with reassuring dark eyes. "You'll be fine as long as you don't go wandering around out in the dark."

Lisa grabbed my arm, steering me toward the door as she tossed back over her shoulder, "Thanks. Fortunately, we left our idiot pills at home."

I dug in my heels as soon as we were alone outside. "Jeez, Lisa. That was really rude, even for you."

She faced me on the cracked concrete path between the empty swimming pool and the stairs up to our motel room. "Me? You're the one with the fake phone call."

"You're welcome to go back in and get Dave's hopes up if you want."

"That's not what this is about." She set her fists on her hips. "You think this chupacabra thing is real."

I took a deep breath to clear my lungs of the secondhand smoke, and to phrase my answer. "I don't think it was a coyote that attacked that cow by the road."

"I suppose it was the comment about burning sulfur that convinced you?"

"That did catch my attention." I noticed it had caught hers, too.

"Did you smell anything like that on the highway?" she asked, repeating Dave's question, but with the weight of our shared memories.

"No. But think about it, Lisa. The brake lights—those could have been glowing red eyes."

"And they also could have been brake lights."

"Okay, what about the footprint? We both agreed it looked like a lizard claw. And this thing is supposed to look like a lizard."

Her brows knit skeptically. "You really think it could be this dog-kangaroo-vampire-bat thing the village people were talking about?"

"Would that be any weirder than some of the things we've seen?" It was strange to be the one using reasonable tones to discuss an unreasonable thing. "I know there's *something* here. Maybe it's related to this . . . whatever it is." I leaned in, dropping my voice earnestly. "We should at least check into it, Lisa. Aren't you even curious?"

"Of course I'm curious, nimrod." She jabbed a finger at her chest. "Evil-genius sorcerer, remember? But someone has to be the Scully to your Mulder."

I gave her an I-don't-buy-it look. One, because there was more to it than that. And two, because . . . "Lisa, you have wake-up voodoo in your shower gel. You don't *get* to be the Scully."

She blinked, and slowly her mouth curved—just one side. She looked as sheepish as I'd ever seen her. "Touché."

This was one of those times when I wished I could read minds. "Does this have to do with your wanting to be normal for a week?"

Her fingers flexed where they rested on her hips, but she didn't reject my question. "Have you considered what this means for us if it is a supernatural creature? Like, is it impossible for us to be normal, even away from home?"

I stared at her, absorbing that, and feeling fear flutter lightly in my stomach. "That is a very uncomfortable thought."

"Yeah, well. That's why I want to be the skeptic." She dropped her arms. "I'm in, but I'm going to keep hoping for the least weird possibility."

"Okay." Because now I was, too. I mean, it *might* be some kind of normal animal. We didn't smell anything weird at the highway. The psychic fence in my dream could be unrelated. Maybe that was a statistically small probability, but what were the chances that, of all the people cruising down Highway 77 last night, Lisa and I were the ones to hit that cow?

Great. I'd worked my way around in a circle, and was back to dreading that I was right about the weirdness here.

"If you don't want to stay," I ventured, though it killed me a little to say it, "maybe Zeke would drive you somewhere you could rent a car or catch a flight home."

With a withering look, she started up the stairs to our room. "Please. Like I'd want to answer to Sir Justin if I deserted you. Not to mention your grandmother, who would curse me, or your mother, who would come after me with a hatchet."

"That's probably true." I climbed after her, pulling the key from the pocket of my jeans.

"And let's not forget, my karmic account is enough in the

red. I don't need to add to my debt by leaving you helpless against *el chupacabra.* Whatever the hell it is."

I unlocked the door, and pushed it open—hard, because it stuck in the humidity. A rush of stale motel smell wafted out. "You're such a pal, Lisa."

She entered ahead of me. "What are friends for?"

# 7

"You've reached Justin MacCallum. Leave a message, and I'll get back to you as soon as I can."

Sitting cross-legged in my pj's on the motel bed, I waited for Justin's voice mail to beep. Lisa sat on her own bed, legs stretched out in front of her as she surfed through the three television channels and stated the obvious. "No answer? He and his buddy are probably out doing bachelor stuff."

"What kind of bachelor stuff can a pre-priest do?"

"Same kind of stuff as any other guy, but with less boobies, I guess."

"Jeez, Lisa!"

The voice mail beeped in time to catch that. Great. "Hey, Justin." I sounded flustered, and not at all as I'd planned. "I'm going to be stuck here in Dulcina for a while. At least until Tuesday."

I caught Lisa watching me with a sardonic twist to her eyebrow. I shot her a silent *What?* and she rolled her eyes back to the TV.

"Lisa gets obnoxious when she's bored," I said into the phone, earning a glare, "so we're going to investigate this local folk legend called *el chupacabra.* Something's been killing the livestock and, um, that's what they think it is."

Ordinarily, Justin would be my go-to guy for information on myths and things. He's getting his degree in the anthropology of magical folklore. I would have been more frustrated at his unavailability when I needed intel, except that I knew his field of study was European legends, so I wasn't sure what he could have told me in any case.

"Anyway. You don't have to call me back. Just keeping you posted. Hope everything is going well." I was back to the signing-off dilemma, only ten times worse, with Lisa a witness to the awkward. "Um. See you soon."

I closed the phone and glared at her. "What?"

"I didn't say anything." She rolled out of bed and headed to the cooler.

"You don't have to. I'm psychic girl, remember?"

She grabbed a Diet Coke and wiped off the melted ice. "Then why are you asking?"

Glaring at the back of her head wasn't very satisfying. "You know what? Someday when you fall for a guy and have to learn all new rules of conversation, I am going to laugh."

She snorted and popped the tab on her can. "I thought you didn't see the future."

"I don't need any hoodoo to know that when you run up against something you can't control, you're going to be a sad case."

"Please." Dropping back onto the bed, she reached for the remote. "Something I can't control. Don't make me laugh."

I grabbed it before she could and turned off the TV. "You don't seriously think you're immune to everything, do you?"

Her expression was distinctly irritated. "No. I just think all that 'you can't help who you fall in love with' stuff is crap. We're human beings, not animals."

"I didn't decide that I was going to fall in love with Justin."

"Sure you did. He's perfect for you. Sensible and steady. Smart. Ready to slay dragons. And jeez, where else are you going to find someone who not only believes in the stuff you See, but has a freaking degree in it?"

None of that was news to me, of course. "So, who's your perfect guy, then?"

"Temporary."

"Like Zeke?" I pried. "Do I detect a spark there? A little thawing of the D&D Lisa level-five ice shield?"

"There is no level-five ice shield," she said in a voice full of ennui. "That's a level-ten spell, minimum."

"Clever plan. Distract me with your nerditude."

She drained the last of her soda and tossed the can in the trash basket. "So, how are you going to find out about this chupacabra thing if you can't ask the square?"

Grumbling in frustration, I tossed my cell onto the bed. "My next phone is going to have a Web browser."

"I'd like to see what job you're going to get to pay that bill."

Stretching out on top of the covers, I felt yesterday's nearly sleepless night catching up with me. "I guess I'm going to have to do my sleuthing the old-fashioned way."

After all, Nancy Drew didn't have any Internet, just a great wardrobe and a sexy roadster. My Jeep was in the shop and I had a suitcase full of cargo shorts and flip-flops. But I would persevere.

✳  ✳  ✳

The phone woke me from a dreamless sleep. In the dark room, I fumbled on the nightstand for my cell.

"Hello?" My voice was hoarse from the smoke in the bar. From the other bed, I heard Lisa roll over and pull the pillow over her head.

Justin didn't waste time on a greeting. "What's this about tracking down the chupacabra?"

"Hang on a minute." I struggled out of the marshmallow bed and grabbed my hoodie from the desk chair. Unlatching the door, I slipped out and sat at the top of the stairs.

"You didn't have to call me back tonight," I said when I was settled.

"Come on, Maggie. *El chupacabra?* Like I could let that go?"

It was difficult to get a read on his mood over the phone. "Did I say I was tracking it down?"

"Why else would you be staying in that town until Tuesday? You really think there may be a legendary monster?"

"The jury is still out. *Something* is killing livestock."

I rubbed the sleep from my eyes, pulling up the details, such that they were. "Goats at first. Someone mentioned a herding dog. And the cow on the road. The woman who runs the bar and hotel here thinks that it's this goat-sucker thing."

"And . . . you think she might be right?"

I leaned my head against the banister. It was two in the morning. Why wasn't he sleepy? What had he and his buddy been up to? "There were a couple of things in the description that could be significant. But no one can really agree on the details." I wasn't quite ready to mention the glowing eyes and smell of sulfur. "You're the one with the degree in folklore. Have you ever heard of this thing?"

"Before this? Just lumped in with Bigfoot and UFOs. Cryptozoology isn't really my thing."

"What the hell is cryptozoology?"

"The study of animals that are rumored to exist, but haven't been proven. Mostly urban legends and folktales." In the background I heard the tap of a keyboard. "The list is mostly pretty crackpot—Bigfoot, the fur-bearing trout, little green men, that kind of thing. Then you get something like the giant squid, which lives so deep in the ocean, no one had ever seen a whole, live one. Just tentacles that got snagged in fishing nets."

"Yeah, but I saw on the National Geographic Channel where they've caught pictures of it, with deepwater cameras or something."

"Right."

"Any proof like that for the chupacabra?"

"Depends on your standard for proof. Grainy photographs, eyewitnesses that didn't really see anything. An unidentified animal carcass that turned out to be a really mangy coyote."

"Lovely." On the other side of the village green, a cat ambled through the light of the streetlamp by the courthouse. "But this chupacabra thing could be like the giant squid. It lives out in the desert, and doesn't come near enough to people to be documented."

"That's one theory." I heard the click of a mouse. "Latin American myths aren't my area, so I did a little Internet surfing. The name *el chupacabra* was coined by a Puerto Rican newspaper in the eighties. After that, reports of a goat sucker killing livestock started popping up in Mexico and the southwestern United States."

He paused, and I could picture him looking up from the computer, all earnest and scholarly. "You know, Maggie, the fact that the legend has spread more through common language than through linear geography is consistent with story lore. Urban legend, like I said."

So cute and so nerdy. "I appreciate your expert opinion."

"My expert opinion is you are either wasting your time, or messing with something you shouldn't." He paused, then stated the obvious. "Not that it will stop you."

"It's that or sit around watching my navel lint accumulate." I kept my reply flippant, though I wasn't fooling either of us. Something in Dulcina had triggered my dreams, and I couldn't *not* investigate.

I heard Justin exhale—more than a breath, less than a sigh. "So, what's your plan?"

Plan. It would be good to have one of those. "First I need to find out as much as I can about the chupacabra legend, and compare it to what's actually been seen around here."

"Have your dreams been any help?"

I sorted my thoughts, still too short on real-world information to put the vague vision in context. "I keep seeing a fence. It's symbolic, not real, and way powerful."

"Protective magic, maybe?"

It struck me, now that Justin had suggested it, that when the guy at the bar had told Dave we'd be fine walking back to the room, it had been more like he was *reminding* him of something he already knew.

"Protective magic would make sense. I could put Lisa on it, if it doesn't contradict her role as the skeptic."

Justin's surprise was entirely fake. "Lisa? The skeptic?"

"Don't you think that's weird?"

"Not really." His voice held a shrug. "You're intuitive. She's very reasoned. She decides whether to believe in things or not. But disbelief doesn't make a thing untrue, which is where she's gotten into trouble in the past."

That was Lisa. All about control.

The air had turned cool when the sun went down, and the coastal humidity was settling into dew. I smothered a yawn and wrapped my jacket tighter, satisfied to have solved at least a part of one mystery.

"Go back to bed," Justin said, in a new, softer tone. "Sorry to call so late."

"I'm glad you did." The words slipped out naturally, without my overthinking them. "I miss you." Distance made the feeling acute.

"I miss you, too, Maggie. Just promise me you'll be careful, okay? Whatever this thing is, supernatural or not, it's a dangerous predator."

"Do you think I'm going to play big-game hunter and go after it? Give me a little credit, Justin."

"I give you a lot of credit," he answered. "You're brave and brilliant, and if someone is in trouble, you'll rush right in where angels fear to tread. Just be sure to take backup."

I was speechless a moment too long. "Text me with updates," he said. "I'll call you tomorrow afternoon."

"Okay."

"Sleep tight, Maggie."

"You too." I closed the phone and held it against my cheek, the lingering electronic warmth a symbolic connection to things far away. Not only Justin, but everything familiar.

A salt-scented breeze stirred my hair, and I brushed it back, gazing out on the sleeping town. Even the Duck was quiet now, and the only lights were from the streetlamps on the square and the small red beacon atop the water tower. Dulcina, it said. No high school mascot, because there was no high school.

I tucked the phone into my pocket. In the shadows by the motel pool, I saw the green-white flash of eyes, low to the ground. The cat was checking up on me.

Dusting off the seat of my pj's, I headed for the room. There were worse things to dream about than your boyfriend saying that you were brave and brilliant. Hopefully none of them would show up in my sleep that night.

✳ ✳ ✳

Crossroads again. In the field nearby I could see the shining barbed-wire fence, stretched endlessly across the moonlit desert. I stepped off the road, dry grass scraping my ankles. Weird that I wore my shamrock pajamas even though I was dreaming. Completely impractical, but at least I'd managed to dream myself a pair of sneakers.

Looking up from my Nike-clad feet, I saw twin flashes of red. Not taillights, but eyes. A fist of foreboding squeezed my heart. Was that what Lisa and I had seen on the highway? It seemed stubborn to stick to the idea that it had been a car.

Except for the eyes, the nightmare creature was solid shadow. It was on the opposite side of the fence, and I followed it along the strands of wire, hurrying to keep pace with the occasional glimpse of crimson. Before long, I lost sight of the . . . whatever it was, and stopped running, staring at the fence in frustration.

The barbed wire glowed and gave off an electric thrum of power, mesmerizing and maddening, because I knew that to get a look at the red-eyed creature, to find out if it was the chupacabra, or a figment of my imagination brought on by the power of suggestion, I was going to have to get over the fence somehow.

As I searched for a gate or gap, there came a steady tread against hard ground, too heavy to be a person. I raised my gaze and looked across the fence, where a woman astride a dark horse stared back at me.

She was young, but her flawless skin and aristocratic bone structure made her seem ageless. She was beautiful now, and probably always would be. Thick dark hair fell over her shoulders, reflecting the moonlight like a polished stone. Her posture in the saddle was relaxed but commanding, and her clothes were old-fashioned—jodhpurs, riding boots, and a long-sleeved white blouse, with a scarf around her neck.

*Intimidating* wasn't quite the word. I was in my pj's, and she had a rifle across her saddle. The fence lay between us, and the imagery was clear: she belonged here, and I was infringing on her territory.

"Nice fence." Inane, yes, but I wasn't sure where else to start.

My words seemed to surprise her, but after a moment she answered evenly. "You can see, then, that this land is protected." Her accent was Hispanic, but more refined than the Tex-Mex blend I'd heard at the Duck Inn.

I eyed the barbed wire, shining in the dream moonlight. "Yeah, I got that."

"Then what are you seeking here?"

The challenge was unmistakable. The only other time something in my dream had looked back at me, it had been a really *bad* something. But this woman spoke of protection, and seemed to be the one responsible for the fence. So even though I didn't appreciate her tone, I kept my own mental voice civil.

"I was following something."

Her black brow arched. "A white rabbit with a pocket watch, perhaps?"

Her sarcasm set my teeth on edge, but I was unable to make myself say *el chupacabra* to this woman, whether she was a figment of my imagination or not. "There was something running through your pasture over there." I pointed to her side of the fence.

"That's impossible."

"Why?"

"Because this is my domain."

"But this is *my* dream," I countered.

The woman blinked, and her horse danced beneath her. She brought it under control with a sure hand on the reins. "Who *are* you?"

A wind came up, cool and damp against my bare shoulders, and blew my short hair into my eyes. I pushed it away, and the woman was gone.

Another gust, and I looked up to see clouds swelling across the night sky, extinguishing the stars and crowding in on the moon. I shivered at the omen. A storm was coming. Real or figurative, I didn't know.

# 8

I woke easily in the morning. Between one breath and another, I became fully conscious, staring at the cracked plaster of the Artesian Manor ceiling. My head was distinctly unmuddled and non-achy.

There must be something terribly wrong with me.

It was easier to concentrate on that—wondering why I didn't have one of my psychic hangovers after such a vivid dream—than to sort through what it meant. I could remember the vision clearly, but it raised more questions than it answered. Who was the woman? What was the red-eyed creature? And why did I see it when she couldn't?

I heard my name and realized I hadn't woken sponta-neously; Lisa's phone must have rung and she'd gone outside, like I'd done last night. I could hear the murmur of her voice through the window. She sounded almost *friendly*. I didn't need my mojo to know it was Zeke on the line.

Back in high school, D&D Lisa had a cutting wit, but she could be amiable if she decided you were worth the trou-ble. Since the incident with the demon Azmael, though, her sarcasm had more bite. It was like she'd decided she didn't deserve any friends, and her prickly demeanor kept every-one distant. I knew her history, and her need for atonement, so I was immune, but I wondered what things were like for her at Georgetown. Lonely, I'd bet.

The girl on the phone outside was more like the old Lisa. I wondered which came first: Had Zeke slipped through her guard because she'd decided to be "normal" (for Lisa, any-way)? Or was she acting more like old Lisa because she'd de-cided to let herself like Zeke?

Since I couldn't hear her conversation clearly enough to eavesdrop, I flung back the covers and went to the bathroom to wash up. Lisa came in while I was brushing my teeth, and she tossed her phone on the bed.

"How is Zeke?" I asked, mouth full of foam.

"Fine." She pulled the rubber band out of her hair and combed through it with her fingers. "His grandmother wants to meet us. That should be interesting."

I paused, toothbrush clamped between my molars. "Really? Why?"

"She's a pistol. After Granddaddy Velasquez died, she ran the ranch alone for fifty years, and still hasn't completely given up control of it."

"Good for her." I spit and rinsed. Eyeing my humidity-frizzed hair, I gave up and brushed it into a headband. "Want to get some breakfast?"

"You go." She grabbed clean clothes and headed to the shower. "I'm not sure I can handle another round of the chupacabra follies just yet."

I picked up the room key and my cell phone. "Suit yourself."

"I usually do."

Her skepticism didn't seem to have let up any overnight. I wondered if that was Zeke's influence, too. I thought about telling her about my dream, but figured it could wait until I came back. The Lisa follies were also hard to handle, at least on an empty stomach.

* * *

The Duck Inn was more crowded than I expected on a Sunday morning. The neon signs were dark and the jukebox was quiet. Sunlight fell on Formica, and coffee cups had replaced beer bottles, but other than that, the men who hunched over propped elbows or sprawled with their denim-clad legs out and their boots crossed at the ankles looked pretty much the same.

I walked to the bar, my flip-flops slapping the hardwood floor. There was a guy behind it today, and as he turned, my step halted. He was the man who'd told Dave we'd be fine on the walk to the room.

"Where's Teresa?" I said to cover my surprise.

He set a mug in front of me and filled it with steaming coffee. "Not even she can be here twenty-four-seven. I'm Hector." His thin, craggy face creased with a friendly smile. "What can I get for you, little missy?"

He was the only one who said that with any irony, and I liked him for it. With an exaggerated sigh, I reached for the cream. "Where to start?"

"Why not start with some breakfast, and go from there."

"In that case, I'll have one of those *taquito* things."

"You got it."

The coffee was good, strong enough to take the polish off a spoon. Hector put in my order, then returned to wiping the scarred wooden bar. "You're not having much of a spring break, Miss Maggie."

"Not what I'd planned, no." I didn't question how he knew my name. I would bet money that most of the town knew my bra size.

He flipped his towel onto his shoulder. "But sometimes things happen for a reason."

My brows made an involuntary climb toward my hairline. My gran said that all the time. "What do you mean?"

With a shrug, he straightened the napkin holder. "Just that we don't know the big plan. Maybe this is where you're meant to be."

"You sound like my Granny Quinn."

"She must know what she's talking about." He grinned.

I narrowed my eyes, tilting my head to look at him from an angle. "What did you mean last night when you told Dave we'd be safe on the way back to our room?"

He shrugged. "Just that it's a short walk."

"Fine." I let him be mysterious, for now. Maybe he knew about the protection that the psychic fence represented; maybe he just observed the effect. "So, what's your take on this chupacabra business? Fact or fiction?"

"Depends what you mean by fact." A plate hit the

pass-through from the kitchen with a clatter, and he retrieved it, answering with his back to me. "Something is killing livestock. I can't say what it is."

Someone plopped onto the seat beside me. "What what is?" It was Dave from last night, wearing a T-shirt and jeans. He hooked a boot heel on the rung of the barstool. "Hey, Hector. Hey, Miss Maggie."

Hector set my *taquito* in front of me with a deadpan expression. "Good morning, Dave." The barman's flat intonation made me snort into my coffee. I had to respect anyone who could do such a perfect imitation of HAL the computer.

"Coffee?" Hector asked.

"Keep it coming." Dave turned to me, and I checked him out in the daylight. He had a Jake Gyllenhaal thing going on, a kind of nice-guy handsomeness that made him look like someone's brother or boyfriend.

"You asking Hector about Ol' Chupy? Wasting your time. He doesn't believe in it."

Hector's craggy features twisted in skeptical humor. "Do I believe in a supernatural bogeyman or an alien space pet? No."

"Alien space pet?" I failed to keep the laughter out of my voice.

His tone was dry. "That's what some people think it is. A pet left by UFOs."

Dave picked up his coffee mug and said pointedly, "*Other people* think it's some kind of undiscovered animal, maybe a crossbreed or something."

I unwrapped my breakfast taco before the eggs got cold. "So, you subscribe to the giant squid theory?"

"The what?"

"People used to think the giant squid was a myth, because it lived so deep in the ocean, but now they know it's real."

He slapped the bar with an enthusiastic hand. "Exactly! There's a hundred thousand acres of nothing out here. Who knows what could be hiding."

Hector shot me a wry glance. "Thanks for giving him ammunition, Maggie."

Dave was on a roll. "The drought makes food scarce, and Ol' Chupy has to come in close to get something to eat. That's when people get a glimpse of it."

I fished for anything more specific than the vague mishmash of description I'd gotten last night. "Have *you* seen it?"

"Nope. My Tía Rosa, though, she swore that it came to her place one night and carried off her puppy. My granddad found what was left of the dog out in the pasture, wouldn't let her see it. Said it wasn't natural. Forty years ago or so, and she's never forgotten about it."

The stark retelling had more impact than Teresa's melodrama the night before. I leaned forward, elbows on the bar. "Did *she* see it? *El chupacabra,* I mean?"

"Swears so." Dave nodded decisively. "Red eyes in the dark, rustle of wings . . ."

I sat back in disgust, and Hector laughed at my expression. "Oh, for crying out loud. That's the same thing everyone says."

"Yeah, but Ol' Chupy is going to get careless. Sooner or later, someone's got to get a clear shot at him, with a rifle or a camera." His eager tone indicated exactly who he thought that person might be. "And that lucky bastard is going to make a fortune."

"Has *no one* ever seen a whole one?" I asked in frustration.

Dave shrugged, sipping his coffee. "Not a live one, anyway."

Finally, a glimmer of hope. "Someone's seen a dead one?"

"Well, sure. There's a skeleton in the museum up the road."

I set down my mug and turned on the barstool to look at him. "A real skeleton?"

"Sure."

"How far is the museum?"

He rubbed his chin and thought about it. "Maybe twenty miles down seventy-seven, going on toward Brownsville. Right on the highway."

Hector spoke up at last, his face comically expressionless. "Tell her what kind of museum, Dave."

"I forget the name," Dave said blithely. "But you can't miss it. Has a big sign that says 'Two-Headed Snake.' "

"Two-Headed snake?" I echoed. What the hell kind of exhibition had a bicephalic reptile for a headliner?

Chuckling, Hector grabbed a fresh pot of coffee to make the rounds among the tables. The stuff was like crack here.

Dave leaned his elbow on the bar, turning to face me. "So. You and your friend sticking around until Buck fixes your car?"

"Yeah. Buck says he can probably do it by Friday. So Lisa and I will be hanging out."

"Well," he said, "there are a few things to do around here. Some people like to bird-watch out on the bay. Got a great restaurant there, too. Better than you might think."

"Well, tomorrow we're going out to the Velasquez ranch." I only mentioned it so that he wouldn't feel obliged to offer to play tour guide.

Dave laughed, either not realizing I was putting him off, or not caring. "Technically you've been on it since you got here. The Velasquez property takes up most of the county, 'cept the town and the highway."

I stared at him. "Really?" No wonder Lisa was being so nice to Zeke.

He nodded. "Most of us who run cattle here lease acreage. My great-granddad was a Velasquedero—that's what they called the vaqueros who worked for the family. His son started with a twenty-acre lease and five head of cattle. My dad owned a hundred. I've got the lease now, though the numbers are down because of the drought."

"A vaquero is a cowboy, right?" Dave nodded, and I went on. "Why are your numbers down? Not because of the . . . whatever Teresa thinks killed her goats?"

"Nah." He sounded casual, but didn't quite fool me. "In a drought, it takes more land per head of cattle to keep them healthy. So a lot of us have had to sell off our breeding stock."

"Oh." Considering how much pride had laced his voice when he talked about how his family had built up their herd, it was a real shame, and I said so.

"Yeah." His smile was, for the first time, unconvincing. "Especially at market price per pound. Doña Isabel has tried to help the tenants, but even she can't control the weather."

Hector had returned with the empty coffeepot and set it on the burner to refill. He didn't rejoin the conversation, but there was a set to his shoulders that said he was listening.

"Doña Isabel?" I asked.

"Zeke's grandmother. Matriarch of Velasquez County."

"Oh." How old-fashioned, yet fitting, from the little bit I'd heard. "I think we're going to meet her tomorrow. Zeke said she was asking about Lisa and me."

Hector turned, and Dave set down his mug. "Summoned into the presence," said Dave. "Wow."

"What's the big deal?" Other than the fact that she owned most of the county, I guess.

"Doña Isabel doesn't leave the ranch." Hector's tone was carefully neutral. "People come to her."

I glanced between them, wondering if they were pulling my leg. "She *never* leaves the ranch?"

Dave shrugged. "I can't remember the last time she did. But, as I said, the ranch is a big place." He stood and fished his wallet out of his pocket. "I've got to run. We're all checking our fences after that cow got on the highway. Not that it'll do much good against Ol' Chupy."

He winked at me as he left, which seemed a little flippant. I guess maybe if you think it's just an animal and not a monster, it's hard to get really worked up. That was the difference between him and Teresa; from what I'd seen, she had worked-up down to an art.

Hector was the mystery. When I quizzed him on the chupacabra, my gut instinct said that he took it more seriously than anyone. But he said he didn't believe in it. At least, he didn't believe it was an alien space pet.

He cleared away my plate. "What's your plan for the day. The two-headed snake museum?"

I gave him a penetrating stare, as if I could read minds. "Is that the best place to start?"

"As good a place as any, if you're serious about this chupacabra business."

With a sigh, I sank my elbows onto the bar. "I am, but I'm transportation impaired."

"Buck's got a couple of trucks he uses as loaners."

"Yeah?" Since he'd dodged so many of my questions, the suggestion was surprisingly helpful.

He yelled over his shoulder at a trio of men sitting at the Old Guys' table, nearly indistinguishable in their sweat-stained caps and oil-stained jackets. "Hey, Buck. You got a truck you can lend this young lady so she can get around while her car's in your shop?"

The mechanic pushed his cap farther back on his head, talking around whatever he had stuck between his cheek and gum. "Don't see why not." He detached a small key ring from his bigger one and tossed it to Hector. "Just come get it when you need to. Can't miss it parked beside the garage. Big old blue Chevy."

"Thanks, Buck." I included the enigmatic man behind the bar in my gratitude. "You too."

He dropped the key into my hand. "Don't thank me until you've seen Buck's truck."

I slid off my barstool and dug in my jeans for a couple of dollars. "Well, thanks for the breakfast, anyway."

The barman waved me off. "I'll put it on your tab."

"Thanks." I started toward the door, but as I was passing the cash register, I saw a rack of road maps and a brochure with a sepia photograph of a bunch of men gathered with their horses around a campfire. On it was also a woodcut of a design I'd seen on Zeke's belt buckle—a simple cross with two arms, the top one slightly longer than the bottom.

The title on the pamphlet said: *Velasquez Ranch, Then and Now.* I guessed the symbol was the ranch's brand.

Grabbing one of each—a map and a pamphlet—I waved to get Hector's attention. "Add these to my bill, too, will you?"

"Will do, Miss Maggie." He whisked away our mugs and wiped the spot where they'd been. "You be careful out there."

"Will do."

God, now I was even sounding like them.

✳   ✳   ✳

Dave was right. We didn't have any trouble finding the place. Beside the highway, a faded billboard proclaimed: SEE IT HERE! TWO-HEADED SNAKE! REPTILIAN WONDERS! ICE-COLD COCA-COLA! MEXICAN POTTERY!

"This must be it." I kept both hands on the wheel of Buck's "loaner"—a seventies-vintage pickup truck, more rust than blue. It smelled like ancient cigarettes, old boots, and dirty socks, but since it lacked air-conditioning, I didn't notice the odor so much with the wind whipping through the open windows.

"Yeah," Lisa drawled as a long, low building came into view. "I didn't figure there was more than one house of reptilian wonders nearby."

"Nearby" was relative; it was a lot of driving for questionable payoff. If the bones were real, that was a point for the giant squid theory. If not . . . well then, as Lisa had pointed out, it didn't really prove anything one way or the other.

I pulled off the highway into a gravel lot, raising a cloud of fine, pale dust. It settled in a gritty layer onto my

85

sunscreen-coated skin as I climbed out of the truck and got my bearings.

The Brazos Valley Reptile and Curio Museum wasn't in any valley that I could see. The landscape was—surprise—flat and brown. The cinder-block building had a corrugated metal roof, and a chain-link fence enclosing the sides and back, I guess to keep people out, because it wasn't going to do much good keeping snakes in.

A tattered collection of stuffed animals—the taxidermy kind—guarded the front door. A vulture lurked atop a wooden crate, and an armadillo hunkered beneath one of the pottery chimney stoves for sale. On the wall was another large sign, painted in garish red: SEE THE DEADLY CHUPACABRA! THE ONLY COMPLETE SKELETON IN THE WORLD!

Lisa's sneakers crunched on the gravel as she paused to take it all in. "That sign does wonders for its credibility."

"Everyone's got to make a living, I guess." The front door was propped open, and I stuck my head inside apprehensively, worried the place would be slithering with vipers, like the pit in *Raiders of the Lost Ark*.

The tiny foyer was deserted and free of snakes. Live ones, anyway. A glass display counter held an ancient cash register, and the walls were lined with shelves full of rubber snakes, stuffed animals—the fabric kind—and cheap Mexican souvenirs. An ancient cooler, humming noisily in a corner, held the promised ice-cold Coca-Cola.

Everything was covered with a thin layer of grime, and there was a strong, musty smell. At the counter Lisa picked up a placard listing the admission fees. "Five bucks? For a two-headed snake?"

"And chupacabra bones," I said. "Cheap at any price."

To the right of the counter was an open doorway. Lisa stuck her head in and called, "Hello?"

The only answer was probably my imagination, a hiss of protest at an interrupted nap. "They—whoever runs this—must be in the back."

"Maybe." She was full of gruesome glee. "Could a two-headed snake eat you twice as fast, do you think?"

I tried not to shudder. "Thanks for that mental image."

After a last look around, she started in. "Let's just pay on the way out."

Of course I followed her rather than be left alone in the place. Snakes or no snakes, museums creep me out.

I had to pause to let my eyes adjust to the low light. At the end of a short hallway there was a diorama of the local desert. Scrubby mesquite trees, salt grass, cacti, and more taxidermy specimens: a bobcat, a tortoise, and a mockingbird. I eyed the fauna for goat-sucking potential. The tortoise and bird I ruled out right away, but the bobcat could probably do some damage to a herd of goats. A cow, however, would be a stretch.

To the right of the display were three glass cages. Yellowed index cards taped to the front identified the animals inside. The rat snake, the hognose snake, and the black racer were all harmless and beneficial, keeping the rodent population in check.

The black racer flicked his tongue at me through the grimy glass, following my movements with its slitted yellow eyes. He might be harmless and beneficial, but that was still eerie.

"Check this out, Mags," Lisa called from the next display.

On the wall was a mural of a woolly mammoth being hunted by saber-toothed tigers. In front of this grisly scene was a huge bone—like, *Flintstones* huge—helpfully labeled: MAMMOTH LEG BONE.

Lisa read from the typewritten info card. "This says that a rancher found the bone after Hurricane Celia washed out part of an arroyo." She glanced at me, curious. "Is it real?"

"Yeah." I could sense the age and authenticity without touching the thing. Clearly other people hadn't held back, because there was a hand-sized dark spot on the fossil where the bone thickened at the end.

"Remember when we went on that eighth-grade field trip to see the King Tut exhibit? How you fainted in front of the sarcophagus?"

I shot her an irritated frown. "Vividly."

"At least now you know why."

She was right. Even as a kid, art and artifacts had seemed very alive to me. They were observers of everyday domesticity and witnesses to the end of kings and countries. Maybe that was why I've always found museums so unsettling. At least in legitimate ones, that history was contained and safeguarded. Here, not so much.

I moved to the next diorama, where some department-store mannequins stabbed a big lump of fake fur that was meant, I guess, to be a bison. Not exactly a respectful representation of the prehistoric Native Americans. In front was a dusty case full of flint arrowheads, most of which just felt like funny-shaped rocks to me.

The next scene was a burial; the mannequins were having a weirdly macabre doll funeral. Beneath the fly-specked glass of that display case were domestic items—a stone for grinding meal, some carving tools, and what looked like jewelry: small pieces of horn or tusk ornaments, and a necklace made out of delicate bleached bones.

These artifacts were real and old. Seeing them under the thick layer of dust made me sad and indignant. The index card said they were from an excavation of a cemetery site in Velasquez County, believed to be from the grave of a Coahuiltecan Indian, maybe a medicine man or shaman, but no one could be sure.

"These things should be in a proper museum." When Lisa didn't reply, I glanced over to see her pensive face lit by the fake firelight in the diorama. "What are you thinking?"

She shook herself back from wherever she'd been in her head. "About burial grounds. Sacred space."

I stared at the case, feeling like there was something here I was missing. "This stuff was found on ranch land, right? Maybe the ranchers are having trouble because they've violated Indian burial grounds. Like in *Poltergeist*."

She chewed on that. "There have been Europeans here for over two hundred and fifty years. It's a little late for revenge on the long knives, no matter how justified."

"I guess." Continuing through the plywood maze, I rounded the next corner and came nose to nose with a rattlesnake.

I jerked back and the snake made the same motion, cocking his head as if to strike. At the other end of his coils, his rattle tail blurred with the force of his warning.

"Whoa." Lisa leaned over my shoulder to peer into its glass cage. "Does it have two heads?"

"No." I put my hand over my stuttering heart. "One is more than enough." The snake, still buzzing, fixed me with its cold yellow stare, its triangle head poised to attack.

Lisa put out a finger like she was going to tap the glass, but didn't. "It sounds just like the movies, only more so."

I knew what she meant. The sound was blood-chilling, sending the cold of instinctive fear rushing through my veins.

"Let's go find this chupacabra already." I moved off and the snake stopped rattling.

Lisa didn't follow. When I went back to see why not, the rattler started buzzing its tail again. The chill in my gut intensified, a colder dread than the noise itself could provoke.

"It doesn't like you." Lisa stared into the sand-filled enclosure, fascinated.

"It's just reacting to my motion. I'm moving, you're standing still." All the same, I was seriously weirded out, and not just because of the Western movie sound effect.

"You know," she said thoughtfully, "snakes aren't always associated with evil. Some cultures think they can see between worlds. Maybe it recognizes another Seer."

"Yeah, that would be why it looks so glad to meet me." I pulled her away before she could tell me anything else I had in common with a deadly serpent.

The next doorway finally paid off. Inside a small, octagon chamber, was *el chupacabra.*

"Wow," said Lisa, confronted with the grotesque figure that greeted us. "That is one ugly son of a bitch."

I stared at the five-foot-tall sculpture, the "life-sized artist's representation," as the card described it. The legend in 3-D. "No argument here."

The depiction was weirdly hypnotic, a Frankenstein monster made up of parts of other animals. As tall as me, it had tar-black hide and stood on its hind legs, kangaroo style. Batlike wings sprouted from its shoulders, and spines ran down its back. The head was smooth and dome-shaped, and the eyes were violent red, like the forked tongue that poked through huge white incisors.

"Fascinating," Lisa said in her Mr. Spock voice.

I'd brought my pocket camera with me. I much preferred my bigger Nikon, but it was hard to sneak into places where it might not belong. I took a few pictures, but didn't risk the flash. "It's like a gargoyle and a Roswell alien had a love child."

She pointed to the fangs. "And Nosferatu, the original vampire. Funny how the same things come up so often in horror folklore. There must be something about that shape that connects with our human psyche."

"That's very Jungian of you, Lisa."

She went to the wall behind the statue and read the description. "According to this, the forked tongue and huge fangs are for draining its victim's blood. When the eyes glow red, it paralyzes—do you think they mean hypnotizes?—its prey to suck the blood at leisure."

"Nice." I continued around the wall displays, which had a list of sightings, grainy photographs, and other "proof" of the animal's existence.

After all this buildup, the main feature of the exhibit was an anticlimax. The chupacabra skeleton was as big as a pony, but mounted in the same position as the statue by the door—reared back, wings spread, claws out, teeth snarling.

I was disappointed in spite of myself. Limbs were out of proportion, the mass unbalanced and awkward. "This thing has all the psychic resonance of a Thanksgiving turkey carcass."

Lisa leaned close to examine the wings. "Appropriate. I think these are chicken bones wired together."

A metal pipe barrier kept us from getting too close, but I examined the skull as best I could. "What do you think this is? Bobcat?"

"Could be. Or maybe a cougar. They weren't always extinct in Texas." She craned her head to inspect the teeth.

"What a bust." This didn't prove anything. We were back to square one. I turned away, dejectedly scanning the rest of the exhibit.

Directly across from the skeleton was a flat piece of limestone, or other sedimentary rock. Impressed in the surface were two footprints, extremely similar to the ones I'd photographed at the roadside where we'd crashed the car.

The card beside the display said: DINOSAUR? OR *EL CHUPACABRA*? NO ONE CAN BE SURE.

Lisa was still playing dentist, paying no attention as I wandered off. "Check this out, Mags. You can see where they attached the fangs."

I ignored her, and stretched out my open hand toward the fossil. After a moment's hesitation, I placed it into the claw-footed impression. It was old, but not dinosaur old. I didn't get an impression of new violence, like on the road, but there was something there, some energy that wasn't quite . . . normal.

"Hey! You girls!"

We whirled in unison. A man stood by the life-sized artist's representation, his face like thunder. "What do you think you're doing?"

In a guilty rush I blurted, "There wasn't anyone up front."

His skin was tanned as leather, his hair grizzled where it escaped his gray ponytail. "I mean with *el chupacabra*. Those bones are very rare and unique."

Lisa coughed into her fist, and I spoke loudly to cover any commentary. "We were just wondering how you came by them."

"Same way I do all the artifacts here. Folks bring them in, want money for them." His scowl gave him a Popeye the Sailor squint. His forearms were kind of big, too, come to think of it. "I think you'd better leave."

"We'll pay on the way out."

"I don't want you kids messing with the artifacts. You should show proper respect."

This was ironic, coming from someone who kept people's ancient belongings in a case and never dusted them. My ears began to burn, but under his watchful eye, Lisa and I left the chupacabra room like chastised children.

Popeye stayed behind, I guess to check for damage to Ol' Chupy. Under my breath, I told Lisa, "You know what we haven't checked out? Whether there have been attacks like this—what's going on now around Dulcina, I mean—in the past."

"How are you going to find that out?"

"We could look in the archives of the local paper."

"Dulcina?" Lisa snorted. "They don't need a paper. They have the Duck Inn."

"Maybe the Kingsville or Corpus Christi archives. Or the old ranch records."

"You don't really expect me to go to Zeke with this chupacabra story, do you?"

"Why not? Or I will. My cover story can be that I'm investigating a logical source for the legend—"

I'd forgotten about my boyfriend, Mr. Snake. The violent rattle made me flinch, and I stumbled backward into the curio case that held the burial artifacts.

As soon as my hand touched the dusty glass, a shock raced up my arm, an electric vibration that I felt all the way to my back teeth.

I jerked my hand away, rubbing my fingers to soothe the nerves, even though there was nothing physically wrong with them. "What?" asked Lisa, glancing back to check for Popeye.

"There's something in this case." I wiped at the glass, trying to clean it. Among the ornaments of shell and bone was a flat medallion, like a sand dollar. I thought at first that it had the same double-armed cross as the Velasquez brand, but when I leaned closer, I saw that it was different, more delicate. The upright was rounded at one end, and the cross pieces were made up of fragile lines, almost obscured by age.

"Where's Popeye?" I asked, pulling my Canon from my cargo pocket.

"Just around the corner."

I couldn't risk a flash, then. I barely had time to take the picture at all, when our host came around the corner.

"You girls aren't stirring up that snake, are you?" The proprietor peered at us in disapproval, but didn't seem to see me slipping my camera back into my pocket. "Not tapping on the glass or anything?"

"No, sir." I moved to hide the suspiciously clean spot on the curio display case. "What happened to the Native Americans that used to live here?"

"No one knows. They just vanished."

I'll believe a lot of weird things that I wouldn't have a year ago, but this wasn't one of them. "Seriously. Was it smallpox from the Spanish? Or what?"

His squint narrowed suspiciously. "You sure ask a lot of questions."

Lisa had one of her own, completely unrelated to mine. "Are these real snake skins?" She pointed to a dispenser in a corner, like a gumball machine. The clear plastic eggs that normally hold toys or cheap jewelry instead held dry, papery sheddings.

"Yeah," said Popeye. I heard a door opening, followed by childish squeals of delighted horror. New patrons had arrived. The proprietor headed that way, and left us with another warning. "Don't forget to pay for your tickets before you leave."

Lisa put out her hand as soon as he was gone. "Give me a quarter, Mags."

"No. Gross. What do you want that for?"

"Souvenir."

I didn't believe that, but dug into my pocket anyway. So much for my ice-cold Coca-Cola. She took all my quarters, and I went up front to make good on our outstanding debt.

There were two families at the counter ahead of me, which proved that some people will do anything for a rest stop. Outside, two minivans and a Suburban had joined our beat-up truck in the lot, and a compact car full of spring breakers was pulling in. "Good thing we came early," I said as Lisa joined me.

She looked up from the plastic snake-skin eggs in her hands. "I guess we beat the after-church rush."

"What are those really for?" I asked as we headed for Buck's loaner, which got a scornful eye from the spring breakers.

"They're supposed to make you have clearer vision. Take the scales from your eyes, metaphorically."

I climbed into the pickup and waited until she closed her door. "You mean in a spell."

"What else?"

Shaking my head, I started the truck. "I'll never get used to that."

"But you get used to seeing things that aren't there?"

I sighed. "Everything I See *is* there. That's the problem."

Lisa let that lie while I pulled out onto the highway, and then said, "I do regret one thing, though."

"What?"

"We never did get to check out the two-headed snake."

# 9

"So, recap for me," said Justin. I had my cell phone on speaker, so that Lisa and I could fill him in once we got back to the Artesian Manor. "The chupacabra bones were fake, right?"

Lisa sat cross-legged on her bed, eating Tostitos. "The chupacabra bones were fake," she confirmed between crunches. "The mastodon bone was real. The grave-robbing stuff was real. The jury is still out on the two-headed snake."

"The what?" asked Justin, understandably confused.

"It's not important," I said. I was sprawled on my own

bed, the phone in front of me on the polyester bedspread. "Let's stay on track."

He obligingly moved on. "But there was a rock with footprints like the ones you found by the highway?"

"Yeah. They were old, but not like dinosaur ancient."

"Any luck matching either print to a known animal?"

"They weren't in the book I got from the library." By now I was pretty convinced that I wasn't going to find them identified in any field guide. At least, not in any normal one.

Lisa swallowed a mouthful of chip. "But if it makes tracks, doesn't that mean it's just an undocumented animal? Giant squid or whatever."

"It means that whatever it is," I said, "it's real enough to make footprints."

"So, if it's not a natural but undiscovered creature, then what's the alternative?" Justin's tone was rhetorical, but it was a good question.

"A supernatural one. Something that really can disappear, or fly, or shape-shift."

"You mean like an actual goat-sucking vampire?" said Lisa, dryly dubious.

I exhaled in exasperation. "Well, it sounds stupid when you say it like that. But it's not like this is the first 'mythical' thing we've ever seen."

Justin cleared his throat and moved the conversation forward. "So, how is this related to the protective magic you felt in your dream, Maggie?"

"I'm not sure yet. We need to find out whether there's a past event on record: a rise in cattle deaths, reports of wild animal attacks, anything like that."

Justin correctly interpreted "we" to mean "the only one of us with Internet and library access." "Can you give me an idea where to start looking for something like that?"

"Try the online archives for the nearest cities. Corpus Christi and San Antonio are the biggest." I wished I could send him the pictures I'd taken. Since I always have a real camera with me, I never think of using the crappy one in my phone. "The other thing I need to know about is the Coahuiltecan Indians."

"You want to spell that for me?"

I did the best I could from memory. "The guy at the museum said they vanished mysteriously into thin air."

Lisa pursed her lips, and rolled up the bag of chips. "Maybe he thinks they went up in the mothership when the aliens left their pet behind." At my glare, she raised her hands, pleading innocence. "I didn't say *I* thought that."

"Yes, but your sarcasm is inhibiting the seriousness of my chupacabra investigation."

Justin, to my surprise, came to Lisa's defense. "To be fair, Maggie, the whole urban legend aspect does make it harder to take seriously. It's like the boy who cried wolf."

"Whose side are you on?" I asked, even though I knew he was right.

"The side of you guys staying safe. Which means not turning your back on any possibility."

Lisa rolled her eyes and mouthed, "Paladin."

Her phone rang before I could answer. She glanced at the caller ID, then looked at me. "It's Zeke."

"I'll go outside." Picking up my own phone, I turned off the speaker and spoke into it to Justin. "Hang on a second."

I slipped out of the motel room, closing the door behind me, and explained to Justin as I settled onto my usual place at the top of the concrete stairs. "Zeke's the guy whose ranch we're visiting tomorrow. The one who helped us the other night."

"How much do you know about him?" His tone wasn't suspicious, exactly. Just cautious.

"He's okay. Spidey sense says he's a decent guy trying to hold things together."

"Could you ask him about previous weird happenings? It's his family's land, right?"

"Lisa's worried that he'll think we're crazy. Plus, he's not happy about the chupacabra rumors that Teresa the innkeeper is spreading, so we don't want to alienate him."

I didn't mention any other reasons Lisa might be hesitant to alienate Zeke. I might discuss her idiosyncrasies of temperament with Justin, but her love life was just between her and me. Maybe it was the best friends code of honor. But also I knew what a deep vulnerability romance was for her—more so, in a weird way, than the state of her soul or her quest for atonement.

Justin was unaware of my mental sidebar. "So, you think this thing—animal or monster—has been around for a while?"

Refocusing my thoughts, I answered, "Maybe a past wave of attacks was dismissed as a cougar or a coyote. It could be what prompted someone to build the psychic fence, or whatever it is I'm Seeing."

"And the Native American connection?"

"They were here before anyone else." I considered the

artifact in the museum, the powerful charge I'd felt even through the glass of the case. "Maybe they set up their own kind of protection."

There was a pause, and a softly agitated sound, like the tapping of a pencil on a desk, before Justin spoke again. "You know, if that's true, maybe you should just leave it to the protections in place. It could be a surge that will abate again. You could just go on to the beach."

"No, I couldn't." I wrapped my arms around myself, though the evening was still warm. "What if it's not just a giant squid? What if it's even worse than a goat-sucking vampire?"

He saw where I was going. Heck, he probably had gotten there on his own. "You know, that could be the reason Lisa is in such denial about this thing being supernatural."

"Because it might be a demon?" I leaned my head against the stair rail. "I've thought of that. But we don't know there aren't all types of freaky creatures out there. Yetis and werewolves and God knows what else. And this thing was solid enough to leave footprints."

"Azmael was solid there at the end. We don't really know all the rules. Neither of us does." He sighed. "I just wish I was there."

"Me too." I didn't point out that he could have come along in the first place. Or he could have invited me to go with him and meet his friend, see where he grew up.

The sun was setting, and the lights were coming on in the Duck Inn. "How much have you told Henry about all this?"

There was an uninterpretable pause. "He's been pretty curious about our phone conversations."

"Does he know that you chose to study folklore of myth and magic because you believe in it?"

"Not exactly." He clearly wasn't comfortable with the discussion. "Why does it matter?"

That was a good question. "It just seems like you keep the past, Henry part of your life separate from the present, Maggie part of your life. It's a quirk. Quirks make me"—I refused to say "insecure" even to myself—"curious."

I'd never really pushed him to explain how he came to believe in the reality of all this, before he'd met me and my freaky intuition. But even with him helping me long-distance, we seemed separated by more than miles.

"This isn't an over-the-phone type of discussion, Maggie." I can't say he shut me down entirely, but his redirect was firm. "Instead let's talk about how careful you're going to be tomorrow out at that ranch." His voice became protectively chiding, something I took as an expression of his affection.

"I'll be fine. It's not like we're going to be wandering around the desert like Elmer Fudd, hunting chupacabwas."

That made him laugh, but only briefly. "Okay. I just hate . . ." He chewed over his next words. "I know you don't *need* me there, but still."

He didn't need to finish the thought, but it was exactly the right thing to say. Leaning my head against the banister, I pictured his crooked smile, his brown eyes, his hair, always rumpled. "Thanks, Justin."

"Just be careful." His voice was full of unspoken things. "Good night, Maggie. I'll be in touch."

When I went back into the room, Lisa was stretched out, reading one of the library books. "How's Zeke?" I asked.

"He'll be here to pick us up at eleven. We're going to meet his grandmother, then we'll go riding."

I sat in the room's one chair. "On a horse?"

"Unless you'd like to try a bull."

"Have *you* ever been horseback riding before?"

She shrugged. "I went to summer camp once. And last fall some friends invited me to their place up in Maryland."

"Oh." I tried to wrap my head around the idea of D&D Lisa in jodhpurs and boots. She was a long way from her goth days. Instead of dyed black, her hair was a rich reddish brown. After two days in the sun, she had a smattering of freckles on her nose. But her pajama pants were covered with skulls, so maybe not everything was different.

Going to the cubby of a closet, I pulled out the jeans I'd worn to the Duck Inn the night before. They still smelled like cigarette smoke, so I figured horse couldn't make them smell any worse. "Are you learning anything new from that book?"

"Yeah. I am." I heard the rustle of another page. "The Native Americans called this land the Wild Horse Desert. But you know what the Spanish called it?"

"What?"

"*El Desierto de los Muertos.* The Desert of the Dead."

✳ ✳ ✳

I dreamed that night of the fence, of searching for the red-eyed creature. I didn't see the horsewoman again, but I had the sense she was just out of sight, maybe even watching me. Once again I woke with a clear memory of the vision, but no hangover headache. It seemed ungrateful to complain, but there was something really weird going on.

"That's so strange," I said aloud, staring at the cracks in the plaster ceiling.

"What?" Lisa looked over from her bed. She had the South Texas history book and a notebook full of orderly scribbles in her lap.

"I feel great, like I slept a week." I sat up and swung my legs off the bed. "You didn't *do* anything, did you?"

She closed the book with a snap. "It's bad manners to enchant a friend without their permission."

I got up and walked around the room, feeling my way with my extra senses—like trying to track the source of a smell, or find a chirping cricket. "It's two mornings in a row now I've had no psychic hangover."

Lisa watched me pace. "But you're still dreaming. Not like when the Sigmas blocked you."

"I know." Last fall an item had been hidden in my room that had stopped me from remembering my dreams. "This is different. But kind of not."

She joined the search; we got systematic, checking all the drawers, under the beds, even behind the furniture. It didn't take long to explore the whole room.

Hands on her hips, Lisa scanned for something we might have missed. "I could do a general break-curse spell, but that would be a lot of work and energy."

"I don't feel *cursed.*" The strangest thing about saying that aloud was how it didn't really feel strange anymore. My yardstick for "bizarre" had changed drastically.

My eyes kept going to the beds, even though I'd checked underneath them thoroughly, and found not even a dust bunny. Lisa followed my gaze and then slapped her forehead. "I am such an idiot. That's exactly where *I* would have put it."

She reached between the mattress and box spring and pulled free a small drawstring sachet made of red linen. After giving the bag a once-over, she held it out to me. "Tell me what your mojo says. I can't open it without breaking the spell."

I raised my deflector shields, even though I trusted, more or less, that she wouldn't have offered the bag if she knew it was something *bad.* When my fingers met the red linen, a cozy heat flowed up my arm—the warmth of a comforter and a cup of chamomile tea, of sun-warmed meadow flowers and a fat cat purring on a lap.

My eyelids drooped, and Lisa plucked the sachet from my fingers. "That's what I thought." She sniffed it again. "Red is deceptive. It's a power color, but one of those powers is protection. The botanicals are basically comfort, good sleep, that kind of thing."

"Well, this place needs something to counteract the décor."

Lisa reached under her own mattress, and pulled out a matching bag. She tossed them in her hand, as if testing their weight. "Whoever made these is good. I didn't even notice. But then, I'm not a Seer."

"Don't call me that." It sounded like I should be draped in veils and jewelry, reading tea leaves and crystal balls. I didn't like any of those terms: *psychic, Seer, clairvoyant.*

"Why not?" She cocked her head as she looked up at me from the floor. "It's what you are."

"It's what I *do*," I corrected. "It's just a talent. Like perfect pitch or a photographic memory. I didn't use it for years."

"You didn't use it *consciously*." She sat back on her heels. "But you've always done it. It's intrinsic."

I sank onto the edge of my own bed, facing her. "What about you? The things you can do. They're not intrinsic to you?"

Lisa rose and went to her suitcase and pulled out a silk scarf. "This isn't Harry Potter, Mags. People aren't separated into wizards and Muggles. It doesn't take any special quality to do magic, just knowledge, preparation, the right components, some skill, and a lot of willpower."

I pointed to the bags she was wrapping in the silk. "So anyone with that *long* list of requirements could make those?"

She didn't answer the question directly. "Charm bags are very traditional. It's a simple spell done well, so probably the person who made this had some practice, and a good teacher."

"*You* learned from a book."

"Yes, but I'm D and D Lisa, supergenius."

"And so modest." I took the silk-wrapped bundle. The magic seemed insulated, barely discernible. "So who do you think made them?"

"I think Dulcina has a *bruja*."

It sounded like she said *brew-ha*, but with more spit in the *h*. "What's that?"

"A kind of Latino witch. They do a lot of magic with candles and herbs and prayer. This kind of folksy stuff."

"Could it be Teresa? She strikes me as the eye-of-newt type."

"No kidding." Lisa tucked the insulated bundle into one of the dresser drawers. "She's got white candles behind the bar in the Duck. But she could have bought a protection spell from a *bruja*. I figured if she was a witch, you would notice."

Well, I noticed she was something. But I wasn't getting "witch" in a literal sense. "So, you're saying anyone could learn how to do these bag things?"

Lisa sighed and explained. "*Brujería*—that means witchcraft—is an occult practice that rolls together Latin American folk magic with a veneer of Roman Catholicism. Usually a *bruja* learns the craft as an apprentice to an older woman. Often it goes from mother to daughter."

She grabbed clean underwear out of her bag and slung a bra over her shoulder as she headed for the bathroom. "Lecture over. I'm getting in the shower, unless you want to go first."

I rubbed my head, which seemed very full. "I need coffee more than I need a shower."

"Check it for potions before you drink."

It occurred to me to wonder if the woman from my dream could be the one responsible for the charm bags, as Lisa called them. But it didn't feel right. She wanted me gone. I sensed that clearly. She wouldn't plant something in our room that would make us comfortable for our stay. It had to be someone else. Someone with a talent for magic.

As weird as it seemed for Lisa to be wrong about anything, I wasn't sure she was right about the anyone-can-cook theory of sorcery. I understood where it was coming from—the same illogical place that said if the chupacabra was just an animal, it would mean Lisa could leave behind the magical side of her life. The reasoning followed, then, that if the ability to do magic was inborn, then it wasn't something Lisa could control.

Welcome to my world. I was learning *some* control over my freakitude, but I couldn't just drop this ability like a hobby that had become inconvenient.

The discovery of the charm bags made the nature of the chupacabra—giant squid, magical monster, or even, as Justin and I had discussed on the phone, a demon type of thing—a moot argument in at least one way. There *was* a supernatural mystery here. We couldn't get away from it.

The truly worrisome question was, had I really stumbled upon it, or had it found me?

# 10

Zeke arrived at the hotel to drive us to the Big House. It sounded like we were making a prison visit, but that was what everyone called the Velasquez family abode: the Casa Grande. Which sounded like a Mexican restaurant. Couldn't really win in either language.

I'd brought my backpack, hauling everything I might need for the day: sunscreen, change of clothes, MP3 recorder, both cameras—the Nikon, and the Canon that fit in my pocket. Zeke grunted under the surprising weight of the backpack as he stowed it behind the seat in the truck. "Did you pack for a week?"

Lisa explained, "Maggie believes in being prepared for anything. Flood. Famine. The Second Coming."

She made me sit in the middle, with my feet on the axle hump, since my legs were shorter. I dug between the cushions for the seat belt, as Zeke headed northeast out of town.

"Did you find something to do yesterday?"

"We hung out, mostly," said Lisa. Which was more or less true, except for our excursion to the curio museum. We'd snacked in our room and read the library books on local history. "How was your family dinner?"

"Nice."

I stared out the window while they exchanged pleasantries across me. Wherever a live oak tree spread its branches, I could see clumps of dark red cows, hanging out like college students at a Starbucks. From last night's reading, I knew they were Santa Gertrudis cattle, bred for their heat tolerance.

"We also went to the two-headed snake museum," I said, broaching the subject I really wanted to talk about.

"Really." There was laughter in Zeke's voice. "What made you pick that grody old place?"

At least if he kicked us out of the truck, we were only a few miles from town. "I wanted to see the chupacabra skeleton."

Zeke's knuckles tightened on the steering wheel, but he kept his eyes dead ahead, like the road held the secrets of the universe. "I see Teresa's been talking."

"Not just her," I said. Honesty compelled me. "Just about everyone in the bar had an opinion."

"Look, don't mention it to my grandmother, okay? She doesn't like all that superstitious garbage."

Lisa and I hadn't discussed this beforehand, but she followed my investigatory lead. "Any superstition," she asked, "or just the goat sucker?"

I saw him flick her a glance, and his grim frown relented. "Any that comes from Teresa. Abuelita is a traditionalist—old-school Catholic—and Teresa . . . She's got a different tradition."

Lisa leaned forward at that. "You mean *brujería*?"

He flexed his hands again on the wheel. "Yeah."

"So you do have a *bruja* in Dulcina." She glanced at me, satisfied to be proven right.

I turned to Zeke, incredulous in spite of myself. "You're saying Dulcina isn't even big enough for a Dairy Queen, but you've got your own witch doctor?"

He gave a short laugh. "Every little town has its quirks."

"I bet that just thrills your grandmother," I said.

"Doña Isabel doesn't go to town much."

"Yeah, I heard that."

The curve of the road demanded his attention. "My uncle and I cover the day-to-day business; he does the networking deals up in Houston, I run things here. But of course my grandmother has the last word on any major concerns. The housekeeper takes care of what few things can't be delivered, doctors make house calls, and there's a chapel there on the ranch. She's got everything she needs."

"She has her own church?" I asked.

"Chapel," he corrected. "She likes to hear Mass in Latin."

My eyebrows shot up. "They still do that?"

He smiled wryly. "They still do for my grandmother. And

a lot of the workers who live on the ranch attend there, too. Not everyone lives in town."

"How many people work for Velasquez Ranch?"

He didn't have to calculate. "Maybe a hundred. We lease a lot of the land to independent ranchers and farmers."

Lisa craned around me to stare at him. "Just how big is your property?" I realized that although I'd heard it from Hector and Dave in the bar, this was news to her.

"The state owns the highways and the right of way. Other than that . . ." Zeke made a sweeping gesture that encompassed the vista, uninterrupted until it fell off the horizon.

No wonder doctors made house calls for Doña Isabel. If I were old and rich, maybe I'd make people come to me, too.

\*　\*　\*

The Big House was, in fact, a *huge* house, three stories and a tower, built in a Spanish Revival style with red tile and whitewashed stucco, framed by palm trees and live oak. Lush vegetation in riotous color encircled it; I could glimpse a swatch of blue water through the trees, and the breeze that stirred my hair was cool and damp.

Zeke parked in the gravel drive. We climbed out of his truck and I put my camera to use as he showed off the place, recording the arches that delineated a patio below and balcony above, and the red-roofed tower over that.

"What's on the weather vane?" I indicated the ornate metal arrow on the very top of the building. "An airplane?"

"A dragonfly. It's kind of a good-luck symbol." He pointed to the corner of the tower. "See that bracket? They put a lookout and a Gatling gun up there during World War Two, to watch for U-boats in the Gulf of Mexico. This is actually the highest point for miles. Now there's a cell phone antenna there."

"You're kidding," said Lisa.

He grinned. "The rent paid for a new barn in the north forty."

A woman appeared on the porch. Her black hair was shot through with silver, and she wore an apron over a neat skirt and blouse. Zeke took the three stairs in one bound and greeted her casually. "Hey, Connie. Is my grandmother back from Mass?"

Connie—the housekeeper, I was guessing—included us in a friendly smile, but her eyes missed nothing—jeans, frizzy hair, sneakers. "She's freshening up. Show your friends in, and I'll bring them some iced tea while you see if she's up to receiving them."

Lisa and I followed Connie and Zeke into an open foyer, where an arched doorway led to a formal parlor with portraits lining the walls. I only glimpsed them, though, as Zeke led us down a terra-cotta-tiled hallway to the back of the house. Another arch opened into a bright and airy room, with huge windows looking out on the sand dunes and the calm Gulf waters.

"Hang tight for a sec," he said. "Do you mind?"

"No problem," said Lisa. Like the front room, this one was full of old furniture, but pieces that actually looked comfortable. As Zeke and Connie left us, Lisa tested the settee.

I wandered toward the bookshelf opposite the windows. No paperbacks or recent bestsellers, but some classics and a few titles in Spanish. There were also framed photographs. I picked up a heavy silver frame, and studied the black-and-white picture. A young woman stood beside a dark horse; she was elegant in jodhpurs and riding boots, and a white blouse with lace at the collar. Her thick dark hair was tied back with a scarf. Even if the clothes and the horse hadn't been the same, I would have recognized that bone structure, those deep black eyes.

"Lisa! This is her."

"Who?" She joined me at the bookshelf and I showed her the snapshot.

"The woman I saw in my dream! That's her exactly."

A voice interrupted, both feminine and commanding. "You mean, 'that is she.' "

Lisa and I turned. The woman in the entry stood straight as a queen, her presence somehow shrinking the room. Her face was lined with age and experience, but the architecture was unmistakable: it was the same face as in the photograph, and the same face from my dream.

Hadn't I said she'd be beautiful even in old age? Her thick hair was iron gray, pulled back in an elegant French twist. She could have been on the cover of a 1950s *Vogue* with her brown tweed pencil skirt and crisp white blouse.

Until she moved, I hadn't noticed her cane. While Lisa and I stared, she went to an armless chair and sat as if it were a throne. Her bright black gaze studied us, avidly curious and deeply suspicious.

"Now. Tell me. What is a pair of pretty young *brujas* like you doing in a place like this?"

# 11

Lisa and I exchanged glances in the "what the hell?" silence that followed the question. With a minuscule twitch of her head, as good as telepathy, Lisa deferred to me. I aimed for a nonchalant but polite tone as I addressed the waiting matriarch. "Isn't that an ironic question under the circumstances?"

"Is it?" She raised a perfectly arched black brow. "You are on my land, within my sphere of protection. I think it's a very good question."

Lisa lifted her own brow, matching the older woman arch for arch. "It sounded rhetorical to me, *señora*."

The lady narrowed her eyes, and the corners of her mouth tucked in. "There is a thin line between pert and rude, *niña*. You should err on the side of caution."

I broke in quickly, because I was sure Lisa's reply wouldn't be cautious at all. She hadn't felt the power in the electric psychic fence, but I had. "You'll have to excuse us, Doña Isabel, but the last"—what was it?—"*bruja* that I met tried to kill me."

Somehow she managed to look down her nose even while seated. "Since you survived, I suppose that speaks in your favor."

My mouth opened, but no sound came out. Doña Isabel continued as if nothing were odd in that. "You might as well sit down so we can have a civilized discussion."

Warily, I perched on one end of a chaise with a heavy oak frame. Lisa stood stubbornly for a moment; then curiosity must have gotten the better of her and she sat as well. "Did you see Maggie in her dream, too?"

"I saw her in *my* dream." She corrected Lisa as if she found her a bit dim. "In fact, I dreamed of *two* powerful young women. I assumed you were a threat, but I see now that you are largely . . . what do they say? Clueless."

Since we were, I didn't take offense. I was too busy being awed and fascinated by this woman, and the way she controlled the conversation. "Clueless about what? Specifically, I mean."

"Your nature." She looked at us each in turn. "Your potential for harm."

My stomach dropped. "What do you mean?"

Lisa spoke, with a challenge in her voice. "You mean *my* potential for harm."

Doña Isabel met Lisa's eye, her gaze unyielding. "Yes. You have great intelligence and curiosity, and great power. That is a dangerous combination. But you are not as monstrous as you fear."

Lisa blinked, the blood draining from her carefully expressionless face. "Not *as* monstrous?" I noticed she didn't deny the "as you fear" part. "Don't spare my feelings, *señora.*"

Doña Isabel waved a dismissive hand. "Please. I am an old woman. God showed me my gifts a very long time ago, and I haven't time or patience for your novice insecurities."

I decided I'd better make some attempt to direct this interview, if I was going to learn anything about what was going on here, both in a situational and cosmic sense. Was she a witch—a *bruja*? Or just a Seer like me? Was she Good? Evil? Neutral?

"Doña Isabel," I said. "I've sensed the protection around this area. It must be your doing—"

She cut me off with a stately shake of her head. "Not mine. I am only the instrument of God's will."

"Of course." Old-school, Zeke had said. He asked us not to upset his grandmother with superstitious stories, but that promise seemed moot, given his *abuela*'s psychicness and all. The chupacabra was out of the bag. "But if you've Seen *us,* then maybe you've Seen the other thing, too? A strange creature that's been killing livestock?"

She rose to her feet. Her walking stick was elaborate, dark wood carved with dragonflies down its length. The design distracted me for a moment, and I thought about the weather vane. If dragonflies were good luck, it seemed an oddly superstitious thing for her to carry, unless she just thought the design was pretty.

Her straight, cool posture drew my gaze back to her. "There is nothing strange on the land. The coyotes are growing bold because of the drought, that is all."

So Zeke hadn't been able to keep her completely in the dark. I wonder how he thought he could, even if he didn't know about her abilities.

I rose automatically, still full of questions. "But if you know about the cattle—"

"Enough." She rapped her cane against the floor, an old-fashioned but impressive gesture. "This land is under my protection." The statement was both a fact and a warning. "Nothing happens on this land without my knowledge. For one hundred and fifty years my family has been here, and I am tied to this place like a mother is tied to her child."

She spoke softly in her richly textured voice, her accent a grace note. But her words reverberated like an oath, and I saw a flash in her black eyes.

*You're wrong.* I pressed my lips together, swallowing the words. It wasn't good manners that held my tongue. It was the power of her belief and my complete lack of ammunition against her denial. *"El chupacabra"* isn't much of an argument against "God has shown me the way it is."

"Now," said Doña Isabel very pleasantly, "Ezekiel is waiting for you in the foyer. I hope you enjoy your afternoon."

✳ ✳ ✳

The dismissal was so complete, Lisa and I were outside in the hallway before I even realized I was moving. I caught sight of my face in an ornamental mirror, and my gobsmacked expression snapped me back to reality. "Wow. I feel like I've just left the principal's office."

In contrast, Lisa's expression was grim. "I don't know what that does to your chupacabra theory, Mags. Even the witch of Velasquez County doesn't think there's anything going on."

"Well, she's wrong." I glanced toward the door we'd just exited, then lowered my voice. "Do you think Zeke knows?"

"About her denial?" Lisa folded her arms. "Or that his grandmother is a witch?"

"I'm not sure she's a witch." There was a particular *feel* to magic like Lisa did, and even to the charms we'd found in our room. But the vibe that I got from Doña Isabel was different. "I think she's like me. A Seer." One who didn't seem to be Seeing the whole picture. Granted, that was how *I* operated most of the time, but at least I was *looking* for the missing pieces.

Zeke waited in the foyer, where Doña Isabel had said he'd be. He looked a little anxious, but smoothed his features as we appeared. "Ready to go?"

Who was he worried about—her or us? "Your grandmother is very interesting, Zeke."

His brow knotted warily. "How so?"

I chose my words carefully, to judge his reaction. "She's very protective."

He let his guard down, smiling sheepishly. "Well, I'm the only grandson still around."

Lisa slid her hands into the back pockets of her jeans, hips cocked to the side. It was a deceptively casual posture. "I'll warn you, we probably didn't pass inspection."

He grinned. "If you hadn't, I'd already be hearing about

it." Holding open the front door, he gestured to the bright afternoon. "Let's go saddle up."

"Yee-haw," Lisa said, and led the way out and to the truck.

I brought up the rear, resisting the urge to glance over my shoulder one more time.

# 12

Horses are nothing like in the movies.

Maybe it's the way they focus the camera, or maybe because when I watched *Hidalgo*, I was really paying a lot more attention to Viggo Mortensen. But once you're standing next to one, you can't help but realize, horses are freaking *huge*.

"Go ahead and pet her, miss." The stable boss—Zeke had called him Lupe—tied the lead rope for a dark brown mare around the top rail of the barn's fence. Already saddled, she shifted placidly from hoof to hoof, clomping in the sawdust.

Tentatively, I ran my hand down her neck to her shoulder,

a wall of muscle under warm skin and sleek coat. My hand came away dusty, with sweat-damp hairs clinging to my palm.

Horse sweat smelled better than I would have thought, blending with other smells of the stable yard—leather and oats, hay and manure. It wasn't exactly perfume, but it wasn't that bad, either.

"Here." Lupe handed me half an apple. The mare's head followed the fruit, nostrils widening in interest. "Hold it like this." He showed me his open palm, held very flat.

"O-kay." I did as he said. The horse stretched out her lips to investigate the offering, then deigned to accept it, leaving my palm coated with green-flecked saliva.

Lovely.

The mare watched me with an indifferent eye while she chewed her treat. "Does she have a name?" I asked.

"Sassy." Lupe patted her affectionately on the rear end.

"I'm not sure I'm up to a Sassy. I think I'd be much happier on a Gluefoot."

The cowboy grinned, his face a map of sun-weathered years. "Short for Sarsaparilla, miss."

Because she was the color of root beer. Duh. I touched the white mark on her hip—the double-armed cross of the Velasquez ranch—and her skin twitched like she was shooing a fly.

Zeke had brought out his horse—a pinto with artistic splotches of reddish brown on his white coat—and a long-legged black mare that Lisa was brushing as they chatted. She and Zeke, not the horse. Though between the charms in my room, the chupacabra, and meeting Doña Isabel in my dreams, not much else would surprise me today.

I'd never gone through a horse-mad phase as a girl. Any terminology I knew came from reading about Nancy Drew and *The Secret of Shadow Ranch*. I eyed the stirrup, which was about at the level of my shoulder. The saddle was *way* above that.

"How am I supposed to get up there?"

"Get your foot in and jump up," said Lisa. She checked the length of the stirrups by measuring the leather against her arm, then tucked her foot into place, and with an effortless hop, swung her long leg over the horse's back.

"You're just showing off."

Lupe moved to hold the mare's bridle as Zeke came over to help me. "I'll give you a leg up."

That sounded slightly indecent, but I went along with it, putting my foot in his knit hands. "Now, grab the front of the saddle for balance. When I say three, jump with your standing leg, and I'll toss you up."

"Wait, toss? What?"

"One, two, three."

I landed on my stomach across the horse's back. Zeke somehow got my foot in the left stirrup, and I used it for leverage while I wrestled my right leg over. Finally, I was upright in the saddle. As long as I didn't look down, I'd be fine.

Zeke handed me the reins, positioning them between my thumb and palm. "All you have to do is hold them in one hand and move them the way you want to go. Right, left, stop."

I copied his movements timidly. Rather than obey, the mare bent her neck to cast me a disdainful eye.

Zeke's grin flashed white against his tan skin. "Don't

worry. All you really have to do is follow me, and she'll do that automatically."

"If you say so." He returned to his own horse and I tried to find a more comfortable position in the saddle, which was difficult with the torque on my knees and the pressure on my hip bones. Not to mention the really long way down.

Lupe corrected my grip on the reins. "Not so tight, miss. You'll communicate better with her if you're not sitting like a poker. Relax. Not that much," he added, when I slumped in the saddle.

"Sorry."

"This is Doña Isabel's horse." He stroked her neck, and the mare regarded him much more kindly than she did me. If she was the grande dame's mount, that explained the disdain.

"Ready?" called Zeke. Lisa gave her mare a nudge with her heels and brought her alongside his horse, and they both looked at me expectantly.

I sighed, feeling even more out of place. "Ready as I'll ever be."

✳ ✳ ✳

Zeke reined in at the top of a rise; the land ebbed and flowed gently, but you couldn't tell until you were actually riding it. Like an ocean, it seemed to stretch on and on, until it faded into the blue-gray haze of the horizon.

"There you go," he said. "The Wild Horse Desert."

There was a stark kind of beauty to the place—the bleached tan of the ground and the dark umber of the shrub oaks and mesquite. Cacti bloomed with bright yellow flowers, and the irrigated places—cotton fields, stock ponds—were sparse but vibrant green. And everywhere was scattered the dark red of the cattle.

"It's kind of gorgeous, isn't it."

"Yeah. My great-great-grandfather saw the potential here. Got to know it pretty well while he was gun-running up the Rio Grande during the Civil War." Zeke flashed that grin. "We weren't always such a reputable lot."

"I'm not convinced you're reputable now," Lisa drawled, too sardonic to be flirting. *Lisa* and *flirting*—there were two words that had never shared a sentence before.

Easing my right foot out of the stirrup, I tried to straighten my knee, expecting to creak like the Tin Man. From the waist up, I was getting more comfortable with Sassy. From the waist down was a different story.

The horse shifted, maybe smelling the stock pond that I could see about a hundred yards away. "How come some of the ponds have windmills and some don't?" I asked. "Is there electricity run out here?"

"No." Zeke followed my line of sight. "Depends on the well, and the water pressure underground. The reservoir under the ranch has mostly artesian wells—ones that don't need a pump."

"That's how the Artesian Manor got its name?"

"Right. The artesian springs used to be a novelty. The hotel was built by a land developer who used them as a selling point, trying to get people from back east to buy land here."

Lisa scanned the empty horizon with an arched brow. "I can see how well that worked."

Zeke grinned. "Actually, he was moderately successful

before a hurricane wiped out half the town." He nudged his horse with his heels and it ambled forward. "Ready to go?"

Lisa clicked her tongue, and her mare started walking. Sassy fell in alongside, trying to get her nose in front. "So, between hurricanes, desert, and drought, why would anyone settle here?" I asked.

"See that cactus?" Zeke pointed to a plant with broad, fat sections covered in spines. "When you boil it down, it makes great feed for cattle. This place was full of untapped resources when my great-great-granddad bought it."

We were passing an oil pump—a contraption that looked like it had a horse head bobbing up and down on one end as cranks turned on the other. "And plenty of tapped ones," Lisa added.

Zeke's smile turned rueful. "Yeah, that, too."

"So if that's an oil well," Lisa said, pointing to the nodding pump, "then what's that thing?"

She indicated an arrangement of pipes sticking out of the ground like a metal cactus, but covered with spools and plumbing fixtures. Zeke answered, "It's also a well. Just like with the water, how you get oil out depends on how much pressure is in the reservoir. Sometimes you need a pump, like one of those nodding donkeys." He gestured to the horse-head contraption. "And where the pressure is higher, you just need to control the flow into the pipeline. If you don't control the pressure, you could have a seep or a gusher."

"A gusher would be bad, right?"

"Thousands of gallons of petroleum lost," said Zeke. "Or worse, it could catch on fire. And that would be very bad."

"How do you know so much about this?" I asked.

He laughed. "It's genetic. Cattle and oil. That's what Texas is about, little lady."

"Please," said Lisa, letting her horse speed up. "You round up cattle with a helicopter."

I protested. "You're ruining my mental image. I'm already disappointed that Zeke doesn't wear a six-gallon hat."

"Ten-gallon hat," he corrected.

"Whatever."

"You mean six-shooter, maybe." Zeke spoke conversationally, to the rhythm of the horses. "I don't wear one of those, either."

I pointed at the pistol in the leather holster attached to his saddle. "You're packing something." I'd done an article on gun-control legislation for the school paper, so I could tell a revolver from a semiautomatic from a machine gun, and that was about it.

He shrugged. "It's a little big for snakes and vermin, but you never know what you'll find out here."

For the record, I'm pro–gun control. The way I see it, if someone has a problem that can't wait for a background check, they're the last person who needs to be armed. And the only reason you'd need an automatic weapon for hunting is if you expected to get attacked by a battalion of mule deer. But if I lived where snakes and vermin might mosey up to my front door, I'd beat a quick path to Big Bob's Guns and Ammo.

Zeke nodded to the stock pond. "Let's give the horses a drink and then head back. Up for a canter, Lisa?"

"Sure," said pod person Lisa. "Maggie? You okay to follow at a walk?"

"No problem." As if I didn't feel like a third wheel before. "Don't let me hold you up or anything."

"Hold your horse," said Zeke.

"What?"

Before he could explain, Lisa gave her mare a jab with her heels and leapt across the dune. Zeke and his gelding were off a second later. Sassy wasn't happy to be left behind, and I had to put my crash course in riding to the test, sitting back in the saddle and flexing my legs as I held her back.

I watched the two riders crossing the pasture at a gentle lope, puffs of dirt rising from the dry ground with each thud of their horses' hoofs. The afternoon light painted everything in stark colors, and the air smelled of sun and salt and sweat.

"Are you going to behave?" I asked Sassy, my voice as stern as I could make it. She tossed her head, then dropped it and settled into a sulk. "We might as well start our walk."

As soon as I slackened the reins and shifted my weight, she started forward, dragging her hoofs through the sand. I nudged her into a normal walk, gritted my teeth against the pain forming where my butt met the hard leather of the saddle, and turned my thoughts to Doña Isabel.

I pictured her in the portrait, young and willowy, posed with Sarsaparilla's great-granddam, or however many greats made fifty years in horse generations. What must it have been like to be a woman in the fifties—a young widow with two babies—and in charge of all this land? No wonder she had a will of iron.

Sassy changed gaits, and I adjusted my weight without thinking, taking the impact of the trot with my knees and thighs as if I'd been doing it all my life.

But Doña Isabel's connection to the land wasn't just about being its worldly heir. It was a bond of guardianship. That was how she spoke of it, and how I saw her in my dream.

That said, if she was psychic like me, why had she dreamed of me and Lisa but not of the red-eyed creature that I'd seen? She seemed to know about the livestock deaths, even if Zeke thought he was sheltering her. And what was up with that? Didn't he think she could handle it? Even without the mojo, Doña Isabel was obviously a woman to be reckoned with.

Then I ran out of questions, and realized Sassy and I were almost at the watering hole. I *also* realized that I was now riding at a gentle canter, moving in synch with the horse.

My body tensed, breaking the rhythm, and I started bouncing around in the saddle like a paddleball. Sassy reacted immediately to my alarm; maybe she'd fallen into the same trance I had, thinking about her mistress. She bolted from a canter into a gallop, as if trying to outrun the stranger on her back.

My legs clamped to the mare's ribs and my fingers knotted in her mane, which only made things worse. I remembered Lupe telling me to stay relaxed. Unfortunately, trapped and "relaxed" on a runaway horse, I was getting a big 404 error. The only thing accessible was panic.

The desert whipped by in the corner of my eye, a merry-go-round blur. It hurt to hold on, but hitting the ground would hurt even more.

What would Doña Isabel do? *Think*, Maggie.

No, wait. It wasn't thinking that got me into this. I'd been doing fine going on instinct. Use the Force, Maggie.

I reached down with my right hand and grabbed the reins low near the bridle. The scarred tissue in my wrist sent lightning bolts of pain up my arm, but I clenched my fingers and pulled hard to the side. The steady pressure drew the mare's head around, and where the head went, the horse had to follow.

Sassy spun on her own axis, and I felt myself coming up out of the saddle. Pressing my foot into the stirrup, I rode it out—one turn, two, slowing like a top. Finally she stopped, and gave a whole body shudder, like a car that clanks and sputters after you turn off the ignition. I unlocked my fingers from the rein, cradled my aching arm against my chest, and let myself breathe again.

There were flecks of white foam on Sassy's chest, and her coat was now more the color of coffee than root beer. Perspiration soaked my bra and trickled down my back, and the pain in my arm had progressed to burning numbness when I flexed my fingers. But I would recover.

"It's okay, girl." I leaned forward to stroke her neck with my left hand, which was shaking almost as much as my right. "We're okay."

She blew out a breath and dipped her head. We had come out of warp speed in a maze of mesquite trees. The mad rush had turned my sense of direction upside down. Everything looked bewilderingly familiar; the scrubby trees were identical to the ones I'd seen on the entire ride. The cacti looked the same, the cows on the horizon looked the same. It was a flat, open canvas of dry desolation.

Where were Zeke and Lisa? They must have seen me galloping past the watering hole. Zeke, at least, was an experienced rider and should have been hard on our heels. But there was no sign of either of them. Just like on the highway, I felt as though I'd slipped out of time and space. Me and Sassy, and my Spidey sense going off like an alarm clock on finals day.

The horse stood stiff-legged and trembling, and I realized it wasn't just the crazy gallop that had her wound tight as a bowstring. A carrion wind stirred the leaves of the mesquite and eddied sand around the horse's hoofs. The stink of death and decay.

The smell came from where the land rose slightly, hiding what lay on the other side of the rise. I tugged on the reins, but Sassy rolled her eyes and didn't budge. Her meaning was clear: if I was crazy enough to check out the stink, I was going to have to do it without her.

First I had to dismount without landing on my ass. You would think that going down would be easier than going up, but no. I swung my right leg over the horse, clung to the saddle like a life preserver while I worked my left foot free of the stirrup, then dropped down. My legs trembled as if I'd climbed to the top of the Empire State Building, but I stayed on my feet.

I staggered up the rise. Beyond it, the ground dropped away into a drought-empty pond, nothing but cracked earth at the bottom. That, and what once had been a cow and her calf. I think.

Both carcasses were covered with a carpet of fat black flies. Two turkey vultures flapped back at my approach, but they were too brazen, or too full, to take off. Other scavengers had been there, also, and left bloody pieces of the calf scattered, like messy children with their toys. The cow's red-brown hide had been torn in huge gashes. Dark slimy things spilled out, soaking the ground and turning the bed of the empty pond to mud.

The putrid stink was so heavy that I almost missed the other smell, a rotten-egg odor that was barely perceptible, like the top note of a sick perfume. The buzzing of the flies was as thick as radio static. One of the vultures hopped forward to pluck out the cow's eyeball with a soft, wet pop, and my skin went prickly hot with nausea.

I took short, shallow breaths through my mouth, the refrain of don't-puke-don't-puke-don't-puke running through my head, covering all sound until a gunshot split the air. I jumped, the stab of adrenaline like a splash of icy water. The vultures lumbered into the sky with a rustle of greasy black feathers as Zeke lowered the pistol he'd just fired.

He stared at the carnage in the dry pond, his nostrils pinched, white lines of tension around his mouth. Lisa came up the rise after him, and stopped when she saw what lay below. "Oh my God."

I shuddered. There was nothing godly about this. Nothing natural, no circle of life. Something very *bad* had done this.

That certainty made me turn to Zeke more fiercely than was tactical. "You can't tell me *this* was done by a coyote."

"Who knows, after the scavengers have been at the bodies?" He ran a shaking hand through his short hair. "Maybe a cougar has come back into the area. Or a wolf. They're notorious cattle killers out in Yellowstone."

"Come on." Frustration—not to mention freak-out—had cut short my temper. "What are the chances of that?"

"Better than the chance it's some kind of fairy-tale monster," Zeke snapped, color coming back to his face.

"Bogeymen—*stories* of bogeymen," I edited, trying not to alienate him completely, "they've always been around, Zeke. Only the names change. Maybe the tales are based on something. This kind of carnage, and that smell, like rotten eggs . . ."

Zeke pointed across the carnage in the pond, to a horse-head pump, placidly nodding up and down. "The smell is hydrogen sulfide—impurities in the gas coming from an oil well. It's sure as hell not the breath of *el chupacabra.*"

"I'm not saying it is—"

But he had a full head of steam now. "You can smell the wells all over, even when you don't see them. Stinking oil wells and real, live animals that have eyes that reflect the light. That's all. The rest is superstitious bullshit."

I simmered, *so* tempted to tell him what I knew about superstitious bullshit, that a legendary animal would be the *least* weird thing I'd seen. After what I'd been through in the last year, I would be *relieved* if we were dealing with an alien space pet.

Teeth clenched on all the things I could say, I turned to Lisa, ready to put her on the spot. Before I could speak, though, she went for the preemptive spin control.

"Give Maggie a break, Zeke. She learns in reporter class to investigate all angles of a story, no matter how bizarre. Right, Mags?"

"Right." I ground out the word, only because I realized that she was trying to defuse the situation.

Zeke looked from her to me, processing Lisa's words and seeing their logic. Then he dropped his angry stance with a hard exhale of apologetic frustration.

"I'm sorry, Maggie. I just don't know what to make of all this. I'm trying to hold things together, and all the irrational grumblings in Dulcina aren't making it any easier."

His words gave me insight into his denial. When you were trying to keep a lid on general hysteria, maybe the first step was clinging to a stronghold of normalcy, no matter what the evidence to the contrary.

"Why don't you talk about this with your grandmother?" I asked. "She doesn't seem like someone who needs sheltering."

His jaw tightened and he shook his head. "It upsets her, I can tell. Abuelita has some strange ideas about things, and I'm not going to let that kind of foolishness distress her. She's not a young woman."

It didn't surprise me that Zeke failed to connect his grandmother's strange ideas with the weirdness going on at the ranch. He was a logical, modern guy who herded cows in a helicopter. Not the kind of person who believed in the Sight, or chupacabras, or *brujas.*

He brushed a couple of flies off his jeans and got back to business. "I'd better get the tag number from that cow so I can let the owner know what's happened."

Forcing myself to glance back at the mess, I asked, "They aren't yours?"

"No." Zeke pointed to the brand—what was left of it—on the cow's flank. "That's the Bar S. One of our tenant ranchers." He glanced at me. "You've got your camera, right?"

Lisa chuckled. "Maggie's always got her camera."

I shot her a look, but answered Zeke. "You want me to take some pictures?"

"It might help with the insurance claim. If you don't mind."

He added the last in a sheepish tone, as if he was embarrassed by his previous, uncharacteristic discourtesy. It was hard to hold a grudge. Especially when he was asking me to do something I needed to do anyway. As he went back to the horses to grab his radio and call Lupe, I steeled myself to face the carnage close up.

"Way to back me up there, Lisa." My voice was much colder than I meant it to be.

She eyed me, and I noticed that her face was ashen, even though her expression stayed unperturbed. "It won't do any good to convince him we're crazy."

I cast a quick glance toward the horses, and hissed, "Lisa, you can't pick and choose. We both swallowed the red pill on this one. There's no going back into the Matrix now. We can't unlearn what we know."

"That's not what I'm doing, Mags. But what *do* we know? It leaves footprints and may or may not smell like sulfur, may or may not have red eyes?"

"At least you could give my dreams some credit."

She took a breath and let it out, resuming control. "All I'm saying is, Zeke is funny about this stuff, and way defensive about his grandmother. If he kicks us off the land, you won't be able to investigate anything."

Unable to argue that point, I pressed my lips together. "Okay. That I will accept. Now let me get this over with."

I pulled my Canon from under my shirt. The cord had rubbed my neck raw during Sassy's mad gallop, but I was glad I hadn't brought my Nikon. I might have broken a rib with it thumping around. Or worse, broken the camera.

I tried to detach myself as I took the pictures, and it helped get my fear under control. Lisa wasn't the only one good at pretending this didn't still freak her out.

# 13

The first obstacle after Zeke dropped us off at the motel was the stairs up to our room. Some action hero I was.

Using the banister, I hauled my aching butt up to the second floor, and sanctuary. I fumbled with the lock, went in, dropped my backpack, and fell onto the bed. I was filthy, but at least the dirt wouldn't show on the monstrosity of a bedspread.

Lisa came in a minute later and closed the door, which I'd left standing wide open. "You are really out of shape."

"How is that a surprise to you?"

"I thought that since you're a mighty demon slayer now, you'd exercise occasionally."

"I'm not a demon slayer." Except by circumstance. "I'm a reporter."

"Right." I heard the tap run; then Lisa appeared at the bed and held out a glass of water and two ibuprofen. "Zeke asked me to go out to dinner with him."

That surprised me, but not for the reasons you'd expect. "You can eat after that?"

Her raised eyebrow was eloquent. "Eating really isn't the point."

I was delighted to have something to distract me from the gory mess we'd found that afternoon. "So, you really like him?"

She snorted and headed for the bathroom. "Not the point, either. I'm just going because it will give Doña Isabel nightmares."

The door closed before I could call bullshit on that.

Speaking of romance . . . I found my phone and checked for word from Justin. I was disappointed not to have any messages. This wasn't clinging-girlfriend behavior; I wanted to know if he'd found any records of past weird incidents on the land. What I'd said to Zeke back at the pond rang true. Monsters in the dark are a constant across time and cultures. Only the names of the bogeymen change.

✳ ✳ ✳

By the time Lisa got out of the shower, the ibuprofen had started to do its own magic. I was back to work, too, with one of the regional history books in my lap, jotting a to-do list in the spiral notebook on the bed beside me.

"Looking up Great-granddaddy Velasquez, the gun-runner?" Lisa asked, toweling dry her hair.

"No. I was looking for something I skimmed last night, about the Native Americans who used to live here. The book doesn't call them the Coahuiltecans, but it must mean them. They did disappear, but not into thin air."

She sat on the bed, a wide-toothed comb in her hand. "What's the story, then?"

"Same old thing. A bunch were killed by European diseases brought over by the settlers, others by neighboring tribes. The rest went into the Spanish missions, and were absorbed into the settlements."

"But no mention of them being chased off by the chupa— Are we really going to keep calling it that?"

I looked up from the book. Her purple camisole matched her purple and green striped underwear. I assumed there would be more to the outfit eventually. "It's as good a name as any, for the moment."

"Fair enough. Not any more ridiculous than calling it the giant squid theory, I guess."

"Especially since I don't think it's a giant squid." I doodled on the notebook. My arm still ached, but my fingers weren't numb anymore. "It's just a feeling I've got."

She tapped her comb against her leg. "You're going with extraterrestrial pet, then?"

I gestured to the notebook. "I only put two columns. Natural. Supernatural. There's no third column for extraterrestrial."

She worked on combing the tangles from her wet hair. "So what does this have to do with the Native Americans? I don't see a column for vengeful spirit, either."

"It's this medallion we saw." I got out my Canon and

thumbed back through the gory stuff until I got to one of the pictures I'd taken at the snake museum. "What if it was protection against something *like* the chupacabra? I was hoping Justin would call if he found out something about past animal attacks. Maybe there's some kind of pattern."

"Maybe he and his buddy are having too much fun with their other school chums to spend all day in online newspaper archives."

I narrowed my gaze. "Just because *you* have a hot date . . ."

"I can stay here if you want," she volunteered a little too quickly.

"Don't be such a chicken."

"Excuse me?" Her brows drew up in affront.

"It's just a date. And he likes you." I flipped my notebook over so she didn't see the part of the to-do list that said: *Get Lisa to convince Zeke of Chupy.* "I'm sorry I said you were putting your head in the sand."

Her expression turned bleak. "Maggie, I summoned a demon. I'm going to be paying for that the rest of this life and the next. I guess maybe I *have* been keeping my head in the sand, hoping for the natural explanation, even past the point where it's logical." She sighed. "That's why I need you. As long as you keep getting into these messes, it keeps me from getting complacent."

"Um . . . thanks?"

Her mouth curved in a rueful smile. "That, and you're the only one who knows me and likes me anyway."

I looked at her levelly. "Lisa, that's only because you don't let anyone else see the real you. You should give people a chance. Maybe starting with Zeke. He's Doña Isabel's grandson, after all. He can't be completely oblivious, even if he chooses not to believe in all this superstitious bullshit."

Her brows twisted wryly. "You can see why that might be a problem."

"Come on. You're D and D Lisa, supergenius. You thrive on a challenge."

"Well, that's true."

I unfolded myself from my place on the bed and headed for the shower. "So go have a good time. Tomorrow we'll get back on the chupacabra trail."

# 14

Lisa left shortly after I got out of the shower. I threw on a T-shirt and a clean pair of cargo shorts and went out to the landing to call Justin. I was starting to think of it as our spot. He didn't answer, so I hung up and sent him a text message instead.

**Survived horse and chupacabra. Call me.—Maggie**

As I typed, the sun set, lowering a plum-colored curtain, leaving only a soft glow on the horizon. Headlights cut through the shadows as the parking lot of the Duck Inn began to fill with cars and trucks.

Something was up. Even if this was the only restaurant/bar in a hundred miles, it was still a Monday night, and it looked like the whole town, maybe the whole county, was rolling in. So I swatted a mosquito, stuck my phone in my pocket, and headed there, too.

The clang of the cowbell over the door went unnoticed. The tense babble of voices inside had a runaway feel, like a flooded river, and anger and fear pushed against my skin. The air was thick, but it wasn't the cigarette smoke.

"What we need is a plan." The speaker was Bud Man from the other night, the one who didn't believe in the chupacabra. He stood near the bar, raising his voice over the others. "We can't just run off half-cocked."

I hung back under the restroom sign. The lights were on and every booth and chair was full; people stood around the walls, leaning on the pool table and the jukebox. Ignore the beer signs, and the whole thing looked like a shabby town hall meeting at the beginning of a lynching.

"Planning takes time." The speaker was a balding man with a sweat-stained hat on the table in front of him. "We can't afford to lose any more cattle."

"Or goats." Teresa grabbed center stage and, like a Wagnerian prima donna, launched into a chorus of I Told You So. "I was the first one to lose livestock, and I warned you all. A whole herd of goats—"

"Three," interjected Bud Man. "Your herd had three goats, Teresa."

She jammed her fists onto her hips. "But I *did* tell you all that this would happen. *El chupacabra . . .*"

The volume of the chatter surged—annoyed groans, shouted down by protestations and testaments.

"Quiet!" The balding man yelled over the noise. "This isn't getting us anywhere."

But the chaos only escalated, voices loudly topping each other with suggestions, demands, and a lot of finger-pointing.

I recognized Hector, the barman from Sunday morning, watching the fracas from behind the bar, his arms folded and his face grim. Weaving through the crowd, I squeezed into a spot at the counter.

"What brought all this on?" I had to shout in the din.

"Your gruesome discovery." He popped the tab on a can of Coke and put it beside a glass of ice. "And a similar one 'bout ten miles the other direction."

I had to stand on my tiptoes and lean across the bar to hear his answer. "Killed on the same night?"

Hector nudged the shoulder of a lanky cowboy taking up space on one of the barstools. "Show some manners and give the lady your seat."

The guy slid from the vinyl-covered stool and I climbed up where we could talk with only a little shouting. "Seriously, Hector. How many livestock deaths does this make?"

He paused carefully before answering. "It's hard to tell. Animals die out here. Dogs get bit by snakes and bobcats raid chicken coops. But the rumors started after Teresa's goats were killed. Then there were a couple of calves. I think your cow on the road was the first adult, but now two in a night has people worried."

"Does Zeke know?" I didn't think he would have gone out with Lisa if he did.

A sharp rap dropped the roar of voices to a murmur. Bud Man set down the bottle he'd banged like a gavel. "Listen, people. We need to trust the Velasquezes. They're not going to just sit and do nothing."

"*Doña Isabel* wouldn't have done nothing." The bald guy spoke again, his challenging words echoed by a few nodding heads. "But you know as well as I do, her son doesn't ride anything but the desk in his office in Houston, and Zeke is too young. He's full of newfangled ideas. We need action."

"Jorge." Bud Man spoke kindly, but firmly, to the bald man. "My family were Velasquederos—five generations, just like yours. We have to work with the family."

Jorge pressed his lips together, but didn't back down. "Well, maybe you don't mind losing your cattle to *el chu-pacabra,* but I do." He turned to the crowd. "Who can afford to lose another two head of cattle? Maybe it will be three tonight, or four. We need to go out and patrol our herds."

I glanced at Hector. "They're not serious."

" 'Fraid so." A worried frown lined his face.

Bud Man made a grab for the reins of reason. "*El chu-pacabra?* Come on, Jorge. You're talking about a fairy tale. . . ."

"Doesn't matter what it is." It was Dave, the young guy who'd told me about the two-headed snake museum. "A forty-five slug will put a hole in Ol' Chupy, same as in a coy-ote, same as a bobcat."

His cocky statement met with rousing agreement. The easy acceptance that this was what they should do—ride out as an armed party in the middle of the night, like *Wild Wild West* meets *Dracula*—rang my alarm bells. It wasn't just the freaky gene talking; this plan had disaster written all over it.

"This is crazy," I said to Hector. "What do they think they're going to accomplish?"

"They're scared, Maggie."

"Which is exactly why they shouldn't be riding around in the dark with an arsenal."

"Well," said Hector calmly, "if you think it's such a bad plan, then stop them."

"Me?" The suggestion, posed so reasonably, made me blink. "I'm just a city girl who's never gotten closer to a cow than unwrapping a hamburger. How am I going to convince them that rushing out of here like a bunch of Transylvanian peasants with pitchforks is a *really bad idea*?"

I didn't notice how the noise had fallen off until my own voice was the only thing I heard. I glared at Hector, who should have warned me.

"You've got a better plan?" Teresa's scorn dropped heavily into the well of offended quiet.

My gaze went around the room. I needed a logical argument, a reasonable alternative. Something that kept them out of danger, but didn't sound like inaction.

"Wouldn't it be easier if you rounded up your herds?" I judged from their expressions that this wasn't complete nonsense, so I pressed my luck. "Your stock is all spread out over the Velasquez property, right? If you consolidate them tomorrow, during daylight, then you can patrol more efficiently."

"But the chupacabra only comes out at night," said Teresa.

Which was my point. Bud Man nodded at me in approval, and turned to Jorge and his friends. "She's right. With all our stock spread out, we can't cover everything."

Teresa flashed me a thwarted glare, then addressed the assembly like Patton marshaling his troops. "If you are afraid, then stay home and wait to see what turns up dead tomorrow. But I'm telling you, *el chupacabra* won't stop until it destroys all your herds. If you want to try and kill this thing once and for all, you should go now. Don't waste any more time."

Jorge took up the flag. "My dogs are out in the car and my horse is in the trailer. I'm going out tonight, whatever the rest of you do."

Dave stood up, scraping back his chair. "Anyone who's scared to go out alone can ride in my truck."

Men rose to go, teaming up or striking out on their own, making haphazard arrangements based on local place names like Lady Acre and Back of Morrow Creek. I pulled my cell phone from the pocket of my shorts and flipped it open.

"Who are you calling?" Hector asked.

"Lisa. She's with Zeke at some seafood place up the road."

"They'll never get here in time." He nodded to the door. "Folks are heading out now."

This was my dilemma: I knew there was *something* out there, animal or monster. Maybe even a demon. Whatever it was, anything capable of gutting a cow was going to be bad news for a human.

So how could I let these people go out there after it? If something happened to them, wouldn't that make me responsible? I, at least, had some idea of the possibilities. They had none.

My mouth seemed to come to a decision before my brain did. "Hey, Dave," I called across the quickly clearing room. "Can I ride shotgun with you?"

He looked me up and down in amusement. "You serious, city girl?"

The mass exodus to retrieve trucks and guns and dogs had

all but emptied the bar. Mostly it was just Teresa and Hector and the Old Guys at their table. And me.

"What does a girl like you think you can do against *el chupacabra*?" Teresa's scorn could have peeled the wood veneer off the walls.

"Maggie." Hector's voice was full of bemused concern. "This wasn't what I meant by doing something to stop them."

Determined, I hopped down from the barstool. "I'm a reporter." It was as good an excuse as any. "This could be a story. I'm going."

Dave sized me up again. Behind him, the Old Guys were watching avidly what happened next. "A reporter, huh?"

"Yeah. I can't really fire a shotgun, but I've got a camera and a knack for getting the picture."

Teresa started in. "This is serious business, missy. No one should make a profit on *el chupacabra.*"

"Why the hell not?" Dave asked. Then to me, "You really think you can get a picture of Ol' Chupy?"

"*No one* has ever gotten a picture of *el chupacabra*," Teresa said. "Its hide is as black as the night and it hides in shadow. It can disappear on the wind and—"

"If anyone can get a photo," I told Dave with certainty, "I can. And I'll give you ten percent of whatever I sell it for."

He rubbed his chin thoughtfully. "Fifty."

"Twenty-five."

"Go get your gear."

As I headed out the back, I caught Hector shaking his head. If he cared to lecture me, he'd have a point. Instead of stopping the runaway horse, I'd jumped right on its back.

Figured. It had been that kind of day.

When I returned—wearing jeans and a T-shirt, my back-pack slung over my shoulder—the Old Guys had gone and Hector was waiting for me with a fat turkey sandwich and a thermos of coffee. "I figured you hadn't had any dinner."

"You are my hero." I stuck the plastic-wrapped sandwich in one of the side pockets of my pack.

I hadn't realized until he was out from behind the bar how tall and lean he was. He held out a denim button-down shirt, worn but clean. "You'll need long sleeves. The mosquitoes are fierce."

"Thanks. Is Dave out front?"

"Yeah." Hector studied me soberly. "Do you really know what you're doing, Maggie? Whatever they call it, this thing is a dangerous predator. Folks won't have reckoned that it may not be easily killed with a man-made weapon."

It was strange—stranger than my usual strange, I mean—that his grasp on the situation didn't surprise me. Doña Isabel's ability, her supernaturalness, had hit me the moment I'd met her. Even before that, if you count my dream. But Hector's otherness worked its way into my subconscious with a dozen shared looks and chosen phrases. He was more than met the eye.

"Do you know what the chupacabra is?" I asked.

He shook his head. "No. I'd tell you if I did."

"Would you tell me if I was an idiot for going with Dave?"

"Yes." His smile was small and quick. "Dave is all right. Don't let his big talk fool you. He knows his weapons and he knows the land."

"Okay." I grabbed the thermos from the counter and tucked it under my arm.

"Just keep your head, and you'll be all right." He walked me to the door and held it open. I glanced out to see Dave waiting by a large, late-model pickup. On the other side of the parking lot, the Old Guys were still watching events unfold.

"Teresa's keeping the Duck open all night for those coming and going from patrol." Hector glanced down at me, his expression sober but reassuring. "I'll see you when you get back."

I realized why I'd taken an instant liking to him. With his soft-spoken confidence and long, grave face, he reminded me of Bishop, the android that Lance Henriksen played in *Aliens.* Which doesn't sound like a compliment to his character unless you love that movie as much as I do.

Did that make me Ripley? That was a grim thought before I headed out into the dark with a creature capable of eviscerating two thousand pounds of beef. What could it do to a hundred and twenty pounds of slightly psychic college coed?

# 15

Four hours later, I'd had a historical and sociological revelation. The dominant role of the male in the rise of Western society was, undoubtedly, a result of their ability to pee outdoors. They took it completely for granted; otherwise why would Hector have thought it a kindness to give me such a large thermos of coffee?

"You okay there, city girl?" Dave and I sat on the hood of his pickup, which gave us a panoramic view of the pasture. It wouldn't have been comfortable under any circumstances, but given my saddle-sore rear end—not to mention the other thing—I was past discomfort and sliding toward misery, with agony yawning below.

"I'm fine," I lied, trying to shift so that the metal wouldn't dig into my bones and my jeans wouldn't squeeze my bladder. "But I've ruled nature photographer and surveillance operative out of my career plans."

Dave chuckled and swept the terrain with the night-vision scope on his rifle. The man was a serious hunter. He'd told me all about it during the first hours of our stakeout: deer, wild turkey, duck, and boar. The truck was full of saddle tack and fencing wire, but he also had a GPS locator, the night-vision scope, and, of course, the gun rack.

As he scanned the landscape, I did, too. The same way that my eyes grew accustomed to the moonlight, my sixth sense had begun to discern discrete patterns in the night, separating them from the background. There was a large group of cows to our left, and a smaller group over the hill. Not far away was the rhythmic movement of a pump jack, like a heart sending blood through the vein of the well.

I checked my watch. Twelve-thirty. I hadn't heard from either Justin or Lisa, but that wasn't a surprise, since I wasn't getting any cell reception in the pasture.

"So, Dave. You really think that—what?—twenty men will be able to keep watch over thousands of acres of pasture?"

He sipped his coffee and considered the question. "Well, Ol' Chupy never liked to come near people. I figure just our being out here might keep him away."

One could always hope. I gestured to the rifle in his hands. "Are you good with that?"

"Hell, yeah. I was a sniper in the army. Wanted to be career, but my dad got sick and I came back to work the cattle."

His profile, lit by the three-quarter moon, was easily visible. "Why not just sell them off?"

"Nah. It would have broke my dad's heart. Every time one of the kids from here moved off to the city, he would talk about how the cowboy is a dying breed." Setting the rifle across his knees, he reached for the thermos. "By the time he died, I figured I was kind of invested. Maybe I'll sell off someday, but it's not bad for now." He winked at me over his cup. "Ladies think cowboys are sexy."

"Sure. Because the smell of cow crap and horse sweat is so hot."

"Well, some people think so." He put the empty cup back on the top of the thermos. "You ever fire a weapon?"

"No. My family are pen-is-mightier-than-the-sword types."

"Peaceniks. I gotcha."

I'd held my own in a catfight with a demon. But that was more explaining than I wanted to do, so I let it pass.

Dave jumped down from the truck. "Come on. I'll teach you the basics."

I stayed where I was and gave him a dubious look. "Why would I want to learn how to shoot a gun?"

"A rifle," he corrected me. "Lesson one is: Don't call it a gun unless you want to sound like a newb." When I still didn't move, he held it out like an invitation. "Might as well. What else are we going to do?"

With a suffering sigh, I slid off the hood, my sneakers sinking into the sandy soil. Dave put the rifle in my hands, standing behind me to position it properly.

It was heavy. My arms felt the weight. My *instinct*, though, felt its deadly power.

"Don't be afraid of it." He adjusted my stance so that the weapon was closer to my body. "Put your cheek against the butt and close one eye. Look here, through the scope."

I did as he said, lining up the crosshairs on a mesquite tree. With the night-vision on, I could clearly see a rabbit peeking out from the cover of a thorny bush. "Cool."

Dave took the rifle back and demonstrated the next steps. "Make sure the safety's off, pull it into your shoulder so the recoil doesn't bruise you, and squeeze the trigger."

"No problem," I drawled.

He set it on the hood and opened the truck door to get another gun—weapon—from the rack inside the back window. "This is a shotgun," he said, bringing it back to me.

"Not a shotweapon?"

"No, Miss Smarty-pants." It was like Elmer Fudd's gun, with two big barrels. Dave broke it open and pulled out one of the cartridges. "These are the shells. They're filled with buckshot—actually, these have birdshot in them—and gunpowder." He reloaded the shell, closed the gun, and held it out to me.

I brought it into position the way he'd shown with the rifle. Dave corrected me. "Don't put your face so close to this one. It's not a question of aiming so much as just pointing in the general direction."

"Okay."

"It's got a big kick, so hold the butt in tight. That way it'll just push you back instead of slamming into your shoulder." I adjusted my position; strangely enough, I did feel more powerful. Not because I could blow something away, but because I could maneuver this dangerous instrument and make it do what I wanted.

"That's it," said Dave. "You're a natural."

"I don't think so." I handed the weapon back to him.

"Why not?" He took the shotgun and laid it on the bench seat of the truck, then closed the door. "Because it's not politically correct?"

I climbed back onto the hood with a shrug. "I guess that's just not my kind of power."

After the cab light had come on, my eyes needed to readjust to the darkness. Dave sat beside me, the rifle across his knees, and leaned back on his braced hands. "Isn't this more fun than getting drunk with a bunch of frat boys on South Padre Island?"

"Oh, yeah. It's a real dream." I stared into the night and tried to concentrate on something serene and dry, like the desert. "Getting eaten alive by mosquitoes, with my bruised butt on this truck and my bladder about to pop."

"Is that why your leg is jitterbugging? Why don't you just go?"

At first I thought he meant go home. But he nodded toward a mesquite bush and I realized he meant *go.*

"What . . . outside?"

"No, I mean at the rest stop just over that hill. Of course outside."

"I can wait."

Dave took another look, all the way around us. "Nobody here but the cows, and they won't mind."

"*I'll* mind. What if there are snakes?"

He held out the gun in his hands. "Want to take the rifle?"

I shook my head. I reminded myself that I was a competent and strong woman. I'd faced down killer demons and the cheerleading squad. Now I even knew—basically—how to fire a rifle. I had no intention of going all girly at this point, so it was a total surprise when I heard my own voice asking, "Will you check for snakes first?"

"Sure." He was clearly the kind of guy who gets spiders out of the bathtub, like my dad did for my mom.

I fished in my backpack for a flashlight and some tissues and stuck a bottle of Purell in my pocket. Just because I'd never peed outside in my life didn't mean that I wasn't prepared.

"Don't use the flashlight," Dave said. "It'll ruin your night vision."

"You're the expert." I dropped the flashlight back into my pack. We headed for the cover of the mesquite bushes, Dave with his rifle slung over his shoulder.

"So, seriously," he asked conversationally, "how much do you think you could get for pictures of Ol' Chupy? A thousand dollars?"

"I have no idea."

"How much for its carcass, I wonder?"

"You know, if it really is some kind of undiscovered species of animal"—which I didn't really believe anymore—"then it would be criminal to just shoot it."

"But if it's a space alien—"

He broke off in the same instant that I noticed the ground vibrating under my feet. The rumble ran up through my legs, shaking my vitals and finally reaching my ears. Holy crap. That was the last thing I expected. "Earthquake!"

"Stampede," Dave shouted, and shoved me toward the pickup. "Run. Get to the truck."

"But—"

"Run!" he repeated, and unslung his weapon from his shoulder.

I stumbled toward the truck in a surge of adrenaline. The rumble grew to a roar, like a violent rainstorm pounding on a shingle roof. I glanced back once, as the cattle crested the rise to the east, a living avalanche of meat and hoof and horn, their wide eyes reflecting the moon.

The herd bore down on us, their fear flying out ahead of them like a cold ocean wave, icy on my skin. Something terrible drove them.

I fell against the pickup; Dave grabbed the back of my jeans and hoisted me up onto it. Vaulting up beside me, he faced the oncoming stampede, kneeling with his legs braced apart for stability.

"Hang on to your hat," he said as the truck was swamped by kazillion tons of hamburger on hoof.

Calling with terrified voices, the cows flowed around the truck like a river rushing around a rock. I clung to the hood as the pickup bucked and swayed like a raft on the rapids.

"They're going around!" Dave shouted.

I must have looked as terrified as I felt, but it wasn't all my own fear. I felt caught up in the animal panic of the herd. "It isn't that. It's what's coming after them."

The stampede roared past and wheeled to the west, the dust in their wake thickening like hot, dry fog. My head was full of the echo of their pounding hooves, the musty smell of cow, and the feel of the pickup's hood buckling under my knees. But none of my senses was as alert as my sixth, which said we weren't done yet.

Perched behind Dave on the hood of the truck, I squinted into the dark. "Do you see anything?"

He raised the rifle, nestling it into his shoulder and peering through the night scope. "Not yet. Wait for the dust to settle."

Movement caught my eye, the slink of a predator, barely more than a swirl in the haze. I pointed over his shoulder. "There!"

He swung the weapon around and searched through the scope. "Gotcha," he whispered in excitement. Then I felt the tension in his body change. "What the hell?"

"What?" I demanded.

"I don't believe it." Dave sounded thunderstruck, too amazed yet for fear. "It's real. Looks just like the stories."

A gust of wind parted the dust, and two eyes, red as stoplights, glinted out of a nightmare shadow. It was four-legged like a dog, but with a thick tail and meaty haunches like a lizard. I saw no wings, but the creature was so indistinct in the dark, it was easy for my mind to shape it into what scared me most.

"You think you can get a picture?" Dave asked.

Camera. Duh. Picture of a lifetime and I was gawking like I'd never seen an unnatural monster before.

I scrambled for my bag, which fortunately hadn't been bucked off the pickup during the stampede. "I'm going to try to take a picture without the flash. Is it moving?"

"No. Just . . . watching us." The slight tremor in his voice was his first sign of apprehension. That was unnerving in an ex—army ranger type.

To hold off my own nerves, I concentrated on my

camera, tweaking the settings to accommodate the low light, worried about getting a picture before the thing ran away. Belly down on the hood of the truck, I braced my elbows to keep the camera steady in my shaking hands. Sighting parallel to Dave, I brought the red eyes into focus manually.

The whirr of the camera seemed unnaturally loud, and I realized that all the nighttime noise had disappeared. No nocturnal birds and no mosquitoes buzzing. Only Dave's breathing, almost as quick and scared as mine, and the low, steady pulse of the pump on the well.

I blinked to clear my vision, and in the span of that instant, the crimson spots vanished from the lens.

"Son of a bitch!" said Dave, lowering the gun.

No eyes and no shadow. My heart jumped against my breastbone, because as terrifying as the creature was to look at, it was much worse not being able to see it.

"Where did it go?"

"I don't know." Dave scanned the pasture through his scope. I could sense the serious freak-out rising up in him. "It vanished. It was there, and then it just . . . wasn't."

"I have a *bad* feeling about this."

He took a deep breath, and seemed to take a firmer grip on his bravado. "It probably just dropped down behind that dune. That thing is real, and real things can't disappear into thin air."

That was some screwy logic, but he was right in a way. Supernatural creatures have to adhere to supernatural rules; the trick is knowing what they are. If disappearing wasn't against this thing's rules, then *re*appearing might not be, either.

"We should get in the truck," I said.

"Yeah." Dave's distracted tone wasn't very reassuring. He climbed down from the hood, still aiming at the spot where the chupacabra had been.

"Seriously, Dave. A *really* bad feeling about this." That was an understatement. My skin prickled with the certainty of immediate danger.

"Stay there," he ordered, walking steadily toward the dune. "Get the shotgun out of the cab and keep it with you."

Sure. Like I was going to stay back at the truck with the figurative womenfolk. Looping the camera strap around my neck, I slid to the fender and jumped down.

Before I even got my balance, a nightmare claw flashed out from under the truck. It wrapped around my ankle, and yanked my foot out from under me. I hit the unyielding ground and the air rushed out of my lungs, nothing left to scream with as razor-tipped talons ripped through the denim of my jeans. The thing dragged me across the ground, pulling me toward the shadows under the pickup, where red eyes gleamed in the darkness, and teeth like needles reflected the desert moon. I stared into the horrific maw of God knows what, unable to think anything except, *Wow,* I didn't see *that* coming.

# 16

I scrabbled at the dirt with my fingers, fighting for traction, a handhold, anything to stop the relentless force pulling me under the truck. Breath knocked out of me, I struggled to grab enough air to scream as my mind spun its wheels on the fact that I was about to get eaten by *el chupacabra*.

*El chupacabra.* That was just so wrong.

My captured leg was about to disappear into the darkness; I had to do something. Bracing my free foot on the bumper, I pressed until my thigh muscles shuddered. The grip on my ankle tightened and twisted, torquing my knee while sharp claws cut through the leather of my running shoe.

The pain wrenched a cry out of me and panic snapped loose, reason kicking in. I grabbed the strap that had tightened around my neck and pulled my camera to me. The light on the flash was green. Green was good. This creature had never shown up in the daytime. Maybe those huge red eyes were the reason why.

I squeezed shut my own eyes and hit the shutter button. Crimson flashed through my lids; the chupacabra let out a piercing scream and released my foot.

"Get out of the way, Maggie!"

Dave's voice seemed to come from far away. I shoved with the foot braced against the bumper, got clear of the tire, and rolled to my left. There was a shot, another inhuman screech, then the rush of a heavy body flying past me.

Another yell, this one from Dave. I crawled to the door of the truck, hauled myself up by the handle, and yanked it open. The cab light spilled over the scene. I saw Dave pinned by something the size of a huge dog, but with dark, leathery skin and spines running down its back. The beast's tail whipped back and forth as it tried to get at Dave's throat. He deflected the snapping teeth with the rifle, and his bent knee up against the monster's belly kept the back claws from slashing open his gut.

I grabbed the shotgun from the bench seat. Five minutes of instruction didn't qualify me for this, but I couldn't give my brain time to think more than one moment ahead, or my neurons would short-circuit on the impossibility of what was happening.

Reaching onto the dashboard, I pulled on the headlights, illuminating the scene. The chupacabra reared back with a shriek like the unoiled hinges of Hell. Hauling the shotgun in tight to my shoulder, I aimed and squeezed the trigger.

The blast tore out of the weapon, and I stumbled backward at the recoil. The shot ripped through the creature's side in a spray of dark droplets. I saw the thick hide blister and smoke. Then it was gone, moving faster than my eye could follow. If it had been a natural animal, it would have been dead, or dying. Maybe the fact that I could glimpse it at all was proof it was at least injured.

Tossing the shotgun into the cab of the truck, I hurried to Dave at a limping run. He lay on the dried grass, holding his shoulder with a bloody hand. His mouth was moving, but all I could hear was the ringing in my ears and the refrain of ohmygod, ohmygod running through my head.

"How bad is it?" I asked. His denim shirt was in tatters, covered with blood and black goo. It was hard to tell which was which. He said something I couldn't make out, but it sounded emphatic enough that maybe he wasn't about to die. "What?"

He grabbed me and shouted in my ear. "I just got attacked by a gawd-damn chupacabra. How do you think I am?"

"Bad?" I had to ask, because in between the moaning and cursing every time he moved, Dave didn't look nearly as freaked out as I was to have been grasped in the literal jaws of death.

"Are you kidding?" He grinned like a maniac. "I'm going to be a freaking millionaire!"

\* \* \*

Adrenaline and elation got Dave as far as the pickup. I kept him talking about his plans while I bandaged the deepest of his wounds with the military surplus first-aid kit I

163

found in the truck. It beat the hell out of the little one in my Jeep, and I was definitely going to have to get one of those.

Forget a first-aid kit. The way my life seemed headed, I was going to need a whole new skill set.

"We'll pitch the story to everyone." Dave sounded punch-drunk. "Get a bidding war going."

"Sure thing." I tried not to cringe as I tied a pressure bandage around a particularly deep gash, then looked at the pattern on his upper arm and over his shoulder. "Oh my God, Dave. That thing really *bit* you!"

"You're shitting me." He craned his head to look. I'd helped him out of his shirt; under that his wifebeater was splotched with red. "Son of a bitch. Do you think it will scar?"

"I don't even know if this thing is poisonous. Or if it's going to transform you into another one, like a werewolf. Jeez, Dave." He laughed, not taking me seriously. But at the very least he should have been worried about tetanus or rabies or the bubonic plague.

His head fell back against the bench, his adrenaline high fading, but not his big dreams. "I'll betcha I'll get on *The Tonight Show* for sure, now."

"I've got to get you to the hospital first," I said, checking to see if I'd missed any cuts that were more than superficial.

"First," he said, grabbing the flashlight from the dashboard, "we gotta get out there and find that thing's sorry lizard carcass."

"No way." I put my hand on his chest and pushed him back. "You can't even stand up."

"Sure I can." He slid off the truck seat, and would have kept going, straight into a heap on the ground, if he hadn't grabbed on to me. I staggered under his lucky-not-to-be-dead weight and managed to get him back into the truck.

"Okay," he wheezed, holding his bandaged shoulder. "Maybe we'll just mark the spot on the GPS so we can come back in the morning."

"Great idea." It was easier to agree than to point out that after the hospital was done stitching him up, I doubted they'd sanction another chupacabra hunt.

I buckled him in, then climbed behind the wheel, proud of my battlefield composure until I found that my hands were shaking too badly to get the key in the ignition. Resting my forehead against the steering wheel, I took a second to remind myself how to breathe.

*Come on, Maggie. Sensible action.* It was absurd to fall apart at that point. Not to mention impractical. What if Ol' Chupy came back pissed?

I couldn't dwell on that. I'd think later, in the safety of my motel room, about the way my weirdometer had redlined when the thing had grabbed me. There was *weird,* and there was *bad,* and then there was a whole other magnitude of *worse.*

✳   ✳   ✳

It wasn't difficult getting to the hospital in Kingsville. Once I reached Highway 77, I simply turned north and kept going. The hospital was visible from the highway, four stories looming over a darkened neighborhood. I pulled in, woke Dave as gently as I could, and got him inside. The hardest part was convincing him he shouldn't mention *el chupacabra* to the ER staff.

A nurse in Saint Patrick's Day scrubs took charge and whisked him back to the triage area, exiling me to the waiting room with nothing to do but fret. At least there was a bathroom.

I washed my hands and face and checked my phone messages. Lots of texts from Lisa, of escalating worry, but when I called her back, there was no answer.

And still not a single message from Justin.

In the icebox of a waiting room, I found some coffee that had been on a burner too long. I wrapped Hector's denim loaner shirt tight around me, and tried to get comfortable. Before long, despite the subzero temperatures and a crappy cup of coffee, I dozed off.

At least, I assumed I slept, because one moment I was huddled on a polyester tweed sofa, trying to keep my teeth from chattering, and the next I was sitting in my Granny Quinn's kitchen, the smell of chocolate chip cookies warming me from the inside out.

"I am dreaming, right?"

Gran poured a dose of steaming amber-brown tea into a china cup and slid it across the table to me. "Unless you've developed a sudden talent for astral projection."

"God, I hope not. I'm freaky enough already." I reached for the sugar bowl and ladled in a teaspoon. I like my tea supersweet when I'm in shock, or possibly having an out-of-body experience.

I took a bracing sip before eyeing Gran again. She wore a light green sweater set—her signature color—and her bright red hair looked as though she'd just had it done. Except for the lines of experience traced around them, her green eyes were exactly like mine. Fitting, I guess, since I'd inherited the Sight from her side of the family.

"So is this really you?" I asked. "Or is it like a projection of my subconscious into the shape of you, because I need advice and comfort?"

She sighed in exasperation. "Must you overanalyze everything? You should *think* a little less and *listen* a little more to your instincts."

"I always listen to you, Gran." I grabbed a cookie and ate the majority of it in one bite. All my troubles were easier to contemplate in the familiar comfort of my grandmother's kitchen.

"Maybe that is why I'm here now," she said, pouring her own cup of tea with unperturbed calm, "telling you what you already know."

"So . . ." I let my inflection go up expectantly. "What do I already know?"

"The nature of the beast."

Groaning, I sank my head into my hands. I was as bad as Lisa and Zeke—I wanted so badly to resist the obvious evidence, not to mention the knowledge in my gut. "What are the chances that I could be hundreds of miles from home, and stumble across a . . ."

I broke off, unable to say it out loud. But Gran didn't let me avoid it. "A what?"

"A chupacabra."

"Why do you persist in calling it that ridiculous name? You know what it is."

Outside the house, the wind rustled the trees, and I shivered. "Something Evil. Capital *E*."

She sipped her tea. "It's always easier once you call a thing what it is."

I searched her gaze, looking for answers, or at least reassurance. "Is this kind of thing going to keep happening to me, Gran? Am I some kind of magnet for everything weird and wicked?"

"I can't tell you what I don't know, Magdalena." There was a tap against the window and I jumped. "It's just the wind, dear. Drink your tea."

The china was painted with blue dragonflies. I raised the cup to my lips just as a clap of thunder rattled the house. My hand jerked and the cup fell from my grasp, shattering on the tile.

The tea spilled across the floor and collected in a warm, dark pool. Puzzled, I rose from my chair and went closer. The liquid had thickened, sinking into the floor as if the tile had become porous. Reaching out a hand, I touched the pool, and my fingers came away coated in crimson.

Blood. I rubbed it between my fingers, as a hand closed on my shoulder. With a startled cry, I jerked awake, striking out at whatever had me in its grip.

"Hey!" said Lisa's voice. "It's me!"

Wildly I looked around, trying to remember where I was. The waiting room walls, industrial beige. The smell of stale coffee. The rough texture of the sofa beneath me, and Lisa, standing in front of me in her date clothes, looking angry and relieved and pissed at the same time.

I ran my hands over my face and through my gritty hair. "What time is it?" The room was empty except for us. "Where's Zeke?"

"About two-thirty. He's talking to the doctor about Dave. Are you out of your mind?"

Trying not to grimace at the pins and needles of restored circulation, I uncurled from the couch. "You're going to have to give me a frame of reference for that question. It's been a long night, and in no way lacking in crazy."

Her gray eyes darkened like thunderheads when she saw the shredded hem of my jeans. She pulled back the denim to expose some wicked purpling bruises.

"What were you thinking?" she hissed, strangling back her outrage. "What would I tell your mother if anything happened to you?"

I refused to be drawn into an argument. My emotions were as spent as my body, nothing left but the dregs. "Anytime you're ready to get over yourself, that's cool with me."

She drew a breath to snap back, then paused to examine her options: bitch pointlessly at me some more, or find out new information. "Fine."

My brain caught up a bit. "How did you know I was here?"

"I didn't." She sat in the chair catty-corner to me. "Jorge Gonzales was attacked, too. They brought him here, and Zeke and I came to meet them."

Pushing myself straighter, I glanced toward the ER doors. "Is he going to be all right?"

"Don't know yet. Am I forgiven for flipping my shit when I saw you sacked out here, looking half dead, too?"

"Yeah. I guess."

Zeke appeared in the doorway, his expression grim and tired. He saw us in the corner and headed over.

"How's Dave?" I asked when he reached us. "And Jorge?"

He rubbed his neck, as if trying to ease an ache. "Jorge lost a lot of blood, but he'll pull through. They're going to keep Dave overnight. As soon as it's light, we'll send a party out to find the carcass of the thing that bit him so it can be tested for rabies."

"Rabies?" asked Lisa. I tucked the tattered end of my jeans under the sofa. After my talk with Gran, I was pretty sure disease wasn't a factor, and I had too much to do to be stuck in the hospital getting shots. "And what do you mean, carcass?"

Zeke nodded. "Rabies would explain why this animal kept attacking things it normally wouldn't. Carcass, because Maggie shot it."

"Hold on," said Lisa. "Maggie *shot* something? With a gun?"

"Shotgun," I corrected automatically.

Zeke kept on target, which happened to be me. "I expected you to be the voice of reason, Maggie. Not join the ranks of delusion."

"How can you still say anyone is delusional?" I was too tired for real anger, but I had to defend myself. "Forget the name, Zeke. There really is something out there. You saw Dave's bite, right?"

"Damn straight! And Jorge getting twenty stitches in his leg." He was pissed enough to shake me out of my pique. "You could have been killed. I feel responsible for you girls."

"Us 'girls'?" Lisa asked, in a warning tone.

He scrubbed a hand through his hair. "I feel responsible for all of these guys, but you two are like guests. Not to mention a couple of tenderfoots."

There was enough irony in the word *tenderfoot* that I didn't take offense. I knew what he didn't—that we were more used to life-and-death situations than we appeared.

"Zeke," I began tentatively, because the middle of the night in a hospital waiting room didn't seem like the perfect place to reveal the full scope of our freakitude. "You're assuming we're a couple of normal college girls."

His brows twisted with tired humor. "Obviously not. What kind of normal college girl goes on a stakeout for the *National Enquirer*?" He dug his keys out of his pocket. "Anyway. It's done. Let's get back to Dulcina. If I never hear the word *chupacabra* again, it'll be too soon."

I didn't move. "It's not done, Zeke. The chup— The *thing* isn't dead."

He frowned. "What do you mean? Dave told me you shot it. He saw the blast hit it."

"What time did Jorge get attacked?" Dreams and gut feelings weren't going to convince Zeke. I had to come up with something concrete.

He checked his cell phone call log. "Around one."

"Dave and I were attacked about twelve-thirty. So it had to be alive afterward."

Still scowling, he looked from me to Lisa and back again. "How is it possible that you shot the animal full of buckshot, and half an hour later it's tearing up someone else?"

I was ready to tell him everything, even if he left us stranded here at the hospital, maybe in the psych ward. But Lisa spoke up first. "Did you ever read any Sherlock Holmes?"

His brow knit in confusion. "No. But I've seen the movies."

"Holmes always says, whenever you eliminate all the possible explanations, whatever remains, no matter how improbable, must be the answer." Lisa unfolded her arms, her body language unbending. "Jorge and Dave both said it was impossible that they were attacked by a cougar, a wolf, or any

171

animal they'd ever seen before. If those things are impossible, then it must be something else."

Zeke processed that for a moment, then rubbed his hands over his eyes. "Okay. Tomorrow we'll round up the cattle, and post guards all around the corrals."

"And you should talk to Doña Isabel," I said. "She's been here so long, she may know—"

"No." He cut me off. "I'll listen to you on this, Maggie. But I'm not going to my grandmother with a crazy story about an unkillable monster."

"Don't you think—"

"No." There was no arguing with him. Everything—his tone, his expression, his posture—said that to continue would be like hammering against a wall.

Instead, I capitulated. In the morning, I'd simply figure out how to work around him.

# 17

Zeke drove us back to the Artesian Manor, more or less in silence. I didn't want to push my luck by discussing the real nature of the chupacabra; I was happy he was listening to me about it not being dead. Small victories.

Backpack over my shoulder, I hauled myself up the concrete steps while Lisa and Zeke said good night. I was amassing an impressive category of aches: saddle-sore butt, wrenched ankle, and the familiar pain in the overstressed scars of my wrist. My heart was hurting a little, too. There was still no word from Justin and I was starting to worry. He wouldn't have said he'd help, then leave me hanging. Romance aside, he was just too responsible for that.

I shed Hector's denim shirt and hung it on the back of the desk chair. As I did, the collar flipped up, and I was startled to see embroidery on the underside, where it wouldn't be noticed. What was the point of that?

Lisa came in and locked the door, and I called her over. "What does this look like to you?"

She peered over my shoulder at the stitching on the underside of the collar. "Is that the Velasquez brand?"

"That's what I wondered." I'd thought that about the medallion in the museum, too. There was a similarity in shape, though this one was much more like the double-armed cross than the lacy outlines on the artifact.

"Where'd you get this?"

"From Hector. He's the guy who works the bar when Teresa's not there." I traced the thread with my finger, feeling a slight echo of the energy from the charm bags we'd found that morning. Had it only been that morning?

"Can a *bruja* be a man?" I asked.

Lisa made a doubtful face. "They're supposed to be women. It's a kind of balance for the male-dominated Church."

Maybe Hector was married. I didn't remember him wearing a wedding ring, but that didn't mean he wasn't.

I was too tired to try to find out in the middle of the night, so I dropped the shirt back over the chair. "There's nothing else we can do tonight. I'm going to take a shower."

Lisa sat on her bed with a groan. "Please do."

She didn't have to be specific. The smell of blood and sweat was going to haunt my dreams. Grabbing clean undies and a sleep shirt from my suitcase, I headed for the bathroom, then paused in the doorway. "We're going to have to talk about the chupacabra, Lisa."

She cracked open an eyelid and looked at me. "I know that the giant squid theory is out."

"By a mile."

"It was a nice hope while it lasted." She rose and fished her own pj's out of the dresser drawer. "Go shower. That cloud of mosquito repellant is making my eyes water."

After all her denial, she accepted the news more calmly than I'd thought she would. Figured. Lisa never did the expected.

✳   ✳   ✳

When I came out of the bathroom, scrubbed and blissfully clean, I knew immediately that Lisa had been busy. There was something in the air, the feel of something otherworldly at work.

Before this trip, when I'd encountered a magic spell in progress—which was a wild phrase to have to incorporate into my vocabulary—it had been the psychic equivalent of an electrical storm, raging and crackling, and very hard to miss. What I felt here was more like the static charge on a dry winter day.

"What are you up to?" I asked, almost too tired to care.

She had a towel spread on her bed, where she seemed to be putting together another charm bag, like the ones we'd found that morning. One of those was lying on the nightstand, unwrapped from the silk scarf.

Lisa picked up a sachet in each hand. "It's red pill or blue pill time." She held up the sleep-good charm. "This one you said was influencing your dreaming, maybe protecting you from seeing the bad stuff."

"That's my theory." I pointed to the new bag, made of unbleached cotton. "What's that one?"

She offered it on her other palm. "If you really want to get a look at what's prowling around down here, it will—theoretically—make your dreams more clear and insightful."

I squinted at the bundle, then at her face. "You just whipped this up?"

"More or less."

"What happened to ingredients and preparation and energy source and a partridge in a pear tree?"

She exhaled impatiently, ticking off on her fingers: "Symbolic or practical materials, focus of intent, and power source. That's for serious sorcery. But this kind of charm bag is just . . . Ye Olde New Age Gift Shoppe stuff. It enhances a tendency. You already have psychic dreams, so it doesn't have to work very hard. The spark, in this case, is your ability."

I took it from her and felt a slight, nonthreatening tingle. "What's in it?"

"Among other things, the sheddings I got at the two-headed snake place."

Eew. As if that wasn't bad enough, I had to ask, "Among *what* other things? Anything that would make me fail a random drug test?"

"You don't smoke it, you moron. Just put it under your pillow." She shrugged, as if my decision didn't matter. "At worst, it doesn't do anything."

"Modesty doesn't really suit you, Lisa." If she made it, it would work. But if it gave me some answers . . .

The bag was a little crunchy and had a musty smell. That would be really nice under my pillow. "What's this about, Lisa? Why the turnaround?"

"Fine. Don't trust me." She folded up the remnants of the ingredients into the towel and carried it to the bathroom. "I don't care if you use it or not."

Of course she did. It was an act of trust. She'd made it as a sign she was on board, no matter what I discovered. By accepting it, I accepted her peace offering.

Lisa should come with an instruction manual.

I put the sachet on the mattress and covered it with two pillows, then climbed into the marshmallow of a bed. The last thing I did was carefully place my phone on the nightstand, but not before checking one more time for a message.

✳ ✳ ✳

I fell into the dream almost eagerly, with the anticipation of learning something important. I'd settle for any glimmer of light at the end of this tunnel of ignorance. Finding myself back in the desert, the same place I'd been all day and all night, was a major disappointment.

Mesquite and sage bushes, endless rise and fall of the dunes. I sighed. "Same song, forty-second verse."

"Are you sure?" I heard the clop of horse hooves on dry ground, and turned to see Doña Isabel—as young and strong as she looked in her portrait—leading her mare. She was still taller than me, more so even than in real life. I wondered if that was her projection or my perception.

"What happened to the fence?" I asked.

Her face was sculpted in haughty, smooth perfection. "You're inside now. Isn't that what you wanted?"

I took the question as rhetorical. "So the fence really is your doing?"

She set her mouth impatiently. "I have told you. This land is under my protection. Why are you still seeking in your dreams?"

"There's something here, Doña Isabel," I said, urgent but respectful. "I don't know why I can see it and you can't, but you have to believe me."

"Bah." She tossed her head, a girlish gesture that made me forget I was really dealing with an old woman. "I do not *have* to do anything, *chica*. I've been guarding this land since before even your parents were born."

A cool breeze touched my cheek. The horse stomped a hoof and shook her bridle as shadows crawled across the ground like in fast-motion photography. Gray clouds rolled over the sky and then settled onto the coastal plain in a damp mist that eddied through the dunes.

Doña Isabel dropped her gaze from the sky and moved to mount her horse. "Go home, Magdalena. You don't belong here."

She pulled the mare's head around, and the horse sprang forward at the touch of her booted heels. They disappeared into a swirl of fog and I hurried after. I slid down a sandy slope, into a gully between dunes, where I hit a dark patch of soil and stumbled, unable to move.

My bare foot had sunk into what looked like a tacky puddle of tar. I tried to pull free, but the ground sucked at my leg like a thirsty mouth.

"Doña Isabel?" I called into the mist. "Are you there?"

No answer. I managed to free part of my foot before it was

drawn back down with a wet, hungry sound. Something vile and viscous oozed out from the earth around my ankle, dark as old blood.

A fat raindrop splattered onto my cheek. It seemed warm in contrast to the enveloping fog. I touched the spot, and my fingers came away slick and red.

Gross.

Another drop fell into my outstretched palm. There was a rumble of thunder, and the red rain began to fall in earnest. It soaked my clothes and matted my hair, running down to sting my eyes and seep between my lips.

The dry earth drank the rain down greedily, softening into mud, and I pulled against it with all my strength. My calf slid out, then my ankle, but what came with it this time was no longer an amorphous ooze. A distinct claw, five razor-tipped digits, wrapped around my ankle like a vise. With every drop of blood that struck it, the leathery dark skin seemed harder, and more distinctly *real*. Something else emerged, too—a domed head and bony brow. Huge red eyes blinked away the tarry sludge and the creature's mouth gaped wide, lined with silver white teeth.

I screamed as it pulled itself out, its claws flexing on my ankle as it licked the thick crimson stain off my skin. Logic said to wake up, but was overpowered by the part of me that shrieked and flailed against the grip of the nightmare.

A kick of my free foot caught the creature in the eye. With a hellish cry it reared back, shark teeth coated with blood. Could it kill me in my dream? If it did would I simply never wake up? I kicked it again and there was a sound like splintering wood.

That didn't make any sense. Neither did the smash of glass, or the yelling that wasn't coming from me, or the way the light snapped on like someone had thrown a switch.

Suddenly I was sitting up in my bed at the Artesian Manor, disoriented as hell, my throat aching from the scream that still rang in my ears. I wasn't about to be eaten, but I couldn't figure out why a bar fight had broken out in my room.

The motel door stood wide open, and a familiar-looking casualty staggered amid the wreckage of an ugly ceramic lamp. Lisa grappled with another guy—a complete stranger, big enough to make my tall friend look like a petite flower—and she seemed to be winning.

Pepper spray. I had some somewhere. I scrabbled in the nightstand drawer, hoping I'd been smart enough to keep it handy.

"Stop! Hey, Lisa. It's us." That memorable baritone voice cut through my panic and confusion.

I twisted around, caught in the sheets, and saw that half of "us" was indeed my boyfriend, who was supposed to be half a country away. He had one hand propped against the wall near the light switch, and the other held his head as if he was afraid it might come off.

"Justin?" I gaped. "What are you doing here? And who is . . . Hey!" His companion had ducked Lisa's fist, then grabbed it to keep her from swinging again. "Don't hurt her!"

"Hurt *her*?" The guy spared me a glance, and it was his downfall. Lisa's left hand popped him in the nose. I winced in sympathy as his head snapped back and hit the open door.

"Jeez, Lisa." I managed to get myself untangled from the covers. "Is it two-for-one concussion night?"

She stood back, fists still at the ready, the cord of her earphones hanging around her neck. "What?" she said, not at all defensively.

The stranger held his nose, blood dripping through his fingers. "I think you broke it."

"Please," she scoffed. "If I did, you would know it."

I whirled toward Justin, but the door caught my attention first. "Oh my God! You broke down the door."

"It really wasn't that hard." He gingerly felt the top of his head. "Unlike the lamp Lisa hit me with."

"You *broke* the *door*."

Now he got my point, and looked abashed. "We knocked, but there was no answer. Not until the screaming started, anyway."

"Nightmare," I said succinctly, because I heard footsteps on the landing. It was a good thing the threat wasn't real, or Lisa and I would have been murdered in our beds and our skins made into a suit by now.

The barrel of a shotgun appeared first, then Teresa, swathed in a rumpled housedress. "What the hell is going on here?" She took us all in with a ferocious glance, gesturing with the gun. "Who are these boys? I thought *el chupacabra* had come to steal you girls away, and now I find you having some kind of orgy?"

"There's nothing going on, Teresa." I raised my hands in the universal gesture for "don't shoot me." The corner of my eye caught Justin's friend—it couldn't be anyone other than Henry—climbing to his feet without any help from Lisa.

"Then why aren't you wearing any pants?"

I dropped my arms and tugged down the hem of my *Battlestar Galactica* T-shirt. "It's a funny story, really."

Justin stepped up and did his thing. His trustworthy Boy Scout aura was so genuine, it was like a superpower. "It's my fault. We got here late because we took the wrong road out of San Antonio. When no one answered our knock, I worried. Especially after Maggie told me about *el chupacabra.*"

Teresa's eyes narrowed, but she stopped making conversational gestures with the shotgun. Then she saw the damage to the room. "What happened to my door? And the lamp! Who's going to pay for that?"

"We will," I assured her. "You see, after everything that happened tonight, I had a nightmare, and when I screamed . . ."

". . . I got a little overenthusiastic with the heroism," Justin finished. It was the right tack to strike with her—brave men, rescuing the little ladies—even if Henry's bloody nose didn't support the image very well.

Teresa sighed, and moved the gun to the crook of her arm. "Well, you girls can't stay here. Meet me in the office and I'll give you a new room. *Two* new rooms," she added, with a warning look at the guys.

When she left, I turned to Justin, raising a cynical brow. "I'm glad you're on our side."

"Come on." Lisa's tone was an audible eye roll. "I can't believe you're letting these two sexists off that easy." She pointed at Justin. "Forget property damage, assault, and scaring the crap out of me. Sir Galahad came here to rescue you. He thinks you're a damsel in distress."

"Don't be stupid." Justin didn't waste any charm on Lisa. They knew each other too well.

I finally looked at him properly, without yelling and punching and armed innkeepers to distract me. His short brown hair was unkempt; his jeans and T-shirt were rumpled and creased. There were shadows under his eyes and a trace of stubble on his chin. It was almost dawn, so it didn't take a genius to figure out there'd been all-night travel involved in his getting there.

Which made him the most awesome boyfriend in the world.

"There's a difference between 'help' and 'rescue,' " he told Lisa, proving my point. So what if he sounded a bit defensive. I was willing to excuse a little crankiness.

Henry had pulled out the desk chair and taken a seat. He was tall, dark-haired, but it was hard to tell anything beyond that, since I hadn't seen him without his face obscured—first by Lisa's fist, and now by a wet washcloth he'd gotten from the bathroom.

"So what's your excuse?" I asked.

Whatever his face looked like, his voice was an impressive, deep, Vin Diesel sort of rumble. "Road trip."

Lisa blew out a disbelieving *"Pfft,"* and I figured I'd better redirect. "I'm Maggie. If you're wondering. And this is Lisa."

He took in Lisa's skull and crossbones pajama pants and her black tank top with *Did I ask you?* emblazoned across her breasts. "I guessed that."

She bristled, and folded her arms pointedly. "And *you* are?"

Justin made a belated introduction. "I thought you'd have figured out by now. This is my friend Henry."

Her mouth opened, and for a second no sound came out. "This is the future friar?"

Henry looked her up and down. "And you're the sorceress?"

Lisa's gray eyes narrowed dangerously, and her tone grew icy. "I prefer the term *evil genius*. The sorcery is incidental."

Too many things had besieged me at once. I hadn't even processed the dream or its ramifications or the confusion of Justin's arrival, and now there was his mystery friend to fit into my sleep-muddled head. "You told him about us?"

Justin didn't seem to understand my consternation. "It was hard to explain the necessity for the trip without clueing him in on the particulars."

Lisa's lip curled. "That explains it. He came to see if you're crazy, Mags. That's true friendship for you."

Henry pointed to his nose. "And this is the thanks I get."

I couldn't deal with the battle of the best friends. The adrenaline rush of the room invasion was fading and the nightmare was catching up. I could feel a headache looming, waiting to land on me like an Acme anvil.

"We'd better not keep Teresa waiting," I said, rubbing my forehead with the heels of my hands.

Lisa grabbed a jacket and slipped it on over her tank top. "I'll go. You gather up our stuff."

Justin stared at Henry until he got a clue. His friend made an elaborate show of checking his nose for blood, then got to his feet. "Why don't I go, too, and take care of our end of things."

"Nice job, Captain Subtlety," Lisa told Justin as she slipped on her flip-flops and headed out after Henry.

"What happened to your leg?" Justin asked the moment they were gone.

I looked down. My ankle was a Technicolor mess of pur-ple, green, and yellow. "It looks worse than it feels." Which wasn't strictly the truth, but the dull throb wasn't sufficient to stand out from the barrage of other crises.

He followed me as I went to the vanity and bundled toiletries into a clean towel. "Not really an answer to my question."

"I'd rather just tell the story once." Back to my suitcase, where I dropped the bundle in and took out a pair of shorts. "Assuming you want Henry in on the discussion."

Justin sank onto the bed, watching me collect the rest of our stuff. "I'm confused. Maybe it's just because I haven't slept. But when you were talking the other night, asking if I'd told Henry about us—well, not about us, but about the weird stuff we've seen—I thought you were hinting that I should."

I stared at him stupidly while my pounding head processed his meaning. "So you told him about me and Lisa, and the demon and everything?"

"I told him about you, your Sight, and Lisa studying magic to try and combat what we've encountered." He leaned for-ward, peering closely at my face. "Is that a problem?"

"No." It was ironic, though, in a be-careful-what-you-wish-for way. Justin kept a lot of his past—stuff Henry knew, because he'd been there—private from me. But at least I had the weirdness. That was our thing. Now he'd told Henry, who just happened to be studying to be a priest. There are limits to my self-assurance. Forget thinking I was crazy—what if my boyfriend's best friend thought I was going to Hell?

All of which was inconsequential next to the fact that I was sure now that we were dealing with a demon, even if I'd yet to say it aloud. The forces of darkness tend to put things into perspective, generally speaking.

Suddenly my hands were shaking too badly to do up the zipper of my bag. Justin, observing this, took over the task. "How's your headache?"

I squinted at him. "Is it that obvious?"

He took me by the shoulders and steered me to a seat on the edge of the bed. "That must have been some dream."

"Yeah." I wasn't ready to go into detail just yet. "How's *your* headache?"

"I'll live." His smile was sheepish. "If I did have delusions of riding to your rescue, shining armor or whatever, that piece of slapstick put an end to it."

I grinned a little, reading more into the admission than just his embarrassment. He'd totally been doing the dauntless hero thing in his head.

I'd jab a sharp stick in my eye before I'd admit this to Lisa, but the white knight thing didn't bother me that much. Like she always said, Justin was Lawful Good. A paladin. It was his nature to try to protect me when my own crusader nature made me rush in where maybe I shouldn't.

"I have a confession, too," I said, swinging my legs across his lap and pointing to my bruises. "I got that doing what I promised you I was too smart to do."

His fingers were warm as he laid them gently on my multicolored ankle. "I didn't need any psychic powers to know that. Does it have anything to do with the nightmare?"

"Yeah." I sighed. "We have a lot to catch up on."

He set my feet back on the ground, stood up, and offered me a hand. "Well, let's find Lisa and Henry and get going."

I accepted his help up off the bed; the pounding in my head made it hard to see straight. "They may have canceled each other out, like matter and antimatter."

Justin picked up my backpack and suitcase. "In that case, we'll just look for the smoking crater."

The last thing I grabbed was the denim shirt from the back of the desk chair, throwing it over my T-shirt, since the predawn air would be cold. As soon as I did, the throbbing in my skull disappeared. The tension evaporated from my neck and shoulders as if someone had lifted a weight off them.

It was the same feeling I'd gotten from the charm bags, which were still wrapped up, safely insulated, inside the dresser. Whoever had made the charms had made this shirt. I was going to figure out who that was—and not just to thank them.

At the moment, though, I had to admit I was pretty darn grateful.

# 18

Our new room looked pretty much exactly like the old room, except in mirror image and with a door still on its hinges. It occupied the upstairs west corner, and Teresa had put the guys in the downstairs east corner. Hardly subtle.

The four of us dumped our stuff in our respective quarters and reconvened in Lisa's and my room to catch each other up. The guys' story was short: insane decision to come down and help us look for *el chupacabra,* standby flight to San Antonio, rental car down to the middle of nowhere.

For our part, I recapped the accident, the reports of dead livestock, the bogus bones in the two-headed snake museum, and ended with the stakeout with Dave. Justin prompted me for details while Henry listened silently, his chair tipped back on two legs, his arms folded across his chest.

When I finished, Henry said, "Okay, let me see if I've got this straight. The village people think that an urban legend is killing their livestock, and you all believe it because Maggie has . . . a feeling?"

Lisa, who had spent the last three days being the skeptic, was now the first to jump to my defense. "If you're coming in at intermission, you're just going to have to take some things on faith."

Henry raised a brow at her phrasing. "As strange as it seems, I'm just playing devil's advocate. You're asking me to believe a lot, with no actual proof."

Justin nudged me. He was sitting on the corner of my bed, since there was only one chair. "Show him your ankle, Maggie."

I got up and propped my foot on the edge of the desk, displaying my war wounds. Henry grimaced in sympathy. "Ouch." Then he peered closer, giving me a view of his profile. He missed tall, dark, and handsome by a nose—an impressively Roman nose that owed nothing to Lisa's fist. When he looked up at me in surprise, the blue of his eyes was startling, an odd match with the rough angles of his face. "It looks like a handprint, but the fingers are too long and thin."

Justin nodded. "Whatever grabbed her had opposable thumbs. So unless there's a five-foot-tall carnivorous raccoon out there, I think this counts as tangible evidence."

"Fine. But evidence of what?"

The three of them looked at me, and I delayed the inevitable by digging under the stack of library books for my spiral pad of notes. "The way we figured, it could be two things. One: a rare, reclusive creature that has come near civilization because of the drought."

"And you're ruling that out," Lisa confirmed.

"Right. It moved way too fast for anything natural." I drew a line diagonally across that column. "Two: a supernatural creature. Like Bigfoot, or the Loch Ness monster. Maybe there really is a goat sucker."

Justin shook his head. "How could something exist without leaving behind any evidence besides a couple of footprints?"

"Maybe some magic keeps the monster from being photographed or documented?" I suggested.

"Even after death?" Justin asked. "Nothing in the fossil record?"

"If it's supernatural," said Lisa, "maybe it doesn't die."

"Everything with a body dies."

Henry listened with a bemused expression. "So, Justin. You don't believe in Bigfoot, but you believe in spirits—angels and demons and psychic girlfriends?"

Justin smiled ruefully, as if realizing it didn't make sense. "Because they shouldn't be proven, but are. At least to me."

Lisa had that debate-team look in her eye. "But Thomas Aquinas says that God can be proven by reason."

"But not by physical evidence," said Justin. "And also, that's God, not angels. And definitely not *el chupacabra.*"

I pressed my hands to my aching head. "Focus, you guys!

We don't have time to argue about the number of angels on the head of a pin. Let's come back from the theoretical extreme, okay?"

After a startled moment, Justin cleared his throat in apology. "Sure, Maggie."

I flipped my notebook to a blank page and sat down cross-legged on the bed. "The problem is, there are a lot of factors. There's the chupacabra." I wrote it down and circled it. "There's Doña Isabel, who is a Seer, and some kind of guardian of the land. And there's someone else we don't know about yet. A *bruja*."

"A witch?" Justin looked over my shoulder as I circled each word on the page. "That's a lot going on in one place. No wonder you're having such a hard time figuring it out."

"Thanks for the vote of confidence." I connected the dots into a triangle on the paper. "The problem is, I don't know how they all link together."

Lisa contemplated the page as well. "You're sure Doña Isabel isn't the *bruja*? Even if she never leaves the ranch property, she could have had someone here in town put those charm bags in our rooms."

"Charm bags?" asked Henry, sounding as if that was one blithe magical reference too many.

"Yeah," she said. "Check under your bed before you go to sleep."

"It's not her," I said, before things could get off track again. "The two protections—the one on the room and the psychic fence around the ranch—*feel* different." I struggled for a comparison. "It's like the difference between a folk song and Handel's *Messiah*."

Justin had picked up the pamphlet on the Velasquez ranch and was thumbing through it. "Doña Isabel is this guy Zeke's grandmother?"

"Yeah. Matriarch of the ranch. The whole county, basically. Way powerful."

"What's with the holy cows?" Henry pointed to the sepia photo on the front cover. "Why do those cattle have a patriarchal cross on their backsides?"

"That's the Velasquez brand," I said. "The double-armed cross."

Justin read from the first page. " 'Raphael Velasquez chose it to honor the French Oblate missionaries who rode from ranch to ranch to deliver the sacrament and the Word.' " He looked up. "There's a job for you, Henry. Put your polo pony to good use."

Lisa swiveled to stare at Henry. "Polo pony?"

"Let's focus, people." I jumped up to think on my feet. "We need to figure this out. We've got until sundown. That's it."

"So this thing can't come out until night?" Justin asked.

"It's photosensitive. That's how the camera flash saved me."

He watched me pace the tiny space between the beds. "Is it intelligent?"

"The thing in the pasture seemed more instinct than intellect. But it's not neutral, it's not just a hungry animal. It's Evil." My mind went again to my dream and I wrapped my arms around myself, unable to stop a chill. "It doesn't just eat to survive. It wants to kill, to consume. In my dream I saw—" I broke off and rubbed my eyes with my hands. "There was blood, and it was soaking into the ground and somehow making this thing more solid. More real."

Silence met my words, thick and heavy. Henry spoke first, and actually sounded shaken. "No wonder you were screaming."

I smiled ruefully, appreciating the sympathy, even if he didn't believe my dream meant anything.

Lisa broke in. "Am I the only one who noticed that Maggie just called this thing Evil? Otherworldly, destructive-for-the-hell-of-it-type Evil?"

"I just always assumed it was," said Justin. "We haven't encountered anything supernatural that wasn't."

"Hello." I pointed to my freakish brain. "I resent that. And so does my tea-leaf-reading granny. Lisa might have something to say about it, too."

Lisa leaned against the wall, deliberately indolent. "Evil geniuses make it a policy never to apologize or explain."

Justin rubbed his face, looking fatigued. "What's the next step, Maggie?"

"I need to speak to Doña Isabel. She knows a lot more than she's telling." I stretched my arms over my head and tried not to groan. Everything ached. "Lisa, what's Zeke's plan for the day?"

She checked the clock on the nightstand. "He's supervising the roundup. They were going to start as soon as it was light. In fact, Zeke will be picking me up any minute now. I said I'd help however I could."

I glanced at the window, where gray light edged the floral curtains. "It's dawn now. The Duck will be open, and I can get some coffee, then head out to the Big House. The guys can get some rest, and we can all meet up later."

Justin's hand on my arm stopped me before I got any momentum. "One more thing." His backpack lay on the floor near him. He pulled it over with his foot, and took out a small notebook. "I searched for info on previous animal attacks, like you asked. Livestock getting killed by wild animals wasn't uncommon until all the apex predators got driven off and hunted to extinction."

His dedication was admirable, but he looked half dead with fatigue. "Can't this wait until you've gotten a couple of hours of sleep?"

"No, we need to talk about it before we do anything else." He flipped open the notepad. "So to narrow things down, I looked for anything in Velasquez County that happened around a drought. Two events stood out. One was an anecdotal story from the eighteen hundreds, about the ground getting so dry that cracks opened up large enough to swallow whole cows."

I sat on the edge of my bed, thinking about my dream, about sinking into the ground and the monster crawling out. "Okay. What's the other one?"

"The last thing I found was in the nineteen fifties. Also a drought. Also mutilated cattle, blamed on a cougar. But it stood out to me because a cowboy died."

"The fifties?" Doña Isabel would have been at the ranch then. She'd have been about the age she appeared in my visions. "Did it say where this happened, exactly?"

"No." He pulled a folded map out of the notebook. "I planned to plot all the past and present incidents and see if

there was a pattern. But I couldn't narrow down any locations."

"I know how we can find out." I stood up purposefully.
"Meet me in the Duck in fifteen minutes. It's time to turn the
inquisition around."

If anyone knew the chupacabra's social schedule, it was
Teresa. And if her memory didn't go back that far, I was bet-
ting the Old Guys' did.

# 19

I entered the Duck alone, having hurried to dress and get there before the guys. The bar seemed almost deserted, especially after the crowd the night before. There were only three Old Guys at their table. Hector, as I'd hoped, was drying mugs behind the counter, and I headed his way.

Teresa intercepted me en route, one hand on her hip, the other holding a pot of coffee. "There better not be any hanky-panky going on, little missy."

"Hanky-panky?" I warily eyed the steaming pot and didn't try to go around her.

She gave me a death-ray glare and flipped a dish towel

over her shoulder. "I know what you kids get up to on spring break, but this is a respectable place."

One of the Old Guys called from their table. "Give her a break, Teresa. That girl shot your chupacabra."

"Hmph." She pressed her lips together and went to fill their mugs. "*El chupacabra* is not so easily killed."

I continued to the bar. Hector had coffee waiting for me, a pitcher of cream beside it. "Heard you had some gentleman callers this morning."

"It was an exciting night all around." I climbed onto a stool and put his folded denim shirt on the counter. "You probably heard all about that, too."

"Yeah." He wiped the spotless bar. "Dave's headed home from the hospital already. Carl went to go pick him up."

"That's a relief." I pushed the shirt across the countertop. "Thanks for loaning me this. It was a big help. Especially this morning, when I had a hammering headache."

He smiled at my lack of subtlety. "Hang on to it. I reckon you might still need it."

I checked that Teresa was still busy with the Old Guys, and then gave Hector a narrow-eyed stare. "Lisa said that only a woman can be a *bruja*."

The creases in his cheeks deepened further. "She'd be right. A male witch would be a *brujo*."

"Do you know any?"

"*Brujas*? Just you and your friend."

I stifled my frustrated response as Teresa returned to the bar. Hector, his humor fading to a warning glance, went back to drying mugs.

The cowbell over the back door clanged. I swiveled on my

barstool to greet Justin and Henry. They'd both changed clothes and looked considerably less rumpled. The Old Guys watched their arrival with interest.

They slid onto seats on either side of me, and Henry asked, "Where's Lisa?"

"Getting dressed. Zeke is picking her up in a bit."

Justin shook his head. "I'm trying to wrap my head around the idea of Cowgirl Lisa."

"Hmph." Teresa plunked down two more mugs, one in front of each of the guys. "She thinks she's a smart cookie, that tall girl. She must figure Mr. Zeke will own most of the county when Doña Isabel dies."

Henry and Justin looked taken aback. They weren't used to how eating in the bar entitled Teresa to know, and comment on, all your personal business.

Hector nudged her aside in order to put a tray of glasses under the counter. "Teresa, don't go telling these folks the Velasquezes' private concerns."

"Well, it's not private, is it? The whole county knows." She filled the guys' mugs without asking. "They might as well tell their friend and save her a lot of trouble."

"Tell her what?" I asked.

She flicked her dishtowel over a nonexistent spot on the counter. "Doña Isabel is leaving all the land to the Catholic Diocese of Corpus Christi. Zeke will either have to work for them, or go do something else."

Hector looked seriously annoyed. "You make it sound like Ezekiel Velasquez doesn't do a lick of work around here."

Teresa put her hands on her hips. "You know he wants to put a bunch of airplane propellers all along the coast?"

Justin—who was still sitting with his mouth slightly open

in bewilderment—looked at me for explanation. "A wind farm," I said. "He wants to go green." Which was kind of ironic when you thought about how the other big industry here was oil and gas.

Henry cleared his throat. "Could I get an iced tea instead of coffee?"

Teresa moved off, still in a huff. Hector took away the coffee cup, meeting my eye with a grimace. "Is it true?" I asked him. "Doña Isabel seems so fond of Zeke."

The lines of his face dragged down in concern or regret, and he seemed to choose his words carefully. "I can't explain it to you, Maggie. You'll have to add that to your mysteries to solve."

When Hector left, Justin turned to me, eyes wide. "What was *that* about?"

"I told you there was a lot going on here." I lowered my voice as Teresa brought Henry's iced tea. "Even I don't know the half of it."

Henry took a sip of tea and set it aside. "It's certainly a colorful place."

They exchanged looks—a silent communication I couldn't interpret—and Justin opened the map he'd brought with him. "Let's get these locations plotted and see if we get a pattern."

He smoothed the thick paper, and I saw that it wasn't a road map but a geological survey chart—the kind of contour map used for orienteering and hiking. It was a much larger scale than an atlas, and overlaid by gridlines. "Start with your accident, Maggie. Where did you hit the cow?"

I hesitated over the line for Highway 77, then pointed to a spot that seemed right. "Here. I think."

He marked it with a felt-tipped pen. Teresa loitered

across from us, not bothering to pretend she wasn't paying attention. Justin turned the map toward her. "Teresa, would you mind showing me where your goats were killed?"

She pointed to a spot outside the town's dotted administrative boundary. The entire incorporation of Dulcina was smaller than my college campus. "There. The whole herd."

Marking the spot on the map, Justin turned again to me. "How about the coordinates you got from the GPS system last night?" I read them off; they were faded but still clear where I'd written them on my arm. Justin found the intersection of two gridlines and made an X. "Any idea where you found those cows on your ride?"

"Um . . ." I oriented myself with the curve of the shore and the road that connected Dulcina to the Big House. "Here, maybe." I indicated a small area bounded by a couple of unimproved roads. The topographical chart was much more detailed than a road map, getting in close to show fences and gravel roads as well as stock ponds, windmills, and wellheads.

Justin prompted Teresa with questions about the present attacks, and she was thrilled to be taken seriously. As she recalled the incidents, he marked them on the map and started a legend: _G_ for goat, _C_ for calf, _C_ with a line under it for grown cow. The Old Guys at their table had stopped their talk to eavesdrop. Eventually one of them ambled over to us, peering around Henry's shoulder.

"Don't forget Carl's best herding dog," he said.

Henry rose and offered the barstool to the Old Guy. "Have a seat."

"Don't mind if I do." The Old Guy sat and pointed to a

spot on the map. "There it was. Neck torn right out. Wasn't natural, Carl said."

I made sure my voice would carry over to the table. "We heard there was a cowboy killed, years ago."

Another Old Guy came over, carrying his coffee cup. His cap was embroidered with the USS *Lexington* seal, marking him as a navy veteran. "I remember that. Young guy, riding the herds to protect them."

The first guy chided the second. "Joe, you old coot. You're thinking of that young fellow who got bit last night."

Lexington Joe rubbed his chin, rasping the nearly invisible gray stubble. "No. This was years ago. I was home on leave."

I seized on that. "So this has happened before? Livestock being attacked?"

"Of course. Nothing new under the sun." He held his mug over the counter. "How about a warm-up, Miss Teresa?"

"When was this? Were there a lot of cattle killed?"

He scratched his head under his cap. "I don't reckon I remember. It was after the war, when little Isabel La Tour came from New Orleans to marry young Mike."

"You mean Doña Isabel? Zeke's grandmother?" Everything she'd said indicated a much longer association with the land.

"Yeah," said Joe. "She was a Velasquez cousin. Twice removed or something like that. Her father's father went to the Big Easy to make his fortune, but Isabel spent every summer here. We all knew she'd marry Mike Velasquez, but not for lack of our trying to convince her otherwise."

"Cousins?" I echoed. Eew.

Henry noticed my tone. "Probably not closely related. Franklin and Eleanor Roosevelt were sixth cousins."

"That's right," said Joe. "People's circle of acquaintances was smaller then. No meeting people on the internets and all that."

"So about these livestock killings—the ones from the fifties," I clarified. "Did they coincide with Isabel's arrival?"

He rubbed his chin again. "Not in any remarkable way. No more than, say, you girls arriving now."

Teresa narrowed her eyes at me, looking speculative. I was glad for Justin's redirect. "Where did you say the cowboy was killed?" He slid the map across the bar.

"Lady Acre." Joe pointed to a stretch of land between Dulcina and the Gulf. "That's it right there."

Shoulder to shoulder, we studied the map. The livestock attacks were scattered, seeming random all over the county. The only grid squares that were completely free of marks were the ones that encompassed the town of Dulcina. The other clear area was Lady Acre, with its lone X for the sixty-year-old death.

X marks the spot.

"Why is it called Lady Acre?" I asked.

"Because Our Lady appeared there," Teresa said, matter-of-factly.

I blinked. Not what you expect to hear mentioned so casually. Henry recovered first. "The Virgin Mary appeared in the Velasquez pasture?"

"No, she didn't," Joe corrected firmly. "Doña Isabel had a dream that the Virgin appeared to her, and said to put a shrine there, so that no other deaths would take place."

"Hey, Joe!" One of the Old Guys hollered toward the bar. "If you stand there all day, Teresa will never get over here with the coffee."

With an annoyed huff, Teresa grabbed the pot off the warmer. "Like it would kill you to get off your lazy butt once in a while?"

Joe followed her back to the Old Guys' table. Justin kept an eye on them, and pitched his voice under the cover of the radio in the kitchen and the struggling air conditioner. "Now we know. That's what stopped the killings last time."

I looked around for Hector, hoping for confirmation, but he had disappeared. Figured. What was his problem with direct answers?

Henry reclaimed his barstool, and leaned in to keep his voice low, too. "You're not seriously suggesting the Blessed Virgin Mary really appeared in a dream, then vanquished this chupacabra thing?"

My image of the mother of Jesus didn't really incorporate the slaying of monsters. You'd think she could delegate that to some middle-management cherubim with flaming swords.

"If Joe was quoting her correctly," Justin pointed out, "Doña Isabel didn't say that the BVM would stop the attacks, just that they would stop. Classic semantic dodge."

"So, what's the plan?" Henry asked.

I studied the single X on the map. "Doña Isabel first, but then I think we need to go see this shrine. Maybe I can get a picture of how it ties in." I traced the contour lines that marked changes in elevation. If you stared at them long enough, they started to look three-dimensional.

"You know, Maggie." Justin's voice dropped even lower,

203

so there was no chance of anyone in the bar hearing him. "I didn't bring it up in front of Lisa, but it seems like you've skirted all around the most obvious label for this thing. You said it was Evil, but you haven't named it out loud."

I sighed. "We've all thought it, though. Well, maybe not Henry, because he's still struggling to catch up."

"Thanks," he said. "But I'm not that slow."

Justin ducked his head to hold my gaze. "If this thing is some kind of demon, the next question is, who summoned it?"

I dropped my eyes, picking at the corner of the map. "I haven't really thought that far."

He sat back, looking worried. "Just making sure we're all on the same page."

What he meant was "Just making sure you remember all the other times you trusted people you shouldn't." When I liked someone, I never wanted to think they were capable of bad things. Summoning demons. Deals with the devil. And the problem was, I liked *all* these people. Except maybe Teresa.

Handing me the folded map, Justin went to settle up our drinks, leaving Henry and me alone. I didn't have to touch him to pick up on his thoughts. I didn't even have to be psychic. He was thinking very loudly.

I turned to face him with a statement, not a question. "You don't really believe in any of this, do you."

His gaze was level and appraising. "Like you said, I'm still catching up."

"In other words, you haven't made up your mind yet."

"About you? Or about the Blessed Virgin appearing in visions?"

"Aren't you kind of obligated to believe in things like that?"

He thought over his answer. "I believe in the *possibility* of such a thing. But I'm undecided about the *reality* of it."

I hopped off the barstool, grabbing Hector's denim shirt to take with me. "Well, stick around. It's only a matter of time before you find yourself saying the craziest stuff with absolute seriousness."

He got up, too, and went to meet Justin by the door. I followed more slowly, hoping to spot Hector again and try for some straight answers. I was doomed to frustration this morning. I could only hope that my visit with Doña Isabel would go better.

I wondered if she'd really had a divine vision. She seemed devout enough. I certainly would never rate that. At least, I hoped I never would. From what I could tell, whenever an archangel or a burning bush turns up, it's generally not to say, Hey, go out and have a happy and uncomplicated life.

# 20

Justin slammed the door of the rental car and stared up at the Big House, taking in the arches of the balcony, the red tile roof, and the lookout tower with its dragonfly weather vane.

"So, this is the Velasquez manor?"

"Yeah." My skin was sticky and hot, and I'd done nothing but climb out of the car. I'd gotten used to the breeze from the Gulf, but today the air was muggy and still.

Henry pried himself out of the backseat of the Escort. Since neither of the guys was old enough to rent a car from a major company, they'd had to find what they could, and the subcompact wasn't really built for a person of Henry's height.

Justin nodded toward the porch, where a woman stood like a sentry on a drawbridge. "Is that Doña Isabel?"

"No," I said. The figure was small and plump, her shoes sensible. "That's the housekeeper."

"She looks like she's expecting us," said Henry. "Lisa's boyfriend must have called ahead."

"I didn't tell him we were coming." Just the opposite, in fact. I didn't want him to know.

Justin waved me in front of him. "Ladies first."

Connie watched the three of us approach, her expression forbidding, with no shift to recognition as I neared her. "Hi, Connie. I don't know if you remember me, but—"

"Doña Isabel said you might come." Her gaze flicked over the guys in dismissal.

She gave no indication whether I was actually welcome. "Can I see her?"

The tightening of her mouth wasn't promising. "She said to say that she was in the chapel, and you may find her there, if God means for her to be found."

"Okay." I guess that was the closest thing to an invitation we were going to get. "Thanks, Connie."

"Don't thank me. There are strange happenings here, and I don't like it." She looked up at the sky as if it had personally offended her, then went inside and closed the door, leaving the three of us standing on the drive.

I looked up at the cloudless gray-blue sky, wondering what she saw. Justin shifted his weight, crunching on the gravel. "Apparently she's expecting you, Maggie."

Henry's expression was skeptical. "It's a logical guess, if she's heard any of the past week's events."

"True," Justin said, accepting his friend's cynicism as easily as he did my psychitude. "Which way to the chapel?"

"Good question." A quick scan of the front garden showed a flagstone path leading around the corner, and it seemed as sensible a place to start as any. "This way."

I wound through the tropical plantings of the formal garden to where the fauna became more ruggedly indigenous, full of lantana and hearty daisies. The path split and, with almost no hesitation, I took the way that led toward the water. A tall palm tree rose above a cluster of shrub oak and mesquite, the fronds like a star over a stable. Or in this case, the Velasquez family chapel.

It looked like the Big House—red tile roof, white stucco, and arched entry—like a tiny offshoot of a parent plant. The door stood open in invitation.

I turned to Justin, and Henry behind him. "Maybe you two should let me talk to her alone. She's really prickly, and she's not expecting you."

"Are you sure?" Justin asked.

"Yeah." I had a pretty strong feeling about it. He must have picked up on that, and let me go without further question.

Stepping into the chapel, I had to pause for my eyes to adjust to the cool shadow. The only light slanted through two stained-glass windows on either side of the altar. They illuminated a straight figure on a prayer kneeler, her dark hair covered with a lace scarf, her face lifted to the cross above.

The stone floor was worn but very clean, and the marble altar seemed to glow softly in the rosy light from the windows. There were no pews, just two rows of wooden folding chairs.

I let my footsteps announce me. Doña Isabel kept me waiting another minute, then crossed herself and moved to rise. Her hands grasped the front of the kneeler, the part where you put your prayer book—or in my case, my elbows—and I saw her knuckles whiten as she levered herself up.

Without thinking, I offered her my hand. She disdained my assistance, and once she stood, moved to one of the rows of folding chairs. Taking a seat, she looked at me expectantly. "Well?"

"You knew I was coming. Surely you have some idea why."

"I am not a mind reader, Magdalena Quinn."

I took a seat beside her. "Zeke wouldn't be happy to know I'm here. He says that you don't know anything about what's happening on the ranch, but I think you and I both know he's wrong."

She narrowed her eyes. "You are a very presumptuous girl, to march into my chapel and tell me my own business. Do you think anything happens on this land that I do not realize? I knew the moment you and your friend arrived. I knew about your blundering attempts to test the protections here. Do not presume to tell me what I *should* know."

Great. I gazed at the patient Madonna behind the impatient matriarch, and struggled for a little of that calm.

"In that case, you *do* know about the . . . um . . ." I couldn't bring myself to say the name in front of her.

Doña Isabel waved a dismissive hand. "I know the ridiculous legend that Teresa tells everyone in her bar. *El chupacabra*. She watches too much television."

"Right. Except there really is something here."

"Impossible." She had deflector shields like the Death

Star, but she couldn't completely control the false note in her voice.

"How is it impossible?" I sat forward, the wooden chair creaking underneath me. "Hasn't this happened before? Didn't you do something then?"

She turned to face the front of the church, giving me her profile. "That is precisely why I know it is impossible now. That door is closed."

I thought about my dream, about the things trying to push from their spirit world to this one of flesh and matter. The idea of a door made sense—maybe not one with a lintel and threshold, but some way of crossing from one state of being to another.

"How did you close it before?"

Her voice took the cadence of rote recitation. "I had a vision of the Blessed Virgin Mary, who told me that if I erected a shrine to her, then the livestock killings would stop."

I make it a policy to never knock anybody's miracles. The only thing I know more about than the average person is how little we humans really know about the Big Picture. So in theory, I didn't automatically dismiss the idea that the BVM put the kibosh on the chupacabra monster the last time it had wiggled its way into existence on our physical plane.

Except for two things: The explanation *felt* too easy, and it didn't seem to mesh with any of my experiences so far. And also, I could tell Doña Isabel was lying.

I didn't want to call her on the falsehood directly, so I poked at the other hole in her story. "That's all? You just put up a statue, and the demon was vanquished?"

Was that a tiny flinch at the word *demon*? An instant later her mouth pursed primly. "I did nothing. I was merely the instrument of God's saving hand."

"If that's true"—I thought supplicant, respectful thoughts, in case she was also the instrument of God's smiting hand—"then maybe you could allow that I'm here to help you."

She looked at me in cold disapproval. "You and your sorcery."

I didn't bother to deny that I was the sorcerer. Not only did it not matter, it would be a technicality. Not to mention hypocritical. "Look, Doña Isabel, we're on the same side, no matter what the particulars might be."

She rose and walked back to her prie-dieu before the altar. "Scripture says, Thou shalt not suffer a witch to live."

"Please." I didn't mean to scoff, but that was how it came out. "The Bible also says, Let him without sin cast the first stone."

Her back was to me, but I saw her shoulders stiffen. I got such a clear flash of her emotions—a muddled tangle of guilt and frustration and honest despair—that I was struck by a revelation of my own. Doña Isabel thought of herself as a witch. More to the point, she thought of herself as a sinner.

"Doña Isabel." I knelt next to her, not in a religious fervor, but so that I could see her expression. "Whatever happened back then, keeping it a secret isn't going to help matters now."

Her gaze lifted heavenward, but I think it was more of an eye roll than a prayer. "Impertinent child. You are not my confessor."

"I wish I was," I snapped, losing my temper, "because

then you would listen to me when I say that your guilt is not helping anyone. If this is the same thing that you dealt with fifty years ago—"

"It isn't." She looped a rosary around her fingers and folded her hands.

"How do you know?" Was that even possible? Could lightning strike the same place twice? "Give me a clue, Doña Isabel, please."

She lifted her sculpted, stubborn jaw and fixed her eyes on the altar. "God's work does not come undone."

"What? Like, what God has joined together, let no man put asunder? If that were true, there would be no divorce. . . ." The look she shot me was eloquent. Okay, maybe that wasn't the best argument to use on a woman who still heard Mass in Latin.

I sank back onto my heels and speared my fingers through my hair, as if I could pull the magic words of cooperation out of my head. "It's getting worse."

"Have you not thought that perhaps your presence here is making it so?"

The blood seemed to drain from my head, and I braced a hand on the cold stone floor so I wouldn't fall over. "What?"

She stared down at me, her black eyes piercing. "Perhaps your presence is not a coincidence. But that does not mean you were brought here by the side of the angels. Your well-intentioned blunderings seem to be strengthening the thing, not weakening it."

My stomach knotted itself around that horrible idea. "That's impossible."

"No one went to the hospital before you came." She

positioned herself for her prayers, clasping her hands and turning her face to the altar. "I hope it's not true, but it's something to think about as you leave."

"And in the meantime, you do nothing?"

"I'm doing what I know best." Her voice was placid once more, but I saw that her fingers were white as they grasped the beads of her rosary. "Now leave me to it."

She closed her eyes, and it was like a wall had gone up between us. I climbed to my feet, not knowing what else to try. As I turned toward the door, shoulders slumped, I caught sight of the Madonna in her niche, watching me with serene sympathy.

You don't have to tell me. That could have gone a lot better.

✳   ✳   ✳

I didn't see the guys when I went outside. On a hunch I followed a trail that wound around the chapel to a shaded garden overlooking a salt marsh inlet, where fat dragonflies danced over the tall grass, catching their lunch.

Henry stood with his back to me, gazing at the water. Or maybe sleeping on his feet—I couldn't tell. Justin sprawled on a wooden bench; one arm shielded his eyes from the overhead sun, and the other rested on his chest. I kind of hated to wake him up.

"How'd it go?" he asked, startling me. Henry turned around, too. "Learn anything?"

"About Ol' Chupy? No. About Doña Isabel? Loads."

He sat up, and gestured for me to take a seat beside him. "Like?"

"Doña Isabel thinks I'm a witch and a sinner."

"Well . . . ," said Henry, in a she's-got-a-point tone.

"That's not funny." Not when I wasn't sure he was joking.

Justin shot his friend a look, the kind of silent communication Lisa and I did all the time.

I got back on track. "She also thinks that *she* is a witch and a sinner." I squinted out over the water, replaying the conversation. "It's not just her being a Seer. She was fine with that when I first met her. This feeling is new and it's tied to the chupacabra getting bolder. She can't deny its existence anymore."

Justin leaned forward, elbows on his knees. "So, you think that in the past she did something she now considers a sin? Like maybe worked some kind of spell to vanquish the demon?"

"Maybe." I scrubbed my hands through my hair. "This is like if Luke Skywalker found Obi-Wan Kenobi, but the Jedi just told him to piss off because he didn't believe in the Empire and he'd defeated them fifty years ago anyway. My entire movie has to be replotted."

"So," said Justin. "What's the first step?"

I tapped my fingers on the rough concrete of the bench. "She's sticking to the story about the BVM and the shrine. I think that's where we should start."

He stood and grabbed my hand to pull me up. "Then that's what we'll do."

✳  ✳  ✳

Lady Acre wasn't far from the Big House, if you were going over land. But by the road it was more like five miles. Ten, if you counted where we came to a dead end and had to retrace our path.

"Um . . . turn left," I said, trying to navigate while Justin drove. It didn't help that Texas required a road map the size of a bed sheet.

The next opportunity to turn was a narrow road about a car and a half wide. "Are you sure?"

"All I'm sure of is that if we keep going straight, we're going to end up in the Gulf of Mexico."

Justin turned onto the small road, which seemed identical to all the other small roads we'd already been down.

"Well," said Henry from the backseat. "This looks new and exciting."

I groaned, and crumpled the road map in frustration. "This shouldn't be so hard!"

With a determined frown, Justin checked the rearview mirror, flipped on the hazard lights, and pulled onto the unimproved shoulder. "Give me the chart—the geological survey one."

I slapped the neatly folded map into his palm, maybe a little more forcefully than necessary. Nothing tests a relationship like driving around in circles.

Justin climbed out and stood by the front bumper, orienting the chart on the hood. Henry collapsed against his seat with a moan of exaggerated relief. I shot him a you're-so-not-helping look and got out to join Justin, hardly slamming my door at all.

"We are nowhere near this Lady Acre place," he said.

"Sorry." I mostly meant it.

"Not your fault." His eyes were on the chart, but he brushed my shoulder absently. "I should have let you drive instead of trying to navigate."

I checked that statement for condescension, but decided to take it at face value. He had proven his familiarity with maps; I'd had us going around in circles. If he had said that he should have let *Henry* drive, then we would have had a problem.

"See this mark?" He pointed to a symbol on the chart. "It represents that water tower over there. And this line here is that power line to the east of us."

Shading my eyes, I found the landmarks that he meant, then looked back at the map. "So, we're probably right about here." I pointed to the intersection of a blacktop road and a thinner one coming off it.

"Right." He folded the chart, with the relevant grid squares facing out. Obviously a practiced move.

"Where did you learn to do that?"

"Fold a map? It's a guy thing."

This time he was obviously joking, but I wasn't quite ready to laugh. "Reading a topographic survey chart."

"I was on the orienteering team in high school."

"Your school had an orienteering team?" As sports went, it wasn't the weirdest thing ever, but I'd only heard of timed land navigation trials since I got to college.

Justin shrugged. "It was a boys-only boarding school. They had to channel all that testosterone somewhere. I also did track and fencing."

I glanced into the car, where Henry looked like he was taking a nap, then back at Justin, with an arched brow that would have done Lisa proud. "Do *you* have a polo pony, too?"

"No. I have to borrow one when I play." My jaw dropped, and he laughed, which sounded good after all the sniping in the car. "Kidding. I've only done trail riding at summer camp."

"You're a regular pentathlete." I tried not to sound too impressed. Brains *and* brawn. Just as well he was a bit of a chauvinist, or he might be too good to be true.

He went back to correcting our course on the map, remarking absently, "I've never learned to shoot, so you're one up on me there."

I sat against the hood of the car, wincing and readjusting my bruised butt, when I noticed the sunlight reflecting off something metal, barely visible in the distance.

Several big somethings, actually. Shading my eyes and stretching onto my tiptoes, I made out the shape of one silver pickup truck. The other vehicle was tan, which made it hard to distinguish against the drought-brown landscape. The light bar on the top, though, was hard to mistake.

"Justin?" He looked up, and I pointed to the trucks. "Maybe we're not in the wrong spot after all."

✳ ✳ ✳

There were three other trucks parked in a haphazard arrangement in the pasture, in addition to Zeke's silver pickup and the tan blazer with a bar of red lights on top and an official-looking seal on the door. Not the highway patrol, but the Wildlife Commission.

I let out a breath of relief that Justin, cutting the engine, echoed in words. "Hopefully that means there isn't a human involved."

"Involved in what?" Henry asked, then sat back as I opened the door and the smell rolled in. "Oh. God."

"Yeah," I said. "This isn't going to be good."

The odor wasn't old or putrid yet, but the day was warm and getting warmer. We hiked through the dry grass to where several men were standing around, talking in low, worried voices. While the land had appeared flat from the highway, the trucks actually were parked atop a gentle rise. Justin, Henry, and I reached the crest and stared down the slope into what seemed to be a slaughterhouse without walls.

I counted seven cows, all full grown. Their carcasses littered the ground like debris after a storm. They'd been there long enough for the blood to cake around the slashes in their hides.

"Jesus." I didn't think Henry was cursing so much as praying. His hand twitched, like he'd checked the impulse to cross himself. His face had turned sort of green, and Justin didn't look much better.

When I'd climbed out of the car, I'd automatically grabbed my camera. I glanced around to make sure we were still under the radar, then clicked off a couple of pictures.

"Careful," said Justin, nodding toward a guy in a khaki button-down shirt. "That guy looks official."

"Just look like we're supposed to be here." The camera whirred softly as I zoomed in on one of the cows. "He doesn't know we're not ranchers ourselves."

"Your *Doctor Who* baseball cap might be a clue."

Henry looked sharply at Justin, then at me. "How can you calmly take pictures of that?"

The answer was simple: The camera was a kind of shield. While I was photographing, I didn't have to think about what was in front of me, or use my other senses. But I could only procrastinate so long.

I slowly lowered the camera and looked at the grisly scene again, this time with a discerning eye. The cattle had all been slashed across the throat or the belly, but there didn't seem to be much blood. The ground had soaked it all up. Even though there were more animals dead than yesterday, I didn't see the same wholesale carnage. There was an economical intensity to what happened here.

"This is different from before."

Justin frowned. "How so?"

"It's neater. Before, there were pieces all over the place, and the carcass was more torn up, picked apart." I chose my words carefully, listening to my instinct. "This is just . . . slaughter. Ruthlessly efficient. It knows what it needs now."

"What's that?" asked Justin.

The answer came to me through the soles of my feet. "Blood. This is a bloodletting."

"You keep saying 'it,' " said Henry. "But one creature couldn't have done all this."

I shook my head. "It couldn't."

"Lupe!" We turned toward the voice; I recognized Zeke, even from a distance, calling down the hill. The uniformed game warden stood beside him. "Do you have those ID numbers yet?"

The stable manager called back up. *"Uno mas, Señor Zeke. Un momento."*

Justin looked at me, his expression bemused. *"Mister* Zeke? And I thought the name Doña Isabel was old-fashioned."

I turned off my camera and capped the lens. "They're

forty years behind the times in some ways. And once you meet Isabel Velasquez . . . well, it doesn't seem strange at all."

Squinting into the midmorning sun, I found Lisa leaning against Zeke's truck. Like me, she was wearing jeans, a T-shirt, and sneakers; her chestnut braid snaked down her back, and dark glasses hid her expression as she watched Zeke confer with the game warden.

She waved us closer and we headed over. Keeping her tone low so she didn't interrupt the official conversation, she asked, "What are you doing here?"

"Either I can't read a map," I said, "or other forces are at work. I prefer to think the latter."

As we watched, a third man, his tanned face grimly stoic, joined Zeke and the game warden. Lisa explained quietly, "We were out with the roundup when Zeke got a call about this. The Wildlife Commission was already on their way."

"Do they have a mythological beasts department?"

She smiled without humor. "If Tommy Lee Jones and Will Smith show up in black suits, it will make my day."

Over her shoulder I saw the game warden shaking his head as he addressed the third man, who must have been the owner of the cattle. I strained my ears to eavesdrop.

"Looking at your livestock here, Mr. Garza, I'd think it was a cougar that killed them, as unlikely as that is." Again his head wagged side to side. "It's a head-scratcher for sure. Never seen anything like it."

"What are you going to put in the report?" Zeke asked, sounding testy. He stood with his thumbs hooked in his belt, deceptively casual. But I could see the tension in his fingers.

"Unknown predator, I guess. Maybe rabid. We'll have to do an investigation." The warden glanced between the ranchers, and I realized his brain wasn't as slow as his drawl. "You are insured, I reckon."

Mr. Garza muttered a few choice words in Spanish. Zeke didn't move, except for his hands, which flexed as if itching to make fists. "Just send me a copy of the report."

"Oh, we'll be seeing each other." The game warden put on a pair of aviator sunglasses. "I'll have some men put out cage traps. Tell your guys I'd better not see any home jobs. And to be careful what they shoot at. I know they gotta protect their herds, but it would be a shame to kill a returning Mexican wolf or something equally endangered."

Zeke spoke with remarkable calm. "The only things endangered right now, George, are our cows."

"Well, I heard you're out here rounding up cattle so you can ride herd on them. That's the thing to do. Just don't go shooting anything out of season if you don't have to."

The warden nodded to Zeke—whose family's taxes probably paid his salary—and headed toward his truck.

Zeke pulled himself together. When he saw the four of us clustered by the bumper of his truck, he headed over.

"Well," he said, sounding resigned, "I guess you girls were right about one thing. That monster is definitely not dead."

I made my tone as light as possible. "I thought you didn't believe in the chupacabra."

He blew out a sigh and ran his hand through his hair. "I don't know anymore. I'm at the end of my rope. No one knows what the hell it is, except a whole lot of trouble."

He looked at Justin and Henry, who were flanking me in a strangely protective way. I made belated introductions. "Zeke, this is my friend Justin, and his friend Henry. When they heard we were stuck, with the accident and all, they came down to make sure we were okay."

It was a weak explanation, and Zeke wasn't fooled, judging by the dubious glance he slanted at me as he offered Justin his hand. "Glad to meet you. I'm Zeke Velasquez."

"Sorry you're having troubles," said Justin.

"Thanks."

The exchange was banal, but there was a territorial wariness to the way they sized each other up with that handshake. I remembered what Zeke had said about feeling responsible for us "girls," and Justin had certainly proven his protective nature. Henry, of course, was his wingman.

Judging from her wry expression, Lisa must have sensed it, too. We exchanged a look, and I got back to important matters. "The game warden wasn't big on the chupacabra theory, huh?"

Zeke glared toward the tan truck, his voice bitter. "No. He seems to think that we staged this for insurance money."

"What would be the sense in that?" Henry asked. "This is breeding stock, right? So if all you got was the cost of the animal, you'd still take a loss on all the calves they could produce over time."

Lisa's eyebrows shot up. "Playing polo has given you a real understanding for livestock, Henry."

He shrugged. "I'm a Renaissance man."

I caught the glance that Zeke flicked between them, a little sharper than plain curiosity. "Normally you'd be right," he said. "But the drought has hit us hard. When the pasture

222

won't produce, you have to buy hay and feed, which means breeding can become a losing proposition."

"Which is academic," I said, "because the game warden doesn't know what he's talking about."

Zeke smiled slightly. "Thanks for the vote of confidence, Maggie. But I don't think it would help my case if you told him you thought I was innocent because the chupacabra did it."

"You said you were out of better ideas."

He grimaced, then changed the subject. "How'd you end up out here? Did Lisa call you?"

"We were headed over to Lady Acre to see the shrine, but we had some trouble finding it."

His brow wrinkled in bemusement. "You pick the strangest places to sightsee. How did you find out about that?"

"Teresa told me."

Understanding dawned, and he stared between the guys and me, incredulous. "Is this about that legend, how the Virgin Mary was supposed to have stopped some cougar attacks way back when?"

"We're just going to go check it out," I said.

He set his hands on his hips. "I used to go there all the time with my grandmother. It's nothing mystical. Just a nice, peaceful place where people go to pray."

"Well then, maybe that's all we'll do there." I could be stubborn, too. The Velasquez family didn't have a lock on obstinacy, though they seemed to be making a run on denial.

"Suit yourself. Just be careful." He looked at Justin as he said that last bit, putting the responsibility on him to keep us out of trouble.

As if Justin needed to be told. "Don't worry about it," he said, arms folded.

Zeke nodded, as if that settled things, and turned to Lisa. "I have to get back to rounding up stock and monster-proofing the corrals."

"You don't need to stay here?" She gestured to the carnage and the workers organizing the cleanup.

"There's not a lot else I can do," he said. "I'm leaving men to help Rob Garza out, but we need to get the rest of the cattle penned up before the storm comes in, or the helicopter won't be able to fly."

Lupe called him over, and he gave a be-right-back sign to Lisa before stepping away. She turned to us, pushing her sunglasses up on her head. "What's the deal with this Lady Acre place? What does this shrine have to do with the chupacabra?"

"That's what we're sorting out," said Justin. "Maggie thinks it's a big piece of the puzzle."

"You should come with us, Lisa." I made sure that Zeke, conferring with Lupe and Mr. Garza, was out of earshot. "Your expertise would come in handy. I think there may have been some kind of spell done there to vanquish the demon once before."

She stared at me, grim-faced but not very surprised. "When did we decide that's what it was?"

"I decided last night, but I didn't want to start calling it that until I had to." "Chupy" was a lot less scary.

"Okay. Let me tell Zeke I'm going with you. I'll leave the *D* word out of it for now." She slid her sunglasses back into place. "But don't think the consultation of an evil genius comes cheap."

"Just meet us at the car, Wile E. Coyote."

Justin and Henry fell in on either side of me as we walked back to the Escort, our sneakers crunching the dry grass. Both of them had to shorten their strides to match mine. Glancing back at Lisa, Henry asked, "She's joking about the evil genius bit, right?"

"It's hard to tell with Lisa," Justin answered, then had a question for me. "Is Zeke like his grandmother?"

"Yep. Bone structure of the gods. Denial as wide as the river in Egypt."

"But no . . ." He tapped his forehead. "Psychic super-power."

I stopped walking, forcing them to do the same. "Okay, what's going on? Why the inquisition about Zeke?"

"It's just a couple of questions," said Justin. "Not an inquisition." He exchanged a glance with Henry, then forged ahead. "After Teresa's infodump this morning, I couldn't help wondering how serious Lisa is about this guy."

My jaw dropped open. "There is *no way* she's after him for his money."

He raised his hands, warding off my fury. "No. This isn't about Lisa."

Henry stated the obvious. "It's about Zeke."

"You don't seriously think he's behind this." My voice squeaked with the effort to keep it from carrying.

Their sober faces were my answer. I stared from one to the other, unable to believe they were tag-teaming me. Me! The only one of us with an Evil-meter in my head. "Why on earth would he summon a demon to kill his own cows?"

Justin spoke in a soothing, don't-fly-off-the-handle

tone. "We noticed when the Old Guys were talking this morning—it's only been his tenant's cows. Not his."

"Oh, yeah. That makes it so much more believable." I pointed an accusing finger at Henry. "You don't even really believe in any of this."

"Actually," he said calmly, "I was thinking about old-fashioned insurance fraud."

"Think about it," said Justin. "If his grandmother vanquished the demon before, maybe he has inside knowledge on releasing it."

I gestured wildly behind me, to where Zeke was still working on cleaning up the mess and saving the rest of the cattle. "*He* doesn't even believe in the chupacabra, or his grandmother's Sight. He's only humoring Lisa and me because no one can come up with a better plan."

Justin caught my flailing hand, endangering his life by stepping in close so he could speak almost in my ear. "Here's a better plan, Maggie. Just admit it could be possible, and I won't mention it again."

Lisa was on her way toward us, which must have prompted his whispered compromise. I tightened my jaw, because I didn't want her to hear this about a guy she was willing to spend the day being Dale Evans for. "Fine. If you and Henry will admit that if I say he's a good guy, I'm probably right."

"Yes," he said, squeezing my hand. "You are probably right, and I'm probably wrong. But we'll keep our minds open. Okay?"

I looked at Henry, realizing that I'd put him on the spot, vis-à-vis our tête-à-tête in the Duck Inn. I knew Henry didn't really believe in my Sight. And his stare back at me said that *he knew* I remembered that.

"Okay," he said. "I admit the *possibility* that Maggie knows what evil lurks, or doesn't, in the hearts of men."

Pursing my lips, I gave him points for quoting *The Shadow.* Even bad science fiction movies got credit from me.

Lisa reached us then, stopping warily when she picked up on our mood. "What's going on?"

"Nothing," I said. "Arguing over who gets to ride—"

"Shotgun," called Henry, heading for the passenger side of the Escort. Okay, now he had really pissed me off.

Lisa slanted me a look that said she wasn't fooled a bit, but had decided to let it go. She edged around Justin and me and climbed into the backseat.

Justin was still holding my hand, watching me cautiously. "Are we okay?"

My glare was so tart it made my own face hurt. "Am I really angry at you for teaming up against me? Yes. Will I forgive you for it? Only after I get to hear you say that I was right and you were wrong."

"Deal." He leaned down and kissed me before I could remind him I was still mad. I was much less mad after that, even though the kiss was way too short to make me completely happy.

# 21

Lady Acre was as picturesque as its name. Or it would have been if the drought hadn't turned the surrounding grass to a carpet of faded brown. Justin pulled off a dirt road onto a level parking space delineated with limestone blocks. A weathered sign read: SHRINE OF OUR LADY OF PERPETUAL AID.

As I climbed out of the car, I saw that a path led from the parking area, winding around a small hill the way a stream winds around a rock, and into a copse of live oak and mesquite trees.

The slam of Lisa's door startled a bunch of doves from a clump of grass in the distance. Only then did I realize how still the vista was, and empty.

Henry scanned the pasture, shielding his eyes against the sun. A few gray clouds had started to gather on the horizon, but it remained bright overhead. "Where are all the cattle?"

Lisa twisted her braid up and tucked it under her hat. "They must have been through this area already, herding them up."

I ducked into the car to grab my camera, popped off the lens cap, and took a few pictures of the terrain. Justin looked at me curiously, and I explained, "If I do live through this, I can use them for my photography final."

"You better live through this," Henry said. "We burned a lot of frequent flier miles to rush down here."

Lisa rolled her eyes and headed for the path indicated by the sign. "Yes, lucky us. What would we poor womenfolk have done if you brave, strong men hadn't shown up?"

We followed her to the trail, which was shaded by twisted live oak trees and lined by rustic chunks of limestone. Despite the sultry heat, I could feel a kind of peace knitting around me. Dragonflies darted across the path. An armadillo trundled out of a thorny bush, took one look at us, and dashed off with startling speed.

The hill that the path circled was as steep as anything I'd seen here. The path curved around, then down into a low spot on the other side, a shallow sort of hollow. Fragrant bushes lined the area, and a large, spreading tree shaded a stone bench.

The focal point of the space was a stone-lined niche, carved into the steep side of the hill that sheltered the low clearing where we stood. A grotto is, traditionally, a small cave where people put statues for either decoration or worship. This one hardly qualified as a cave; it was more of an alcove, just big enough for a not-quite-life-sized statue of Our Lady of Perpetual Aid, aka the Virgin Mary.

The recess was lined with a seamless oval of pale rock, which formed a backdrop for the statue of the Blessed Virgin. The stone reflected the diffuse sunlight, surrounding the icon's delicate simplicity with a rosy white halo.

The knoll itself was more prominent than anything around, which meant it was probably all of six feet above sea level. From the top, you might be able to see all the way to the Big House. That would mean looping around and climbing up one of the sloped sides, and it would *technically* mean you were standing on the BVM's roof, but with a telephoto lens, you could get quite a panoramic shot.

Lisa studied the figure's painted blue veil and peaceful face. "She looks good for fifty years old."

"Doña Isabel wouldn't let her get shabby," I said.

She crouched to examine the plants growing in cultivated disarray around the base of the shrine. "Keeping her spruced up might be a way to keep the spell fresh, too."

"Spell?" Henry shifted his weight, as if uncomfortable with the word. "Wasn't Doña Isabel adamant that it was divine intervention that stopped the killings in the fifties?"

"She's not telling the whole story." I was sure of that.

"Someone knew what they were doing." Lisa pointed to the different plants. "Marigolds, calendula, dill, fennel, and rue."

Justin brushed a spring of rue, and grimaced at the smell. "Those are all protective, right?"

"Right. So are aloe, blackberry vine, honeysuckle . . ." She gestured to other flora around the hollow, including a spot in the tree just above Henry's head. "Mistletoe."

He glanced up, then took an exaggerated sidestep.

"You wish." She straightened and brushed off her hands. "The mistletoe and the aloe could have been native. Everything else had to be cultivated."

Henry frowned at the statue, then at Lisa. "So you're saying the Virgin is just an excuse for putting this spell here? A Marian shrine is as good as anything else?"

She shook her head. "Not at all. If this statue was meaningless, it wouldn't work. I think this required real faith to enact it, and to sustain it."

An idea was sprouting from the depths of my brain, where things filter down and germinate while I'm busy thinking too much. "Zeke said people come to pray here frequently. If that recharged the batteries, maybe that's why the spell has lasted so long."

Lisa's eyebrows arched in overstated surprise. "Good job, Mags. You *are* starting to figure this out."

Henry cleared his throat. "But the spell hasn't lasted. The . . . chupacabra, whatever, is back."

"Yeah, but look." Justin pulled the USGS chart out of his pocket and unfolded it to show where we were. "This area is the only one where nothing has been attacked. No goats, no dogs, no cattle. So something is still working."

I peered around his shoulder. On the map I could see the infinitesimal slope of the pasture toward the shore. The contour markings outlined the grassy knoll that held the BVM in her niche, and the shallow depression in front of it.

"Look at this spot." I pointed to the lopsided oval where

we stood. "Doesn't it look like it could have been a pond if there was a spring underground?" It would have been twenty feet across and about a foot deep, but I couldn't shake the image. The smell of herbs and clean dirt filled my head, but so did the nearby dampness of fresh water.

"Could be." Justin compared the chart to the shaded clearing around us. "This low spot is too irregular to have been made just for this shrine. And these trees sort of clumped here might mean a source of water."

"So what happened to it, then?" asked Henry. "Did it dry up?"

"The trees are still alive. So there must be water under the surface."

"That's what I'm getting," I mumbled, more to myself than to them. "Something under the surface."

I stared at the Madonna, willing her to give me some answers, maybe a little wink to say I was on the right track. But the icon's painted face remained inscrutable and as immobile as the granite that framed her.

Tracing the pale rose rock, I followed the curve of the detailed edge. "What would this stone symbolize in the spell, Lisa? If rue and fennel and all that are for protection, what is the granite for?"

Tapping a fingernail against her teeth, she contemplated the shrine. "It's a barrier."

I rolled my eyes. "Well, yeah. I meant symbolically."

"One doesn't exclude the other, dimwit."

Justin jumped in before things got ugly. "Do you mean the granite in particular, Maggie? Because different rocks have different properties."

That's true. Granite isn't rare, but it seemed an odd choice in the rustic environment. Why not make it native limestone, like the bench and the blocks that framed the pathway?

"What do you think of with granite?" I asked.

"Igneous rock," said Justin. "Cooled magma."

Lisa leaned close to examine the pattern of flecks. "The mineral composition is what gives it color."

"And it's impermeable," I said. That was why granite and not limestone. I'd read about this in one of the library books. Water, oil, natural gas—all of it seeps through the limestone under the Texas soil. But granite is . . . "A barrier. Like you said, Lisa."

"You've all lost me," said Henry. "Can I get a crib sheet or something?"

Lisa took up the challenge. "A spell uses the practical or symbolic properties of something to represent what you're trying to accomplish." She plucked off a sprig of rue. "For example, during the Middle Ages, people thought this would magically keep away the Black Death. Which it actually would, if you mixed it in with the rushes on your floor, because the smell kept the fleas away, and fleas carry the plague."

Henry's nose twitched at the herb's pungent odor. "So is it magic or not?"

"The plant is not magical until it's combined with some kind of energy and the practitioner's intent. Then its traits—in this case, warding off disease-carrying insects—become part of the spell. Warding off a demon."

She gestured to the plants and the niche itself. "These components are just plants and stone and some painted plaster until you add power and intent. And true faith is a deep well for both those things."

That was why I didn't think just anyone could perform spells like this. Maybe it isn't as simple as being born a wizard or a Muggle, as Lisa said, but there has to be some spark inside a person, some connection with—I don't know . . . the elements, or the universe, or God. Maybe you don't have to be born with it, or maybe we're all born with it, but it isn't as easy as baking a cake. Even if Lisa does make it sound that way sometimes.

Henry turned to Justin, who'd been listening soberly to her explanation. "Doesn't it frighten you, how much they know about this stuff?"

Justin answered with certainty. "After the things I've seen, I'd be more frightened if someone on our side *didn't* know about this stuff. Lisa is scary, but she has her uses."

"Thanks, Galahad," drawled Lisa. "You're a pal."

As they talked, I ran my hand along the smooth inside of Mary's granite backdrop. I thought it would stop at ground level, with the icon's pedestal set in front of it. But as I followed the curve of the shell, I found that it kept going.

On my hands and knees, I silently apologized to Mary as I dug to discover how deep the stone went down. The soil around the statue's base had been improved for the flowers; it was dark and loamy and easy to brush aside.

"Maggie?" Justin asked in alarm. "What are you doing?"

"Hey!" Lisa bridged the distance to the shrine in one jump. "Do you really want to be tearing up Doña Isabel's shrine of vanquishing?"

"I'm not digging past the granite." Sitting back on my

heels, I brushed my hair out of my face with the back of my hand. "Look. The rock goes all the way under the statue." The pedestal was carved in one piece with the stone underneath, and the soil filled in around it, incorporating it with the earth.

I started to laugh as the three of them crowded over my shoulders to see. "Maybe it really is that simple. Doña Isabel put up the shrine, and it trapped the demon underground."

"By blocking the spring?" Justin asked.

"Yeah." That's why granite—it's impermeable.

He ran his hand through his hair. "So, the demon is . . . was . . . imprisoned in the water reservoir, like a genie in a bottle?"

"Then how is it loose?" asked Henry. "If the shrine is intact, what uncorked the bottle?"

"I've been reading about this in one of the library books." One of the things I like about journalism is getting to learn a little about a lot of different things, but I never thought I'd need so much science to fight Evil.

Drawing in the dirt, I illustrated. "The water reservoir isn't like a big hole in the ground. The liquid seeps through permeable rock, like limestone, until it meets a barrier of nonporous layer." I drew a straight line for the ground, and a squiggly one under it to represent the water layer. "More than one well can tap into the same reservoir. That must be what happened here."

Justin frowned at my drawing. "But there are springs, wells, and stock ponds all over the place. If your theory was right, the demon could have escaped anytime."

"Maybe someone drilled a new well." I felt giddy with

relief. "Nobody had to summon the demon. It was let out by accident."

"Okay." He understood my point, but wasn't conceding yet. "But why don't all the other springs"—he drew lines into my dirt reservoir—"release the demon?"

"I don't know." My bubble of elation popped. "Maybe there is some other component that allows it to escape."

"What about the drought?" said Henry. Then he checked himself, as if he hadn't expected to be taking this seriously. "The past incidents in the records happened during dry spells."

Lisa brushed off her hands. "We need to backtrack. Trace this to the original case. Then Mags and I can do our thing, see if we can get a read on what happened there."

Justin went to the stone bench and spread the map across it. "What was the first attack?"

"Teresa's goats," said Lisa blandly. "Great."

"What about Carl's herding dog?" I wiped my dirty fingers before I smoothed a hand over the chart. "The victims have been getting progressively bigger, right? Goat, calf, cow . . . herd of cows. And finally Dave and Jorge."

"Well," said Lisa, "most men are smaller than cows."

"But 'bigger' in a philosophical sense." Two memories popped up in quick sequence: Dave telling me about his great-aunt's dog, and Buck the mechanic telling me about another little girl who had lost her puppy.

I dug in my hip pocket for my cell phone, in the forlorn hope that I would get a signal. To my surprise, I did— one short little bar. We must have been close enough to the Big House for the antennae on the tower to work. Thumbing through the phone list to a number I'd programmed in on

Saturday, I hit Send and crossed my fingers, while the others watched curiously.

"Hey, Buck," I said, when the call connected. It sounded flimsy, but I put it on speaker. "This is Maggie Quinn."

"You don't let any grass grow under you, do you. Your Jeep's not ready yet."

"That's okay. I was wondering. About your granddaughter's puppy."

There was a pause, full of static from the country music radio in the background. "The new one she got from Mr. Zeke?"

"No. The one that was killed."

"Lord, girl. Why do you want to know about that?"

I floundered for a reason. Usually, even when I didn't have a lie prepared, my mojo kicked in and something convincing came out of my mouth. Not this time.

"Is this about that chupacabra business?" he asked. "Teresa was going on in the Duck this morning about you city girls poking your noses around, stirring up the Chupy and making things worse."

"Oh. Really?" Her, too?

"Yeah, but she doesn't always know what she's talking about. What do you want to know, little missy?"

"Where you found the dog. Was it anywhere near a pond or a spring?"

He paused to think. "It was out past my daughter's barn, which has a stock tank. Does that count?"

I didn't know, but I had him give me directions anyway. As I relayed them aloud, Justin found the place on the map.

"That isn't far at all," he said, after I'd thanked Buck and closed the phone. "If we go across the pasture, it wouldn't be more than a couple of miles."

"You mean, walk all that way?" My horse-abused thighs ached just thinking about it.

A gust of wind caught the edges of the map, a moment of relief from the stagnant heat. The paper flapped madly then subsided.

Justin folded the chart. "We'll drive to the barn and then walk across the pasture where the dog was found. But we'd better get going. This heat is going to brew up some serious rain when that front blows in."

I thumbed my camera back on. "Just let me grab a couple of pictures before we go."

"Don't take too long." He and Henry headed back up the trail to the car.

They were barely out of sight before Lisa turned to me. "So what is the story on the future friar?"

We hadn't been alone since the guys broke into our room and we hadn't had a chance to discuss the new addition to the Evil-fighting team.

"What do you mean, what's the story?" I snapped pictures of the shrine and the plants so I would remember what was here. Compulsive, yes, but with everything so spread out, there was no running back to check my memory.

Lisa stared at me in disbelief. "You mean you haven't done your touchy-feely thing?"

I made a disgusted face. "Don't call it that, Lisa. Gross."

"Don't you want to know if he thinks you're going to Hell?"

"Definitely not." I had been extremely careful not to brush against Henry without my deflector shields on maximum. "Plus, it's cheating."

She sat on the bench. "How do you figure that?"

I fiddled with my lens as I spoke. "I can't really read the people I'm closest to. Which is usually a good thing, because I definitely don't want a flash into *your* psyche."

"Well, no. Because then I'd have to kill you to preserve my secret plan for taking over the world."

"Exactly. And Justin—he doesn't talk about his history. But if Henry knows something about Justin, and I flash on that, then I'll feel underhanded."

"Yeah, but I know you're curious."

"Of course I am. But I want *him* to tell me." I capped the lens and turned off the camera. "Besides. What if I found out something I didn't want to know?"

"Like what?"

"Like he isn't serious about me."

Lisa fell over on the bench, covering her eyes with her arm. "Oh my God, Maggie. If that guy was any more serious about you, he'd have your name tattooed on his butt." She lifted her arm. "He doesn't, does he?"

"No! Well, not that I know of." I laughed, in spite of everything: romantic uncertainty, chupacabra demons, witches, and saints. "Can you picture Justin with a tattoo?"

"No." She grinned broadly. "Zeke has one."

I gaped, shocked in spite of myself. "On his butt?"

"Here." She pointed to her bicep. "Jeez, Mags. I'm not that slutty."

Justin appeared on the trail. "Are you girls going to sit there giggling all day? We're burning daylight."

"Just a sec," I yelled back. Lisa started laughing again, and I nudged her off the bench with my foot. "Shape up. We've got work to do."

She rolled to her feet, dusted herself off, and we started back to the car. "Don't worry about Henry, Mags. He's probably as threatened by you as you are by him."

"Yeah. Worried I'll corrupt his friend."

"Worried you'll come between them." She made an exaggerated thinking face. "Or maybe he's hoping he can talk Justin into joining the priesthood, too. Do you think they get a recruitment bonus, like stockbrokers?"

"Jeez, Lisa." I checked the sky for thunderbolts.

"Well, if he does, at least the outfit is kind of hot."

"Can we talk more about my problem and less about how you're going to Hell?"

She shrugged, lowering her voice as we neared the guys, who were waiting impatiently by the car. "Look at it this way. Henry may represent a normal, demon-free life. But you have plenty of things to offer that he can't."

"Like what?"

She shot me a pitying look. "Duh, Mags. If you have to ask . . ."

# 22

The Escort hit a pothole in the gravel road, hard enough that Lisa and I bounced out of our backseats.

Henry rubbed his head and squinted at Justin. "I'm not sure this is what the rental company had in mind when they said unlimited mileage."

Justin adjusted his grip on the steering wheel. "Almost there."

The road ended at a barn and corral that had seen better days. It was a hodgepodge of wood and corrugated metal. Most structures on the ranch seemed to be more about function than beauty.

Justin set the emergency brake and turned off the engine. "Everybody remember where we parked."

Lisa climbed out and scanned the empty pasture. "It's strange not seeing any cows."

By the corral was a windmill, squeaking as it turned in the faint breeze. The rusty blades ran a pump, which filled an aluminum stock tank; the water was green with algae and surrounded by mud and a lot of what you'd expect would be left by loitering livestock.

"The clouds are getting really thick." I swatted a mosquito intrepid enough to venture out, now that the sun wasn't blazing down.

"We'd better get moving." Justin pulled the map and a compass out of the cargo pocket of his khakis, which was both nerdy and completely awesome. "West is that way."

"Yeah," said Henry. "I could have figured that from the big ball of fire in the sky."

Justin shot him a look. "It's behind the clouds, and I want to be accurate."

"You carry around a compass?" Lisa asked.

"Doesn't everyone?"

"I do." There was one hanging from a clip on my backpack. Flashlight, Swiss Army knife, first-aid kit, a bag of unprocessed sea salt . . .

"You sure you want to carry all that, Maggie?" Justin eyed my backpack with misgivings.

"It's got my stuff in it." I resettled it on my back, nodding to his map and compass. "You like to know where you're going. I like to be prepared for anything."

Lisa slapped her arm. "I don't suppose you have any mosquito repellant in there."

I pointed over my shoulder. "Exterior pocket. Right side."

Henry laughed and Justin shook his head. "Suit yourself."

"I walk all over campus with this thing. How much harder can this be?"

As soon as I said it, I wanted to bite my tongue. Why is it that you can never hear the ring of famous last words until they're already out of your mouth?

✳  ✳  ✳

It turns out that walking overland, even on the mostly flat and visually unchallenging terrain of the coastal plain, *was* harder than sprinting between classes on a paved campus.

For one thing, while the dog days of summer can be barking hot in Avalon, it didn't compare to the sauna heat of a March afternoon in South Texas. Especially as the clouds collected overhead like steam on the lid of a pot.

With the sun in hiding, the mosquitoes became a fierce, bloodsucking army. They made guerilla runs through the aura of Off, undeterred by T-shirts or jeans. I slapped at a quarter-sized insect on my leg and got a palm smeared with blood and bug parts.

The long grass caught at my sneakers and the short clumps made for uneven walking; I had to keep my eyes on the ground and my Spidey sense tuned to the direction we were going. The backpack seemed to be increasing in weight with every step. My legs ached, my skin was slimy with sunscreen and bug spray, and I didn't think I'd ever smelled worse.

"How far do you think we've gone?" I asked.

"Maybe half a mile," said Justin. God. I was in sad shape.

The others had to keep pace with me, and no one else seemed to have broken more than a token hot-day sweat. I comforted myself with the thought that their legs were all a lot longer.

Lisa called from behind me. "Does your freakometer give you any idea how much farther?"

" 'Freakometer'?" asked Henry, who wasn't up on the Maggie vocabulary.

"She thinks *clairvoyance* or *ESP* sounds silly," Lisa explained.

"And *freakometer* doesn't?"

"Hey, Henry." I was anxious to change the subject from me and my weirdness. "What did you guys do to almost get kicked out of college your freshman year? Justin won't tell me."

My boyfriend walked backward so he could glare a warning at his buddy. "He doesn't want to talk about that."

Henry laughed. "It's kind of a funny story."

"No," said Justin firmly. "It's not."

"It wasn't in college, though. It was high school." He ignored his friend's death stare. "Because the whole reason we volunteered to work on the haunted house was to get near what's-her-name, the one with the pom-poms, and her sister."

Justin thought about it, maybe a little too long for my liking. "You're right. It was high school."

"Wait a minute," I said between gasps for air. "What about the pom-poms?"

"The pom-poms aren't important," said Henry. "We went to a parochial boys' school. We grabbed any excuse to be around any girls at all. We weren't picky."

"Which was how Henry convinced me to work on the

Halloween festival at the church in town," Justin said, contributing his version of events. "We were supposed to work up a labyrinth—like a haunted house, but instead of Dracula and the *Saw* puppet-head guy, they wanted vignettes of the lives of the saints."

"Oh, yeah," muttered Lisa. "That'll definitely bring the kids swarming."

"It was supposed to be for *little* kids," said Henry. "Only Justin was so distracted by this girl—"

"Don't blame that on me."

"Okay," Henry admitted. "*We* were so distracted by actual female-type people that weren't nuns, we missed that part of the instructions."

Lisa snickered, and Justin's glare made her cackle harder. "It's nice to know you're human, Galahad."

"Anyway," said Henry, "the girls were in drama club at the public high school, and Justin and I figure the way to impress them is to get all these books about special effects and pick the most exciting scenes from the saints' lives. Which, unfortunately, was usually their martyrdom."

Justin's voice was dry. "You'd be surprised how many saints met a truly gruesome—and, it turns out, traumatizing to small children—death."

Henry's laugh was gravel-deep and contagious. "There were all these little kids peeing in their pants and screaming for their mamas. We even heard that a woman went into labor, but that turned out to be just a rumor."

"I thought *Brother Mathias* was going to go into labor," said Justin, "with a whole litter of kittens."

Henry's laughter faded, but not the humor behind it.

"Anyway. The vestry of the church vowed to never do a fundraising event with the school again. Which was what really had Brother Matt's girdle in a twist."

Watching them laugh together, I realized that I couldn't compete with their friendship, and I didn't want to. Justin needed someone to keep him from being too serious. For years that had been Henry, and now it was me, and that didn't have to be mutually exclusive.

It would be better, however, if Henry didn't think I was nuts for seeing things that he didn't believe were there.

Or smelling them. I halted so abruptly, Lisa crashed into me.

"Hey. Brake signals next time."

"Do you guys smell that?" I sniffed the air, and the others did the same. We must have looked hysterical to the gophers and jackrabbits.

"Sulfur?" asked Henry. "Isn't that a little . . . clichéd?"

I exchanged a glance with Lisa, who rolled her eyes. "You would be surprised," she said.

"It's hydrogen sulfide," I corrected. "Zeke said it's a byproduct of oil and gas production."

"Coming from there, maybe?" Lisa pointed to a complicated arrangement of pipes and wheels and valves sticking up out of the ground. It was taller than Henry, and painted bright yellow. Hard to miss.

"Maggie . . ." Justin said my name in a tone of significant enquiry. "Didn't you say you smelled the sulfur—hydrogen sulfide, I mean—by the cows you found yesterday?"

"Yeah. And we were near a pump jack last night." I looked at him, realization dawning. "I haven't been factoring the smell into the appearances, because I just thought it was the oil wells."

"But it could be the oil wells *are* the factor."

We were finishing each other's thoughts, a good sign that we were on the right track. I sped up, even with the weight of my backpack. The others kept pace across ground that grew rougher as we went.

"Look at these cracks in the dirt," said Henry. "Is this from the drought?"

I stepped across one that was almost six inches wide. "Do you think this was what the records were talking about? Cracks opening up big enough to swallow cows whole?"

"None of these are that big," he said.

"But they *are* big." I stopped as we reached the wellhead. It wasn't a moving pump, but one of the metal tree-looking things, with spools and valves and fittings all over it. That meant that the pressure of the oil and gas in the reservoir underground was higher than the air pressure above. Without the wellhead to control the flow . . . What had Zeke said? There might be a seep or a gusher.

Spreading from the base of the upright pipe was a bog of dark, thick mud and a meandering puddle of water. About twenty feet by three feet, it wasn't that impressive, but the smell was powerful. Not just the rotten-egg odor, but a tarlike stink of creosote.

"Is it a spring?" Justin nodded to the iridescent sheen on the puddle. "That doesn't look like water."

"It's an oil seep." Henry crouched beside the shallow pool. "That would explain the smell. We had them in California. Like the La Brea Tar Pits."

He held his hand over the liquid and a bright red warning light flashed in my brain. "Don't touch that!"

Jerking back, he looked at me in confused alarm. "What?"

"I don't know. I saw this in my dream." My heart tripped double-time in fear, but also in realization. "This is it. It's not the water. It's the oil." I smacked my forehead, killing another mosquito. "I'm such an idiot! It was so *obvious.*"

"You always say that," said Lisa. "Because even a moron can see things in retrospect."

"Shut up a sec." I slipped off my backpack and dumped it into Justin's hands. "Hold this."

I dug through the stuff in the outer compartment and found the pamphlet that Hector had given me. The clouds had gotten so dark that I had to take off my sunglasses to read. "There was something in here. A passing reference . . ."

"To what?" asked Lisa, as she and Henry watched.

"Here: '. . . the profits the Velasquez ranch saw from the demand for oil and gas, both found in rich reservoirs trapped under the geologic *salt dome* under the Texas coast.' " I looked up to see if they were suitably impressed.

Lisa stared at the oily puddle with a grim frown. "So, you're saying the demon is trapped in the oil reservoir."

"Salt dome?" Henry asked. "Why the emphasis?"

"It's a barrier," I said. "It seems to either ward off demons or break their connection with the material world."

"Salt is a component of holy water," he said pensively. I wasn't even sure he realized he was speaking aloud. "It's dissolved in the water before it's blessed."

Henry's expression was pinched with doubt. I'd seen that

look on other people on our adventures, when they found themselves starting to take something seriously instead of just going along.

"So this is how the demon is getting out?" asked Lisa. "The drought cracked the ground and let the oil seep out around the pipe?"

I nodded. "The pipe runs down to the reservoir below the salt dome, so bingo . . . chupacabra escape route."

Henry brushed at his pants leg, sending a cloud of mosquitoes into the air. Justin cast a worried look at the sky. "It's getting really dark, guys. We'd better start back."

Grabbing my camera from its padded compartment, I ignored the way his words resonated with my Spidey sense. "Let me take some pictures real quick."

He set my backpack down, away from the oily ground, and looked at Lisa. "Do you think your boyfriend knows there's a La Brea Tar Pit in his backyard?"

"I'm sure he doesn't. That thing could kill cattle, even if it doesn't lead straight to Hell." She pulled her phone from her pocket and checked the signal. "Two bars. We must be near the Big House."

"Why?" asked Justin, swatting at a bug. Since we'd stopped moving, the mosquitoes had gotten braver, diving in through the repellant, not at all affected by the fumes from the seep.

"There's a cellular relay on the tower." She moved her thumbs over the text pad on her phone, pausing only to slap at the line of insects on her arm. "Zeke may be out of range. Coverage sucks except in this five-mile radius."

A mosquito whined in my ear while I tried to take a

picture of the oil seep. The light was so bad, I had to use the flash to get any detail. It might as well have been dusk. Another bug stung my leg and I shook it off as I took one last shot.

"You realize what this means." I lowered the camera and put the lens cap on. "Nobody summoned the demon. The drought is the common factor every time the chupacabra shows up."

"You want me to say it now?" Justin slapped his neck, his fingers coming away bloody. "You were right. And I was wrong."

Lisa glanced between us. "Right about what?"

Justin looked sheepish. "I was worried about your guy Zeke."

She blinked, and then gave a bitter laugh. "Oh, sure. Because if he likes me, he must be the type who'd summon a demon."

"That's not what I thought at all," he protested.

When she turned her glare on Henry, he slapped a mosquito from his arm and shrugged. "Don't look at me. I just figured it was insurance fraud. Of the nondemonic kind."

"Nice. You guys are just . . . just such . . ." She brushed at her hair with both hands. "God! These bugs are driving me nuts. I can't even argue right!"

Justin swatted at the air in front of his face. "Okay, look. Maybe we can talk about this somewhere else. Because chupacabra or not, I'm getting bled dry here."

That turn of phrase shook awake the instincts that should have been paying better attention. "Yeah." I hurried to secure my camera in the backpack. "We should get out of here."

Justin grabbed my pack from me and swung it onto his own back. "Don't argue," he said. "Just run."

"Okay." The insects were thick around us; I could barely hear him through the whine in my ears. "I'm running."

Henry and Lisa didn't have to be told. They were both fast, and got ahead of us quickly. Justin waved them on, and they took off, the long-legged pair of them, racing for the car.

I'd never run a half a mile in my life. My lungs burned and there was a stitch in my side like a knife through my ribs. But every time I stopped moving, I was instantly swarmed, mosquitoes landing on me by the dozens.

A sharp pain on my neck. I clapped my hand over the sting and felt a squish, and something else—something awful—run up my arm. Incredible that in the midst of so much physical misery, the psychic shock could even register.

I looked at my hand and the smear of greasy black. No legs, no wings. Just sooty, viscous goo that began to dissolve in the salt of my sweat.

"Oh my God." I was so shocked I forgot how to move my legs. Justin overshot me and had to come back.

"What's wrong?"

I showed him my hand. "These aren't mosquitoes."

"What was your first clue?" He grabbed my arm and pulled me back into motion. "Come on. We're almost there. I see the barn."

As soon as he said it, I realized I could *smell* the barn, and cow shit had never smelled so good.

I heard a sound through the whine of the mosquitoes and looked up to see the rental car, four-wheeling toward us like the armored cavalry in a Ford Escort.

Henry, at the wheel, fishtailed to a stop, and Lisa leaned over the front seat to open the back door, shouting, "Get in!"

Like we had to be told twice. Justin pushed me through and jumped in after. Henry gunned the engine, taking off almost before Justin got the door closed. He was sprawled half on top of me, which would have been nice under other circumstances, like if my lungs weren't about to explode and the speed over the bumpy ground wasn't rattling us around like dice in a cup.

"Hey!" Justin yelled through the bucket seats. "Dale Earnhardt. Try not to kill us."

If Henry eased off the accelerator, I couldn't feel it. "What the hell?" There was a note of hysteria in his voice. I think he was at the end of his ambivalence. "I mean, really. What the unholy, bloody hell was that?"

Lisa craned around to look at us. "You guys okay?"

Justin tried again to sit up, with more success. "Maggie?" he asked, searching my face anxiously. "Say something."

My heart was pounding so hard I was worried the top of my head might blow off. "You think," I wheezed, "this is what . . . they mean by . . . 'don't mess with Texas'?"

"We're okay," he told Lisa, still gripping my hand tightly, which was incredibly hot and uncomfortable, like wearing an oven mitt while in a sauna. Not that I pulled away.

Through the back window, I saw that under the charcoal sky, the swarm was a visible mass, preparing for an offensive.

"What's the plan?" Lisa asked. "There is a plan, right?"

"Back to Dulcina?" said Justin. "Can we make it?"

Henry was adamant. "Hell, yes." The wheels of the Escort kept scattering gravel. "We're not stopping until we get to a church and a priest."

"Guys!" It took all my breath to break in. "We can't lead these things back to town."

"You think they'll follow us there?" Lisa asked.

I blinked the sweat out of my eyes. "We can't risk it."

Henry skillfully avoided a ditch-sized pothole. "Do you even know what those things are?"

"Demon mosquitoes. I think they're the same stuff as the chupacabra, only a zillion little ones instead of one big one."

"Did it shape-shift?" asked Justin, like this was a perfectly reasonable possibility.

"How should I know? I didn't even think they could come out during the day."

"Look at the sky," said Lisa. "It's hardly daylight, the clouds are so thick."

"Guys." Henry nodded to the road. "Intersection ahead. I need a decision."

"Back to Lady Acre." As soon as I said it, I felt the *rightness* of the choice. Henry took the turn in a hail of gravel. Justin gave a grunt as I fell against him, my elbow landing in his ribs.

The road was only a car and a half wide, which was a problem, since there was a big silver pickup coming straight at us.

# 23

Henry swerved the Escort onto the shoulder and the truck did the same. The wheels spun on the dirt, then caught some traction and we were back on the road.

Lisa twisted in her seat. "That was Zeke. He must have got my text."

"Stop the car," said Justin.

Henry's foot was already on the brake. Lisa jumped out, waving her arms like she was waving in an airplane. The truck's brake lights were bright in the gloom; then, after a beat, the reverse lights came on, too.

Lisa stuck her head back in the car. "Drive. I'll tell him

where we're going." She slammed the door and ran for Zeke's pickup, which had returned to the gravel road.

"Not sure how she's going to explain this to him," said Justin.

We watched until she climbed in; then Henry stepped on the gas. "I don't know why," he muttered. "Mosquitoes from Hell. What's not to understand?"

Justin slapped a pair of bugs that had made it into the car with us. "How are there so many of them?"

I looked at my shirt, which was spattered with squashed bugs and blood and tiny black spots of demon spooge. They were staying dead, which was good. It meant they could be killed.

"Half of them are normal mosquitoes. Ow!" I slapped at another that had crawled out of my hair to bite me. I missed, and not one, but two buzzed off. Justin smashed them against the window, leaving a pair of black streaks.

"Did you see that?" I asked. "Every one that bites us instantly breeds another."

"That's impossible," said Henry. He looked in the rearview mirror. "Isn't it?"

I eyed him askance. "You're really not getting the demon concept, are you?"

"Impossible is relative," said Justin. Against the false dusk of the storm clouds, a darker mass seemed to move parallel to our flight. "Just keep driving."

✳   ✳   ✳

When Henry stopped by the trail to the shrine, the three of us looked at each other for a heartbeat of "What now?"

"Should we wait them out in the car?" Henry asked.

"I don't think we can." I could see—or maybe See—the insects coming, descending from the sky like a plague of Egypt. "We'll be trapped."

"That settles it," said Justin, grabbing my hand. "Let's go."

"Lisa and Zeke aren't here yet."

"They'll catch up." He opened the car door and pulled me out behind him.

The demon bugs were on us in an instant. They buzzed in my ears and tangled in my hair, stinging my neck and arms. Justin beat at his clothes, trying to keep the fiends from finding their way in. He pushed me toward the trail, sounding more like a drill sergeant than a boyfriend. "Let's go."

More running. Henry led the way down the path through the live oak trees, and Justin brought up the rear. Between the cloud-darkened sky, the heavy air, and the tremendous effort just to move one foot in front of the other, I felt like I was underwater. I could barely hear Zeke's pickup pulling into the trailhead.

The infernal insects kept stinging. They tried to fly up my nose and get in my eyes. I ran blind, swatting at the air. I tried to hold my breath but couldn't last, and sucked in a compulsive gasp through my fingers. Something horrible and bitter hit the back of my throat, making me gag and spit.

Oh, God. Impossibly, a chill ran through my overheated body. Had it gone up or down? I couldn't tell.

"What's wrong?" asked Justin.

"Bug," I wheezed, and then spit again.

"Did you get it out?"

"I think so." I was panting as we reached the hollow in

front of the shrine. In its circumference the air seemed thinner, cooler. Easier to breathe. My legs tried to collapse underneath me, my bruised ankle screaming, my arm aching, but Justin hauled me back onto my feet.

"Keep walking. Your heart has to slow down." He was winded, too—even Henry huffed like a steam engine. And I wasn't dead yet. Go, me.

"Now what?" asked Henry, catching his breath.

I propped my hands on my knees, still wheezing. Still worried. "I don't know." At least I could think. The swarm had thinned to an annoyance, and when I slapped a mosquito on my arm, all that was left was a smear of wings and legs. No goo.

But all around us, the hellish buzz droned on.

Lisa and Zeke came tearing into the glade. As if he'd crossed some invisible line, I felt a shift when Zeke entered the grotto clearing, a charge in the air. Immediately he began pelting me with incoherent questions. "What the hell? I thought the chupacabra . . . And now Lisa says it's a *demon*?" He gestured to the gauntlet we'd all just run. "What the . . . How . . . Jesus!"

"There's no time to explain." I caught his eye, hoping he would calm down enough to help, but not enough to start to rationalize again. "Just work with us for the moment, okay?"

"They're not coming in." He looked around us, as if the absence of the swarm was as incredible as its existence. "Why are they not coming in?"

"Because your grandmother knew what she was doing," said Lisa.

Zeke stared at the four of us, from Lisa's unruffled

confidence and my red-faced exhaustion, to Justin's steadfast reassurance, to Henry's tightly reined panic.

"Oh, you have got to be kidding me." His laugh verged on hysteria. "You expect me to believe that the Virgin Mary can save us from monster mosquitoes?"

"Pull it together, Zeke." Lisa's voice was as sharp as a slap. "You've just got to trust me."

He searched her gaze, seeming poised in indecision. I held my breath—figuratively, since I was still operating on an oxygen deficit. From the moment he'd stepped into the circle of the grotto's influence, I *knew* that Zeke's cooperation was vital.

"Okay," he said, without taking his eyes from Lisa. After a beat, he seemed to settle into the idea. "We can't stay here forever."

Nor could we let the demon swarm pack up and head somewhere else. I didn't even want to think about a mutant mosquito migration.

"We all need to be on board with this." Lisa looked hard at Henry, who'd been quiet since they'd shown up.

"Let's just get on with it." He pulled his eyes from the circling swarm. "What are we supposed to do?"

"We have to invoke the protection that Doña Isabel put in place here." Lisa rubbed her forehead as she thought out loud. "It's not necessarily about the Blessed Virgin Mary specifically, but that's the icon that Zeke's grandmother chose to represent the defensive force over this spot."

Zeke gave a humorless laugh. "Have you not met my grandmother? It's *all* about the Blessed Virgin."

"I mean for the work she did here." As Lisa reasoned

things out, she settled into a fast, academic rhythm that I wasn't sure we were supposed to follow. "It's probably not a coincidence that she chose an icon based on the Virgin of Guadalupe, who is the Marian apparition particular to Mexico." I saw Justin and Henry exchange looks. "Which some people think could be an adaptation of a pre-Aztec goddess whose persona was rolled into the Virgin Mary during the conversion of Latin America."

Zeke held up a hand. "Just stop talking." Startled, she did. If the situation hadn't been so dire, I would have enjoyed the look on her face as Zeke continued. "This is crazy. I think you all may be nuts, and I wouldn't even try this if I hadn't seen *that*." He pointed at the swarm around us, and the rising pitch of their whine. "But I think I know what I'm supposed to do."

He went to one of the oak trees, where a wooden cabinet had been attached to the trunk. He opened it and took out a handful of colored votives in cheap glass holders, a piece of pink chalk, and a box of waterproof matches.

"Your grandmother taught you this?" Justin asked, watching him set up the candles on the flat rock in front of the icon, then use the chalk to draw the Velasquez double-armed cross in the center.

"Abuelita used to bring me here all the time as a kid. Part of my spiritual education, she said. If ever I was in trouble, I should come here and pray the way she'd taught me." He cast a wary eye on the swarm, which seemed to be pushing against the invisible barrier. "She always did the whole rosary, though."

The dentist-drill whine of the insects had become so loud

that I could feel it on my skin. "If you know a shortcut," I said, watching the dark specks coalesce, "do that one."

Nodding, he lit the first candle. It flared five inches high, and Zeke jumped back with a stifled sound of surprise. After a steadying breath he continued, but his hand shook as he moved the match to the next wick.

Justin, Henry, and I were standing close, keeping watch in three directions. Justin spared me a glance, though, and whispered, "You okay?"

I wiped the sweat from my upper lip and felt heat radiating from my cheeks. In the same hushed tone I answered him, not wanting to distract Zeke and Lisa. "That's a really bizarre question under the circumstances."

He quickly scanned my face. "You don't look so good."

My stomach was doing somersaults and my heart seemed about to pound out of my chest. Was that different from any other time I'd been standing ten feet away from something that wanted to kill me?

"I'll be okay," I said. Zeke was about to light the last wick. My scarred and aching arm gave a pang of memory. "Why is it always candles?"

"Light and heat," Justin murmured. No question was rhetorical with him.

Henry finished the answer on my other side. "Fire keeps the darkness away. The Holy Spirit came down in tongues of flame. It can destroy, but it also purifies." At my stunned look, he smiled ruefully. "I understand that part."

The last flame sprang up into a thin pillar of light, then settled down with the rest of them to behave normally. Zeke looked at Lisa. We all steeled ourselves as he began.

"*Ave Maria,*" he said, in a beautifully natural accent, "*gratia plena; Dominus tecum.*"

The Latin wasn't really a surprise. Doña Isabel was nothing if not old-school. But I wasn't really feeling it, and glanced at Lisa to indicate as much. My mojo-meter had pinged more strongly when Zeke had merely stepped into the hollow.

"Guys," said Justin, looking skyward. "There seems to be a weakness to air assault."

Sure enough, the protective circle was now obviously a dome, the ceiling of which was gradually lowering. That made sense if it was contrived to protect more from below than from above. But we were screwed all the same.

Lisa crouched beside Zeke, speaking urgently. "You've got to sell it, Zeke. How would your grandmother say it?"

"It isn't how she *says* it." Henry's head was craned back, watching the swarm push at the defenses. "It's how she *means* it. Not that I'm telling you your business or anything."

She shot him a glare, and turned her attention quickly back to Zeke. "You've got to believe it, Zeke. Faith is a powerful element of the—"

Henry broke formation and moved Lisa out of the way, taking her place. "*You* think she's a rolled-up Aztec hybrid whatever. But that's not what she is to Doña Isabel. So go over there and let me do the one thing that I actually *get.*"

Kneeling in the dirt beside Zeke, Henry turned to face the image of the Blessed Virgin Mary and waited. Zeke eyed him warily for a moment, then did the same. The drone was so loud I couldn't hear their quick conference, but when Henry started in earnest, his deep voice welled up beneath the high-pitched whine of the insects and drowned it.

*"In nomine Patris, et Filii, et Spiritus Sancti."*

They crossed themselves in tandem and my hand twitched in reflex, even though I hadn't been to Mass in ages. Henry set the stage, but it was all Zeke's show when he started the *Ave Maria* again. The words rolled over the space like a heavy fog, rising into the air and sinking into the ground. Maybe it was his Tex-Mex accent that gave the Latin the natural timbre, made it seem as if the prayer belonged only to him and not to a bajillion Roman Catholics all over the world.

Or maybe it was this speech in this place, in this situation, that belonged just to him. Maybe it was because Doña Isabel had originated this. Maybe the place recognized him.

*"Sancta Maria, Mater Dei, ora pro nobis peccatoribus, nunc, et in hora mortis nostræ."*

Pray for us now and at the hour of our death.

Not a real cheery ending under the circumstances.

The last words of the Hail Mary rang out, and I waited for something to happen: The fiend flies to go up in smoke. The icon to raise a hand in benediction. But my stomach still churned, the droning whine continued, and the dark swarms still closed in from overhead.

Zeke sat back on his heels, looking up expectantly, then frowning at the anticlimax of his work. "Nothing's happening."

Lisa and Justin glanced at me, but this time Henry was the confident one. "What do you expect?" he said, climbing to his feet. "Instant gratification?"

"Well, yeah." That was exactly what I'd expected. Wrath of God. Plague of frogs to eat the plague of insects.

"Look at all the factors," said Lisa. "It's been fifty years since this spell was set up, and it wasn't designed for this. It's not an exact science."

Henry looked down his Roman nose, unimpressed by her reasoning. "It's not a science at all."

Zeke stared at them, and I could see the window of his open-mindedness closing. "You people are crazy. Hell, I probably am, too."

They were speaking normally, and I could hear them clearly over the buzz of the swarm. "Hang on, guys."

A breeze from the east caught a strand of my hair and blew it across my face. The clouds above us thinned, spread by the gentle wind like a clump of jam over toast, and pale rays of light struggled through the haze.

"Look at that." Justin pointed to the dragonflies darting around the perimeter, feasting on the mosquitoes like it was Thanksgiving come early.

The sky turned from charcoal to mottled gray to a veiled yellow glow, and the cloud of demon mosquitoes thinned. I imagined I could see each one going up in tiny puffs of smoke as the sun intensified, until all that was left for the dragonflies to eat were the real mosquitoes who'd been caught up in the mob.

Light and heat.

Zeke laughed in disbelief. "You have got to be kidding me." He laughed again, with relief, grabbed Lisa, and kissed her, which was awesome. "Man, do I owe my grandmother a big thank-you for making me learn Latin."

Lisa grinned, and Henry and Justin slapped each other on the back like they'd won the big game, which struck me as funny, in a remote kind of way.

I seemed to be watching them from a great distance, the glare of the sun making it hard for me to see. My skin was cool, but inside I felt like an overheated engine.

This was not good. See, I *knew* exercise was bad for you.

Justin, his face lit with giddy triumph, scooped me up in a hug and twirled me off my feet. My stomach lurched, and when he set me down, my knees wouldn't hold me up.

"Maggie?" He caught me before I hit the ground, all the exhilaration running out of him to be replaced with concern. "Are you all right?"

I peeled my tongue off the roof of my mouth. "I don't feel so good."

Lisa touched my face. "Her skin is all clammy."

"Heat exhaustion," said Zeke. "Get her into the shade."

"Henry, go get some water from the car." Justin half carried me to the largest live oak tree, and I flopped down under it gratefully.

"I've got an ice chest and Gatorade in the truck," said Zeke. "We'll get those, too."

I closed my eyes, since they wouldn't focus anyway. I felt cool fingers on my throat, and heard Justin's voice again. "Her pulse is racing."

Maybe I was dying of heatstroke. Maybe I'd lost too much blood. That would suck, to have survived the Hell prom and sorcerous sorority girls only to be bled dry by demon mosquitoes.

"Maggie. Listen to me." Justin gave me a little shake and I forced my eyes open. He leaned over me, his face pale and grim, the worry in his dark eyes very stark. I had never seen him like this. I must be in really bad shape. "Do you think you could have swallowed that bug?"

"Oh yeah." That would explain a lot. My body was so heavy, it felt as though I was sinking into the ground.

"Swallowed a *demon* bug?" It was weird to hear so much fear in Lisa's voice. "Damn it, Maggie! Why didn't you tell us?"

Jesus was going to be pissed she'd cursed in front of his mom. Lisa was going to be pissed if that was the last thing she ever got to say to me.

Because I *was* sinking into the ground. Instead of oil seeping up, I was seeping down. I grabbed for Justin's hand, but my fingers were too weak to hold on, and he slipped from my grasp as darkness swallowed me greedily down.

✷　✷　✷

I landed with a jolt. There was pavement under me, and smooth, unbroken gray-blue sky above. Sitting up, I rubbed my elbow—can you skin your elbow in a dream?—and got my bearings. My head still pounded, and there was a strange heaviness in my chest, but I could move now, and I started by getting to my feet.

I recognized the landscape. I was at the crossroads. The roads ran endlessly, and from each direction, as far as the four winds could blow, came a host of nightmares.

They came on wings and claws and crawled on bellies, through the air and over the ground and up from under it. Too fast and too many for my brain to grasp except in terrible fragments. Yellow eyes and icy breath. Talons and teeth. Scales, fur, and flesh. Two legs, four legs, eight legs, and bodies that bore no form a human mind could reckon.

And I had nowhere to run. The horrors streamed around me and came together in front of my eyes, flowing into a molten heap, piling on, up and up, framed by the leaden sky.

The individual creatures melted and came apart, like pieces finding their matches, melding together into a whole. It rose up above me, forming a head, torso, arms, and legs. Eyes came together to form the eyes, a thousand tongues were ringed by millions of teeth. Which I saw, as it opened its mouth to speak.

*You have no power here, human child.*

Boy, just when you think things can't get any worse.

I shifted my weight to both legs, my knees too weak to rely on just one. The pain in my ankle grounded me, spiked through the terror seizing my brain.

"Are you the demon?" I asked, meaning the chupacabra. "The plague of this place?"

*We are all demons. And we know your name.*

# 24

Think, Maggie.

I could feel the immeasurable *Evil* of the creature pulling apart my sanity, stripping off layers of reason, like a black hole, a gravity well with no property but destruction.

Something darted through the edge of my vision, but I couldn't look away from the abomination in front of me. Infinite eyes blinked at me in succession, delighted by my fear.

Again the motion, the glimmer of unseen sunlight on iridescent wings. A dragonfly zipped across my line of sight. Suddenly, unbelievably, I could smell my mother's perfume.

I could see the jumbled mess of books in my father's study and hear Brigid's gurgling baby coo. I could taste Gran's strong tea, with lots of sugar and milk.

I could feel Justin's lips on mine.

The memories grounded me, made me remember who I was. I was a sensible person who didn't let fear control her.

What was sensible in this situation?

The answer came to me in Lisa's voice. *Not everyone gets the chance to face her demons so literally. Don't waste the opportunity.*

So I did what I always do when I can't think of anything else: I started talking.

"Are you Satan?"

All the eyes blinked at once. I'd managed to surprise it. And then it made a nauseating sound, like the hiss of snakes and whine of locusts. I realized it was laughing.

What do you know. The devil had a sense of humor.

The dragonfly landed on my shoulder, and I didn't shoo it away. I wanted to faint, or run, or puke. But the unfathomable concept in front of me was no longer ripping my mind apart. My bravado didn't extend to thinking that was my own doing.

The mouths spoke again. *We are Chaos and Nightmare. No creature rules us.*

"So . . . Hell is a democracy?"

There was a restless stir through the body. They didn't find that very funny.

*Do not confine us to human terms. We are indefinable in your philosophy.*

That was disheartening, but it—they—were too irritated for it to be entirely true.

"So I'm guessing Milton got it all wrong? That whole fallen angel thing must really piss you off."

Teeth snapped and fur bristled. *We are not fallen. We are as we were when the* Ruach *moved through the heavens and brought the universe into being. We are perfect.*

Ruach. I didn't know that word, but I got the context. "So, you were created Evil? You didn't rebel and change sides?"

*Your mythology is constrained by what your human mind understands. You understand rebellion.* Its agitated parts settled, giving the impression of a sigh. *We are as we have always been. For what creature could rebel against God?*

That was an uncomfortable question, coming from the host of Hell. What about free will?

"Then what *is* your nature?"

*We destroy. We negate. We oppose and create balance. Without death, there would be no life. Without pride, there would be no accomplishment. Without lust, no creation.*

The scary thing was how, on the surface, that made sense.

The dragonfly took off, zipping around my head before disappearing. "So you oppose. And yet you've banded together so we could have this little chat? I'm flattered."

The snake tongues flicked, tasting the air. *You should be. You are special, Magdalena. The Enemy has given you a great burden.*

"Burden?" I shifted uneasily.

*You have accepted a gift with a great cost. Your Sight marks you as different, set apart. As long as you continue to use it, you will never have a peaceful, normal life.*

Hadn't I just thought that?

*Already those you love are pulling away from you, knowing that you must travel your path alone, and far from home.*

Now, that was overselling the point. I wasn't alone. I never would be. Hell wasn't the only place that knew my name.

"You are so full of crap."

Tongues hissed and claws flexed. Eyes blinked and flashed.

"My 'mythology' got one thing right. You are the prince—democracy, anarchy, whatever you are—of lies."

*Nothing we've said has been a lie.*

"Twisted words, then." I concentrated on anger, let it burn away the confusion that I couldn't afford here. "I know how your kind works."

*You understand nothing. You are an ignorant child, sparring with shadows.*

"Oh, really." I folded my arms. "If you are all so equal, why do some of you come into the physical world at all? Why try to cross the line between spirit and matter unless it's to become better—more—than the others?"

The body rippled with the unrest of its members, and I pushed my luck. "Who has succeeded? That one?" I pointed randomly to a tentacle, and the clawed arms turned to their comrade and ripped it to bits.

"Whose idea was it to meet me here in my dream?" The mouths tried to speak, but the parts were no longer working together. The tongues shrieked their own sounds, the eyes rolled, and the limbs tore at each other.

"You don't fool me. Every one of you wants to rule. Not just your world, but mine, too."

The squabbling worsened, rising to a frenzied pitch. The

noise pierced my ears. I covered them with my hands and squeezed my eyes shut. The air shuddered, as if with a silent clap of thunder, and when I looked, the body of demons had flown apart, disintegrated, and disappeared, no sign they'd been there at all.

"You should try to wake up now," said Gran's voice.

I whirled, and found myself in her kitchen, a steaming cup of tea waiting for me. Gran set the pot on a trivet and reached for the sugar bowl.

My heart squeezed in my chest. "Are you really you?"

"Are we going to have this conversation again? There's really no time for it."

"But there's time for tea?"

"There's always time for a cup of tea. It will cure what ails you."

"What does ail me?"

"You aren't dreaming, Maggie-mine. You are dying."

I searched for a joke or a lie in her eyes, but saw only calm resolve. Sinking into one of the chairs, I let out a sigh. "Well. That would explain why I feel so awful."

Gran pushed the teacup to me. "You need this."

I lifted it and saw the dragonfly painted on the china. It was the same cup I'd seen in the last dream, but never in real life. "I don't recognize this tea set."

"Yes, you do."

"No, I don't."

"Maggie, this is your safe haven. There is nothing here that you don't already know."

I gestured to a nonexistent outdoors. "What about the theology lesson?"

"That's different. The crossroads is the intersection of

the worlds of spirit and of matter, and things meet there that shouldn't."

"So those were really a bunch of demons rolled into one, just for the purpose of schooling me?"

"And themselves. They know what you fear now."

Which wouldn't be as much of a problem if I ended up dying. "How much of what they said is true?"

"All of it and none of it. Drink your tea."

I lifted the cup to my lips, but the smell made my stomach clench and roll. I set it down, and saw that the saucer had become the bone medallion from the two-headed snake museum. "How did this get here?"

Gran looked Heavenward for patience. "It's in your mind, and so it's here."

I sank my head into my hands, my elbows on the table. "If I'm going to die, I'd really like some answers before I go."

"It would help if you remember where you really are."

"Doña Isabel's grotto." As soon as I said it, the glade appeared through the window, and Doña Isabel herself appeared in the chair across from my gran. At least they didn't acknowledge each other, because that would be weird.

"But you didn't construct the spell on your own," I said, pointing to the matriarch of Velasquez County.

"No. I am not a witch."

"So someone helped you."

Doña Isabel didn't deny it. "You have to see the patterns, niña." She held a saucer in one steady hand, a dragonfly cup in the other. "How do the lines connect?" she asked.

Gran pushed my own cup across the table to me. "You need to drink your tea."

I ignored her, which I never would have done in real life. "What lines?" I asked with a rising urgency, feeling my time running out.

"Listen to your *abuela*," said Doña Isabel. "And drink your medicine."

Gran was suddenly standing beside me, and I had a flashback to childhood as she grabbed my nose until I opened my mouth. Instead of cough syrup, though, she poured tea down my throat. It was tepid and unbearably salty, which didn't make sense unless I remembered that I had a body somewhere, and friends who were smart enough to figure out how to save one astral-projecting psychic not-so-supergirl.

The liquid hit my stomach and immediately began to come back up again. Lurching out of the chair, I fell to my hands and knees, retching up the salt water and with it the black, viscous substance of the demon that I'd swallowed. Only it seemed to have grown, because the blackness kept coming, spreading in a pool like the one at the Velasquez ranch.

"Gran?" I gasped between heaves, clammy with nausea and fear. I thought this was my safe and happy place.

"You brought it in," I heard her say as the pool reached out dark tendrils to wrap around my arms and drag me under. "And the only way out is through."

The blackness enveloped me, clogged my eyes and ears and nose, and dragged me down.

# 25

There was a tunnel, and a bright light at the end of it. From far away, I could hear a voice calling my name.

"Maggie?" My favorite baritone voice. Not gravel deep, not tenor smooth, but pleasantly in between. "Can you hear me? Come back, baby."

"Wake up, Mags." Someone slapped my cheek, hard enough to sting.

Only Lisa called me Mags.

"Hey!" Justin protested sharply. "Watch it!"

"Well, don't call her baby. Could you pick a more chauvinist endearment?"

"I'm not the one hitting my unconscious friend."

I cracked open an eyelid, blearily focusing on the familiar faces above me. Justin and Lisa argued over my prone body. I saw Henry by my feet, and sensed Zeke somewhere near my head. My chest hurt and my throat burned like I'd swallowed battery acid.

"What happened?" I croaked, my thoughts hazy, as if some part of me hadn't caught up with the rest.

They were so busy glaring at each other, it took a moment before they realized I'd spoken. Then Justin, with a wordless sound of relief, yanked me into his arms, holding me so tight that my abused body creaked in protest.

"Ow, ow, ow!"

"Sorry!" He would have let me slip back down to the ground, but I found the strength to wrap my arms around his waist.

"No. It's good to feel stuff." He was hot and sweaty, his neck red with sun and exertion. Nothing had ever smelled so good.

Lisa flung herself to her feet and paced away from me, as if to hide her discomposure. When she turned back, her wan face had flushed with relief disguised as anger.

"What is the matter with you?" she asked. "Did we not talk about how I didn't want to call your parents to tell them of your demise by supernatural creature?"

"I love you, too, Lisa," I said, without lifting my head from Justin's shoulder.

She opened her mouth, then pressed her lips together with a scowl. "Whatever."

I tried to get my bearings, which wasn't easy after the

disorientation of my head trip. We were still under the tree in front of the grotto. The sky was light again, but mottled with dark-bottomed clouds. Not a chupacabra or mosquito in sight. Water dripped into my face and my clothes were soaked. I shivered and touched my soggy and sandy hair. "Why am I wet?"

"We had to get you cooled off." Zeke twisted open a bottle of sports drink. "Sip this slowly. You don't want to throw up again."

"Again?" On the ground was a water bottle, uncapped and on its side, a little bit of liquid left inside. Next to it was the package of sea salt I kept in my backpack with the rest of my don't-leave-home-without-it stuff.

There was a sudden, musical sound, so mundanely incongruous with my otherworldly adventures that it took me a minute to figure out what it was. Zeke pulled his cell phone out of his pocket, checked the caller ID.

"I'd better get this." He stood and walked a few steps away to take the call.

I sipped my Gatorade and grimaced as it went down. "Why does my chest hurt so bad?"

Lisa looked at Justin, who looked at Henry, who was finally the one who told me. "You stopped breathing for a minute or so. Justin had to give you mouth-to-mouth until you started again and Lisa could get you to swallow the salt water."

I stared at my friends, who couldn't get along except when it came to saving me. "Thank you," I said inadequately.

Lisa waved a hand and Justin gave a no-big-deal shrug. Like it would kill them to admit that they'd worked together.

Zeke closed his phone with a snap, his expression grave. "I've got to go. It seems that while the sun was behind the clouds, the chupacabra was busy all over. I've got two more dead heifers, and they haven't heard from the guys out in the west quarter yet." His tone was frustrated, and not just at the situation. I hoped that he wasn't backsliding into denial. "I should have been there."

"You can't be everywhere." Lisa dusted off the seat of her jeans and gathered up the empty water bottles. When she looked down at me, her composure was fully in place. "I'll go with Zeke so I can report back. We'll reconvene before night-fall at the Duck."

I smiled, in spite of everything, at the Scooby-Doo-ness of the plan. "See you then."

"You sure you're going to be okay?"

"I'm fine." To prove it, I lifted a hand to Justin, and he helped me to my feet. "See?"

Zeke waited impatiently by the trail. "We need to go, if we're going."

As soon as they were out of sight, I sank onto the stone bench with a groan. Being stoic is hard work. No wonder I never bother to hide anything.

"What time is it?" I asked.

Justin checked his watch. "About three."

"Really?" It felt like we'd been there for days, even allow-ing for my perceived time in dream space.

"Yeah. We have four and a half hours until sunset. De-pending on how long the sky stays clear, I guess."

That was a big if. I shivered in my wet clothes, despite the warmth of the afternoon.

Justin sat and put his arm around me, rubbing my shoulders. "We should get you some dry clothes."

"I have a shirt in my backpack."

He smiled slightly. "Of course you do." Fishing in the pack, he found the shirt that Hector had loaned me, and dropped it over my shoulders. I began to feel better, and even if I still didn't understand Hector's role in all this—Mysterious but sage old man? *Brujo?* Red herring?—I wasn't going to look this denim gift horse in the mouth.

Henry rubbed his head as if it ached. "Okay. I know I came late to this party. But I have a *lot* of questions."

"Join the club," I said.

He paced as he shot off a rapid-fire inquisition. "If there's more than one chupacabra, does that mean there's more than one demon? Does that swarm mean there are a bajillion demons? How are we going to fight that?"

The only way I was going to be able to sort through the junk drawer of info in my head was to take each piece out and examine it individually. It was too overwhelming otherwise.

"I think it's all one demon." I turned that nugget over, mentally testing its shape. Yes. It felt true.

"One demon that can be in more than one form at a time?" Justin asked.

"How can it have a form at all?" The inquiry volleyed back to Henry. "Isn't a demon, by definition, incorporeal? From the Greek *daemon,* which means 'spirit.' "

I slid my arms through the sleeves of the shirt. "This is still just a working theory. A demon's natural state is spirit, like you said. Nonsubstance. And then you have human beings"—I knocked on the bench beneath me—"and everything we can see and hear and touch. Our natural state is matter. Substance."

Henry nodded. "I'm with you so far."

"This is the easy part," warned Justin.

I went on. "If a demon wants to affect our world, it requires power. The amount depends what it wants to do. Influencing something nonphysical, like someone's emotions or mental state—which is probably how you're used to thinking about spirits, Henry—takes less power. Directly affecting the physical takes lots more power. Usually not cost effective.

"Actually *becoming* physical is the most costly of all. It takes huge energy, because it's transforming a stable *non*-substance into something that's not a natural state—matter. It's like chemistry: it takes energy to go against the balanced equation."

Henry's eyes had glazed over. "No offense, but I became a theology major so I wouldn't have to deal with the physical science stuff."

"I'm not sure you can separate the two." I'd had almost a year since my first eerie experience to mull this over. "The universe is about balance. Molecules want to be neutral and grab up atoms that balance their charge. Our nerves fire because of positive and negative potentials in the neurons. Too much emotional high or low and we become manic or depressive."

I wrapped the warm, dry shirt more tightly around me. "This is what I think. Good and Evil are opposing forces, and they have to stay balanced or everything breaks down. Maybe that's why God can't just smite serial killers or stop earthquakes."

"Can't?" Henry raised a brow.

"Fine. Doesn't. Because Team Good cares about the consequences, respects what breaking the rules would do to existence."

Here I did think about my vision, opened the lid on the box where I'd tucked it for now, to be fully analyzed later, when I had the luxury of time to freak out. "It's the nature of Evil to destroy. Team Evil wants power at any cost. They'll annihilate humans, each other, even the universe."

Justin blinked. "I can't decide if that's brilliant or deranged."

Henry's expression was assessing but otherwise impenetrable. He seemed to see past my intellectualization to the disquiet left by the nightmare. "You got all that from a dream?"

"Well, and that Matt Damon movie *Dogma*, where that one demon planned to end creation just to get what he wanted."

The roll of his eyes broke the tension. "Nice."

More used to my illustrative style, Justin moved on to the important stuff. "So, your theory is that our demon, the chupacabra, steals power for transformation through blood. That's why its prey have gotten bigger, and it seems to be multiplying."

"Right. Ol' Chupy is stuck underground. Somehow it gets a little bit of itself out of its prison in material form. It's like a space probe. It can go out, feed, and beam back the energy to the mother ship, because it's really all the same entity. There's an alchemy principle that Lisa says and I can't remember."

Justin supplied it. "As above, so below."

"That's it."

Henry chewed on that. "And it could generate all those mosquitoes because they're small. A thousand bugs might have the same mass as one chupacabra."

"Pretty good," I said. "For someone who'd rather give up women than take a physics class."

He didn't take the bait. "So how did the demon get trapped?"

It figured that eventually he'd get to a question for which I didn't have an answer. "Maybe it's always been here. Since before history. I think that artifact in the museum wasn't put in the ground as part of a burial. It was put there for the same reason as Doña Isabel's shrine—to keep the demon contained."

" 'Before history' isn't the same thing as 'always,' " said Justin.

"What do you want? Last night I was still trying to convince myself it was a giant squid."

While we'd been talking, I'd finished the bottle of Gatorade and managed to stop shaking. Even better, my legs had decided to work again, which was nice of them, considering I hadn't abused them so badly since high school gym class.

Once I was on my feet and sure I was going to stay there, I looked at the guys. "Ready? I want to get back to town and—" I broke off, my attention caught by something rhythmic and familiar. "Are those hoof beats?"

"Yeah." Justin grabbed my backpack. "Let's go look."

Instead of going out via the path, which would take us

around the grotto's hill and back to the car, the three of us hurried through a gap in the trees that shaded the shrine, and found ourselves in the pasture, facing east.

The wind had picked up, and whipped my hair into my eyes. I pushed it back and saw a horse, galloping riderless across the desert dunes. I recognized the root-beer brown of the horse's coat, and saw she had an empty saddle on her back. "That's Sassy!"

"Who?" Justin asked.

"It's Doña Isabel's horse." The mare had kept going, headed—if I had my bearings right—back toward the barn.

Justin's mouth tightened and we exchanged grim looks. "Henry, maybe you'd better bring the car."

Henry ran to the Escort, and Justin and I hurried to backtrack Sassy's path, following the dirt road. As we neared a cluster of palm trees, I felt a pull of urgency and sped up the pace as much as my tired legs would stand.

Doña Isabel lay crumpled on the ground, unmoving. Her hair was disheveled and her clothes tangled from her fall. I dropped to my knees beside her, relieved to see her breathing.

She stirred as I bent close. *"El Diablo,"* she murmured. *"No vi que no esta muerta."*

Justin knelt on her other side. "Don't move, Doña Isabel. We'll call an ambulance."

Her eyes opened and focused on my face. "Magdalena. *¿Usted entiende? Está en la sangre."*

I heard tires on the dry road, then the slam of a door and running footsteps. "Is she okay?" asked Henry as he joined us.

Justin frowned. "We need to get her to the hospital."

"No!" Doña Isabel shook her head emphatically. "No hospital. I cannot leave. The storm is coming."

She tried to sit, and I put a hand on her shoulder. "Don't get up. You need to get checked by a doctor. You fell off your horse, and at your age . . ."

Her black gaze was sharp as a raven's, which put to rest my fears of a head injury. "My bones are old but not broken." Grabbing Justin's arm, she beckoned to Henry as well. "Help me up. You may take me home, then call the doctor." When the guys stood unmoving, she gestured imperiously. "Come along. The day is fading."

After a silent conference of significant glances, we gave in. Justin and Henry helped her up, and she allowed them to assist her into the front passenger seat of the Escort. Her white-knuckled grip on their arms was the only indication that she wasn't merely out for an afternoon stroll.

Justin closed her door, and I started to open the back one, then paused. "*Sangre* means 'blood,' right?"

"Right," said Henry.

It's in the blood. Nothing enigmatic about that.

Doña Isabel tapped on the glass, and when she had our attention, swept her hand to indicate the road home. We scurried to obey. The day, as she said, was fading.

# 26

Connie was waiting when we arrived at the house; I'd called her from the car, and she'd called Doña Isabel's doctor. I'd also left a voice mail for Zeke, and a text message for Lisa, trying to cover my bases.

The matriarch was whisked away in a flurry of activity. When the furor died down, Henry, Justin, and I found ourselves in the front parlor, with the prim antiques and the staid family portraits. The guys sat—carefully—while I paced and scratched at mosquito bites.

"Aren't you exhausted?" Justin asked.

"I think better when I move." I certainly had no shortage

of things to think about. I played my dream over in my mind, searching for any clue. The problem was, there were so many parts of it that I wasn't ready to revisit.

"Hey, Justin. What does *Ruach* mean?"

He had picked up a book from a side table, and looked up from it in surprise. "That's very random."

"Just something I heard and I can't remember where."

"*Ruach* is Hebrew for 'the breath of God.' " Henry's brows knit, making his nose look, if possible, even more Roman than usual. "*Ruach Elohim.* Literally, the Breath of God. Figuratively, the divine spirit of creation. Where did you hear that?"

My mind cleared, relieved to attribute the word to something I should know. "I remember now. *Indiana Jones and the Last Crusade.*"

I turned to resume my pacing, and bumped into a chair. Something clattered to the floor, and I thought at first I'd broken some priceless antique. Other than Doña Isabel, that is. But it was only the matron's cane.

"Dragonflies again." They were carved down the length of her walking stick; I remembered seeing them the day we'd met.

"What dragonflies?" asked Justin. I hadn't realized I'd spoken aloud. "The ones in the pasture eating the mosquitoes? That's what dragonflies do."

Henry sank lower in his chair. "We used to call them mosquito hawks back home."

"No. I'm seeing them everywhere—on the stained glass in the chapel, on the weather vane on the tower." The motif had worked its way into my subconscious as well, appearing with significance in my dreams. "The first day we came to the house, Zeke said something about it being a kind of good-luck symbol."

Justin frowned. "That's a new one to me."

Connie reappeared, ending the discussion. She eyed the three of us with disapproval, then summoned me with a nod, like an executioner. "Doña Isabel wants to see you. The boys can wait here."

I followed meekly behind her as she led the way out of the room and up the stairs. On the second floor, at the end of a long hall, she tapped on a large wooden door, then stepped back so I could enter.

The room was sunny, with windows facing the water and a décor that reflected the sea and sky—driftwood browns and transparent blues. The heavy, dark four-poster bed didn't fit the theme, but it was so massive, it had probably been there for generations. Gauzy curtains softened the frame, and Doña Isabel reclined against a mountain of fluffy white pillows.

Her eyes were closed and her breathing even, so I took the opportunity to investigate the numerous prescription bottles on the nightstand. My gran claims that the older you get, the more chemistry it takes to keep you running. But Tamoxifen and OxyContin? I didn't think those were in your average geriatric medicine cabinet.

"Did your grandmother teach you to snoop in a lady's private belongings?"

I straightened and found Doña Isabel watching me. "So you really are unwell."

She turned her gaze to the windows, where the water was gray and uneasy. "No. I am dying." My alarm made her laugh dryly. "Not right this minute."

"That's a relief." I was still frustrated by her blind denial, but now I understood. Admitting the demon was loose meant admitting she was weakening. "You don't have to apologize, you know."

"Apologize?" Indignation strengthened her voice. "For what should I apologize?"

Her reaction evaporated some of my goodwill. "For hiding your head in the sand while people's lives and livelihoods were at stake?"

"I have not been hiding my head. I have been in constant prayer and meditation. I went out this afternoon to . . ." She trailed off, setting her jaw.

"To what? Check the shrine yourself?" She smoothed her sheets with a trembling hand, and I pressed the issue. "I know what you did there. The spell. Why be so secretive?"

She gave an unladylike snort. "I do not need to make my confession to you."

Strangling a dying woman might invalidate my membership in Team Good, so I kept my hands by my sides. "Confess what? That you stopped a monster from slaughtering your cattle? Trapped a demon that had gotten a toehold in this world?"

"But I sinned in the process. Which is why the protection did not last."

"It did, Doña Isabel." I moved then, and covered her hand with mine. Her skin felt cool and paper thin. "It lasted because of your faith and commitment. But the demon has found a new way out, and you have to help us stop it again."

She shook her head, still staring out the window. "I am too old. When I die, the Church will get this land and a new protection will be in place."

"Doña Isabel, it can't wait." She glared at me, greatly outraged. "I mean, I hope you live a long time yet, but the chup—the demon is multiplying every time it appears."

Lying back, she closed her eyes. "Then you must do something about it. You and your sorcerous friend. I cannot help you. My weakness will only corrupt your efforts."

I had reached the frayed end of my patience. "What has happened to you? You told me you were God's instrument. Now you would rather lie here and feel sorry for yourself because you're old and sick and scared to meet your maker."

"What are you doing?" The voice from the doorway was so twisted with fury, I didn't recognize it until I whirled and saw Zeke staring at me, far beyond infuriated. Lisa stood behind him, her hand covering her mouth as if she wished it were mine. Didn't we both.

"How dare you talk to my grandmother that way?" He stalked into the room. I took an involuntary step backward, because he seemed to have grown larger with strength of purpose. He snatched my arm—not tightly, but it was my right arm, my injured wrist. Pain made me gasp as he hustled me to the door.

"Get the hell out of my house and off my land."

"Ezekiel!" Doña Isabel's sharp protest had no effect.

Lisa followed us into the hall, speaking calmly. "Zeke, slow down. Think about the big picture."

"The big picture is that she got my grandmother injured. Abuelita wouldn't have gone out there this afternoon if she hadn't visited this morning." I guessed Connie had filled him in.

We were on the landing now, and I could hear footsteps coming up the steps. Zeke seethed as he pulled me along. "What kind of person yells at a sick old woman in her bedroom?"

I wanted to apologize or to explain. I didn't regret anything except the yelling. But his grip on my arm was making it hard to form coherent words.

Justin appeared at the top of the stairs, Henry right behind him. They assessed the situation in a glance, and squared up for a fight.

"Let her go." Justin's tone was an unveiled warning.

Zeke did, with no air of concession. His angry gaze held mine. "If anything happens to my grandmother because of this, Maggie Quinn . . ."

Justin took a threatening step forward, until his shoulder was touching mine. "Don't talk to her like that."

Zeke looked at him then. "Stay out of it. This isn't your business."

"If you touch her again, it's going to be my business."

I raised my hands in a placating gesture. "Zeke, I shouldn't have spoken to her like that. But she is involved in all this. You can't keep pretending she's not. You saw what happened at the shrine today. Who put the protection there? Who taught you how to invoke it?"

He swept that away with a frustrated gesture. "I don't know what I know anymore."

"But you were *there*," I repeated, a little desperately. "You saw what happened."

"I saw the sun come back out and I saw dragonflies eating mosquitoes. That's what dragonflies do."

Lisa spoke again, her voice unhurried. "Zeke, come on. You're not stupid or blind."

"This is why my Abuelita warns against *brujas.*" He clearly included her in his condemnation. "They lead you astray. Confuse your mind about what's true and real." He focused his fury on me again. "If anything happens to my grandmother, it'll be your fault, Maggie."

Justin stepped in front of me, ignoring Henry's restraining grip. "You need to just back off. She's risked her life to help you and your ranchers."

"Did I ask for her help?" Zeke thrust out a hand, and I thought he was going to push Justin, but he merely pointed to the stairs. "Just leave. Go home, to where you belong." He turned to Lisa. "You too. I never would have pegged you for the decoy type."

She froze, and stared at him, a gray-eyed ice queen. "It's a dirty job, but someone had to do it."

Zeke's anger cracked just a bit, enough to show his hurt. Then his composure was back. "Just go." He turned and left us standing in the hall. "Be out of here when I'm done talking to my grandmother."

Justin set his jaw, catching my hand in his. "Let's go, Maggie."

I held back, anxiety overshadowing every other emotion boiling in my gut. I *knew* that the Velasquez connection was vital, and if Doña Isabel couldn't or wouldn't help us, then we needed Zeke, whether he liked it or not.

"Pick your battles," Henry said, as if he'd read my thoughts. But then, I'd never had much of a poker face.

He was right. There was a demon out there that

could be in two places at once. I could stay here and beat my head against the wall of Velasquez stubbornness, or I could get busy and do something about it. If only I knew what.

* * *

Outside, the wind thrashed the tops of the palm trees and whipped the leaves of the bougainvillea into a fuchsia froth. Thick gray clouds slipped across the sky, moving too fast to build up like they had earlier. But behind the patchy cover, the sun continued its inexorable journey west.

I marched across the drive, trying not to think about how badly I'd messed up. When I reached the car—the poor, dirty Escort—I leaned against it and covered my face with my hands. "God, I've screwed this up."

"Don't let him get to you," said Justin. The wind stirred his hair, where sweat and sunscreen had spiked it up. "You did the right thing. You are *doing* the right thing."

"Am I?" I pressed the heels of my palms to my forehead. "Because things have gotten drastically worse since I got involved."

Trying not to think about my vision was impossible. That was the problem with demons that lied using carefully phrased truths. It really messed with your head.

"Maggie." Justin pulled my hands from my face, his dark eyes full of warm reassurance. "Things *always* get worse. They would have even if you'd gone on your way. Only then, no one would have known what to do about it."

"*I* don't know what to do about it."

Lisa cleared her throat. "Not to deepen your guilt-spiral or anything, Maggie, but I should tell you what Zeke and I found at the north forty. There are two more men in the hospital. One may lose his leg."

"Oh, God." I tried to run my fingers through my hair, but it was snarled with tangles and dirt. "We could be swarmed tonight. By things a lot bigger than Hell-spawned mosquitoes."

Lisa had a talent for shaking me out of self-pity. "So maybe it's time to quit whining and make a plan."

She was right. Sensible action. Or if not sensible, then at least forward motion. Standing in the gravel driveway of the Big House wasn't accomplishing anything.

"Okay." I took a breath, and a grip on my composure. "We can't count on Doña Isabel to tell us what she did last time, so we'll have to work from scratch. The Dulcina library is open"—I checked my watch—"for another hour."

Justin dug the car keys out of his pocket. "You think they'll have books on demon vanquishing?"

"No, but they'll have the Internet." I opened the back door and leaned on it for support. "It's a place to start."

"Hang on," said Henry, stopping my momentum. "You're not thinking of taking on this thing yourself?"

"What do you suggest?" said Lisa. "Exterminators don't cover demonic vermin."

"I suggest a *priest*." He looked at Justin, almost in accusation. "I can't believe you haven't thought of that."

"Do you have any idea what kind of red tape is involved in getting an exorcism?"

"How can you even joke about that?"

"I'm not joking!" Justin shot back. "I am dead serious. We've all got the scars to show how serious we are."

"How do I know?" Henry gestured to us in angry frustration. "Your friends discuss magic like it's a science experiment. It's not kid stuff. We have no business messing around with it."

Since I had gotten everyone into this, I figured it was time for me to fight my own battle. "*No one* has any business messing around with this stuff. But if not us, then who? Henry, you've had actual coursework in Good and Evil, and you didn't believe us until you saw with your own eyes."

His gaze narrowed defensively. "There's a difference between the possibility and the reality."

"I know." Boy, did I. I'd had the Sum of All Demons in my head, calling me by name. The way I saw it, I was the *most* entitled to freak, but they were looking to me for leadership.

"Yes, we're in over our heads," I said. "Maybe there's someone in the world who actually understands how all this works, who's fully equipped with the armor of righteousness and the flamethrower of smiting or whatever else is in the arsenal of Team Good. But unless they're hiding behind a mesquite tree somewhere, me, my freaky brain, my sorcerous friend, and my paladin boyfriend are all that stands between Hell and Texas."

I hadn't meant to make a speech. The silence as they stared at me made my ears start to burn. But I couldn't back down. "So . . . that's what we're going to do, dammit."

Henry gazed at me for another moment, then unfolded his arms and opened the car door. "Fine. You guys get your game on at the library, and I'll talk to the village priest. If he doesn't call the nuthouse, we'll all meet at the Duck Inn."

"Deal," said Justin, in a tone that implied he'd be proven right in the end. Which was a pretty good guess.

Henry got in the car and slammed the door. This should be a real fun trip back to town.

Lisa shot me a wry look. "Nice speech, Braveheart."

"It worked, didn't it?" I opened my own door. "Come on." I used a phrase of Justin's, which seemed especially appropriate at the moment: "We're burning daylight."

# 27

The library was about to close when Henry dropped us off. Justin worked his you-can-trust-me magic, and the next thing I knew the librarian was leaving us to lock up after ourselves when we were done with our research.

"I'm glad you're on our side," I told him.

He gave me a sidelong glance. "People trust paladins."

My turn to look sheepish. "Well, you are. Chivalrous, righteous. Occasionally prone to chauvinism . . ."

He grimaced in apology, but not really. "Sorry about that."

Lisa headed for the single computer. "You two go flirt somewhere else. I've got to figure this out with none of my own books and notes."

I couldn't guess what sites she was planning to tap for research, but I hoped she'd clear the browser cache when she was done. I didn't want to be responsible for giving the woman who ran the place a heart attack when she logged back on.

The selection of books was so limited, "stacks" should probably be singular. Justin headed that way and I went around the corner to the "museum" part of the Dulcina Library and Velasquez Ranch Museum.

What was this rural fixation with museums? Snake museum, ranch museum. At least this one was meticulously clean. On one wall was a grainy, sepia-toned photographic mural of a group of cowboys, rugged and worn, posing by a campfire. The other walls were hung with pictures of the ranch and portraits of people I was beginning to recognize from my reading—the founder of the ranch, the first Miguel Velasquez; Rafael, who'd built the current house; a wedding portrait of his grandson and Doña Isabel. He looked very serious. Her expression was serene, but with a vivacious light in her eyes.

The last portrait was of Doña Isabel as an older woman, maybe in her forties. She was still beautiful, but there was a marked difference in her gaze. The vitality remained, but it had matured and hardened into the steely determination that now impressed and infuriated me.

Underneath the wedding portrait was a Bible on a heavy wood stand. The placard said it was a reproduction of the Velasquez family Bible, with a facsimile of their genealogy in the front. I flipped to the first page. My grandmother had something like this, with the birth, marriage, and death dates of the Quinns going back two hundred years.

The pages held handwritten notes, each in a different ink and script. It was in Spanish—so was the Bible itself—but names are the same in any language. The recorded lineage began with Carlos Velasquez—born in Andalusia, Spain, died in the Mexican colony of Texas in 1826—and ended with Ezekiel Velasquez, born twenty-three years ago.

Zeke was the last of the line. Everyone else had died or moved away from the land. Was that why Doña Isabel was leaving the land to the Church, because she didn't trust Zeke to stay and be the warden of the demon trapped beneath the ground?

The rest of the room was filled with antique tack and ranching equipment: saddles and spurs and branding irons with the Velasquez double-armed cross. I traced the cold metal with my finger. The pattern was all over the ranch, on every gate, every barn. If it was a symbol of protection, the origin seemed obvious. But what about the dragonfly motif? It couldn't be coincidence that the Velasquez family had incorporated it into their house and I'd seen it in my visions.

In the center of the room was a couch—leather stretched over a dark wood frame, and about as comfortable as sitting on a snare drum. But I sat anyway, just for a moment.

"You're not going to sleep, are you?" I opened my eyes as Justin sat down next to me and tried to get comfortable. "I guess not on this thing."

"Hey. Did you find anything on the shelves?"

"I gave Lisa a couple of books I thought might help. Then she told me to go away."

"That's Lisa for you." And speaking of best friends . . . "I'm sorry you argued with Henry. I know he was part of your normal, pre-Maggie life, and now that's kind of gone."

He gave me an odd look. "What makes you think that my life was completely normal before I met you? I was the one who convinced you that *you* weren't. Normal, I mean."

I hadn't thought about it that way. "You've never told me when—or why—you started to believe that some folklore is more than mythical."

He let out a reluctant sigh and leaned forward, elbows on his knees. "It's not a very happy story. And it kind of sounds crazy."

"Like I'm one to throw stones?" I reached for his hand, interlacing our fingers. If he didn't tell me now, he'd have to pry himself loose. "I want to know your sad stories, *and* the happy ones. Even the embarrassing ones with pom-pom girls."

The corner of his mouth curved, just slightly. "Okay." Then he sobered, and ducked his head, though his fingers stayed knit with mine. "I told you my parents were missionary doctors, and they died overseas?"

I nodded. "Treating an epidemic of tuberculosis in Africa."

His gaze on the floor, he spoke evenly, with the distance of time. "My godfather told me they'd died of TB. But when I read Dad's journals, there was more to it. The people of the village were convinced that a witch doctor had put a curse on them. Dad didn't buy it, but since no one was responding to treatment, he and the village's own shaman did a kind of countercurse. Dad figured it couldn't hurt, and maybe there would be a placebo effect. And there was. Almost immediate improvement, and no new outbreaks for over a month."

"That sounds like more than just the power of positive thinking."

"Yeah." He ran his free hand down his grubby khakis, pointlessly smoothing the wrinkles. "Then the village's shaman died suddenly, and Dad copied down some strange symbols he found sketched in the dirt around his house. Right after that, Mom got sick, and . . . that's the end of the journal."

"You think they were cursed?"

His crooked smile was rueful. "Crazy, right? I had no reason to think so, except when I copied out the symbols from Dad's journal and stuck them on the bulletin board to study, I caught the chicken pox. Even though I'd been vaccinated for it."

"Which can happen."

"Right. Easily rationalized. I never told anyone but Henry what I thought, and only because I felt so guilty that he came down with the flu the very same week. I didn't even think he remembered, but he brought it up when I said I was coming down here." Justin shrugged. "You were both so curious about each other, I figured it was time for my two worlds to merge."

His words rang a bell in my head. "Two worlds to merge?"

"Yeah. Old life, new life." He looked at me closely. "What is it?"

A charge ran through me—a good one, like a connection coming together to complete a circuit. "Something Lisa said about *brujería* rolling together New World traditions and Old World religion. You looked up those Native Americans that disappeared from here when the Spanish came, right?"

His brows drew together. "It was a common story,

unfortunately. Smallpox took a lot of them out. The survivors went into the missions, or married in with the settlers. Most of the families who have been here for a long time have at least a little of the Coahuiltecan bloodline."

Invigorated by discovery, I went to the facsimile of the Velasquez family tree in the Bible. "When Isabel said *sangre,* maybe it didn't refer to the blood that was fueling the demon, but about the blood*line.*"

I bent to decipher the faded and ornate script. Carlos Velasquez's son, Miguel, married Angelina Ventura, whose birthplace was Texas. Their daughter, Dulcina, was the town's namesake. She married a man from Louisiana, and eventually her line would return with Doña Isabel, her cousin several times removed.

Justin read over my shoulder. "So, Velasquez came here, carved the ranch out of the desert, married with the locals, anchoring the family to this Native American blood."

"That's why Doña Isabel is such a powerful guardian. It's her lineage." I went back to the drum seat and sank onto it. "Oh, man. I think she's willing the ranch to the Church because she thinks that will protect it from the demon. But the Church has no link to the land."

He pointed to the Velasquez brand. "What about this? They chose the patriarchal cross to honor the missionaries, right?"

"Let me check something." I headed back to the library proper, and found my backpack on the floor by the desk where Lisa was working.

"I'm not done yet," she said, without looking up from the screen. "This Internet connection must be run by carrier pigeon."

"Ignore us." Pulling out my smaller camera, I thumbed back to the pictures I'd taken at the snake museum, until I found the one of the bone medallion in the case.

"What does that look like to you?" I asked Justin.

"A flower?" He squinted closer at the tiny screen. "No, the leaves look more like wings." Then he glanced at me in surprise. "A dragonfly."

"It was right in front of me the whole time." I'd felt the protective force of the artifact even through its case. I'd seen the dragonfly on Gran's china—twice—and when I'd been facing the demon coalition.

The bell on the front door jingled, and Henry came in, looking disappointed. Even Lisa stopped working. "No luck?" she asked, though the answer was obvious in his slumped shoulders.

"No." He sank into a Cat in the Hat chair that was way too small for his big frame. "I thought the priest was going to call the loony bin. I'm glad I didn't tell him my real name."

Since I hadn't expected anything different, I didn't let his arrival distract me now that I knew I was on the right track. "Justin, you said you'd never heard of the dragonfly being a good-luck symbol?"

"No. But it *was* associated with shamanism and supernatural powers. I remember in one of my early classes . . ." He grabbed a book from the stack beside Lisa—*Dictionary of Native American Pictograms*—and continued talking as he flipped the pages. "Survey of Ancient Symbols, I think. Here." He read from the book. " 'The dragonfly was considered a messenger of change or enlightenment.' "

Henry levered himself out of the kid-sized chair and came over to the desk. "A messenger of enlightenment?"

"Check this out." I grabbed a page from the pile of scrap paper by the card catalog and sketched something like the emblem on the medallion. Then I darkened the lines so that it was a sort of stylized dragonfly, with a bulb at the end of the vertical stroke and two thick horizontal lines crossing it where the wings would be. A double-armed cross.

"The Velasquez brand," said Lisa, sounding impressed.

Without a word, Justin handed the book to me. Under *D* for *dragonfly* was almost the exact drawing I'd just made.

The text continued beneath: " 'Used by Indians who were Christianized to tell others that they still kept the old ways. A symbol of someone with a foot in both traditions.' "

"That's how the spell at Lady Acre works, right?" Justin directed the question to Lisa. "The combination of traditions?"

"That's what *brujería* is. Old World religion and New World folk magic."

The guys and I looked at her expectantly, waiting for her to explain in more detail. When she didn't, I prompted, "Well? How do we repeat it?"

She began with a heavy sigh, and I realized how tired she was. We all were. "This is how I would do it, not necessarily how it was done. Once all the cattle are secure, so that they can't be used as food—I hope Zeke is still working on that, no matter how mad he is at me. I mean, us—then we have to put the demon back into the ground."

Picking up the pad and pen, she made a hasty visual aid: a big blob under a solid line, with lots of little blobs above it, attached to tethers like astronauts are attached to the Shuttle when they go for a space walk. "Maggie says it's all one entity, and we can use that. We'll bind the parts to the whole, and as long as there's more spirit-type underground than there is solid-type above, the chupacabras on land will be pulled back to the mother ship."

"Then what?" asked Henry. "Cap it with another shrine?"

Her scowl deepened. "I'm not sure. The problem is the power source." She tapped the notepad. "I've got a list of things I need for a binding spell. But the power source to actually work with the sorcery and make it stick? I don't know."

Justin leaned against the desk. "Faith was enough for Doña Isabel the first time. Is it enough for us?"

Lisa looked doubtful. "There was only the one manifestation back then, right?"

My thoughts had circled back to my original interpretation of Doña Isabel's word *sangre*. "If blood is what gives the demon power to transform to solid matter, could the same power source put it back?"

"Blood is tied up with life force and vitality," said Justin, defaulting into academic mode. "In ancient Rome the cult of Mithras bathed in the blood of a bull to gain the animal's energy. Aztecs offered the blood of their enemies to their gods. In the temples in Jerusalem, offerings were made to Yahweh to purify sins."

Henry cleared his throat. "Would it be too obvious of me to mention the Eucharist? The blood of Christ grants eternal life."

The answer was a fingertip away, if I could just reach it. I wanted to pace, but the children's bookshelves were in the way. "Remember how last fall, in order to undo the Sigma's spell, we had to counter with the exact opposite? So the flip side of killing is self-sacrifice: stealing blood versus offering it."

"You guys are being too literal," said Lisa, then checked her words, "in a *weird* kind of way. Think symbolically. It represents the essence of who you are. You swear oaths, sign away your soul with it. Blood pact, blood brothers, blood kin . . ."

"Bloodline!" I shouted, then covered my mouth, a lifetime of library habits kicking in.

Justin easily followed my realization. Quickly, he explained our discovery next door in the museum. "The Velasquez bloodline is tied to the land all the way back to prehistory. That's why the combination of old and new traditions is so important. Doña Isabel's faith, plus the native magic older than the Velasquez name."

Henry looked doubtful. "So, you're saying the family has superpowers when it comes to protecting the land?"

"Not superpowers like webslinging or laser vision." I sank into one of the kiddy seats. "But power. Yeah."

After a beat of silence, Lisa stated the obvious. "Too bad we pissed Zeke off so bad."

"We've got to find that *bruja*," said Justin.

"You could look in the phone book under 'witch' " was Henry's suggestion.

"No," I said, climbing purposefully to my feet. "We go where you find everything in this town. The Duck Inn."

✳   ✳   ✳

As the four of us headed across the square to the bar, I was surprised how windy it had become. A plastic bag blew across the street and tangled in the low chain that circled the town green, whipping around like it was trying to get free. Overhead, the clouds were fluffy on top, but gray and heavy on the bottom, like cotton balls dipped in paint. Toward the east, over the gulf, the sky was dark as ink.

The red Escort—looking hard used with its layer of dirt and grime—was parked in the lot, and beside it was my Jeep, still sans its top.

Even topless, it was good to see my trusty steed. Since I'd met Sassy, the Jeep had gone from an "it" to a "she" in my mind. I ran—okay, limped—over and caressed her safari-brown paint.

"Would you two like to be alone?" asked Lisa.

No one pointed out the significance of the Jeep's return. Theoretically at least, we could leave. None of us—not even Henry, as new as he was to all this—seemed to consider that an option.

"Let's go get the keys," I said, figuring Buck would be at the Duck, too. The three of them followed me inside, and we weren't disappointed. Buck sat at the Old Guy table. He, and everyone else in the bar, turned to stare as we came in.

"Hey, Buck."

"Figured you'd be by eventually, little missy." He dangled a set of keys from his fingers and then tossed them to me. "You're all set, except for the top."

I considered that a pretty significant omission, especially considering the rain blowing in. But what was I going to do.

"Thanks, Buck." I gave the rest of the Old Guys—Carl and Joe and the guy whose name I didn't know—a tired smile, and turned to the bar, where Teresa was drying mugs. Lisa,

Justin, and Henry had gone to one of the booths, letting me handle her.

I didn't mess around this time. As Teresa paused in her drying to watch me approach, I imagined gunslinger shootout music playing. Which was silly. We were all on the same side. But it was definitely time to start shooting from the hip.

"Where's Hector?" I asked.

"He left a few minutes ago." Teresa flipped her dish towel over her shoulder. "But he said for you to wait for him. He'll be back."

That I wasn't expecting: a direct, no-nonsense answer to my question. But then, Hector had never been unhelpful, just unforthcoming with information.

"So, he *is* the *bruja—brujo,* I mean."

Teresa gave me a pitying look. "You are slower than I thought, city girl. I thought you knew that."

I'd suspected it, but I just didn't know how closely he was woven with Doña Isabel and the ranch.

The door opened, banging in the wind, and I turned at the ominous sound. Hector came in, wearing a rain slicker. Under one arm he carried a cardboard box, and he had a shopping bag in the other hand. He scanned the bar purposefully, and when he found me, indicated with a jerk of his head that I should follow him to the table that Lisa and the guys had staked out.

I met him there, not angry, exactly, but frustrated. "You could have just told me you were the *brujo.*"

Surprise registered through his distraction. "I thought you knew." He set down the box, and nodded to Justin and Henry, who'd stood up, either out of respect or wariness.

"You knew about all this," I accused him indignantly.

"About the past appearance and the shrine and the spell—and you didn't say anything?"

"I promised Doña Isabel that I wouldn't. I was bound by my word to her, but I did try to help you." His expression was guarded. "After we worked on the shrine, our agreement was that I would maintain the protections on the town, and she would watch over the ranch. I don't know why her protections are failing now."

"Doña Isabel is sick." Anxiety made me abrupt. "She's being treated for cancer."

Hector's stricken face made me wish I'd delivered the news a little better. But he collected himself and gestured to the paper that Lisa was holding. "Is that your shopping list?"

She quickly processed the fact that he knew what we were up to. After a lock-jawed moment, she handed over the page. "It's the part I've worked out."

Giving it a cursory scan, Hector returned it along with the handled shopping bag. "Most of the items are in there. What isn't, you won't need." He picked up the box. "Let's go. We don't have a lot of time."

"Hang on," said Justin, before Hector could turn away. I was very aware of all eyes, and ears, on us. The bar was pretty full, mostly with women, and even a couple of kids. Justin must have picked up on the significance before I did. "If you're responsible for protecting the town, can you leave?"

He nodded. "Everyone here will be fine. Come outside with me and I'll tell you the rest."

The four of us trailed him out of the bar and over to his pickup truck, where he stowed the box on the seat. "Things aren't good at the ranch. Isabel just called and said Zeke has gone missing."

"Missing?" I glanced at Lisa, whose face went quickly impassive. "Are they sure?"

"I haven't set foot on the main ranch in forty years. She wouldn't call me if the situation wasn't serious." Hector climbed behind the wheel, his expression grave. "Meet us at Lady Acre after you've found Zeke."

"Me?" I put out a hand to stop him from closing the pickup door. "Hector, I don't even know where to start."

Soberly, he met my eye. "Start with the main corral. He left from there to run down some stray calves."

"Then how does Doña Isabel know he's in trouble?"

"Do I really need to explain that to *you*?" He started up the truck. "You will know what to do, Maggie. Just find him and meet Doña Isabel and me at Lady Acre." Looking past me to Lisa, he nodded. "Then we'll put our heads together and do what needs to be done."

My fingers still grasped the door. "You think she'll come?"

"She'll come because of Zeke." The creases by his mouth were etched deeply. "He's the only thing she loves more than this land."

He put the truck in gear, and I had to relinquish the door and step back as he drove off. The others waited by the Wrangler, Justin grimly worried, Henry with a knot of confusion between his brows, as if he was still struggling to keep up. Only Lisa was busy; she'd put the shopping bag on the hood of the Jeep and was sorting through what Hector had given her.

"It's all here," she said, sounding more numb than surprised. "I can work with this stuff."

"Lisa." I waited for her to look at me, but she didn't. "Are you all right?"

"I don't think any of us is going to be all right if we don't get going."

Justin and I exchanged a worried look. Henry didn't miss it, as he glanced between us. "I know I'm clueless, but if the family is special, like if the Velasquez bloodline really is what keeps this thing at bay, then what will happen if the demon manages to spill Zeke's blood?"

"It won't be good," said Lisa, climbing into the backseat. "Let's go get our stuff."

We'd left our backpacks and duffels at the library. I drove the Jeep over and parked on the side street; Justin and Henry had simply jogged across the square, and got there before us. Besides reclaiming our gear and quickly locking up after ourselves, there were a couple other things I needed to do before we hit the road. First, I called my buddy Dave with a request. He was home from the hospital, and eager to help out against Ol' Chupy.

I also appropriated the branding irons from the museum. They clattered loudly when I threw them into the open trunk compartment of the Jeep, drawing Henry's frown of disapproval. "You know that's stealing, right?"

True, and I felt kind of bad, mostly because it was a library. "If I survive the night, I'll return them."

He shook his head. "You say that very lightly for someone who stopped breathing once already today."

"Battlefield humor."

Justin set my backpack in the rear floorboard, and eyed the branding irons. "What are those for?"

"I'm not sure yet. I'm still tweaking my strategy."

I handed him the keys and got into the backseat beside a grim and silent Lisa. Henry swung into the shotgun seat. "There's a strategy?" he asked. "We're not just winging this?"

"There's always a plan." Justin climbed in and started the engine. "It gives us a place to start before everything goes to hell."

# 28

The Jeep hit a bump in the gravel road and I grabbed the front seats to keep from going airborne. I'd been leaning between them to give Justin directions to the main corral, which we'd passed on our way to the stables the other day.

"This road goes right by the corral. You can't miss it." I sat back and looked at Lisa, whose head was bent over the bagged herbs and potions she was sorting through on her lap. "Hey," I said, lowering my voice so the guys wouldn't hear. "I'm sure Zeke knows you weren't really a decoy. He was just mad."

She kept her eyes on her task. "Evil geniuses never apologize or explain."

My lips pressed together to hold back a choice reply. Like how stupid that was. Relationships were all about offering, and accepting, explanations.

Ahead I could see a clean white glow that rivaled the storm-curtained sunset. Justin eased off the gas. "I don't know what that is, but they can probably see the lights from orbit."

I leaned forward to check it out. Zeke might have been pissed, but he must have believed something I'd said, because the corral was spotlit like a diva at center stage.

The enclosure was essentially a board fence covered with a corrugated aluminum roof, which sagged between its posts. Inside the enormous covered pen, a dark red sea of cowhide moved under incandescent bulbs. Around it, banks of halogen work lamps created an island of artificial daylight in the gloom.

"Heat and light," said Justin. "Bane of cockroaches and chupacabra demons."

Henry shot him a wry sort of look. "You have way more of a sense of humor about this than I would have thought."

Justin's eyes found mine in the rearview mirror, and he smiled slightly. "Maggie's bravado has rubbed off on me."

He pulled the Jeep into a space between the trucks that ringed the corral. Around the perimeter, men on horseback stood guard like a posse around a wagon train. I couldn't decide which was the bigger anachronism—the outriders with their shotguns and walkie-talkies, or the huge generator chugging away next to the graying wood barn.

"There's Dave." I unfastened my seat belt and climbed out, going over the side of the Jeep. My sneakers squished when I landed; the ground all around the corral was soft and . . . let's just say *fragrant.*

Dave stood on a tailgate, directing traffic. When he saw the Jeep, he climbed down and headed to meet me. "Hey, sharpshooter. I got the stuff you asked for. Best I could, anyway."

"Thanks." I looked him over critically; most of the cuts and bruises were hidden by his shirt. "How are you feeling?"

"Like shit." He grinned. "But if you think I'm going to let that razor-toothed son of a bitch have the last laugh, you've got another think coming."

Thunder rumbled across the Gulf. I could still see the dark pink horizon, but the storm clouds were lowering, sandwiching us between earth and sky.

While I quickly introduced Justin and Henry, Lisa climbed, uninvited, into the bed of Dave's pickup. "Where did you get all these bags of rock salt?"

"Maggie said to bring all I could find. I raided the feed and tractor store and every barn on the way here."

When I'd given Dave the instructions, I'd really had no idea how many cattle we would have to encircle. Now that I saw the corral—a quarter of a football field and full of cows—I was extremely relieved about the generators and the lights.

Henry pointed to the Velasquez brand on the arch connecting the gateposts. "Do all the corrals have that on them?"

"All the big ones where we've rounded up the cows. They belong to the ranch."

"Dave." I caught his attention, and lowered my voice. "We need to find Zeke."

Dave called over his shoulder to one of the men watching the cattle. "Hey. Lupe. How long has Zeke been gone?"

The stable boss joined us, not looking at all surprised to see me or Lisa. "He went out after those calves that run off. Maybe an hour ago? He'll be back."

Lisa jumped down from the truck. "He didn't go by himself, did he?"

Lupe gave her a don't-be-stupid look. "Mr. Zeke wouldn't run down a calf by himself at night, even if there wasn't no chupacabra out there."

Justin got my attention, brushing my arm. "Henry and I will load a couple of bags of salt in the Jeep."

I explained our plan to Dave—at least the go-out-and-rescue-Zeke part. He initially protested, but when he tried to get Zeke on the walkie-talkie with no success, he shut up and started offering me guns instead of arguments.

"At least take the shotgun," he said, pressing it into my hands. "You know you can shoot that."

"Dave, I don't need a gun." I pushed it back to him. "I'll just shoot my foot off or something."

"You can't go out there with nothing but rock salt," he said. "What are you going to do? Season it to death?"

That was one way of looking at it. When I'd encountered the demon Azmael, even after it had become real and solid, like these monsters, the salt—unprocessed and as close to the pure mineral as possible—had worked against it, both as a barrier and as a weapon.

Henry was throwing bags of the stuff behind the rear seats of the Wrangler. The branding irons from the museum clattered against the frame as the twenty-pound bags tested the newly repaired suspension.

"We'll be fine, Dave." There was a flashbulb pop of lightning to the east, and a rattle of thunder a few seconds later. "But we've got to go."

He unhooked his radio and handed it to me. "Keep me posted." Then to Justin he said, "Go slow over the terrain. It's not as flat as it looks. The pasture is dry as tinder, and the heat from the car exhaust can be enough to spark a fire, so avoid long grass if you can."

"Thanks." Justin helped me clamber into the back, where I dropped down beside Lisa. She was busy digging something out of her pocket, but I couldn't see what.

Dave stepped back, shaking his head. "Don't know how in hell you're going to find him."

"You and me both," said Justin as he got behind the wheel. Henry was already in the passenger seat.

"I'm on it," said Lisa. "Let's go already."

Lupe had pointed the direction of Zeke's departure. Of course Zeke Velasquez wouldn't ask anyone else to ride out in his stead. I didn't know if the big daddy chupy—the demon hive mind—was smart enough to lure him off on purpose. But it couldn't have planned things any better.

Justin turned the ignition and pulled out, leaving behind the anxious lowing of the cattle and the island of light around the corral. "What's your plan?" I asked Lisa.

She was busy threading a key onto a piece of thick black string. "I need something sticky. You got anything in your bag of tricks, Mags?"

"You're the witch," I said, already reaching for my backpack.

"You're the one lugging a suitcase everywhere we go." She eyed the stick of Trident I offered and made a better-than-nothing face. "Give it a chew, will you?"

As I did, she plucked a long chestnut hair from her braid and started winding it around the key. "What are you doing?"

"I'm making a cowboy detector out of something personal of Zeke's and something personal of mine." She held out the wrapped key. "Gum me."

I took the wad out of my mouth and stuck it where she pointed. "You have Zeke's key? Just how friendly are you?"

"It's to his house in town. He gave it to me if we wanted to watch his satellite TV while he was working. That was before all Hell broke loose and started eating people."

Justin watched in the rearview mirror and Henry had turned around in his seat. "What's that supposed to do?"

"Sorcery is symbolic, remember? This represents me and Zeke, and the nature of the charm is to try and bring us together in actuality." She pushed her thumbprint into the gum, holding her hair in place, and leaned over the console to hang the string on the rearview mirror. "As this is," she said, "so should we be."

The words were simple—no Latin, no poetry. It was still a brass key with a nasty wad of chewing gum and hair on it, but to my other Sight—the weird one—the parts seemed to knit together to form something more than their sum.

"That's really going to work?" asked Henry.

"Shut up and watch."

The key swayed with the motion of the Jeep for a moment, but then a pattern emerged—a distinctly diagonal swing.

"He went thataway," said Lisa, pointing to the northwest.

Justin eyed the landscape. There was no sign of Zeke, but the movement of the key was very clear. "Okay," he said, in a here-goes-nothing tone, then turned the Jeep and stepped on the gas.

I held on to the seat and glanced at Lisa. "I get the components. But what fuels the spell?"

She gave me a humorless smile. "Desperation."

Or our needing to find Zeke and his being in trouble, if you believe in help in times of peril. Which I do. I mean, leaving aside all that valley-of-the-shadow-of-death stuff, we were dealing with a demon manifesting as a *pack* of freaking *chupacabras.* The balance was tipped so far toward Team Evil, I figured some help from the bullpen would only even things out.

A quick course correction jostled me out of my thoughts. "Everyone keep your eyes peeled," Justin said as the key started swinging in confused circles. "He might be close."

I stood up in the back, grabbing on to the roll bar for balance. The wind whipped through my hair, and the lightning ripped through the clouds, the thunder not far behind.

Not just thunder. Hoofbeats. I braced myself only an instant before a huge, dark beast came tearing across our path.

# 29

Justin slammed on the brakes and I fell forward across the roll bar. Only Lisa's quick grab at my legs kept me from somersaulting over.

"What the hell was that?" Henry yelped.

The empty saddle registered first. Long legs, waving tail, three-beat gait. I recognized the mare, even in the eerie gray-green twilight. "It's Sassy," I wheezed.

"Again? Has she got it in for you?"

The wind carried a whistle; the mare bucked and checked her stride. She circled around as if pulled by an invisible lead rope, compelled by training or herd instinct, or a connection to her rider.

"Follow that horse," I said. The tires spun on the sand, then we shot forward. I slammed down into my seat, adding to the bruises on my butt.

Nothing like field-testing the suspension right out of the gate. Justin struggled to keep the horse's flicking tail in sight as she wove around cactus clumps and mesquite thickets. I looked over my shoulder to the west, where dark fingers of cloud closed like a fist over the setting sun, leaving the desert in shadow.

Lisa's grip on the seat tightened. "Is this as dark as it was when the swarm came out?"

"Darker." The world had turned into a black-and-white movie.

"Over there." Henry pointed to Sassy, who was lengthening her lead on us. "She's headed around that copse of trees."

Justin's jaw set in concentration. "Gotcha."

Sassy rounded a patch of mesquite. The moment she was out of the Jeep's headlights, something leapt from the thicket and dragged her down. The horse screamed in terror as the thing on her neck flashed silver-white teeth and glowing red eyes.

"Hang on." Justin cut the wheel and shot the headlights onto the fallen horse, illuminating the horror that crouched over her, its leathery skin like night given substance. It hissed and flinched from the light. There was a shot, and the monster exploded into a cloud of gooey black droplets.

Zeke limped into the spill of the Jeep's headlights, a pistol aimed at the ground to his side. Sassy got her legs under her, whinnying in pain and fear, a trio of gouges in her shoulder. The cowboy caught her reins and shielded his eyes with his hand.

It was very *Wild Wild West* meets *The Thing*. Especially as, just out of the high beams, the monster that Zeke had shot was reassembling itself. A black, oily cloud struggled against the wind, coiled around hot coals for eyes, and spun out into limbs and talons. It was working fast, probably fueled by the power boost from the blood that dripped down Sassy's neck.

"Jeez," said Henry. "Every time I think I've seen it all . . ."

"Drive right for it." I knelt backward on the seat, leaning over into the cargo compartment. With my Swiss Army knife, I punctured the bag of rock salt and filled my palms.

"You ready?" Justin asked, putting the car in gear.

"Go!" He slammed on the gas. Lisa grabbed the back of my jeans to keep me from flying out of the Jeep as it bucked over the dunes.

The nightmare-shaped mist blew out of the path of the headlights, then rode the backdraft straight at me, the claws already solid and gleaming in the soot-dark cloud. I flung my handfuls of salt onto it and heard a satisfying sizzle as the half-formed creature evaporated.

Justin pulled to a stop with Zeke and the horse in the safety of the headlights, and set the brake. Lisa scrambled out over the side of the Jeep.

Zeke's eyes were glazed, his voice numb with shock. "Why won't these things die?"

"Duh," said Lisa, when she'd reached him. "Magic."

He blinked. A whole grab bag of expressions flitted across his face—surprise, relief, chagrin. But rather than express any of these aloud, he wrapped his free arm around her, pulling her into a fierce, tight embrace. After a moment, she reciprocated.

Aw.

"What do you know." Justin watched, both hands still gripping the steering wheel. "Human after all."

"That's sweet." Henry's tone didn't match his words. "Except if we get eaten while they're making out."

The wind blew against my cheek with a wet splat. I thought it was a drop of rain, but when I touched the spot, my fingers came away smeared gooey black. "We've got to go."

Justin honked the horn and shouted over the windshield. "Get in the car, guys."

Zeke dropped his arm from Lisa's shoulders and holstered his pistol on Sassy's saddle. The mare's head was down and her hooves planted, her ears twitching on the alert.

I stood and scanned the twilight for hard-edged shadows or the gleam of red eyes. "Where are the others?" I asked Zeke. "Lupe said you rode out with two guys."

"I sent them back to the corral, and led the . . . things off this way."

"We've got to get to the grotto." Justin put the car in gear but kept the clutch down and the brake set as Lisa climbed in. "Is it far from here?"

"Far enough," said Zeke, "with those monsters out there. You can follow me." He swung into the saddle with a wince. If the mare had spooked and thrown him, he had to be hurting, but he gave a wan smile. "Try to keep up."

He rode ahead of the Jeep, careful to keep Sassy in the beam of the headlights. Full dark had fallen around us. The hair on the back of my neck lifted with the intangible static charge of otherworldly forces nearby.

Lightning flashed overhead, and the shriek of more than

one chupacabra reached my ears before the thunderclap. Did that mean the monsters were closer than the storm? I couldn't remember the formula for calculating the distance of a sound. One one thousand, two one thousand. How few thousands meant we were screwed?

✳ ✳ ✳

I could *feel* the grotto before it came into sight, like a psychic lighthouse in the storm. The lights of Hector's truck were a beacon against the night and all the forces of darkness. It was like coming home and finding your parents had left milk and cookies for you, times a thousand.

Zeke galloped in ahead of us like the Pony Express. Justin pulled up to the edge of the hollow, stopping so that the headlights shone between the trees that edged the space, illuminating Mary in her hillside niche. Hector stood beside the big shade tree, gesturing to us urgently. "Come on. You'll be safe in here."

I grabbed my backpack, Lisa snatched up her duffel. Justin got the branding irons, and Henry threw a twenty-pound bag of rock salt over his shoulder with little visible effort. As always, I felt a demarcation as I stepped into the sunken clearing, but even more so with a campfire burning brightly, waiting for us.

Doña Isabel knelt by the icon, the beads of her rosary moving through her fingers as her lips moved silently in prayer. Zeke wrapped Sassy's reins around a low tree branch and hurried to his grandmother's side. "What are you doing here, Abuelita? You should be in bed."

"Don't interrupt her," Hector said. He handed a box of matches to Lisa and me both. "Maggie, you light the candles

I've placed along the eastern half of the circle. Lisa, you light the western ones. Hurry."

We dumped our stuff and did as he said. The grotto was ringed by a hundred or more white candles—short and fat, spaced about a foot apart. We'd walked through them from the Jeep. On my hands and knees, I went to work lighting them, using one match until it singed my fingers, then striking another.

Outside the circle I could sense a building presence, watching and waiting. Beyond the truck lights and the campfire, a pair of red eyes stared into our haven, the rest of the demon lost in the shadows. A flash of lightning made it scream, and the sound echoed from the other side of the grotto.

"Keep going." Justin had come up behind me. He grasped one of the branding irons like a club. "I'll watch out for them."

My shaking hands could barely hold the flame to the candle long enough for the wick to catch. Lisa had completed her half of the circle, and Hector stopped her before she could continue into mine. Maybe we each had an assigned task. Was that how it was with Hector and the town, and Doña Isabel and the ranch? If each hadn't carried out their separate duties all this time, would the spell have collapsed?

More than one person had said that Doña Isabel never left the ranch. I had taken that to mean "as good as never," but was it possible she could literally never set foot off the property?

Finally, I had only four candles left. I extended the match to make it three when I heard an unearthly sound, a scraping of claws down Lucifer's blackboard. The corner of my eye glimpsed movement, shadow on shadow, and Justin yelled, "Duck!"

I flattened myself on the ground. The chupacabra leapt at me, bringing a foul smell, like new asphalt. There was a whoosh and then a thud of metal hitting meat. Justin had swung his iron weapon over my head and knocked the creature back.

The monster was the size of a German shepherd, its hide like wet ink, its teeth translucent, luminous in the dark. Gathering itself, it lunged at Justin. He parried its stiletto claws, then thrust his weapon at its heart. The double-armed cross at the tip of the branding iron didn't stop, but tore into the creature's thick black hide, running through it like a sword.

The demon shriveled, screaming, around the iron, curled up like burning paper, and disappeared. I wished I wasn't about to puke with fear, so that I could enjoy how awesomely cool that was.

Justin shook any dusty remnants off the iron. Catching me staring, he pointed to the candles. "Get back to it."

Still, I didn't miss his small, crooked grin. I struck another match to finish my task. When I lit the final candle, the whole circle flared up, flames shooting into the air like bars on a cage. The golden light spread to a uniform glow, then disappeared.

"Whoa." I let Justin haul me to my feet. My eyes should have had to readjust to the darkness, but they didn't. "Did you see that?"

"Yeah. I see it." He didn't mean the light show; I must have witnessed that with my *other* Sight. Justin was talking about another Chupy bearing down on us, eyes blazing and claws like Ginsu knives.

He raised the branding iron to club the demon, and Hector gave an inarticulate shout of warning. I caught Justin's arm as he started to swing forward. "Don't break the circle!"

The momentum of his arm carried me around, straight toward the chupacabra and all its teeth. I closed my eyes, certain I was going to break the plane of the candle ring, sure the demon was going to tear into me. But Justin jerked me back against him, and the demon hit the invisible barrier of the circle and bounced off with a furious cry.

"She did it." I breathed the words in awe, not sure if I meant Doña Isabel or Our Lady of the Holy Force Field. Whichever or both. The main thing was, we were safe for the moment.

A strobe of lightning showed the chupacabra demons retreating to regroup. I took the chance to get my bearings inside the hollow. I had no idea what had happened on the other side of the circle, but Lisa was wrapping Henry's bleeding arm with a bandage from the first-aid kit in my backpack.

"Did one of them get you?" I asked, worried about what the blood of a slightly self-righteous theology major would add to the chupacabras' power.

"Um, no." He looked embarrassed. "I was supposed to make just a little cut."

Lisa tied the gauze so tightly that he yelped. "I told you guys. Blood is very powerful. The protective circle needed a *small*"—she chided Henry with a stare—"voluntary donation."

Justin stared at his friend in bemusement. "So, what happened to sorcery is a slippery slope and all that?"

"It went out the window when I saw the teeth on those things." He tested the bandage and lowered his voice, just between the four of us. "Besides, I couldn't let the old guy do it."

Lisa wiped a pocketknife on her jeans and glanced toward the shrine, where Hector and Zeke were helping Doña Isabel to her feet. "That old guy knows his stuff. But to bind these pieces of demon and imprison the whole thing, we're going to need a Velasquez."

Hector and Zeke eased the matriarch to a seat on the stone bench; her face was ashen beneath her caramel skin. Grabbing a bottle of water from my backpack, I hurried to her side.

"Here, Doña Isabel. Drink this." I suspected that only her own iron will was keeping her upright. "Lisa, there are some smelling salts in that first-aid kit."

She dug in her own duffel instead. "I've got something better."

"No, no." Doña Isabel waved a weak hand. "I need nothing."

Lisa handed a small bottle to Zeke, who held it to his grandmother's pale lips. "Drink up, Abuelita. It'll help."

She did, thanks to Zeke, and grimaced at the taste. Immediately, color returned to her cheeks and her sagging shoulders straightened. Brushing the iron-gray hair from her face, she stared at Lisa with dignified disapproval. "Sorcery."

Holding the bottle, label out, Lisa responded, "B-twelve, sugar, and caffeine. I don't mess with what works."

Doña Isabel cleared her throat and glared at Hector, whose smothered smile creased his long face with humor. "Yes. Well. I feel better now. We can proceed."

Hector's levity vanished, and we exchanged glances—him and Lisa and me. "Isabel, the rest is for the youngsters to do."

"No." She placed her hands on her knees, as regal as a queen. "It is my responsibility. I was too stubborn and frightened to see before. I denied my own failings. But now I will make it right."

Lightning and thunder, like the heavens themselves were agreeing. In the eerie silence that followed, there was a low pop, and then a hissing rush of air. I looked at Justin in alarm. "What was that?"

He shaded his eyes from the headlights and peered into the darkness. "Something just punctured a tire on the Jeep."

Henry picked up the other branding iron and joined him at the perimeter. "I didn't think they were that smart."

Neither did I. Animal cunning was all I'd seen so far. But maybe the more of them were out here, the more of the hive mind was in play.

And the storm was about to break. "Lisa, get ready with the witch-fu. Guys, keep a lookout."

"Everything's ready in my pack." Even as she answered me, her eyes were on Zeke. "But we still need a Velasquez."

He held her weighted gaze for a long moment, then knelt by Doña Isabel, his hand covering hers. "Abuelita. I don't see what else you can do. I don't understand half—a quarter—of what's going on, but if all it takes is the Velasquez bloodline, you have to let me help."

She shook her head violently. "I will not leave it to you, Ezekiel. You are so young, and the sacrifice is too great."

Hector laid his hand on Doña Isabel's shoulder. She tensed, but let it stay. "When your *abuela* took on the guardianship of the ranch, she linked herself with this place.

It meant she could never leave, never give it up, or the demon would be free."

"It wasn't such a hardship," she said. "I love this land. My blood runs through it like the oil under the ground. But your aunt and uncle, they wanted to sell shares in the ranch, and hire a company to manage the land and the cattle. When I wouldn't agree, they left to build their lives elsewhere. And I stayed here."

Zeke processed this quickly. "That's why they give you your chemotherapy here at the house. Why doctors have always made house calls. Because you really can't leave the property."

"That," she acknowledged with some dry humor, "and because I'm terribly rich. It isn't all torture."

"But you've never been to any of my cousin's weddings, haven't seen half your grandchildren." Zeke's face was anguished in the firelight. "Why not just tell me?"

"I never regretted my decision," she answered. "But I want you to have every option open to you."

There was a simultaneous clap of thunder and a flash of lightning, and a fat raindrop hit the ground, an advance party for the deluge. "The only problem is, here and now, we're running out of options," I said.

Doña Isabel wrapped her hand around Hector's arm and used him to stand. "I'm ready."

Man, I hated to be the one to break bad news. "*Señora*, the reason the demon was able to get free—I think it's because of your illness."

Lisa wasted no time on sugarcoating. "What Mags is saying, Doña Isabel, is that the only thing you have left to sacrifice is your life. If you do this, you'll die."

Even Doña Isabel blinked at Lisa's bold-faced statement, but she recovered quickly. Zeke stood up, protesting. "Oh no. That's not going to happen."

She quickly regained her resolve. "I'm already dying, Ezekiel."

"You're under treatment," he countered.

Lisa added, "If the sacrifice kills you, Doña Isabel, it might seal the demon away permanently, or it might be free as soon as you're gone. I don't know."

"It doesn't matter." Zeke put himself physically between his grandmother and Lisa. "What do I have to do? Pledge to stay here forever? No problem."

"If you take this on," Lisa warned, "you will never be able to leave. Not a toe off the Velasquez property. No dates, no Spurs games, no movies until they come out on DVD."

Their gazes locked, and a whole conversation seemed to pass between them. I remembered the way he'd held on to her when we found him fighting off the demons in the pasture. He definitely knew what he was giving up.

"I have the whole county," he said. "That's more freedom than a lot of people have."

"Okay." Lisa dropped her folded arms and grabbed her heavy satchel from the ground. "Let's go."

"Wait a sec." I put up my hand as she headed to the edge of the circle. "Where are we going?"

"Zeke and I have got to reach the wellhead with the oil seep. Otherwise I won't be able to reel the chupies back in."

I looked at Hector. He didn't deny this, so I tried a new angle. "Magic is representation, right? What if we had something to *represent* the wellhead? Like . . . paint off the pipe fitting or something. Would that work?"

Lisa considered the question. "Maybe. But it would still mean that someone has to go out there."

Another fat raindrop splashed my hand, and more splattered into the dirt. Sassy, tied safely to her tree inside the circle, whinnied and shook herself. "Guys," Justin called, warning me about the rain. "It's about to be a moot point."

I made my argument quickly. "Out in the truck, headlights on, driving fast. Then back to the safety of the grotto for the actual working."

"Fine, but who's going to—?"

Lisa's question went unfinished as the sky broke open with a flash and a crack and the heavens poured down on us. The campfire hissed and the candles fizzled, and the darkness around us lit with ravenous red eyes.

# 30

The candles guttered and went out. The chupacabras surrounded us, their eyes like a string of unblinking Christmas lights. Justin and Henry backed toward the campfire, weapons at the ready.

Sassy whinnied and danced, pulling at the branch where she was tied. I ran to get her, the raindrops like little hammers, slapping my skin and soaking my hair.

Zeke shouted over the rain. "Hector, get my grandmother to the truck and stay with her."

Hector took the woman's arm, but Doña Isabel pulled away haughtily. "No. I'm still the guardian here. If it is all I can do, then I will pray." She walked to the shrine, where the headlights of the truck illuminated Mary like a halo.

He redirected her over her protests. "God can hear you just as well from the car, Isabel."

Zeke made sure they were safe, then turned to Lisa. "Can we do this thing here in the light from the truck?"

She wiped the rain out of her face. "Yes. Henry, grab that bag of salt and make a circle around us. A thin line will wash away, so the circle will have to be small."

Nodding his understanding, he hefted the bag and poured out the crystals into a line thick enough to hold, now that the first torrent had abated to a steady shower. That meant there wasn't enough salt to make a big circle. Just enough to encompass the fire and the bench where Lisa was setting up the accoutrements for the spell: a brass bowl like a cauldron, a couple of bottles, silk cord, various herbs—

A demon, low like a greyhound, shot into the clearing, straight at Henry, as if to stop him from finishing his task. Sassy yanked the reins out of my hand and leapt forward. She came down on the monster with both her front hooves, stomping it into a greasy black pulp.

I grabbed a handful of salt from the stream Henry was pouring and ran to obliterate anything left of the demon. "Maggie!" called Justin. "Stay in the light."

A second monster flew out of the darkness like a bat-winged harpy, its talons reaching for me. Justin swung the branding iron, tearing the creature's membranous wing. It fell, flailing, to the ground and he pinned it through the neck with a sizzle.

It wasn't as neat as the chupy he'd pierced through the

heart, but it got the job done. I salted it, too, just to stop the sounds it made.

"They're getting stronger." Justin wiped his face with his sleeve. "And smarter."

Sassy snorted a warning to any chupacabras that might infringe on her patrol. I caught her reins and praised her, stroking the strong column of her neck, and she pushed her nose against my shoulder.

After that, my next action seemed inevitable. Someone had to get to the wellhead and back. The Jeep had a flat tire, and the pickup truck's headlights were the only defense besides the guys with the branding irons.

"I hope you're up for another run," I whispered.

Lisa held Henry off from closing the circle, and looked at me expectantly. "I'm going to go get your missing ingredient," I said. "You have what you need to begin the binding, right?"

She started to speak, then stopped, searching for alternatives to my plan and finding none. "It doesn't have to be big," she finally said. "Any piece can make the connection."

Justin saw the horse's reins in my hand, and realized what I meant to do. "No way, Maggie."

Zeke's protest was more confused. "You said you'd never ridden before yesterday."

Neglecting his sentry duty, Justin caught my hand tightly in his. "I'll go. Or Henry. Either one of us."

"Why? Because you're the boys?"

"Because you've been on a horse only once before!"

This was a sensible argument, but when he reached

for the mare's reins, she bared her teeth at him and danced away. Henry tried to catch her, but she tossed her head at him, too. I clicked my tongue, and she came trotting right to me.

"This is crazy." Justin wasn't talking about the horse's behavior. In frustration he turned to his friend. "Henry, help me out here."

Henry shook his head. "I'm sold. It's got to be Maggie the horse whisperer."

Grabbing me around the waist, Henry tossed me up onto Sassy's back like I weighed nothing. Then he slipped the leather strap of his branding iron onto my wrist and showed me how to hold it like a polo mallet. "Backswing and follow through. Keep a smooth arc. You'll have more power swinging forward than backward."

"Fix the stirrups," said Zeke. "You don't want her sliding off."

Henry held the horse's bridle while Justin, jaw set in a tense line, shortened one stirrup, then the other. I watched him, studying the strong line of his neck, the taut muscle where it met his shoulder. "I have to do this, Justin."

He looked up at me, some of the anger running out of him. "I know you do. Or else I'd sit on you to keep you from going."

I smiled, because he totally would, too. "Don't worry. I'm brilliant and resourceful, remember?"

"And insane."

"That, too."

He stood by Sassy's shoulder. When I leaned forward to get the reins, he caught my sleeve and held me there, close enough that his breath warmed my cheek as his eyes searched mine. I don't know what he found in my gaze, but I saw all kinds of things in his. His fear for me was fierce, and so was the other thing I saw, the thing we hadn't said yet, but somehow didn't really need to.

"I'll see you when you get back," he said. Then he kissed me, not long enough to be ridiculous, given our dire straits, but so intensely that my head spun, and I had to grab on to the saddle horn or fall off the horse before I ever got started.

He stepped back and I sat up, just a little dazed. Now I had to live through this so we could do that again, without the horse in the way.

Sassy stamped her foot, ready to be off. Handing me the reins that I'd dropped while I was distracted, Henry put a hand on my knee and whispered something suspiciously like a benediction.

"I thought you weren't a priest yet," I said.

He looked up at me, his expression wry. "Anyone can pray, Maggie. You might keep that in mind."

Zeke watched me, his hands on his hips. "Whatever you did when we were riding the other day. Do that again."

"Okay." I met Lisa's eye. "Start the spell."

I heard the scream of a chupacabra, and Henry whirled, ready to fight it. I kicked my heels against Sassy's flanks and she surged forward. It probably didn't inspire a lot of confidence the way I had to grab at the pommel to keep from tumbling backward over her butt.

So much for my badass cowgirl exit.

✳  ✳  ✳

Sassy's hooves hit the earth with the rhythmic roll of a tympani. I'd put on a brave face at the grotto. But out in the dark, forward momentum was the only thing keeping me from collapsing in panic. The rain lashed at me, but I put my head and heels down and took the force of the gallop with my legs as if I had years of practice.

We were moving fast, up to speed, when a demon tried to come up on our flank. I swung the branding iron like Henry had shown me, in a smooth, hard arc. The blow caught the thing in the head and it tumbled into the darkness.

Another winged monster dove at us from above. I lay low on Sassy's neck as she zigzagged to avoid it. We were rock stars. Nothing could catch us. That was my positive visualization as I clung to the saddle.

I knew the moment that Lisa and Zeke started the spell. There was a change in the air, like a shift in the atmospheric pressure, distinct from the storm around me.

The winged chupy flew past us as if drawn on a current, and another beast followed on the ground. They didn't try to attack me, which seemed like good news. But as the wellhead came into sight, in a flash of lightning, I saw that the creatures had massed in front of me, blocking the way.

The spell was working, drawing all the demon's parts together. Too bad the hive mind had picked a spot between me and the wellhead to assemble.

Sassy didn't need to be told there was bad news ahead. We trotted to a stop, both of us winded, both of us scared stiff.

The demon bodies began to weave themselves together like macramé, but their limbs didn't stop where another one began. They melted together, fused into a horror that bore no resemblance to anything I had ever seen or dreamt.

The amalgamation of demons in my vision had been strange and awful, but nothing compared to the misshapen wrongness of this one. There were three heads where only one should be, and a gaping mouth at the navel, and limbs emerging from all over. Claws bristled on the ends of talons, but also on the body, the tongues, the heads. It was too horrible to take in, but I couldn't look away.

Sassy planted her hooves, her breath steaming in the rain. I pushed my hair out of my face and settled my feet in the stirrups, balancing my weight. "Okay, girl. We have to get past that thing and to the pipe fitting behind it. Ready to rumble?"

She snorted decisively. I braced myself as she lunged to the left from a standing start. The atrocity in front of us galumphed into our path, moving surprisingly fast. I barely touched Sassy's reins and she cut the other way, trying to get around.

The demon sprouted more legs on its bottom and scuttled over like a bug. Not fast compared to Sassy, but big enough to make one hell of a goalie.

Nothing for it. What would Viggo do? Aragorn wouldn't be daunted by some butt-ugly Uruk-hai. He'd take Andúril and shove it through the monster's heart.

Man, being the kick-ass brawn was way harder than being the smart-ass brain.

Sassy gave another snort, as if to ask what we were waiting for. I flexed my fingers on the wooden handle of the branding iron, feeling the pull of scarred tendon and hoping my grip would hold.

The nightmare charged, lurching forward on legs of all different lengths. I kicked Sassy into motion. The terror and adrenaline were too much to hold inside. They tore out of me in a yell, and I raised the branding iron like a lance.

The monster pitched backward. As Sassy bore down,

I drove the iron into the mouth on its belly, straight through, and felt a clang, an unyielding stop, all the way to my spine.

The demon had backed up to the wellhead and lured us in. Sassy cut to the side, and no amount of instant-rodeo mojo could counter the laws of physics. I flew off her back and fell against the spongy flesh of the demon.

My yell turned to a scream as the teeth raked my arm; how had I ever thought this thing was stupid? The malformed mass was dissolving around the branding iron, and at the same time my blood dripped into the oil seep, the greedy ground drinking it in with rain. With one dying action it had fed its rebirth.

Something new was already burbling out. I scooted away and tried to stand. I had to use the wellhead to pull myself up by my left hand and get back on my feet. A piece of pipe fitting—a threaded ring of some kind—popped off in my fingers. I hoped it wasn't important and stuck it in the pocket of my jeans.

The double-armed cross of the branding iron was wedged into the pipes. My right hand wouldn't wrap around the handle—not without setting all my nerves on fire—so I grabbed with my left, but it still wouldn't budge.

Defenseless and horseless. Things kept getting better and better.

Would the others know I was in trouble? Would Sassy go back to them or do the smart thing and run to the barn? Would Doña Isabel or Zeke sense something?

Rain stung my skin like needles. I backed away from the writhing black mass that oozed out of the ground. This was a new demon, still unformed. The eyes opened, and it moved forward on stiltlike legs, trying to divide into a second body like some kind of mitosis.

But the demon couldn't separate—not into distinct creatures, and not from the ground. It was still bound by the spell. Go, Lisa.

Holding my aching arm against my chest, I broke into a limping run, intent on putting distance between me and the growing monster.

Lightning branched across the sky, illuminating the land like a camera flash. The image seemed to stay on my retina even as the thunder rumbled. The grotto wasn't too far away. I could make it on foot as long as the demon stayed tethered.

The hoof beats were close by the time I heard them over the pounding of my heart in my ears. Sassy was coming back for me. I was too out of breath to call to her, so I limped faster, until something caught my ankle, and I pitched face-first into the dirt.

An impossibly long arm had snaked out to capture me. I felt a bite, and realized with horror that the claw had a mouth at the center of it. I screamed and kicked, but pulling just made the teeth dig in deeper. I could see the demon grow thicker and stronger as it sucked my blood like a tick.

Then Sassy's beautiful neigh; her hooves trampled the appendage into demon paste, severing the connection.

"Thank God." I was praying, all right. Henry would be proud.

I reached for the stirrup to pull myself up, and found it

was occupied by a tennis shoe. From Sassy's saddle, Justin leaned down to offer me a hand. I caught it gratefully, and he hauled me up behind him.

"Are you happy?" I shouted over the noise of Sassy's hooves carrying us back to the grotto. Feeling myself slipping from her back, I wrapped my arms tight around Justin's waist; with him there, the cowgirl magic seemed to have vanished. "You got to ride to my rescue after all."

He answered without a shred of self-congratulation. "Ask me again when we're actually safe."

The lights of the trucks in the grotto made an aura in the drizzle. I realized that the storm must be moving off. When the lightning flashed, the thunder took its time rumbling. I didn't know if that was good or bad.

What *was* bad was Lisa and Zeke's situation when we reached them. I could tell as soon as we got to the hollow. The old folks had emerged from the truck, and they watched anxiously from outside the circle, unable to break the line to assist. Hector shot me a quick look of relief when we rode in. Doña Isabel, however, didn't take her eyes from her grandson.

Henry helped me off of Sassy's back. "Interpret for me, Maggie." He sounded frustrated with his own helplessness. "I can't tell what's going on."

Inside the circle, I could see that Lisa had combined the ingredients into the brass bowl, where they smoldered. A silken cord wrapped it vertically, bridging the embers three times. Zeke and Lisa faced each other over it, her hands covering his as they cradled the brazier between them.

"The burning stuff will represent . . . um, wholeness, I think. The cord is symbolically binding. Zeke's hands are actually in contact with the bowl, and that looks like his blood smeared on the rim. He's trying to take control—"

Justin interrupted. "I explained all that as it was happening. He means, what's going wrong."

So even they could see it. Zeke's skin looked gray beneath his tan, Lisa was goth-pale with exhaustion. The cord across the mouth of the bowl was charring and the only thing that seemed to be fueling the spell at the moment was their combined willpower. Even the campfire inside the circle was burning out.

"Come on." I grabbed Justin's hand and trusted Henry to follow. Limping up the side of the knoll that sheltered the icon of the virgin, I reached the top and found an excellent view of the pasture, all the way to the wellhead I'd just visited. "Watch."

The next flash of lightning illuminated, for a terrible second, the monstrosity squeezing itself into existence, slowly but relentlessly. Henry said something, which was drowned out by the roll of thunder. It was probably just as well.

"That's what they're trying to keep together. It's fused, and bound to the rest below the ground."

Justin stared into the darkness where the monster struggled, half in and half out of the earth. "But as long as it doesn't feed anymore, it will stop growing, right?"

"For as long as Lisa—Zeke, really—can hold it together." I could look down into the hollow and see them at work. "Stubborn as she is, I don't think even Lisa has enough willpower to keep it going much longer."

Justin asked a very good question. "Then how are they going to have the strength to put it back in the ground?"

Lisa spoke up from below us, annoyance lacing her weary voice. "Whatever you guys are discussing up there, you want to get on with it?"

"How is this a balance?" demanded Henry, surprising me with his anger. "This thing is kicking our asses." He threw up his hands and shouted to the black sky. "Come on, God. How about cutting the side of the angels a freaking break here?"

Somehow, I had the energy to be shocked. "Is that how they're teaching priests to pray nowadays?"

Justin cast me a desperately humorless glance. "If we were ever in need of divine inspiration, it's now."

Be careful what you wish for. When the lightning flashed again, I could see in my mind's eye the terrain laid out in front of me like a contour map. The grotto, the wellhead two miles away—they both got a cell phone signal because they were close to the Big House, with its cellular relay in the tower. The tower was the first place I'd seen the dragonfly. A dragonfly like the origin of the Velasquez brand I'd just shoved into the wellhead. Suddenly the lines of the pattern all connected in my head.

"Maggie!" shouted Lisa. "Where's that piece of the pipe fitting?"

"Hang on!" I turned to the guys, seized by—I fervently hoped—true inspiration. "We need the storm back. This *Ruach Elohim* . . . can we summon it?"

The same guy who'd just asked God for a freaking break

gaped at me, horrified. "You can't *summon* the Breath of God."

"She means invoke." Justin corrected my vocabulary. "And yes, we can."

Henry narrowed his eyes. "Far away from here, Brother Mathias is having six litters of kittens right now, and he doesn't even know why."

I nudged him down the hill, back toward the grotto. "Get Doña Isabel to start praying for the storm to come back. You help. It's time to put all that righteousness to work."

"The storm—"

"Henry, you have to trust me."

He stared at me a moment longer, until Lisa started yelling again. Then he hurried to do as I said.

Turning to Justin, I wiped sweating palms on my soaking wet jeans. "You said we can invoke this . . ." I couldn't say it twice. I was already terrifying myself.

He dug into the cargo pocket of his trousers and pulled out the map and a pen, explaining quickly. "*Ruach* is Hebrew for 'spirit,' or 'breath.' The Kabbalah is a system of mysticism which says every Hebrew letter has a secret meaning that can be invoked for enlightenment."

I glanced down the face of the hill, where below us, Henry was helping Doña Isabel to kneel in front of the shrine. He knelt, too, leaving Hector the only one monitoring Lisa and Zeke. "Lecture less, Professor. Magic more."

"Okay, okay. The letter that corresponds to *Ruach* is *Shin.*" Bracing the folded map on his left hand, Justin drew a symbol like a twisted *W* over our location. "By inscribing it, we can invoke the qualities it represents."

I waited for something to happen, looking warily up at the sky. The rain had fallen off to a drizzle. "It didn't work."

He pointed to Doña Isabel and Henry. "Intent." And to the map and letter. "Ingredient." Then he pulled a lighter from his pocket. I was beginning to think he was as compulsively overprepared as me.

"Power source. Because the other thing that *Shin* corresponds to is flame."

Handing me the lighter, he held the map steady while I lit the corner. It shouldn't have burned at all, since it was so soggy. But the flame caught and raced across the paper as if it were soaked in lighter fluid instead of rain.

In the silence of my held breath, I could hear Henry's deep voice intoning his own invocation, and Doña Isabel's Amen.

Where was the earth-shattering kaboom? You'd think something like the Breath of God would give you immediate results. But I guess it didn't work that way.

Then my hair tickled my cheek as, almost imperceptibly, the wind changed direction. The sky was too dark to see the clouds, but I could feel the shift in the atmosphere, circling the storm back around.

A crack of lightning arrowed from the sky, and sparks bloomed from the metal dragonfly weather vane atop the Big House. The tower, tiny on the horizon, was lit for a moment like a photo negative, and then the electricity arced across miles of desert, completing a circuit with the double-armed cross that tipped the two feet of iron rod I'd wedged in the wellhead. The effect was like a match hitting a fuse.

344

The explosion rocked us back, even from this distance. A pillar of flame shot into the air, three hundred feet or more, until I thought I heard the clouds sizzle.

The spout of fire looked like a piece of Hell on earth. And writhing, tortured, at the base of it was the demon, slowly being eaten away by the flame.

# 31

I was never, ever going to complain about not learning anything useful from my dreams. Even when it came from the unlikeliest source.

Zeke and Lisa had dropped their concentration, the bowl, and the spell. "Oh my God!" cried Zeke, staring at the jet of flame shooting into the sky. It was so big, it looked within spitting distance. "What happened?"

"Oh my God," echoed Henry, helping Doña Isabel to stand up. "It worked. The storm came back."

The matriarch looked up the hill to where I stood, still reeling like everyone else. "What have you done?" she demanded.

"Heat and flame." Justin sounded dazed. I probably should have warned him what I was hoping would happen.

"What about the binding?" Hector was justifiably alarmed, after all that trouble to hold the demon together.

"Everything aboveground is being consumed," I reported, shading my eyes against the light and heat. "Even the parts that break off. Come and see."

"We can't," said Lisa, meaning her and Zeke. "The rest can burn off, but we have to set the seal on whatever is left underground."

She sounded bone weary. I had never heard that from her. Zeke looked a hairsbreadth from collapse. He swayed on his feet when he bent to pick up the brass bowl they'd dropped. "So let's get to it."

"Wait." Inspiration wasn't done with me yet. "Don't cap it. Call it out."

They stared at me in various attitudes of horror or confusion, depending on how much they understood what I was saying. "What do you mean, call it out?" asked Hector.

Lisa's expression had gone cold as soon as I'd said it, and she answered in a flat voice, "She means, summon the demon."

"Are you out of your mind?" Henry asked. "Look at that thing. That's just the part aboveground. And you want to let the rest of it out?"

"Yes." I flicked a glance at Justin. "Heat and flame. Zeke, you can wait to see what turns up the next drought, or you can vanquish this thing forever."

"You're sure?" he asked. "You're certain this will kill it?"

I let him read it in my eyes. "As certain as I can be."

He turned to his grandmother, and she spoke with quiet confidence. "I haven't been given this vision, Ezekiel. But I know this thing is Evil. Magdalena says this will destroy it. Not bury it, not allow it to grow and fester."

Lisa met his gaze levelly. "All I need is your permission, Zeke. I can do this on my own."

He looked confused. "Don't I need to do it? My link to the land?"

She took the brass bowl from him and set it on the concrete bench. "You've started the spell. I'm not rewriting the whole book, I'm just changing the ending."

He shook his head. "I took on this responsibility. If something goes screwy, I'll be here with my magic bloodline. And I'll take the heat if I have to."

"Zeke," she snapped, "I'm not being noble and self-sacrificing here. I've got nothing to lose, karmically speaking."

I knew what she meant; she was the only one of us who had summoned a demon before. Zeke didn't know that, but he had the unanswerable argument.

"I can't leave you to do it alone, anyway." He pointed to the white circle. "If stepping over that makes it defunct, you don't have a way to redraw it. You used the last of the salt."

She opened her mouth, closed it. Looking thunderous at having no rebuttal, she said, "Fine. Just stay back."

Pulling out her pocketknife, she took the brass bowl in one hand and the knife in the other. The heat of the embers made eddies of mist in the damp air, wreathing her face. Her expression was determined, and in a way, serene.

Far away, the demon pieces, outlined in fire, fought the pull of the well. Hector and Doña Isabel came up to watch, but Henry stayed below with Lisa and Zeke.

Ceremonially—I couldn't hear her words over the roar of the flame—Lisa cut the cord around the bowl. Still speaking, she took the vessel in both her bare hands, shaking the embers so that they flared to life, then raised her arms parallel to the ground, holding the bowl over the campfire in front of her.

"You might want to move," she told the guys, voice taut with strain. Then she dropped the brass bowl into the fire, where it cracked into shards of metal.

Instinctively, I raised my arm to shield my face. I caught Lisa in the same motion, and the guys turning away. Then the light from the fire went from orange to yellow, and a terrible sound, like the groan of an earthquake, bridged the space between the well and us. A wave of dry heat carried an acrid stench, and when I lowered my arm, I saw the demon forced out of the wellhead like a glob of Jell-O through a straw.

It took shape in the pillar of fire, pushing it outward, changing each time I blinked but never really altering, as if my mind was impressing on it the shape of fear. It grew until it loomed over the desert, not just a demon but a fiery god.

"Please, please, God, don't let me have screwed this up." I didn't realize I'd spoken aloud until Justin's arm tightened around me and Hector laid a hand on my shoulder.

The red beast began to writhe and twist, and the roar of the fire multiplied with its agony. As the flames consumed it, the plume became again a narrow jet spewing into the clouds. It grew smaller as I watched, like a lighter running out of fuel, then burned itself out with a whoosh, leaving the desert in darkness once again.

All seven of us stared; the air was unnervingly quiet.

"Is it gone?" Zeke sounded afraid to ask.

Doña Isabel wasn't afraid to answer. "Yes."

She would know. But I felt it, too—a peculiar emptiness where there'd been something nasty stuck to my subconscious. Cleansed by heat and flame.

Justin wrapped his arms around me and kissed my hair, which had to smell wretched. "You really are brilliant and resourceful."

"I have good resources to lean on." I laid my head on his shoulder for emphasis.

With his arm still around me, we climbed down the hill. In the circle, Zeke caught Lisa in a laughing embrace. I saw Hector say something to Doña Isabel that made her unbend enough to smile, and—despite their extreme age—I was a little disappointed there wasn't any hugging going on there, too.

The rest of us made up for it. Justin slung his other arm around Henry's shoulders, slapping him on the back, the way guys do. "So. Are you disowning me after all of this?"

Henry gave a snort. "No. But I will pray for you twice a day instead of just once."

I tucked my filthy wet hair behind my ear. "What about me?"

"You, I'll pray for three times."

Zeke came over, shook both guys' hands, and scooped me up in a tight, grateful hug. "I'm sorry," he whispered in my ear.

"For what?" He set me back on my feet and I grinned my forgiveness up at him. "I would say a lot worse things to anyone who messed with my— Oh my God. Gran will be flipping out."

I pulled my phone from my pocket, slightly amazed it was

still there, and saw that there was no signal at all. I'd managed to wipe out the cell tower, too. Oops.

Hector had helped Doña Isabel down from the hill, and the guys went to share their giddy relief with them. Lisa stayed by me, asking when they were out of earshot, "How did you know the fire would go out by itself?"

"I didn't." I grimaced guiltily. "The idea just came to me and I went for it."

"Divine inspiration, huh?"

"Not really. It was a John Wayne movie. About this guy that puts out oil-well fires. You know the name of it?"

"Can't guess."

I grinned up at her. *"Hellfighters."*

# 32

In the end, the chupacabra was responsible for four hospitalized cowboys, six transfusions, the deaths of eighteen cows, twenty-six calves, a dozen chickens, two dogs, and three goats. Plus one Jeep suspension and *eight* punctured tires.

Zeke didn't have to call for assistance once we discovered the extent of the vehicular sabotage; there was no shortage of folks already on their way to check out the Cecil B. DeMille spectacular and its equally amazing disappearance.

Dave was the one who filled me in on the events back at the corral. The cowboys who had gone out with Zeke made it back okay, but their calves were lost, after all that effort. A couple of chupies had tested the defenses, seeming to get stronger and more daring, until suddenly they fell back into the night and didn't return. Not long after, they'd seen the pillar of flame, and designated some guys to stay with the cows, and some to go check it out.

Oil well blowouts were bad news. They *never* put themselves out. By the time we got back to Dulcina to pick up the Escort and our luggage, word was spreading that nothing short of a miracle had occurred at Lady Acre. Our Lady of Perpetual Aid had done it again.

No matter who, or what, gets the credit, the way I figure it, there were a number of forces at work, maybe more than even my freaky brain will ever know. If my vision was to be believed, Team Evil had an infinite number of forms and faces. Why shouldn't Team Good?

Since I had to wait for all new tires, the four of us—Lisa, Henry, Justin and I—ended up spending the rest of the week at the Big House. When I'd called my parents to tell them about the change of residence, Dad had an intense relief in his voice that meant Gran had told him something was up. He'd even looked the Velasquez Ranch (and family) up on the Internet. Mom, rather than being suitably impressed by my new associations, despaired that I was *never* going to have a normal coming-of-age experience.

She did not ask about the dispensation of the bedrooms. Despite the copious space in the Big House, Connie, the housekeeper, had doubled us up: Justin and Henry in one room, near Zeke, and Lisa and I way down the hall by ourselves. Not that I was much of a chaperone, because the second night we were there—the first night was solely about making up for forty-eight hours without sleep—I hinted very broadly that I wasn't doing bed checks.

Our room was decorated in a kind of Spanish colonial style—heavy wood furniture and opulent covers on the twin beds. Lisa was brushing her hair upside down, and turned her head to look at me through the strands.

"Thanks for enabling me in sin, Mags. But Zeke's got this old-fashioned code about respecting his grandmother's values while in her house or something."

Which seemed about right for Zeke. "She is a Seer, after all. There wouldn't be any hiding it from her."

Lisa flipped her hair over and sat on her bed. Her gaze rested on a painting of a lone cowboy riding through the snow. "He said he'd like to come up to Georgetown to visit me."

That he wanted to see her again was not a surprise to me, since I had a working pair of eyeballs. "What did you say?"

"That I'd think about it."

"Lisa, for a supergenius, you can really be an idiot."

Her jaw clenched mulishly. "He doesn't even know me, Mags. I mean, jeez. I'm a lot to handle. And not in a good way."

I swung my legs over the edge of the bed so I could face her. "Sooner or later, you're going to have to let someone in. It may be Zeke, it may not. But everyone deserves to be loved."

"Even Hellbound novice sorcerers?"

I came to a sudden decision and stood up. "Even psychic girl detectives who seem to be demon magnets."

Slipping on my flip-flops, I zipped up my hoodie and headed for the door. Lisa called after me, "I won't leave the light on."

Thanks a lot for making me blush. Fortunately the hall was long enough for it to subside. I knocked on the guys' door, but when Henry's bass voice said, "Come in," I found him alone, reading a book.

"Sorry," I said. "I was looking for Justin."

He gave me a "duh" look. "He went for a walk. We thought you girls were going to bed early."

"Not yet." I was wearing my pj's, but if he thought I always wore pants with purple hearts all over them, I wasn't going to correct him.

"Hey, Maggie." His voice stopped me as I was about to close the door. "What did you see, when you were unconscious the other day at the shrine?"

I tried to look nonchalant and not wary. "Why do you ask?"

"Indiana Jones." At my baffled expression, he explained. "When Indy is going through the traps at the end of *Last Crusade,* his dad says he has to pass through the 'breath of God.' He never uses the Hebrew word."

My stomach seemed to sink, and my hand tightened on the doorknob. "You're sure?"

He smiled. "I wanted to be an archaeologist when I grew up, until I found out they don't really carry bullwhips."

Then his expression grew sober and rather kind. For the first time, I could see the future priest in him. "Look. Justin's got the anthropological background. Lisa seems to have the practical end of things. But if you ever need to talk out the spiritual ramifications . . ." He cleared his throat. "I know I'm still just a theology major, but at least you can talk to me without getting excommunicated."

I was hugely touched. "What changed your mind? Besides the big chupacabra teeth, I mean."

"Oh, I still think you're living dangerously. But I've seen now that you really do have a gift, and you really don't have a choice but to use it. To paraphrase Saint Paul, 'To whom much is given, much will be required.' "

I did him one better. " 'With great power comes great responsibility.' Spider-Man."

\* \* \*

Justin had gone all the way out to the garden behind the chapel, where he sat on the wooden railing, looking over a marshy inlet. The air was cool coming off the water, and I zipped up my jacket as I leaned on the rail beside him.

"Are you avoiding me?" I asked.

He dropped his arm over my shoulders. "Just the opposite. I was sending you psychic messages to come out and meet me."

"I haven't seen you much today."

"Sorry. I guess after near-death experiences, it would have been more boyfriendly to spend some quality time with you."

"Nah." I turned and jumped up to sit on the rail, too, my back to the water so I could face him. "I interviewed Doña Isabel today. It's going to make a great article."

"I asked Hector a ton of questions about *brujería*. It's rare that an outsider gets so much insight."

"Productive day." I swung my legs, gazing at the moon-silvered garden. Darn it if I wasn't going to miss this place a little.

"Justin." I said his name without looking at him, but I could see from the corner of my eye that my tone had caught his attention. "Do you help me with all this weird stuff because of some kind of Bruce Wayne need to avenge your parents, or absolve your survivor guilt, or something like that?"

He blinked. "I'm helping you because it's the right thing to do. But even if it wasn't, I'd brave Hellfire and more for you, Maggie."

Something twisted pleasantly in my chest, as if my heart were doing a happy little dance. But I had at least one more thing that needed saying.

"You should know, I don't think this is the last time this is going to happen."

The corner of his mouth turned up in that crooked smile that I loved. He slipped his arm around my waist, resting his fingers on my hip. "You say that like you think it makes a difference to me."

"That just proves you're as crazy as I am."

His arm tightened, and my balance became very precarious. "No, that just proves I'm crazy about you."

Right then, a normal life seemed *way* overrated.

Eventually, I did make it back to my room, but it was long after Lisa had turned off the light.

# ACKNOWLEDGMENTS

I'd like to thank the folks at the Kenedy Ranch Museum in Sarita, Texas, for their work preserving the heritage of South Texas ranching, in particular the lives and legacy of the vaquero, and the King Ranch Museum in Kingsville for insight into the cattle industry, past and present. Dulcina and the Velasquez family are completely fictional, but I was inspired by the rugged and hardworking people who fed America as it manifested its destiny across the West. All mistakes made and liberties taken are my own.

My thanks, also, to the great folks at Random House, who have been so supportive of the books, and to my editor, Krista Marino, for her insight, patience, and general awesomeness. Also awesome is my agent, Lucienne Diver, who gives me advice and encouragement and doesn't laugh too hard when I say something dorky.

Thank you, also, to all the readers who have written or stopped by my blog. Not to mention the librarians, booksellers, and bloggers who have stocked, recommended, and reviewed my books.

Finally, to my mom, and everyone who supported me with infusions of coffee, words of encouragement, and kicks to the rear. Most especially: Cheryl Smyth, Candace Havens, Shannon Canard, Marion Smith, Peter Clement, Delilah Peeler, and K. Hudson Price.

And, best for last, my husband, Tim. You rock, babe, and not just at Guitar Hero.

ROSEMARY CLEMENT-MOORE loves ancient and modern history, Jane Austen and Madeleine L'Engle, the Food Network, the SciFi Channel, and Guitar Hero. She used to live on a South Texas ranch with horses, cows, coyotes, skunks, and mosquitoes of hellish origin. Since moving back to civilization with her husband and dogs, she is most grateful that there is a Starbucks within walking distance and she no longer has to shoot rattlesnakes from her front porch.

*Highway to Hell* is her third book featuring Maggie Quinn. You can visit Rosemary at www.rosemaryclementmoore.com.